The Final Mayan Prophecy

By Paul Skorich and Tony Perona

ISBN: 1469902036
ISBN-13: 978-1469902036

DEDICATION

(Tony) To Marjorie Miles Vogel, 1931 – 2010,
and James E. Vogel,
for being quite possibly the world's greatest in-laws

(Paul) To my beautiful wife Laura, whose encouragement and love has made such a difference in my life.

ACKNOWLEDGMENTS

Tony:

First, I once again thank God for blessing me far more richly than I deserve, and my wife Debbie for putting up with me in general. Also my daughters Katy and Liz and my son-in-law Tim for their support. Tim, in particular, read over this manuscript and offered suggestions.

Second, I thank my co-author, Paul Skorich, for his vision of this project and for asking me to work with him on the original screenplay and then this novel.

Third, I thank a number of people for their expertise, particularly Michael A. Black, Jeff Stone, and Josh Wood, who provided experiences I do not have. Thank you, too, to the folks at the Metropolis Starbucks (now closed), who provided encouragement and caffeine.

None of my stories would have made it to print without my author friends who are kind enough to read my work and offer thoughts, suggestions, and advice. I especially appreciate my critique partner, Phil Dunlap, who helped shape the novel form of this manuscript, and my friends at the Indiana Writers Workshop who were with this story from its beginnings as a screenplay to its evolution as a novel. They are Teri Barnett, Pete Cava, John Clair, June McCarty Clair, Nancy Frenzel, Lucy Schilling, and Steve Wynalda.

Paul:

I would like to thank Tony Perona for his talent, hard work and dedication. He took an idea and made it come to life and I pray our friendship and collaboration will continue in the future. May his gift grow and bring enjoyment to an ever increasing number of readers.

Chapter One

The Yucatan Peninsula, Mexico
December 17, 2012
12:02 p.m. local time

Time to Solstice: 90 hours, 09 minutes

Manuel Patcanul approached the gathering of Mayan elders carrying no notes. Notes might make them think he had not committed the substance of the plan to memory. In fact, he had been working on it so long he knew the details intimately. The plan was not the issue; the tactical elements were. Though the vision had been theirs, how to do that fell to him. What if, at this late stage, they did not approve of his methods?

The thirteen elders sat in a large circle, each of them on a stool, even spacing between them. They wore feathered ancestral headgear and traditional embroidered loincloths. Though it was broad daylight, each held a long, lit torch. At the center of the circle burned the sacred fire, green smoke rising from the special mix of jungle roots and tropical vines that took the place of the blood sacrifice formerly required by the gods. At least, that was what he had been told. Perhaps one day he would be an elder himself and know the truth. Or perhaps not, given that he walked in two worlds. His decision to be both Maya and modern, respectful of the past and yet serious about success in the twenty-first century, had caused him to be considered a traitor by a minority of the council.

The leader of the council, fortunately, saw him differently. To him, he was the man to bring their vision to fruition. He was a respected professor of Mayan studies at the University of Mexico, and it was precisely his ability to straddle the two worlds that made him indispensable.

He bowed low before the circle and the leader. "You have summoned me," he said in the modern tongue of the Maya. It was a derived language, similar to the ancient tongue but bastardized since the Spanish conquest of the 1600s.

"We are four days from the end of this era, from the birth of Kukulcan," said the leader, his brown face and chest painted in warlike black and white. "Have you located the birth mother?"

"Not yet, but we are watchful. We have Chichen Itza under constant surveillance as your vision dictated. My sister is there during the visitation hours, as am I, and the Maya who work for us also act as our eyes."

"Are they Cruzol?" asked a high-pitched voice, interrupting him.

Manuel turned to see who it was. A short man standing ramrod straight as though to appear taller, stared at him. Like the chief elder, he was aged but feisty. Manuel recognized the man as having at one time headed the secret rebel Mayan movement. "All Cruzol," he acknowledged.

The man nodded proudly and returned to his seat.

"When the mother comes," Manuel continued, "we are prepared to secure her safety. Do you require additional detail?"

At great sacrifice to his career, Manuel had taken a leave of absence from the university. The elders had asked him to accept a position they were confident would come open at Chichen Itza, and when it had, Manuel felt compelled to take it. He now supervised the restoration of current ruins and the excavation of new ones. How could he have refused the elders? He was Maya and knew the 5,126-year Mayan calendar ended with the winter solstice. Legends held that their god-king Kukulcan would be born at this time. Born out of the mouth of the feathered serpent. He had no idea how that would come about. Rationalizing the secular modern world to ancient legends required faith on his part, but the more the fifty-three year-old the studied the various world myths, the more he could see a coalescing pattern that defied explanation.

The gray-bearded leader smiled, exposing missing teeth. In the developed world, such a smile might be associated with lesser intelligence, but Manuel knew that not to be true here. This Mayan elder knew far more about higher things than he.

"We are confident of your abilities, Manuel. You were not summoned here to be challenged."

Manuel bowed again. Was he being dismissed, with so little questioning?

"We've had yet another vision," he said, before Manuel could decide what to do. "Before this era ends, the door will open to where the Book of the Thirteen Gods has been hidden."

"The Book of the Thirteen Gods?" Manuel could not help but express surprise. The great 16th century Mayan prophet Chilam Balam, when talking about the end of the world, made reference to such a book. But it had long been interpreted as the prophet's own vision of the events that would take place, not as a physical artifact. "How will it be found?"

"It is not an accident that Chichen Itza is the seat of power at this time. The answer you seek will be made clear as events unfold. The Book will be essential to King Kukulcan, and therefore you must secure it as well. But beware. Others seek it, too. And their intentions are to use it for evil."

Manuel contemplated this. "Who else seeks the book?"

"The one who is in total opposition to the King—and he has servants."

"Is the King in danger?"

The elder straightened his thin shoulders. The woven cloak symbolizing his rank in the Council almost slipped from them. "Not at this point. Only at birth, when the King is also of our world, does he become vulnerable. Before that, he has the protection of the ancients."

Manuel blinked. There were so many questions to ask. He opened his mouth.

"Go, Manuel. We release you to your mission. You will experience success, but not always in the way you expect. I cannot say more."

Manuel did not move. "May I have the blessing before I go?"

The creases in the leader's forehead deepened into a frown. "Close your eyes."

As Manuel lowered his head and felt the man's hand upon him, he heard another elder announce to the gathering, "A blessing!"

Suddenly there was an outpouring from all assembled. The cadence was different than that of the usual blessing, and what words he could detect, especially those mumbled by the leader, were not ones he had heard before.

The council went quiet. Manuel felt the leader's hand lift from his head. He opened his eyes and searched those of the elder.

"What …?"

"Goodbye, Manuel. I shall not see you again."

Manuel hesitated. He bit his lip in frustration. But he knew from previous encounters the elders did not elaborate once he was dismissed.

He bowed. Manuel walked away from the fire, through the hut-like palapas that formed the village, through a path in the jungle, and then onto a modern road where he had left his car. As he got into the vehicle, he noticed that the jungle had swallowed up the trail he'd used. Again from past encounters, he knew it would not appear until he was summoned again.

If he was summoned again. If he was alive to be summoned.

Chapter Two

Xcaret eco-park, Mexico
December 17, 2012
1:00 p.m. local time

Time to Solstice: 89 hours, 11 minutes

Rebekah Sagiev watched her husband slip the climber's pack from his shoulder and pull out a granola bar for each of them. He was never without the black, pod-shaped pack. Even the first time she'd met him, three years ago in Cancun, he'd had it.

"Want me to unwrap it for you?" Jonas asked, holding out the bar.

"Of course I do. I'm so helpless." She snatched the bar out of his hand, ripped back the wrapper, and took a bite. "I'm pregnant, Jonas, not handicapped."

"I'd have made the offer even if you weren't."

She stood on her tiptoes and kissed him. "You're right. Sorry."

Rebekah knew not to give him any more grief. They'd argued over whether or not she should come to Mexico to celebrate the grand opening of the Hotel Kukulcan, and she'd won. Though Jonas had been the lead architect on the hotel's atrium, a major achievement in his young career, she had just started her eighth month of pregnancy. If she hadn't been so determined, she would still be in Philadelphia.

"Let's check out the cemetery," she said, "and then if you want to rent gear and go for a swim in the river, I'll watch your pack." Jonas' climber's pack was little more than a man-purse to her. A devoted climber, he kept his rope and a few other climbing necessities in it, but the pack also held his keys and wallet. She liked that fact that he always had it with him. There was enough room for her stuff, too.

"You don't want to go swimming?"

"I don't want to do too much today. I'd rather save my energy for the trip to Chichen Itza tomorrow."

"I'm not sure Chichen Itza's a good idea."

"Professor Patcanul has already agreed to show us around. Besides," she added, squeezing his hand, "you owe me for not being able to see it when I was here as a grad student."

He grinned. She'd given up that tour for a first date with him. "I can't believe it's been three years now."

It was difficult for her to believe, too, even if the Maya-influenced atrium design he'd been researching at the time was now completely constructed. She'd been a doctoral candidate in archeology at Tulane University, on leave in Cancun from participating on a dig at the Ek Balam ruins. She'd noticed his broad shoulders and friendly smile when they'd bumped into each other at a Starbucks. He'd bought her another latte to replace the one she'd spilled, and they had sat and talked for a couple of hours. It was a big plus when she learned that Jonas was of Jewish descent. Rebekah had been born in Israel but become a naturalized United States citizen at a young age. She married him a year later.

And shortly they were going to be parents, the kicking baby reminded her. She caressed the part of her expanded belly the foot was smacking. "Settle down," she told him.

"I think I'm remarkably calm, considering the grand opening is in two days," Jonas said.

"You know I'm talking to the baby. And you're anything but calm. You're not sleeping well. I should know. I'm up every hour going to the bathroom."

"Nerves." He finished his granola bar and put the wrapper in his backpack.

"And visiting a cemetery is going to help, how?" She pointed to the "Bridge to Paradise" hill that held more colorful tombs than she could count.

"Something to do. From an architect's perspective, it's an interesting construction. Structurally, the seven levels of tombs are cut into the hillside to represent the seven days of the week, and there are three hundred and sixty-five tombs, representing the days of the year. The main entrance has fifty-two steps, like the number of weeks in the year."

"Which adheres to the Gregorian calendar, not the Mayan."

"You know I'll never understand the Mayan calendar."

Rebekah nodded. In her opinion he had a mental block against it. "I think the cemetery looks like a giant, garish beehive," she said. "And the Maya didn't even have cemeteries, so this post-Hispanic. It's not all that old, relatively speaking."

Jonas sighed. "Let's take a look anyway."

Rebekah trailed him to Xcaret cemetery. When they reached the passage that led to the very center of the hill of tombs, Rebekah noticed the baby was no longer kicking. She searched the spot where his foot had been, but she couldn't feel it anymore. Closing her eyes, she felt for his presence. The sensation—the connection she had with the baby—was strange, something she didn't completely understand, but she knew that he was there, and he was okay.

Jonas stooped to enter the passage, which had been designed for people significantly shorter than his six foot frame. He looked back and found her frowning. "What is it?"

"It's nothing. The baby must have gone to sleep. He's gotten quiet all of sudden." She felt his arms envelope her.

"About time. He's been active for hours."

"Hours? He's been agitated since we landed yesterday. He gives me short breaks now and then. I hope this one is a little longer than most."

"Why didn't you say something? Is that why you didn't sleep well last night?"

She massaged the spot where the baby's foot had been, looking for it again. "If I'd said something, what could you have done about it?"

Jonas put his hand next to hers. "I would have lectured him on keeping his mother up at night."

"A lot of good it would have done. Everything is fine. Let's keep going." But even as she denied it, Rebekah was worried. She had been having strange dreams. And it wasn't so much that the baby had gone quiet, it was the suddenness when they entered the Bridge to Paradise.

It's probably nothing, she thought.

Chapter Three

Deep in the Syrian Desert, Western Iraq
December 18, 2012
9:10 a.m. local time

Time to Solstice: 77 hours, 01 minutes

Fareed Mohammed was used to dangerous assignments, but driving what he suspected was a nuclear weapon through the Syrian Desert was a little more danger than what he was used to, so he'd demanded a large fee. Fareed was a former member of Saddam Hussein's elite Republican National Guard army, but now he worked for himself. Though it had been a long time since the fall of Saddam's regime, the contacts he'd made there still helped him secure a number of lucrative assignments. Like this one. The man next to him in the truck was Hakim, no last name, and the maybe-nuclear weapon was his. Fareed remembered Hakim from his days in the RNG. Hakim was a brutal man, charismatic but cold-blooded. Knowing that, Fareed had hesitated taking the assignment when Hakim approached him, but the money won him over.

His decision-making was also shaped by the fact that another person was willing to pay even more money. The man's name was Vhorrdak, and he was also very interested in the maybe-nuclear weapon. Vhorrdak claimed to represent the purchasers, who were worried that Hakim would double cross him. The elaborate exchange in the desert Hakim had demanded left the purchasers in a bad position, he claimed. Hakim could provide a counterfeit weapon at this meeting, knowing it would take time for the purchasers to verify the authenticity of the weapon. Hakim could reach safety before they determined the truth. The bulk of the payment came upon the verification, so Hakim had reason to be fair, but the initial amount was substantial. So among other things, Fareed was acting as a double agent, trying to establish whether Hakim had the weapon at all, and if he did, if it was in the back of this truck.

"How much farther?" Hakim asked.

Fareed looked at the odometer. “Fifteen kilometers. About thirty minutes.” The converted M939 five-ton cargo truck Fareed drove had been provided by Hakim. A robust truck for most Iraqi conditions, the M939 had three powered axles and six sets of tires, but Fareed drove it more slowly than it could go. For one thing, there were no roads in this area of the desert, at least none Hakim wanted them to take, and the truck was not known for its off-road performance. For another thing, his lack of knowledge of what was in the back made him cautious. Fareed knew that well-constructed nuclear weapons could be jostled and even shot without being detonated, but he had no idea if this one was well-constructed. If it was a nuclear weapon.

“So, are you going to tell me what is back there?” Fareed asked.

“You are better off not knowing. If I told you, I would have to kill you.”

This was not the first time Hakim had mentioned killing Fareed. He always said it in a way that made it seem like a joke, but before Fareed had heard it more than once he began planning a self-defense strategy. Both men were well-versed in hand-to-hand combat, but in a contest of equals, the bigger man would have the upper hand, and that would be Hakim. So Fareed had insisted on carrying a personal weapon, ‘in case they ran into trouble.’ Though Hakim had agreed to it, he’d made Fareed remove the Glock 26 from his ankle holder and place it in a box on the floor between them. Still there for Fareed, but not easily accessible. Fareed had a back up, a neck knife hanging from a chain around his neck. Hakim had seen it when he patted Fareed down, but he’d let it go. Fareed could pull it from his neck quickly, and the kydex neck sheath came off easily, but in that time Hakim could do a lot of damage. If it came to a fight, Fareed would have strike first.

“It must be valuable, to require such an isolated spot for an exchange.”

“Suffice it to say the buyers were willing to pay plenty for it.”

“And you do not bluff, that much I remember about you.”

Hakim laughed. “I can bluff, but do I seem like the type who wants to live my life in hiding as a result?”

Fareed smiled. An absolute affirmation from Hakim would be difficult to obtain, but this came very, very close. The weapon was real, and Fareed was driving it across the desert. "No," he said. "You seem like the type who would want to enjoy his money."

Fareed permitted Hakim a moment to gloat. As he did, Fareed leaned his left foot firmly into the side of his boot, where he had implanted a device that signaled Vhorrdak positively about the authenticity of the weapon.

"So who are we meeting?" Fareed asked.

"You are full of questions."

"And you give few answers. Do you not think I should have some idea of what trouble we might run into? It is to your advantage to clue me in. It could end up saving your life."

Hakim seemed to consider that for a moment. "They are a group of Syrians."

"What kind of group? Do they represent Syria, or are they Syrians representing other interests?" This was a serious question on Fareed's part. While he was doing what Vhorrdak had asked, he didn't necessarily trust the man. Was Vhorrdak acting for the Syrians, for himself, or for someone else? If too many parties knew about the weapon, that would be bad. Such indiscretion could attract the attention of the Americans. They would do anything to prevent a dangerous weapon from falling into the hands of certain countries, like Iran. Iran desperately wanted nuclear capability, and the West desperately wanted to prevent it. So buying—or stealing—a nuclear weapon would be perfect. Who knew how Hakim had gotten hold of it? But if the Americans had discovered it were up for bid … well, they would want to prevent a sale.

"It is not yours to worry about. I have checked them out."

Fareed took in a nervous breath. The Hakim he'd known in the short time they'd been assigned together at Saddam's opulent Abu Ghrayb palace was not a savvy man. Fareed knew what Vhorrdak had arranged up ahead, because he had helped in making the contacts and employing others. But if the Americans had learned of the transaction, it could get complicated. Vhorrdak warned him one of the other two drivers was now a mole.

* * *

Hakim didn't like the questions this hired truck driver was asking. Though the questions were logical and Fareed provided sufficient reason for asking them, they still made Hakim more than a little suspicious. Good thing he had the upper hand here.

In fact, Hakim considered that he'd held the upper hand for a long time. It was why he didn't care that Fareed was driving so carefully that they were running behind. He had a schedule to keep, of course, but the cargo, hidden beneath the plain muslin cover over the truck's flatbed, was too important to those in the rendezvous vehicle for them to criticize him for any lateness on his part.

Hakim didn't know a lot about Fareed. He knew that he himself had come to the Republic National Guard because he'd proven himself a master in fighting and weaponry, but he was never sure about Fareed. The man was skilled, no question about it, but he was not ruthless. He had learned that about Fareed at Abu Ghrayb. Opportunities to betray others and make advancements had come to both of them, but Fareed had been the cautious one. Everything was a case-by-case basis with him. With a quick promotion, Hakim had moved on and had not seen Fareed again until he was looking for a discreet, skilled fighter who would be willing to take this assignment with little information. Fareed had entered the picture, and Hakim remembered him. He felt a cautious man might make a good driver. Or a good sacrifice, if things turned bad.

It was after he'd been promoted away from Abu Ghrayb and into a set of highly trusted guards surrounding Saddam that this journey had started. When Saddam began preparation for the expected American invasion, Hakim had been moved with a few other loyal commanders to a secret location in the Zagros Mountains in 2002. Though none of them was supposed to know what they were guarding, Hakim had become intensely curious once he got there. The cave, with a small entrance off a sparsely traveled path high in the mountains, was far larger and deeper than it appeared. To a Kurdish shepherd moving flocks to higher, richer pastures in the summer, it was a thirty sheep cave. Not worth using for refuge during a cold night. They were, in a sense, invisible.

But something valuable existed deep below that narrow entrance.

It hadn't been long before Hakim befriended the three scientists they protected. Contact was limited to minutes at a time, only when they came out from the isolated enclosure to have a smoke, but Hakim could see the man in charge liked him. He was accustomed to such glances of admiration. Hakim was taller and burlier than most of his countrymen, the kind of man he believed women fantasized about, the kind of man other men secretly wished they were. It had brought him friends and lovers he'd exploited over the years, and he wasn't above using his appeal again to discover the secrets of the guarded compound.

In the desert heat, Hakim unconsciously unbuttoned his shirt. He thought back to how reticent the shy scientist had been, forcing him to try something he'd never tried before. When months of friendship proved fruitless, Hakim seduced him. He didn't know if the scientist had been seeking a man for a lover, or if Hakim's powerful presence had overcome the man's hesitance. Not having women around for so long a period probably helped. But it had worked. And with his eyes closed, it hadn't seemed so bad.

Finally he learned what they guarded: a nuclear weapon so expertly hidden it had remained undiscovered, despite the invasion by the Americans and the death of Saddam Hussein.

When it became apparent to Hakim that even his contacts in Baghdad had forgotten him—or perhaps they were dead—he decided the time had come to take matters into his own hands. Without hesitation he killed the soldiers and the scientists. He closed up the faux back wall of the cave and travelled the Middle East underground to see what arrangements he could make. It had taken years to penetrate the secrecy of the organizations he needed to make the deal.

When the arrangement had almost been finalized, a middle man entered the picture as a broker for the Syrians. Vhorrdak was well-connected and seemed legitimate, but Hakim could not read him. It did not help that the man wore sunglasses all the time. He found the dark shades unnerving, especially since there was a subtle red glow he could detect behind the black lenses. Did the man really have red eyes, or was it a tactic to distract him? Now that Hakim thought about it, he could not picture the man's face. The details escaped him. They were like the sands that trailed behind him now, specks he knew were there but as he stared at them, they became part of a great cloud obscuring the distance.

* * *

Fareed saw it before Hakim did. At first he thought it a mirage, wavering in the heat. Then it became a black spot that slowly resolved itself as he approached. It was a truck of some kind. Of that Fareed was fairly certain. And it was not moving.

"How many kilometers?" Hakim asked.

Fareed glanced at the GPS unit. "To the rendezvous point?"

"To that truck up ahead. Or are they not the same?"

Fareed quickly corrected himself. "No, they are one and the same." Vhorrdak had warned him to watch for a change. He had nearly ruined the ruse. But as he looked at the basin they were entering, Fareed was beginning to wonder what he had gotten himself into. "Two kilometers. Five minutes."

"It seems we have arrived quickly for as slowly as you have been driving."

"I have picked up the pace. We are arriving on time and in the correct location."

Fareed hoped Hakim believed him. The truck features were becoming clearer and more recognizable as they approached. Like a mirage reflecting their image, it was distinctly recognizable—an identical M939 cargo truck. And, like theirs, the flatbed held something under a plain muslin cover.

Chapter Four

Syrian Desert, Western Iraq
December 18, 2012
9:37 a.m. local time

Time to Solstice: 76 hours, 34 minutes

Vhorrdak watched from a hidden spot on the rocky, desolate crag that rose above the Syrian Desert basin as the first truck approach the second. Not only was he hidden from the drama unfolding some distance away, he was also hidden from the lead sniper, Tabib, he'd hired as a part of his plan to take the device from Hakim. Fareed had vouched for the sniper and his spotter, Mehmet, and had made the initial connection. No doubt, Fareed was an amazing asset, one he would keep until the end. That a fool like Hakim had accepted a tactician like Fareed was so incomprehensible Vhorrdak could not consider it chance. It was one more indication that Vhorrdak's plan was destined to succeed. He could not be stopped.

The meeting place was southwest of the cities of Anah and Hadithah, far from the slim, fertile valley of the Euphrates River, and therefore far from any significant amount of vegetation. The three dimensional ghillie suits of the snipers reflected that, the camouflage blending easily into their surroundings.

Unnoticed, Vhorrdak turned his attention to Tabib. The sniper had placed his right eye to the daytime optic scope of his semi-automatic rifle and followed the first truck as it crossed the desert west to east. The truck had a flatbed covered in a white canvas cloth stretched across a looping frame. Dust flew up behind it, less so as it began to slow.

"Range?" Tabib asked the spotter.

Mehmet consulted his tactical scope. "Eighteen hundred meters and closing."

Vhorrdak smiled. The stationary truck was about a thousand meters away from them, an excellent distance for a sniper. Tabib had provided some strategic input for the ambush. Because the kill would take place in the morning, and the time of year placed the sun at its most southerly point, the sniper had recommended this southeasterly position where the sun was behind them as they looked out into the basin. The second sniper and spotter, who Tabib had hired to complete the ambush, were located equi-distant across the basin on a crag to the northeast of where the stationary truck stopped. The sun was in a slightly worse position for the other two, but Tabib asserted that his sniper compatriot could take out the other targets.

"So that we are of like purpose," Tabib told Mahmet, "remember we are not to kill the driver of the first truck. It should stop short of the second truck. We wait for everyone to get out of their vehicles before we go for the kill."

"It cannot come soon enough." Mahmet moved the binoculars slightly to the left. "We have already been out in the desert too long. I wish to get back to Lebanon."

"At least the hot and dry weather is decent for shooting." Tabib shifted the scope on his rifle toward the stationary truck where the two parties would attempt to switch cargo. "Reading on the position just in front of the stationary truck?"

Mahmet mentally adjusted for the heat and lower barometric pressure to give the .308 caliber projectile less drag. Accounting for the wind was a little trickier.

"Two clicks up, three clicks left."

Tabib made the adjustments. The sniper rested his cheek on the cheek pad and breathed a few times for practice. When the moment came, he would fire during his respiratory natural pause, when he had breathed out and his body was still and relaxed.

"Do you know where the truck is coming from?" Mahmet asked.

"I was told Mosul."

"That does not make sense. The truck comes from a random direction if Mosul was its starting point."

"Next time I will allow you to question the leader of this mission. I choose not to do that. It makes me nervous to be around him."

"In what way?"

"The man has red eyes. He tries to disguise them with dark sunglasses, but it is still noticeable."

"Red eyes? I have never heard of that."

"Believe me, you do not want to look into them for very long, even through dark shades."

Vhorrdak liked that he had this reputation.

"The driver of the moving truck is cautious." Mahmet's voice was low and quiet. Vhorrdak strained to hear it. "It may stop a hundred meters away. What is the cargo?"

"I do not know, but it must be valuable. I was repeatedly warned not to damage it."

* * *

Fareed did not like the looks of this situation. The basin was too perfect for an ambush. What if Vhorrdak decided to take him out? He had never completely trusted the man. Perhaps money had overcome his better senses. He slowed the truck and glanced around at possible places from which they could be attacked. There were many. He hoped Tabib was up there, and that he was not being double-crossed.

"Keep going," Hakim said. He pulled out a Heckler & Koch MK23 pistol and aimed it at Fareed. "I am the superior party here. I have what they want. They will not kill us. They do not know whether or not what they are seeking is in the back of the truck. If they kill us, they take the chance they will never get what they want."

Fareed did not seem to have any other choice than to trust Vhorrdak. He moved forward, stopping the truck twenty meters from the Syrians. They sat for several minutes. No one in the other truck got out. Fareed twisted to face Hakim. "So what are you waiting for?"

Hakim shrugged again. "I am waiting for them to make the first move. Maybe they want to make a statement about who they think is in charge."

There was movement from the other truck. A door opened. Fareed heard satisfaction in Hakim's voice. "See? Everything is going according to plan. The other driver is getting out now."

The two of them watched as the driver and his passenger got out of the truck. They stopped at the middle ground between the two trucks and looked at Hakim and Fareed expectantly.

But out of the corner of his eye, Fareed noticed Hakim moving quickly. He reached for his neck knife, but Hakim was already on him.

"You first," Hakim said, throwing him out of the vehicle. "In case they don't trust us."

* * *

"What are you waiting for?" Mahmet asked.

"The soldier that fell out of the driver's side is my friend Fareed. He is the one we will save."

"It looks like he was pushed."

"The passenger is getting out now. If the readings change when he approaches the kill zone, tell me." Tabib tightened his grip around the M110's trigger and let out his breath.

Fareed approached the middle ground between the trucks. He faced the driver from the second truck. Hakim, encouraged by what felt like good faith, did the same.

Vhorrdak smiled. He had waited a long time for this moment, the first step in his plan to push the world to nuclear war. But he could not let the Americans see it. He closed his eyes and pictured the scene from above.

And then the sky above the basin changed. The sand particles began to swirl and rise, gathering in the air, a sandstorm not touching the ground. Vhorrdak opened his eyes and checked on Tabib. The sniper took his eye off the target for a moment to check the bizarre occurrence. Mahmet noticed it, too.

"Where is it coming from?" Tabib asked.

"I do not know."

He looked back to his target. "No change in conditions?"

Mahmet checked, then answered in the same still tone he had maintained all along. "None."

Fareed, Hakim, and the other two drivers notice the sky, too.

Then in rapid succession, all of them except Fareed hit the ground, the impact of the dead bodies stirring up dust. It caught the wind and spiraled into the air, joining the riot of sand that swirled above them.

Chapter Five

Syrian Desert, Western Iraq
December 18, 2012
9:44 a.m. local time

Time to Solstice: 76 hours, 27 minutes

The sandstorm grew heavier but it was far above the basin. Fareed momentarily focused on the massacre that was around him. He kicked Hakim's body to make certain it was lifeless. Blood flowed out of the mouth, evidence enough for Fareed. Doing his best to avoid the pooling blood, Fareed stepped around the bodies, relieved that his was not one of them.

An M939 truck outfitted identically to the other two drove out from a nearby hill. Vhorrdak's plan was to serve up decoys to the Americans to keep them off guard while Fareed and his top recruit, Ashur, drove the nuclear weapon somewhere else. All of them would be given instructions when needed.

The truck pulled up and five men disembarked. One of them stripped Hakim's dead body of his uniform and dropped it in a large sack with a drawstring top. Another two likewise removed the bloodstained uniforms of their counterparts and placed them in the bag. Ashur jumped out and climbed in the back of Fareed's truck.

Fareed grabbed a small can of fuel and doused the heavy paper bag containing the uniforms. He lit the mess and walked away from it. They watched it burn with intensity.

A commercial cargo truck came rolling out of a cave. The truck was typical of those that hauled commercial freight in Iraq, sturdy but in disrepair. Fareed thought its condition the result of bad roads and roadside car bombs. The truck was driven by his remaining two recruits, both in Iranian uniforms.

Ashur hopped out of the back of the truck Fareed had driven into the desert. He called to the other men, and they helped him transfer the shiny, oblong case with the odd markings on it into the back of the commercial vehicle. Fareed found it to be lighter and smaller than expected, given the size of the truck. But the case was awkward, and they had been warned to be careful.

As soon as it had been transferred, the men moved onto the third identical M939 truck, the one that had come out of the hills. They divided its payload and shifted half of it into the first truck. Fareed knew the contents were little more than junk, vehicular parts twisted beyond usage, but useful for deception. The second truck, the one driven by the mole, had come across the desert with a similar payload.

As he prepared to leave in the commercial cargo truck, Fareed wondered about the dead bodies lying in the sand. Vhorrdak had given him no instructions as to what to do with them, only to burn the uniforms. He decided to leave them be. The heat and the sand would likely take care of them.

Once more he looked at the whirling sandstorm hovering above them.

* * *

Tabib, the sniper, and his spotter, Mahmet, had watched the activities going on the desert basin for far too long for Vhorrdak. He wondered what was taking Tabib so long to execute the next part of his mission. He had been quite clear with the sniper about what was to be done.

"What do you think was in the case?" Mahmet asked.

The sniper looked around before answering. "Something important."

Tabib rolled quickly to his left side, where the spotter was still set up, slightly behind him. Mahmet, surprised by the move, didn't recover quickly enough to block Tabib, who pulled the military survival knife from his ghillie suit. He slashed into Mahmet, ripping down his torso, killing him instantly.

Tabib leaned back up against his rifle and spotted the other sniper. Vhorrdak could see him estimating the conditions as he focused on his next victim. From beneath his sand-colored robe, Vhorrdak pulled out binoculars similar to the ones used by the spotter. He looked across the basin to where the other sniper and spotter were. The other two men had been as interested in the desert proceedings as Tabib had been. That left them exposed, if only slightly.

Tabib's first shot took the sniper out, but the spotter had quick reflexes. He realized what direction the shot had come from and moved behind cover.

Tabib squeezed off another shot.

Vhorrdak was certain it had hit the man, but in the thigh. Still it was a solid hit. Probably a critical wound. Out there long enough without help, the man would bleed to death. But until he did, he was still dangerous. Vhorrdak liked the way this was playing out.

The rifle disappeared behind cover. The spotter had likely retrieved it.

Tabib moved behind the crag out of harm's way. He shot near the spotter's position a couple of times without repercussion. Vhorrdak sensed Tabib's confidence returning, that perhaps he had fatally wounded the man.

Vhorrdak stepped out from his position, exposing himself to Tabib but remaining hidden from the spotter. He knew the color of his robe and the hot, dry conditions made him shimmer like a mirage. He took off his dark glasses to expose his red eyes.

"You got him," Vhorrdak whispered. "He'll die within the hour. Good job."

The sniper stood, surprised at Vhorrdak's presence. Vhorrdak had been counting on that. He liked that he inspired such respect, especially since fear was a big part of it.

Tabib bowed. "Thank you. If I can be of further service, you have only to ask. As you know, I can be trusted to keep the matter quiet."

"Yes. I'm confident of it." Vhorrdak allowed a hint of a sneer to permeate his voice.

A second passed before Tabib processed the sneer. Vhorrdak watched as the sniper dove for the safety of the crag a second too late. His right shoulder jerked, and he gripped it as a wave of pain and nausea washed over his face. He'd exposed himself to the other spotter, who was still able to shoot. And who wanted to kill him first.

"Very confident you will keep it quiet," Vhorrdak repeated.

Tabib lay in the hot dust for a moment, in shock. Blood spilled out of his shoulder. He crawled to the Mahmet's body and pawed at the dead man's ghillie suit, looking for a way to summon help.

"If you find the walkie-talkie," Vhorrdak said, "feel free to call for aid. No one is on the other end."

Vhorrdak left Tabib to rip away at Mahmet's coverings.

In the meantime, the three identical trucks pulled away, moving in directions that skewed from the directions they'd come. The commercial cargo vehicle moved back up into the hills. Vhorrdak was satisfied that everyone who remained was dead or would be, soon.

The wind began to blow through the basin. It picked up the sands and swirled them as though controlled by the deliberate hand of an artist. They covered the body of Hakim, who thought he could sell a nuclear weapon on the black market. They covered the dead soldiers who'd come to get the weapon and were ambushed. They engulfed the dead and the dying ambushers who fell victim to a plot bigger than their insignificant lives.

The sand storm descended from above and followed the trucks along their ways, obliterating their tracks from behind and staying above them, blocking the view of anyone who might be trying to track them.

Chapter Six

Cancun, Mexico
The Hotel Kukulcan
December 18, 2012
6:00 a.m. local time

Time to Solstice: 72 hours, 11 minutes

Standing under a beam twenty-five feet above him in a far corner of the atrium of the just completed Hotel Kukulcan, Jonas Sagiev looked up. Something wasn't right. He slipped the climber's pack from his shoulder. He wouldn't normally be out of bed this time of the morning, but Rebekah's tossing and turning had kept him from sleeping well. She'd said something about having dreams. He figured it was related to the pregnancy. She couldn't possibly sleep well, as often as she had to use the bathroom at night.

It didn't take much to keep him from sleeping, either. He was anxious about the grand opening and would be until the unveiling was official and he saw how the design was received by the architectural press. He decided to check on the atrium. Again. The hotel staff knew him and ignored his haunting the place. They'd probably been glad he'd been sightseeing yesterday. He'd accumulated so many frequent flier miles during the construction phase he could now upgrade to first class for life. The color variation he spotted on the beam, light gray against white, made him think he should investigate it. Even though, he admitted to himself, the upper confines of the atrium were not well lit this time of the morning. It was probably nothing at all.

He opened the backpack and pulled out the long, static rope. The diameter of the rope was a little over a centimeter, but it could support four hundred fifty pounds easily. Jonas's one hundred ninety was considerably less. He tied a figure eight knot in the middle of the rope and held both ends of the rope in one hand. With the other hand he tossed the figure eight high up into the air so that the knot fell over the beam. Jonas ran one end of the rope through the loop and pulled, raising the figure eight until the rope was secured at the top. He tugged it to make sure it was tight.

Pulling two mechanical ascenders out of his pack, he attached them to the side of the rope holding the knot tight against the beam. He slung the pack onto his shoulder. Then, putting a foot in each ascender, he pulled himself up, first right and then left, allowing the ascender to ratchet his feet higher and higher.

Jonas slowed as he approached the beam, distracted by the view. From high up the atrium had an entirely different look, but from any angle it was still an amazing structure. He'd designed it to be a modern take on Mayan architecture. From the outside, the atrium resembled the ancient Pyramid of Kukulcan at Chichen Itza but reinvented with modern features like glass panels that let light flood into the structure. This early in the morning, just three days from the winter solstice, light was not in great abundance. From the inside, the dominant feature was a five-sided Mayan arch, which served as the entrance to the atrium. He used the arch because it was a feature prevalent in almost every ruin found, although architecturally, 'corbelled' arches like the pointed Mayan arch provided less support than semicircular Roman arches, dating from approximately the same time. It was why the walls of Mayan buildings needed to be so thick. Jonas had designed around that weak point by incorporating the Mayan arch within a more structurally sound parabolic arch.

Jonas forced himself back on task. He slipped a hand into his pack and pulled out a flashlight. He was directly under the beam, and when he shined the light upwards, it cast shadows on what appeared to be a grayish mass.

He was just about to go higher on the rope to get a better look when he heard one of the staff members greet Mrs. Sagiev. He spotted her coming across the lobby. Pulling his feet from the ascenders and used rapid hand-over-hand movements, he let himself down until he was about her height from the bottom. He turned himself upside down, his mouth not far from hers.

"Kiss me," he said, puckering his lips.

She stayed clear of his mouth, but smiled. "You didn't leave a note when you left. And you know I don't like you doing the Spider-Man thing anymore."

"I had to check something high up. C'mon, kiss me." She remained just out of reach. "Rebekah ..."

She moved closer and gave him a peck on the cheek. "Seriously, Jonas. It's too dangerous, and we have a baby coming."

He flipped himself over and landed on the ground. Standing next to her in this place that represented such an achievement for him, he felt grateful she'd insisted on coming. He bent down and gave her the kiss he'd been hoping for.

She took a breath. "Wow."

"Yeah."

Jonas pulled on the end of the rope and the figure eight knot fell toward him. He removed the ascenders, untied the knot, and began to gather up his rope.

"What did you see up there?"

"Some kind of gray mass curving out on one of the beams. I thought the workmanship on the atrium had been better than that."

Rebekah craned her neck. "I don't see anything."

"It's not that obvious from down here. If I didn't know this atrium so well, I wouldn't have noticed."

"Talk to the construction manager. Promise me, no more acrobatic stuff."

Jonas paused, not ready to make promises he wouldn't keep if the situation demanded it. Instead he said, "I was just getting ready to look for him."

"Good." She gave him a sideways hug. "Well, Spidey, I'm not sure how long it's going to take for you to finish this up, but don't forget the tour bus for Chichen Itza leaves at 10:30. We can't afford to miss it if we're going to meet Professor Patcanul at 12:30."

"Once I find the foreman, I'll explain the situation and show him what it is. He can take it from there. I'll be back in an hour or so and we can get breakfast."

Jonas pulled her into his arms one more time and kissed her. She ran her fingers down his spine as they embraced, making him shiver.

"I'm proud of you," she whispered.

"I'm glad you're here with me."

Jonas watched her walk away, out the back of the atrium toward the hotel grounds. Then he took one more look toward the beam. What was that thing, and how had it gotten there? Much as he hadn't wanted to admit it to Rebekah, if they didn't have the tour already arranged at the ruins, he would have handled this himself. He wasn't sure the foreman would have the time or inclination to pursue it. He knew they were focused on the finishing touches in the villa area.

He coiled the rope, returning it and the ascenders to his pack. He slung the pack over his shoulder and went looking for the foreman.

* * *

A man in a hotel clerk uniform stepped out from behind the massive lobby desk and looked around. Everyone was busy and no one paid attention to him. Safe for just a few more moments, he figured.

He moved to the center of the atrium, to a waist-high faux stelae. He put the videocamera to his eye and filmed a final sequence in the atrium. At first his hand shook, but then he forced himself to be calm. Life was good. Who would have imagined the architect himself would come into the atrium alone this morning and climb to the very beam that was the target? And how fortunate he'd been there, videocamera in hand, planning for his own safe disappearance during the grand opening party two days from now. Unless there was a technical glitch, he could now edit the video to make it look like Jonas Sagiev had been the one to alter the beam. Barring any last minute unforeseen circumstances, he should be able to keep management busy with some diversions, tiny bits of sabotage that would make them forget the seemingly insignificant complication Jonas had just uncovered. Until the time it would come into play.

The new development would make Vhorrdak very happy.

Chapter Seven

Washington, DC
Office of the National Security Advisor
December 18, 2012
11:05 a.m. local time

Time to Solstice: 68 hours, 06 minutes

Jim Harrington reread the speech he was preparing for his talk at Yale. The speech didn't break new ground; the stated goal was to better explain the President's position on the threat of nuclear proliferation. It had taken on new importance in light of recent events he and his team were monitoring, though few knew about that aspect.

The National Security Advisor swiveled in his chair and looked at the world map on the far wall. The Syrian Desert was one big brown wasteland that stretched from the eastern end of Syria into the middle of western Iraq. He'd never been there, nor did he ever want to be there. In fact, he felt sorry for the people who were. And that included a few more Americans now. Over the last two days the inhospitable land had become the focus of a two-squad, quiet American presence. At least, Jim hoped it was quiet.

He turned back to the document on the computer. The speech, in all likelihood, wouldn't change anything. Iran was still determined to become a nuclear power, however they could arrange it. The situation was volatile and could become more so. Jim added a few notes for the teleprompters—where to slow for expected applause and where to pause for dramatic effect—but overall he thought it was ready, especially since it had been approved by the White House's top speech writer. Jim had always been good at making speeches.

A light knock on the door made him close the laptop instinctively. "Come in."

Travis Black, his assistant advisor, ducked his head as he stuck it in the door. At 6' 10", the man was freakishly tall. "Got a minute?"

"Of course. Have a seat." Jim got up and motioned for his second-in-command to join him across the room, at a small round meeting table. He loved his office. It had two desks and sophisticated electronic equipment with amazing capabilities. It was so much bigger than the hall closet he'd had when he was the assistant, the office Travis now had. Plus it had space for meetings, important since no one could rely on getting a meeting room in the West Wing on short notice.

Black's demeanor betrayed him when he stiffly eased into the chair. His back was straight against the backrest and his feet were flat to the floor. The Assistant National Security Advisor was usually loose and friendly.

"I don't like the look on your face, Travis."

He blew out a breath. "Major problems. That cargo being transferred from the rebel Iraqi? It's gone."

"How can it be gone?"

"We don't know. We know the buyers and sellers met as expected. But now we can't find either. A sandstorm came up and we lost the signal from the mole. Everyone seems to have disappeared."

Jim ran a finger across his lower lip. He realized what he was doing and stopped it. Nervous habits betray, he thought. "A double-cross?"

"Who knows? An informant saw the insurgent's truck leave Mosul, so we know it started as expected."

"Even if it was a double-cross, the trucks couldn't just disappear."

"Special Forces had them on satellite surveillance. We had an inkling there might be a problem, but before we could send the helicopters in, the sandstorm blew up."

"Is it possible the trucks were just caught in it?"

"If so, they'd have tried to get to the natural caves. Until the storm dies down and they get back out, we won't know."

"Hard to trace anything after a sandstorm's been through there. The satellites are still watching the area, of course." Jim leaned back in his chair.

Travis sat quietly, waiting. Jim thought he might make a recommendation, but he didn't.

Jim stood up. "Well, let's keep this close to the vest for now. Stay on it and keep me updated. We have to get that cargo."

Travis started to leave, then turned around. “You should know ... the Pentagon has found out.”

“The Department of Leaks? What do they know? That we can’t find it?”

“Not that, not yet. They know the cargo could be nuclear.”

“Great. We might as well put it on CNN.”

Travis chuckled. “This might be one secret they won’t leak. Word gets out that there’s even the possibility of an unguarded nuclear weapon in the Middle East, and we could be looking at Armageddon.”

Jim looked at the map on the wall. “If it’s real, and it makes it out of Iraq into Iran or Syria, it will be Armageddon.”

Chapter Eight

Chichen Itza, Mexico
Entrance to the Ruins
December 18, 2012
12:40 p.m. local time

Time to Solstice: 65 hours, 31 minutes

Rebekah looked at her watch as she and Jonas rushed to the entrance of Chichen Itza. “We’re ten minutes late. I hope Professor Patcanul hasn’t left.”

Jonas was a few steps behind her. “It’s Mexico, Rebekah. No one is ever on time. He’ll be there.” Jonas glanced at the throng of tourists standing in their way. “If we can get to him.”

Lining the entrance to the Mayan ruins were locals hawking souvenirs. Visitors bargaining for the trinkets meandered back and forth among the vendors. Rebekah almost bumped into a heavyset man wearing a “Kukulcan Rules” t-shirt, weaving out of his way just before collision. Jonas noticed a number of handmade wooden Mayan calendars on display. Wheels spun within a wheel to reveal the complexity of using the ancient time-keeping device. Rebekah had explained the Mayan system of kuns, katuns, and baktuns, and how the repetition of 13 baktuns created an era of over 5,000 years, but he would be hard pressed to explain it. He just knew the Mayan calendar ended in a few days with the winter solstice.

Rebekah stayed ahead of Jonas, maneuvering her large belly through the crowd with surprising ease. He finally caught up with her as she reached the back of the line to buy tickets. She put her hands on her hips and glanced around. “I don’t see him.”

“I thought he was going to leave tickets.”

“I know, but with the line so long and us late, I was hoping he might wait for us out here.”

“Since he’ll be looking for you, why don’t you go up toward the gate while I hold our place in line? If you spot him, you can let him know we’ll be a few more minutes.”

“More like half an hour,” she grumbled. She did what Jonas asked, though, yielding her spot to him while she pushed through to the gate. She disappeared into the crowd.

Jonas eased the climber's bag from his back and examined the faces surrounding him—old, young, white, black, even a few Asians. Most of the Mayan faces were either workers or vendors. A middle-aged gentleman with the stocky Mayan build broke out of the crowd and stood in front of him. His dark face was nearly circular with a broad, flat nose in the middle. His forehead sloped away from his face, exaggerated by coarse black hair combed over the top of his head. When he smiled at Jonas, his teeth seemed almost too white, although Jonas realized it could have been the contrast with the dark skin, not some laser treatment gone wild.

"Are you Mr. Sagiev?" he asked.

"I am. Are you ... "

Before he could get the question out, Rebekah appeared at Jonas' side. "Professor Patcanul?"

The professor's eyes seemed to fix on her pregnancy. "Rebekah. How nice to meet you. Please call me Manuel. I noticed you in line, and then you got away before I could reach you. Professor Davis gave an excellent description of you both."

"We're sorry to be running behind. The tour bus was late getting out of Valladolid. I hope you haven't been waiting long."

"Only a few moments."

"It's so exciting to meet you."

Jonas never quite understood Rebekah's rock-star fascination with archeologists and linguists.

The professor deflected her praise. "Please. I am honored to meet you. Professor Davis has spoken highly of your work. But he did not mention you were with child."

"You know Harry. Buried in his work. I'm not sure he's noticed yet."

"When are you due?"

"Another month, but the doctor thinks the baby might be late."

"I'm surprised you were allowed to leave the country."

Jonas coughed. Rebekah shot him a glance.

"I didn't tell him my doctor I was going. We're only going to be here a few days. I see you've met my husband."

"We were just getting acquainted. Come, we must hurry if we are to stay on schedule. Since I'm with you, you won't need tickets." The professor started off at a quick pace.

Jonas picked up the pack and moved along side him. He stuck out his hand. "I'm Jonas."

"He's the reason we're in Mexico," Rebekah said, a few steps behind. "I wanted us to be together when the hotel opened."

Manuel turned to him. "I understand you're one of the architects on the new Kukulcan Hotel."

Jonas nodded.

"You should be proud of your work. Magnificent job on the atrium. So Mayan, and yet so modern."

"Have you received an invitation to the grand opening? We'd love to have you as our guest. And your wife."

"He's a widower," Rebekah said.

"It is true that I am alone. But it is kind of you to ask. And I do plan to attend."

An awkward silence fell over them as they followed Manuel past the ticket kiosk, past the bookstore and souvenir gift shop, and into the 'NO ENTRY' side opposite the turnstiles admitting visitors into the ruins area. The professor looked to be in his mid-fifties, Jonas thought. Far too young to have lost a wife. He wondered how it had happened.

Manuel spoke softly to a guard in Spanish. The guard looked first at Rebekah, then at Jonas. He swung open the exit gate and they entered.

Rebekah broke the silence. "Thanks for agreeing to give us a personal tour."

"It is my pleasure, but my part will come later, after you've joined a tour led by my sister Diega. She runs a guide service here." He glanced at his watch. "We must hurry to catch up with her."

Manuel rushed them past more locals and their wares. "Diega will probably be at the Ball Court, but only for a few more moments. I know you'll want to see the Pyramid of Kukulcan, and that will be her next stop."

Jonas was struck by the odd, cross-shaped trees that swayed in the hot breeze. He remembered them from his earlier trips, but had never asked about them. Their trunks went straight to a certain height, then stopped and split into two arms, each at nearly ninety degrees to the trunk. "What kind of trees are those?" he asked Manuel.

"Ceiba trees. They are sacred to the Maya. A ceiba tree is believed to be at the center of the Mayan universe."

"They look like crosses."

"Yes. The Catholic fathers appropriated the symbol quickly when they arrived in the 1500s. In fact, there are legends of a talking ceiba tree that prophesies the future, dating back to that time. The tree supposedly had the face of Jesus."

"But it was never really a Christian symbol, was it?" Rebekah asked. "The tree existed before then, if I remember correctly."

Jonas noticed that Rebekah was breathing hard. He touched Manuel lightly on the shoulder and indicated Rebekah's labored pace.

"It depends on whose legend you believe." Manuel changed his gait to a walk. "One version holds that the Mayan elders had kept the tree a secret for centuries. The priests only learned of it when they converted an elder in the inner circle. Once discovered, the Mayan elders hid the tree again. But it didn't stop the fathers from using the legend to their advantage."

Jonas noticed there was no malice in the professor's voice when he talked about the Christians and their conversion of the Maya. "Is that the version you believe?"

"After much consideration, yes, that's what I believe. It explains the source of later Mayan prophecies."

"Really? What prophecies?"

Just as Jonas asked the question, the path broke through the jungle and into the clearing where the ruins had been recovered and restored. In the center, high above all the others, stood the dominant Pyramid of Kukulcan. With the height of a six story building and stone steps leading to the top on all four sides, it stopped Jonas, even though he'd seen it before.

Rebekah clung to him, speechless.

Chapter Nine

Chichen Itza, Mexico
The Ruins
December 18, 2012
12:50 p.m. local time

Time to Solstice: 65 hours, 21 minutes

Manuel was momentarily relieved he could avoid Jonas' question. The story of the ceiba tree had led him to tell more than he had planned for them at that time, but fate often took decisions out of his hands. For now, he would focus their attention on the Pyramid. He also needed to get them over to Diega.

"It is magnificent, is it not?" he said. "Not the oldest of the Mayan temples but certainly one of the most impressive."

Manuel noticed that Rebekah put her hand over her child. She caught him watching her do it.

"The baby is kicking," she said. "I tell him not to be in such a hurry to get out. We need to get back to the States first."

Manuel tried not to show his pleasure at hearing the baby's sex. "You know it's a boy?"

Jonas, now close to his wife, put his hand on her stomach. She moved it to where the baby was kicking. "We thought about being old-fashioned and not finding out until he was born, but we couldn't stand not knowing," she said. "Impatient, I guess. Like the baby."

Manuel trusted the baby would continue to be so. "I'm afraid I must be impatient, too."

Rebekah laughed. "I know, I know, we need to keep moving." She walked toward the Temple. "One of the new seven wonders of the world. I wanted to see it when I helped with the excavation at Ek Balam, but we ran out of time."

"I had seen it shortly before I first met Rebekah," Jonas said. "We met that same night at a Starbucks in Cancun."

Now Manuel smiled. Yes, he was certain it had happened that way. No doubt the celestial sign had also occurred that night. The entry of what would become the Comet Quetzalcoatl into visible range of Earth. Although no one knew it for what it was at the time.

Manuel pointed to a shorter but longer structure far to the left of the Pyramid. “We must hurry over to the Ball Court. Diega said she would try to hold her group there for you, but the tour guides are on a schedule. She will be moving them along soon.”

* * *

Jonas saw a look pass between Manuel and Diega just before the brother and sister hugged, but he had no idea what it meant. Surprise? But she had known they were coming. Relief that they had arrived in time? Maybe, but he thought it was something more. He would have continued to ponder it but he couldn’t stop looking around at the Ball Court they were in. He’d seen it when he’d toured Chichen Itza, but then his interest had been more focused on the Pyramid. Now he could appreciate the other ruins more fully.

“Diega, my friends Rebekah and Jonas Sagiev.” Manuel stretched out his arm toward them.

“A pleasure to meet you at last,” Diega said. She almost bowed as she said it. A bit Asian-like, Jonas thought. But there was nothing remotely Asian about her appearance. She had the same coarse hair as her brother, and as black, though it was longer and parted in the middle. The long hair fell on either side of her face, emphasizing the roundness. Her nose was broad but the bridge was more prominent than her brother’s, and her cheekbones were higher. She wore khaki shorts and a rose colored shirt embroidered with the name of her tour company on it. “Sagiev is an interesting last name. Is it Jewish?” she asked Jonas.

He nodded.

“Are you from Israel?”

“I was born there,” Rebekah said, “but my parents came to the United States shortly after that. I was naturalized with my father and mother when I was nine. Jonas’ family has been in the United States for a long time.”

Diega inched closer to them. “I have an interest in Jewish prophecy. Similarities exist between them and our ancient Mayan prophecies.”

"I have to confess I'm not a practicing Jew, much to the horror of my parents." Jonas pointed to Rebekah. "She knows more about that kind of thing."

"I hope we may talk more later about this."

Diega looked around at the members of her tour group, all wearing matching yellow t-shirts inscribed with the name of an Audubon chapter in Oregon. They had spread throughout the center of the Ball Court. She raised a sign with the name of the tour group and spoke loudly. Her voice had a huskiness to it that penetrated the drone of the side conversations. "If my tour group will follow me, please, we are heading to the Pyramid of Kukulcan." She began walking toward the far end of the Ball Court.

Rebekah leaned into Jonas. "I wish we had more time to spend here. See those hieroglyphics on that section of the wall?"

Jonas could see the area she pointed to, close to them. They were standing near the center of the arena, close to what Jonas presumed would be the visitor's side. The ball stadium was organized like a modern football stadium. The grander side, which had box-like seating above the stone 'bleachers,' was opposite them. The Mayan hieroglyphics Rebekah motioned toward were large and distinct.

"Do you know what they say?"

"I have a general idea. The reliefs show the losers being decapitated, and then their descent into the underworld. The glyphs around them give the dates when the event occurred and what happened. It's tough to read the symbols because so much has worn away."

Manual said, "Professor Davis said you were making great strides in your understanding of the written Mayan language."

Jonas turned in surprise to find that he was right behind them.

"After the tour I will be happy to return with you here," Manuel continued, "although by that time you may find other structures that have more compelling stories. But please, for now, follow Diega. I shall be back at the end of the tour."

"He's a little odd," Jonas whispered to Rebekah after he made certain Manuel had walked away.

"Perhaps, but he's one of the premier Mayan scholars of this century. It's unbelievable that he's going to give us a personal tour of the restricted areas later."

The yellow-shirted tourists had closed in around Diega and the cluster headed across the expanse toward the Pyramid. Jonas took Rebekah's hand and they hurried as quickly as Rebekah's pregnancy would allow. Diega stood in a sunny area near a corner of the Pyramid. One side of the Pyramid was in light; the other was draped in shadow with the exception of a small wedge that was still lit.

"The Maya were particularly advanced in the fields of astronomy, mathematics, and the calendar," Diega said. "The architecture of this pyramid incorporates those elements. You will notice that two of the sides are almost fully in shadow." She crossed between the light and shadow. "In two days, at the winter solstice, they will be completely dark." She moved back into the light. "And the other two sides will be completely in sun."

A few of the more curious tourists followed Diega's movements step by step, talking among themselves. She waited until they quieted. "At the equinoxes, the sun strikes the pyramid in such a way that on the walls of the stone staircase, it looks like a great snake of light slithers down the pyramid. The Maya created all this without the aid of modern computers."

Jonas' first visit had been deliberately scheduled at the September equinox and he'd witnessed the phenomenon. The experience of actually watching the sunlight hit the stones and seeing them shimmer in sequence as they created the 'body' of the snake descending the Pyramid was incredible.

Rebekah nudged Jonas and handed him the camera. "Take a picture of me here," she said. She moved to the place where there was only a sliver of the sunlight remaining on the otherwise shaded side. She was half in the sun, half in the dark.

Jonas put his pack by his feet. He looked through the lens and fiddled with the close-up button.

Diega continued her speech. "This pyramid is dedicated to Kukulcan, the supreme Mayan god. The Aztecs called him Quetzalcoatl."

The crowd buzzed.

"Like the comet?" asked a voice.

"Indeed, the new comet was named for him," Diega said. "How many of you have been up late at night to see it?"

Rebekah raised her hand. Jonas snapped the photo.

"Rebekah, you had your hand up."

"I was answering her question. Take another."

"Prophecies claim that Kukulcan will come again at the end of time, born out of the mouth of the feathered serpent. Some say this comet is his sign."

Jonas took a second photo. He started to hand the camera back to Rebekah.

"The flash didn't go off," she said.

"I didn't use it. We can adjust the balance on the computer."

"Yeah, but the better the photo, the better we can adjust it. Try it again with the flash."

"Have I ever told you you're anal about these things?"

"Just take the picture, Spidey."

Jonas sighed and selected the forced flash option. He positioned for a third photo.

"What do you think about the Mayan calendar ending in two days?" asked a different voice.

"Are all of you familiar with that?" Diega asked. "Our Mayan calendar, which has been accurate now for 5,125 years, ends on December 21st."

There was more whispering in the crowd. Jonas supposed they all knew. He snapped the next photo.

"Do you really think it'll be the end of the world?" asked a skeptical voice.

"Certainly not right away."

To Jonas, it sounded like a laugh line, but the crowd tittered nervously.

Diega continued. "Because the Spanish destroyed so many Mayan records, we are not sure what the ancients thought would happen. One common scenario is that because we Maya view time as cyclic, the end of this era will be the beginning of a new one, marked by the birth of Kukulcan. Another has the beginning of worldwide destruction."

"I guess we'll know soon enough," someone said.
Jonas couldn't see who said it, but he liked the cynical tone in the voice. And he agreed with it. He handed the camera to Rebekah.

"Another messenger of gloom and doom. Y2K all over again," he whispered.

"Shhh." She took the camera and backed through the photos Jonas had taken, squinting in the sunlight. She moved into the shadow so she could see the LED display better. "Hmmm. Would you take one more? This time close up in this area with these hieroglyphics. I worked on similar ones at Ek Balam."

Jonas rolled his eyes, but he took back the camera.

* * *

Vhorrdak wore a yellow shirt like the group of tourists from Oregon. It had been simple to obtain one by following a guest into the restroom. He smiled at the thoughts that would occur to the shirtless tourist when he awoke from his slumber.

Vhorrdak wore dark sunglasses and a ball cap he'd obtained in the gift shop, but he purposefully kept the scruffy beard he'd been working on for several days. If anyone remembered him, they'd remember the stubble, and that would be gone easily. He checked the time on his cell phone. He had only a couple of minutes to make this happen before the time window expired. That these two were poised for another photo could not have been more perfect. He approached Jonas.

"Would you like me to take a photo of the two of you?"

Jonas glanced at the Audubon t-shirt and consented.

Easy, Vhorrdak thought. The two moved back toward the Pyramid. Vhorrdak knew exactly where to position the camera. The sun was causing the shadow to creep across the Pyramid. He aimed where that shadow would be in the next seconds. He made sure the camera was force-flashed.

Jonas and Rebekah smiled, though Vhorrdak hardly noticed. He stepped into the shadow of the Pyramid. It would create the exact effect he wanted to obtain.

He pushed the button, heard the click. His two subjects lit up on the right side of the image. To the left, and more important, were a set of hieroglyphics covered in shadow that, with the lighting the camera provided, would set in motion a series of events he would do his best to control, though he didn't know fully what they would be or how they would all play out.

Chapter Ten

Winslow Indian Health Center, Arizona
Just south of the Navajo Indian Reservation
December 18, 2012
Seconds later

Time to Solstice: 65 hours, 00 minutes

Talasi Evenhema grabbed her briefcase and snapped shut the trunk of her ice blue Ford Focus. She glanced at the sky where dark clouds were gathering. A couple of raindrops splashed on her dark skin. She headed toward into the building.

The Winslow Indian Health Center was a two story, adobe-style medical facility that served the needs of mainly Navajo, but also a few Hopi Indians like herself. The Hopi Indian Reservation was in the northern part of the larger Navajo nation and was surrounded by it. East of the reservation and closer to her people was the Tuba City medical center. Though she would have had more contact with her own people there, she chose to live in Winslow. Winslow had a population of ten thousand, not all that much larger than Tuba City, but it had more of the modern conveniences she had become accustomed to during her medical education and residency at the University of Arizona in Tucson. It also had the advantage of being located on Interstate I-40, an easy drive from Flagstaff International Airport. In case she needed a flight in a hurry, which she might.

Something made her stop half-way from the parking lot to the entrance. The black clouds which had gathered overhead parted. She felt warmth on the side of her neck below her jawbone and put her hand on the unusual five sided birthmark there. A ray of sunlight beamed though the parted clouds and fell on her face. She closed her eyes and breathed in, concentrating.

The vision hit her again. The pregnant woman. The man by her side. And something dark, in the shadows, a force that she couldn't see, but feared. She knew there was a danger. And if she went to it, she would place herself in danger.

This was the first time she'd seen the vision in daylight. Mostly it came at night, in dreams.

Talasi took a step back. Her father had made her memorize the legends of her people, of the end of the world, of a king that would come. He had told her of a prophecy made centuries ago to one of her ancestors, that a descendent would be there at the birth.

But for what reason? He didn't know. The place would be far away, that much he knew. A sign in the sky would be given to the eldest.

She was the eldest. In fact, the only child of her father, also an eldest. When her father died several years ago, the prophecy had fallen to her to fulfill. Either she would give birth to another eldest, or, if the sign came, she must go. He made her promise she would go, that she would believe.

It was not her nature to believe. He'd known that. But he'd made sure she'd had the grants, the loans, and whatever money he could scrape together to send her to school to become the doctor she wanted to be. He told her he believed in her dream and asked only that she believe in his. At the end, his end, she'd made the promise. But she never expected to fulfill it.

Then she started having the dreams. When had the first one been? Almost immediately after his death? The woman hadn't been pregnant then. She'd seen her approach the man. But that was all she saw. Another, half a year later. A wedding. But starting eight months ago the visions came more often. A conception, a baby growing inside the woman. If this was her destiny, could she resist it?

Earlier in the week, she'd read the reports of the Comet Quetzalcoatl, traced its path on maps. It would reach its zenith at the winter solstice, over Cancun. It felt like the sign in the sky.

Talasi returned to her car. She opened the trunk and threw her briefcase back in. The clouds merged again, with no sunlight to be seen. A lightning bolt streaked through the sky from east to west. Taking refuge in the vehicle, she started the engine and drove to the interstate. She knew the way to the Flagstaff airport.

What she wasn't sure of, was how this would all come together. But the signs and circumstances were too powerful to ignore.

* * *

London, England
Early evening traffic near Heathrow Airport

Colin Noble disliked the traffic, but most of all he disliked the job that took him to Heathrow Airport every day. He was a soldier by training, a damn good one. He was particularly good at weaponry, which, in a country that didn't permit citizens to carry arms and even restricted what police could carry, was not a particularly valued talent.

Colin beeped the hooter of his Jaguar at the green Vauxhall ahead of him, blocking two lanes, trying to decide which one it wanted to be in. Idiot drivers.

After Iraq, Colin had found himself needing a job--and taking whatever was available. Which meant security at Heathrow. He felt that at thirty years old and with as much experience as he'd had, he should have been hired into a better position. Searching through bags, questioning citizens, and wrestling the occasional tough guy to the ground were not particularly challenging. Not worthy of his talents. But it paid the rent.

Not that Colin was without resources. Or rather, his father was not without resources. The old man always seemed to have money. When Colin had been younger, his father had passed it off with a preposterous story, that somewhere in the far distant past, one of his ancestors had been a descendent of Mother Shipton, a famous sixteenth century prophetess. The resourceful relative, supposedly also blessed with the gift of predicting future events, had become a consultant of the wealthy and powerful. Until her death at ninety-nine, which she correctly prophesied, she used her visions, the Mother Shipton books, and supposedly the legendary book of Merlin to accumulate massive wealth. Today, his father said, that wealth was in a dozen real estate trusts all over the world.

Colin believed that back in sixteenth century all it took was one lucky eclipse prediction to get a royal appointment. But he was no longer quick to dismiss the family legend. At one time Colin's father had been stingy with the money, but now that he was sick and needed his son's care, he'd become more generous. And his bank balance never fell below twenty-five thousand pounds.

The Vauxhall managed to squeeze into the middle lane, and Colin swerved around it into the fast lane, glaring at the driver. He pushed on the accelerator and zipped ahead, catching up to the faster moving traffic.

Twenty-five thousand pounds was a lot of money. No one at the Bank of England would tell him where it came from. The account had been with the bank for centuries, and the instructions by which money was transferred into the account was held in the strictest confidence. Colin's name had been added to the account, but he was not permitted to know its secrets.

Colin had tested it a couple of times, removing ten thousand pounds at a time. The balance went right back to twenty-five thousand. His father had found out and warned him not to be greedy. But he'd let him keep the money. Colin hadn't spent much of it, other than splurging on the Jag. A soldier didn't need that much.

But now that his father was dying, the old man was starting to hallucinate. In his feverish state he'd talk of the Mother Shipton and Merlin prophecies. Of a king, to be born at the end of time. Colin knew of the Merlin crap, of Arthur coming back. He joked that Arthur could knight him. Sir Colin Noble. But the comment made his feverish father angry. Colin played along night after night, trying to make the man more comfortable.

Another night his father said the Mother Shipton prophecies had predicted one of their descendants would be there at the birth of the king. From the moment he'd seen the birthmark on Colin, he'd believed it would fall to him. He babbled of a sign in the sky to be given, of how the Comet Quetzalcoatl fulfilled that sign, and how Colin would need to find the apex of the path it followed.

More crap, Colin had thought, even as he'd propped up the pillow behind his father's head. Except for the dreams he'd been having lately. A pregnant woman. Her husband threatened. And two others like him. In other dreams, he almost saw their faces. Almost. Instead, he saw their necks and the bizarre, five-sided birthmark he himself had.

Red brake lights snapped Colin out of the memory. He slammed on his own brakes and the Jaguar came to halt behind a Volkswagen banger at a traffic light that had just turned red. He inched up when the amber light also lit, anticipating it would soon go green and the banger would move. He had told his father he'd be there after work, but the afternoon's bad weather had delayed flights and he'd had to work overtime. He'd called, and his father, in a weird, far-away voice, told him it would be all right. To go wherever he was needed. Yeah, like he was needed anywhere else tonight but his father's flat.

The light was taking forever to turn green. Colin glanced in the rear view mirror, into the darkening western sky. The storm had blown over, and the clouds had disappeared. Colin could see the Comet.

Hooters suddenly went off, impatient drivers puzzled by the lengthy red light. Colin glanced up to the traffic signal. The power lines begin to shake. The bulbs of the signal popped, first green, then amber, then red. The light went dead. And yet the power lines continued to shake.

In his mind, the horns became screams. In his mind, he saw the pregnant woman and the man. He heard his father's words and he knew--knew--what his father had meant. Everything felt true, the history and the legends and his father's own prophecies. He had to go. He pulled into the slow lane and then onto the shoulder. He made a sharp turn onto the street and headed back toward the airport.

He had traced the apex of the comet earlier. It would reach its highest point in the sky over Cancun, Mexico, in two days. For whatever reason, for however it would go down, he would need to be there.

* * *

The stranger remained in the shadow of the Pyramid. It was difficult to see him, especially after the flash. Jonas wasn't much of a photographer, but he thought it was likely the picture wouldn't come out well, since the camera was in shadow and he and Rebekah were in sunlight. He stepped out of position to take the camera from the photographer.

"Wait!" The stranger's voice was unsettlingly commanding. Jonas stopped without thinking. "Let me just take one more. I'm not sure that last one will come out well."

Jonas stepped back next to Rebekah. The stranger hardly waited for them to smile before he clicked the shutter button and the flash came again.

* * *

Kung Fu practice area
Henan Province, China
Seconds before

Dark clouds covered the sky above the kwoon where Yan Zhou studied the ancient practices of kung fu. Yan had been confused by his grandmaster's decision to move this morning's exercises outside in such inclement weather. As one of Sifu's top students and a master himself, Yan was expected to lead the lessons. Today was especially unsettling as he found himself under unwavering scrutiny by his teacher. Between the streaks of lightning that flashed from cloud to cloud, the uncomfortable slickness of the grass under his feet, and the glare of his grandmaster, his focus was challenged. Nonetheless, he was determined to maintain his composure.

Yan dropped into a horse stance and continued with Qigong exercises, exercises he'd been practicing since childhood. As his body moved into the familiar forms and he felt his muscles loosen, he warmed fully to the challenges of Sifu watching him closely.

His focus was so complete that the lightning bolt which struck the tree nearest him did not prevent him from completing his next move. He smelled burnt wood before he heard his grandmaster's voice call the lessons to a halt. With one eye on the tree and the lightning in the sky, Yan bowed and moved closer to his grandmaster to receive further instructions.

"The time has come, Yan. You have seen the sign, and I sense you know this as well."

"Yet, I am your *dizi*. It is at your command I will leave."

"No. You are your own master now. You are accomplished in our art, and you have a destiny far beyond mine. I have known this since your father and mother entrusted you to me as a child. And I have been truthful with you since you came of age. It must be your judgment."

Yan breathed deeply. On the day he turned sixteen, his grandmaster had given him a letter from his parents that explained his destiny. How could they have been so trusting of his fate, he wondered? Had they not a trace of fear that he might die before he came of age? This angered him. Who would have known if he had died? And what of the I Ching prophecies? Would the destiny that was supposed to have been his been passed along to another, or would the chain have been broken?

It was a heavy weight, this thing.

"Grandmaster ..." He hesitated, then bowed. "I know the time has come for me to leave."

"You will find a small purse on your bed. There is money enough inside to see you through this task."

Yan wondered at the advance knowledge his teacher exhibited. But he was a practiced master at many things. "Have you any last messages for me?"

His master put his hand on his shoulder, an uncharacteristic move. "You have mastered the enemies you can see, but your true test will come from the enemy you cannot see. Stay true to the test. Any wavering will be a victory for the enemy."

"My master."

Yan bowed and backed away.

"Lift your head, Yan. Turn and walk away. We part as equals."

Still, Yan bowed before he straightened and turned his back on Sifu, an unthinkable action. Yan felt raindrops run down his shaved head, and he ran his fingers over the top, flinging the water down his back and past the five-sided birthmark on his neck.

* * *

The third flash of the camera came and went, leaving spots before Jonas' eyes. He heard a strange, electronic tapping sound. It took root in his brain, the rhythm calling to mind a song he'd heard long ago. Something by AC/DC? Maybe.

As he moved to take the camera from the stranger, he realized it was the stranger's cell phone making the sound. Four repeated taps, a pause, four repeated taps, a pause.

The stranger handed the camera to him. "Excuse me, there is something I must do."

He hurried away before Jonas could thank him, and the spots in Jonas' eyes prevented him from getting a good look at the man.

Rebekah squinted. “That was weird.”

“Agreed,” Jonas said. But even stranger was that he could not get that tapping rhythm out of his head.

Chapter Eleven

Washington, DC
Situation Room, The White House
December 18, 2012
2:11 p.m. local time

Time to Solstice: 65 hours, 00 minutes

Jim Harrington tapped his fingers on the oblong table before him in the Situation Room. He noticed he'd established a rhythm. Four beats, a pause, four beats, a pause. He forced himself to stop it. Another nervous habit. He was here representing the President, and while he wasn't unaccustomed to the role, this was not with the press or some public group. This was the military. Dealing with them was the one thing he hadn't liked about the president's request that he take on this very sensitive assignment. First it was just a small Special Forces group; now, since the SF guys needed to interface with Iraqi military, the Department of Defense was involved, meaning even more people had the potential to learn about this possible crisis. Before, he'd been dealing directly with a colonel in Iraq, now he had to run everything through the DOD. And this was supposed to be kept quiet.

"Hello, Jim."

Jim looked up to see General Clayton Archer enter the room. He came alone.

"Clay, it's good to see you."

"I hear you asked for me personally."

"I did. Have a seat."

Jim liked the affable general. On occasion, the two men played golf at Tantallon Country Club. He knew the white-haired, sixty-five year-old, life-long military man had seen a lot in his day, and nothing fazed him.

The Situation Room was actually a complex of rooms, all equipped with the latest technology. Jim had chosen a smaller conference room since he wanted as few people involved as possible. The room had only seven chairs around a mahogany table and not much standing room. Using the Situation Room also had other advantages as well. It was wired for long distance conferencing, which was a big help in getting reports from Iraq. The monitors could display feed from anywhere, including satellites perched strategically in orbit over the Middle East. Operating the equipment were three Information Specialists.

Jim liked that maps could be pulled up instantly, too. While he was good with geography, this current problem involved locations so precise that maps were necessary to understand the logistics.

"Travis briefed you on the situation, and you've been in contact with our men in Iraq?" Jim asked.

"I have. I'm glad the president put you in charge of this. Your stature will be raised because of it."

"Provided it goes well."

"It will. Once the storm dies down, we'll get in there and find the trucks and the nuke."

Jim shifted in his chair. "If it's a nuke. I'm still hoping it's someone's idea of a very stupid joke."

"The Iraqi who tried to sell it would have been very stupid to go to these lengths, if it wasn't the real thing."

"I know, it's just … the consequences of the whole thing."

Jim let the silence hang between them. The stakes were high in many regards. From simply a political standpoint, to admit that Bush was right—that Hussein had, indeed, managed to secure a nuclear weapon—was anathema for a Democratic president. It was one of the reasons this operation was being kept secret for as long as possible. From a world perspective, should the nuclear weapon manage to reach unfriendly hands, especially in the Middle East, war seemed a too-likely scenario.

Archer leaned forward. "The only way to win is to secure the nuke. We will do that, I promise you."

"Thanks, Clay. I'll hold you to that promise. But I need to know what's being done at all times. Not just because I'm in charge, but because the President wants me to keep him informed. He may be at the economic summit in Europe, but I assure you, this is constantly on his mind. How do you plan to find the missing trucks once the sandstorm ends?"

"It's ten o'clock at night over there. The sandstorm probably won't die down until two or three in the morning. At dawn we'll get our men out there. But it's not as simple as sending helicopters over the area. We think it's Syrians that have the nuke, but at this point it almost doesn't matter. If whoever has it decides to sit on it, finding it will be like starting the search from the beginning."

On the screen behind him, Jim could see the rugged topography of the desert area. "Whoever unearthed the nuke didn't pull this maneuver just to hide the thing again. He wants to get it to the highest buyer. And if the Syrians have it, they'll want to get it out of Iraq. Tell me you're patrolling the borders."

"We are. Jim, I know we're to keep this to as few people as possible, but I felt it was important to bring Major Simmons into this. He's been involved in Iraqi conflicts almost from the day of the U.S. invasion. He knows the territory like no one else."

"If you trust him, I trust him." Jim didn't mean that, but he felt it was important to say. Maybe Archer would make an extra effort to stay on top of Simmons to make sure the trust wasn't violated.

Archer went out and brought Simmons in. He was younger than Jim would have thought. Maybe forty, but he knew looks were deceiving. Simmons had a Middle-eastern look to him Jim hadn't expected considering the European surname. They shook hands.

Simmons asked for the lights to go down and it darkened in the Situation Room. Jim turned his eyes to the map which replaced the topography scene. It showed the countries of Iraq, Syria, Jordan, Saudi Arabia, Iran, Turkey, and the United Arab Emirates. While the borders were well-defined on the map, Jim knew they were not so well-defined in reality.

The major used a laser pointer. "In order for anyone to get the nuke out of Iraq, there are really only two countries they'd take it through, Syria or Iran. The others are either friendly to us, or we have a solid presence there. Iran is probably the leading candidate to want the nuke, but the Syrians won't take it that way. Once it reached Iran, if anyone in authority got wind of it, the seller would have almost no bargaining position."

"Go on," Jim said, although he already had some concerns about their reasoning.

"This is the Syrian border with Iraq. It's nothing but desert for hundreds of miles. We're working with the Iraqis to get troops there. Ours and theirs. You know it's delicate."

"How soon will you be able to get it covered?"

"It's not an easy answer. The sandstorm," he circled a huge brown spot on the map, "is in the middle of the desert, blocking troops to the east, near Baghdad. Plus, resistance to our participation in any form is concentrated in this area." He swooped the laser in an arc, from the southern-most border of Iraq with Syria up to the area nearest Mosul.

"What about the eastern border?"

The major fiddled with the laser. "With Iran?"

"Yes. You acknowledged that they want it, and told me why the seller likely wouldn't take it that way. But we don't want probability, we want certainty."

Major Simmons traced a straight-line route across the desert to Iran. "Of course. To get it to Iran, they'd have to take it through the more populous areas of Iraq, where our intelligence is strongest. We're on top of that."

Simmons had a good point, but straight across Iraq wasn't the only way to get to Iran. "What about the Zagros Mountains?"

"Even less likely," Archer responded. "They'd still have to cross Iraq and into Kurdish territory. The Kurds wouldn't cooperate."

"True, but this time of year there's almost no one in those mountains. Once they got there, driving into Iran would be relatively easy."

"I've been there," Simmons said. "It's never easy in the mountains, and especially not this time of year with the weather."

"The mere fact that we would disregard that course makes it all the more likely someone would try it."

The general glared at Simmons, stopping him from responding. "Leave it to us, Jim. We'll cover the route. If they go that direction, we'll stop them."

Archer's answer didn't leave Jim with a warm feeling. He decided to use the leverage the President had afforded him. "The President will be calling me every four hours for an update until the nuke is found. Make sure I have the latest information to report back to him. In the meantime, talk to no one outside the mission. We have reason to believe rumors are already circulating about there being a nuclear weapon loose in Iraq. To our benefit, the media is certain Bush misled the American public about Iraq having a WMD, so they're likely to disregard the rumors for now. And we're feeding that disbelief. Make sure you don't let anything come to light that would validate the rumor. I'll see you in four hours."

Chapter Twelve

Cancun, Mexico
La Galeria del Sol
December 18, 2012
1:11 p.m. local time

Time to Solstice: 65 hours, 00 minutes

Raz drummed the fingers of his right hand on the counter. His eyes darted to his Rolex every few seconds. He knew the call would come through soon, and he needed to take it privately.

But he had two customers in his Galeria del Sol. The men--gay partners, he presumed from the deference they showed each other--were lingering, asking a lot of questions, trying to engage him in conversation. It meant they were getting ready to make an offer for the Mayan artifact under the protective glass they kept circling. It would be low, and the haggling would take a while.

Under other circumstances, he would have welcomed this. Raz had been successful as a gallery owner because he hadn't opened it to make money. Therefore, he could afford to sit back and inflate the prices. Those who wanted the pieces, like these rich French *collecteurs*, paid his prices. As long as he didn't get too greedy. Over the years, Raz had reflected on the irony of his being able to make money precisely because he didn't need it.

But he couldn't just announce he needed to get lunch and close the store, even if he didn't need the money that badly. He couldn't afford to get a bad reputation. With any luck the offer would be reasonable and he could close the deal quickly.

"*Parlez-vous francais*?" the one with the plumped lips asked. Raz suspected the man had had a collagen injection.

Raz nodded. "*Seulement. Je prefere l'espagnol ou l'anglais*," he lied. Raz was fluent in half a dozen languages, including French, and knew a smattering of others, but he liked Europeans to think he only spoke English and Spanish. Then, if they spoke in their native tongue in front of him, he could feign ignorance and gain an advantage.

The men stood at a counter which held several ceramic pieces under glass. The shorter one with the trendy Versace eye glasses and close-cropped beard took over. He pointed to a bowl. "Tell us a little about this pottery. I assume it's from about 600 A.D."

"Ah, you have a good eye. Indeed, it is. It's a ceramic tripod bowl, likely decorative in purpose. Notice the wonderful shades of reds, browns and blacks."

"It looks like it's had some repair work done."

"Again, you are astute in your observation. There was some chipping, which has been restored, but it's quite authentic."

"Where is the bowl from?" Big Lips asked.

"This type of bowl is only associated with the Maya from the Belize area."

"Is it authenticated?" he pressed.

"That would make it worth considerably more money."

"That is not the question I asked."

Raz assessed the two Frenchmen. If they were agents seeking to confiscate some of the pieces in his shop, they were way better actors than any that had been in his gallery before.

"Obtaining authentication, as you know, carries some risk that it might be recognized by the authorities as having been stolen from a particular ruin. In which case, it may have to be returned."

"Why would we purchase it if it were not authenticated? Your gallery has a good reputation, but please, we seek only the best."

Raz nodded and rested his forearm on the table, glancing impatiently at his watch. "The piece comes with an authentication from a friend of mine who is an expert on Mayan culture at the University of New Mexico in the United States." Such authentications weren't easy to come by, but Raz had some really good blackmail material on that professor, prompting him to authenticate a number of his pieces that were legitimate in every way except in how he had obtained them.

The two men jabbered in French about how good it would look in their conservatory. They mentioned a possible price. Raz gave them his blank stare, but internally he was relieved. It was close to what it was worth. If they went with it, he would get this over quickly. The call could come anytime.

Big Lips made the offer. Raz countered. Big Lips hit Raz's price with the second offer.

Raz exaggerated a sigh. "If I weren't hungry, you wouldn't get it at this low of a price," he groused.

Fashionable Eyewear laughed. “That’s not what we hear. We hear you do pretty well.”

Raz had meant he was hungry for lunch. As if on cue, his stomach growled. It was nerves, really, but what the hell?

“I need lunch,” he said, smiling.

“Then we won’t prolong this,” said Big Lips. He handed over a bank card.

Raz ran it through the machine. Sale went through. Bingo. He boxed up the bowl and handed it to Big Lips. He followed them to the door. “Come back again next time you are in town,” he said.

“We will,” answered Eyewear. “Right before lunch.”

Raz blew out a breath as he locked the door and put out a closed sign. He hurried upstairs using a spiral staircase hidden behind a paneled wall that, once disengaged from its neighboring panel, pivoted in the middle. He closed the door behind him.

The upstairs attic was small by design, just large enough for Raz to stand in. When he’d purchased the house, he’d wanted something he could build into an undetectable, climate-controlled space for storage. He’d done all the work himself, and by timing it with an addition to the gallery, fooled the inspectors. Some of the space was used for storage of artifacts he’d not had time to evaluate, but most of it was used it for artifacts too valuable to be kept on display, hidden for private showings. Or items too hot for anyone to know he possessed them. He had more than a few of those. He kept the light in the attic at a minimum because, though he’d kept the room tight, he never quite got over the fear that someone, somehow, would see it and suspect the hidden attic existed.

He’d also wired the house’s security system himself, adding a few special modifications to protect the attic further. Given the nature of his business, and that this older part of town was picturesque but had some undesirable elements, he felt he wasn’t being paranoid.

The artifacts connected Raz to a long-ago society he dreamt of—so advanced and yet barbaric at the same time—and of a prophecy made by its priests. A prophecy that, once he understood it, he knew he was inexorably linked to.

Now, with Vhorrdak’s involvement, he was doubly linked, placing him in much more danger than he’d anticipated.

Raz leaned against the cool attic wall. In truth, he'd rather not talk to the unyielding Vhorrdak. Raz thought himself relentless, a man determined to pursue what he wanted until he had it. But Vhorrdak's passions were out of human bounds. Working for Vhorrdak, Raz felt fingers around his throat, no matter how many miles separated them. It was why he had to take the call.

Raz slid to the floor. He put the cell phone next to him within easy reach so he could answer it quickly. He didn't like to make Vhorrdak wait any more than a couple of rings. Then he picked up the photographs he'd taken the previous morning at the atrium. He'd always anticipated he would come across the woman, but now that he'd found her, it complicated matters. He had to be even more cautious with Vhorrdak, to hide his true purpose. He hadn't anticipated she would have a husband, or if she did, that he would be with her. For the moment he would keep him alive and humor Vhorrdak. But the woman would be his. He wondered if Vhorrdak suspected his loyalty.

The cell phone rang. Raz put the pictures down, sliding them under the sales receipts from this morning's business. He knew that Vhorrdak couldn't see the pictures, but it made him feel more secure to have them out of sight.

Raz stared at the caller ID. Restricted. He knew who it was, even if it was two minutes late. Still, he would pretend to be relaxed. Just another caller, a potential customer. He flipped open the phone. "*Hola*?"

Raz tried not to be unnerved by the way Vhorrdak's questions formed in his mind as much as he heard them whispered in his ear.

"The time window is narrowing."

Raz's armpits dampened a bit. He sat up straight. "I know there's not a lot of time left. I've got everything set. We'll have his full cooperation."

He paused. There was something unusual about the call, a difference in the voice. Then he knew. He could hear Vhorrdak clearly, no cutting in and out. Or was that only in his mind? "Where are you?"

"Somewhere close, but not for long. I need to be back in the desert soon. I came only because there was one little bit of business I had to attend to. You could not be the one to do it."

What did he mean by that? "But I've been loyal."

His question was met by silence. Raz had no choice but to wait it out. Insisting on his devotion would only make Vhorrdak question it.

The pause might only have been seconds. To Raz, it felt much longer.

Finally Vhorrdak spoke. "Yes. I'm sure you are for now. Don't make me wonder about it. You know how critical it is to get the book. Do not get distracted by other things."

"I know how important the book is to you. It will be ours ... I mean, yours. I will retrieve it for you. It has my complete attention. What other things would distract me?"

How much did Vhorrdak know?

"The baby, of course."

Raz swallowed hard. He checked to make sure the photos were under the sales receipts, not in view. He glanced around the room as though Vhorrdak might be hiding among the treasures. He wasn't. And yet ...

"Why would you think I care about her baby? I'm only in this to gain the book ... for you."

"See to it that you stay motivated that way."

The line went dead. Raz leaned back against the wall. He closed his eyes and breathed deeply.

He'd gotten an answer of sorts. Vhorrdak suspected something, but he still left Raz in charge. It meant he didn't know. That was good.

Raz defiantly uncovered the photographs and looked again at the woman. Pregnant. Ready to deliver.

Which she would, in two days. Whether Vhorrdak liked it or not.

Chapter Thirteen

Chichen Itza, Mexico
The Pyramid of Kukulcan
December 18, 2012
1:12 p.m. local time

Time to Solstice: 64 hours, 59 minutes

Vhorrdak returned to the Pyramid of Kukulcan from the Temple of the Warriors. The call from his mole in Washington was satisfying; his call to Raz Uris less so. He checked the time on the cell phone. Timing. Everything depended on timing.

He could see Rebekah studying the hieroglyphics on the Pyramid. She was precisely in position. He congratulated himself on the excellence of his planning. Everything was as envisioned. He only needed the secrets of the lost book to put the last of his plans in place. Many had died protecting its location in the centuries since it had been hidden from him. No one gave the information up, despite incredible tortures he had devised for the hands of others, since he was limited in his ability to physically harm mortals. Damn his omnipotent enemy for placing that restriction on him. Yet, it only made him more determined to defeat his enemy's plan, which he would do in this waning period of the Earth. He would have his revenge.

Watching the milliseconds advance on the cell phone's display, Vhorrdak picked up his pace. He slipped through the crowd and headed toward Rebekah. She was right where she needed to be. All he had to do was knock her off balance.

Where was the husband? Vhorrdak sensed him more than saw him, just far enough away to prevent interference. He could reach Rebekah, do what he had to do, and be gone before the husband grasped what was happening. By that point, the husband would, by necessity, be more focused on his wife.

Vhorrdak was pleased to see that no one paid him any mind as he got close. He put his left foot in front of his right and deliberately tripped himself. Stumbling, he launched out his hand, caught Rebekah on the shoulder, and propelled her toward the Pyramid.

She put her hand out to brace her fall. And Vhorrdak, scurrying away, depended on the inevitability of destiny.

* * *

Rebekah found herself in a free fall toward the Pyramid. Her first thought was anger, a reaction to the rudeness of whoever had run into her. But she didn't have time to say anything. She found herself tilting toward the Pyramid, and she knew in a moment of horror that she was going to touch it. Other people touched it, she knew, despite the fact that they weren't supposed to—but Rebekah never expected to be one of them.

At the same time, she dared not fall for the baby's sake. Catching herself was the only thing she could do. She put out her hand.

When she touched it, a jolt of what felt like electricity went through her. Rebekah gasped for air. Whether the surge went into her or out from her, she couldn't be sure. She only knew she felt it. The baby felt it, too. Energized, he fought against his confinement.

She pulled back from the Pyramid and steadied herself. Or tried. Her body kept trembling. She looked to Jonas, and he was shaking, too. The whole world was shaking.

Rebekah took a couple steps, trying to get to Jonas, but the shaking shifted her back toward the Pyramid. Under her feet it felt like a tremor. Not a full scale earthquake by any means, but the earth was certainly shaking. And though she didn't want to touch the Pyramid again, she found herself being twisted back toward it. She gave in to the forces of nature and leaned into it.

This time there was no jolt, only a feeling of connectedness, of being one with the Pyramid and instead of falling toward it, she was pulling it toward her. Or was the baby pulling it toward her? She closed her eyes and felt rain, hard rain like hail, plinking down on her.

People were shouting. Rebekah opened her eyes, looking for Jonas. Her vision was cloudy. She willed herself away from the Pyramid, lurching forward. Jonas appeared, elbowing his way through the mass confusion. She could see him looking for her.

"Jonas!"

She tried to wave. Her hands were stung by the hail. Rebekah stared at them and realized the hail was small bits of rock coming off the Pyramid.

Then Jonas was by her side. He clutched her, sheltering her with his broad back. She felt the tiny beating of the rocks stop as he bore the brunt of them. But the bits were still coming down.

The shaky vision began to subside. The noise of the crowd calmed. She felt Jonas moving the two of them away from the Pyramid. Being bent over was uncomfortable. She tried to get out from under him, but he continued to clutch her. She could felt a few stinging hits, and she knew they weren't out of range yet.

She sensed people around her. They were out of the shadow of the Pyramid, into the bright light.

"Are you okay?" Rebekah recognized Diega's voice.

Jonas stopped holding her so tightly and she was able to straighten up.

"I'm okay," she said. She checked the baby. He'd calmed down since she'd let go of the Pyramid. He seemed to be quiet now. She dusted herself off, then began to dust off Jonas' back. She saw a half dozen places his shirt had been torn, a few of them accompanied by flecks of blood. Nothing serious, but he had protected her from harm. She lightly touched his back. "Does it hurt?"

"No, I'm fine."

She hugged him, the baby getting in the way. "Are you sure?"

"Really." He patted her hands, which stretched around him from behind and just touched his ribs. "Are you okay? What about the baby?"

"We're both good."

A number of yellow-shirted tourists had gathered around them, taking pictures. Rebekah realized that with her pregnancy, Jonas' actions looked especially chivalrous. She wondered how long they'd been photographing the two of them.

The crowd was still buzzing. Diega used her walkie-talkie.

"Should we leave the area?" an overweight man demanded.

"Small tremors like this one have been common in recent months," Diega announced to her group. "There are seismic monitors throughout the area, and the authorities have advised us there is no need to worry right now. If the situation becomes dangerous, they will let me know and we will begin procedures to leave the area in an orderly fashion."

Her answer seemed to sooth the crowd, but the talking continued.

"Oregon Audubon Group!" Diega called above the noise. She held up their sign until she had their attention. "If you will follow me, please, we will now make our way to our next destination, the Temple of the Warriors."

Rebekah let go of Jonas and put her hand in his. They fell in step among the sea of yellow shirts following Diega across the expanse. Ahead of them was the largest of the ruins, at least in terms of width. Rows and rows of standing pillars strung out across the front of the temple and for a long way to the right of where the temple ended.

Jonas dropped her hand and put his arm around her waist. She leaned into him. She felt safe again.

But as she reflected on what had happened, she felt that none of it was an accident. But who had stumbled into her, and who was the man who'd taken their photo by the Pyramid? Were they one and the same? She remembered the weird tapping noise of his cell phone and how he'd gone off in this very direction to answer it. She strained to look for him in the crowd. He'd worn the yellow shirt of the tour group.

But he was nowhere to be found. And that had her worried.

Chapter Fourteen

Syrian Desert, Western Iraq
December 18, 2012
10:15 p.m. local time

Time to Solstice: 63 hours, 56 minutes

Fareed Mohammed slipped out of the commercial cargo truck, careful not to wake his companion driver Ashur, who had pulled the truck into the cave shortly after dusk and promptly fallen asleep. Fareed was relieved the man had few qualms about this mission. He had not questioned the mysterious sandstorm that had stirred at the exact time to cover their escape, nor had he shown the slightest interest in the cargo they carried in the back of their truck.

Fareed was not so calm. He was now absolutely certain that their cargo was a nuclear weapon, and the supernatural appearance of the sandstorm made him consider that Vhorrdak had a demon in him. The man looked like the devil himself. He had a broad, almost handsome face, with a smile that could turn to a snarl in an instant. One second you thought you could trust him; the next, you didn't dare. But it was the demonic eyebrows that stood out in Fareed's mind. They were like long, thin, curved triangles, with the short side of the triangle above the bridge of the nose, thinning out through the arch over the eyes until it collapsed to a point on the far side of the face. And then there were those red eyes. The first time they'd meet, Fareed had looked into them. They gave him shivers. At the next meeting, Vhorrdak wore sunglasses, concealing the red glow of his pupils.

He and Ashur were almost two hundred kilometers from the point where the exchange had taken place. The cave was exactly where Vhorrdak had said it would be. If he hadn't been given a satellite phone, Fareed would have believed the devil-man himself might show up to give instructions.

The phone vibrated in his hand. Fareed connected but said nothing, as previously arranged.

"Throw the dogs a dry bone," the voice said. And the call disconnected.

Fareed was certain it must have been Vhorrdak, but the voice, like the transmission, had been scrambled and short. To the best of his knowledge, the Americans still monitored communications in Iraq.

Now it was Fareed's turn to deploy the first of the decoys. Each of the identical trucks had been implanted with a simple device to receive a signal. Fareed made the transmission, changing the final destination of the first truck. Fareed believed that at some point it would be directed out of the sandstorm or the sandstorm would end, and it would become visible to the Americans.

The two who drove the truck did not know that, nor did they have any information that would be useful. They could give a description of Fareed, but little else. They did not know any of his multiple identities. And, Fareed observed, by making him the contact person, Vhorrdak had eliminated any direct connection between these decoy victims and himself.

To Fareed, that meant one of two things. Either it was in Vhorrdak's plans that he would not be captured, or Vhorrdak was planning to kill him after the nuclear weapon was delivered. Fareed was now fairly certain it would be the latter.

So, frightening though Vhorrdak was, Fareed began making his own plans.

Chapter Fifteen

Chichen Itza, Mexico
The Pyramid of Kukulcan
December 18, 2012
2:30 p.m. local time

Time to Solstice: 63 hours, 41 minutes

Rebekah watched as the Audubon group drifted away from the Pyramid, the tour completed. She'd scanned the group during the remainder of the tour but hadn't seen the stranger who'd taken the photos of her and Jonas. It was as if he'd left the group, or maybe he hadn't been a part of the tour at all. Hadn't his yellow shirt been exactly the same as the rest? She could still feel the cold uneasiness that hit when he was near. She would rather have seen him leave with the group than not know where he was.

She stayed by the Pyramid with Jonas and Diega, waiting for Professor Patcanul.

Diega looked at her watch. "He will be here soon."

Rebekah felt anxious for reasons she couldn't explain. To be able to get a tour of the inside of the Pyramid, not open to the public, by an academic she admired was a great privilege. Waiting should be no big deal. She wished the butterflies in her stomach would go away.

Diega noticed her fidgeting. "My brother tells me you have studied here in the Yucatan."

"I have. I did my doctorate in anthropology at Tulane University. We participated in a dig at Ek Balam."

"Really? When?"

"Two years ago. In fact, I met Jonas on that trip. He was here studying Mayan architecture for a building project." Rebekah took Jonas' hand and pulled him close.

"The Kukulcan Hotel," Diega said knowingly.

Jonas nodded. "It opens tomorrow night. We're excited."

Professor Patcanul hurried up to the three of them, coming in from behind Diega before she could make another comment. He held keys in his hand.

"Sorry, but I had a few matters that needed attention. Are you ready to see the Inner Pyramid?"

"Very much," Rebekah answered.

They followed him to the side of the Pyramid where an iron cage guarded the entrance to the inside. He unlocked the gate.

"Climbing the inner staircase is tricky," he told Rebekah. "The passageway is narrow and low and the steps are shallow. Will you be okay?"

"I don't know when I'll have another chance to see it. I'll do the best I can. Jonas can climb behind me to keep me steady."

Diega led the way. Rebekah followed with Jonas behind her and Manuel bringing up the rear. Diega, whose frame was small and compact, went up the stairs easily.

Rebekah soon fell behind and Diega slowed.

"The steps are smaller than you are accustomed to, I am sure," Diega said.

Rebekah braced her arms against the sides of the wall. "I didn't think they would be smaller than my shoe size."

"Back then, without the nutrition we have today, the Maya were quite small. Believe it or not, this passageway accommodated several going up and down the staircase at the same time. Although, probably not quickly."

By the time they were half-way up Rebekah was breathing hard. The ceiling was so low she had to bend over. The baby's weight made it strenuous, and he was being active again.

Jonas stepped onto the stair directly behind Rebekah and leaned in, holding onto her and trying to support her back. "Do you want to go back down?"

"Not a chance. I may be winded, but I'm more excited than ever." Actually, the closer they got to the top, the more her anticipation felt like giddiness.

They finished ascending the staircase. Once Rebekah had cleared the top step, Diega illuminated the large room.

Rebekah and Jonas stared up into the vast, pointed ceiling overhead. "I'm in awe," Jonas said.

"We're standing on the top of the original Pyramid," Manuel said, "which was dedicated to the moon. The outer Pyramid, dedicated to the sun, was built over it. For a long time archeologists didn't know the Inner Pyramid existed."

Manuel began to point out symbols painted on the ceiling and walls, giving short explanations of what they were. Jonas opened his backpack and got out the camera. He began taking pictures.

Rebekah recognized some of what Manuel was showing her, but she couldn't seem to concentrate. She found herself trying to slow her breathing. She was certain that even if she had secured her obstetrician's blessing to come to Mexico, a climb to the top of the inner Pyramid wouldn't have been approved.

"This is the vestibule where sacrifices were made to the moon goddess," Manuel said. "We're not sure how much it was used after the outer Pyramid was built, but you can see they left some of the important artifacts. The second room is called the sanctuary."

The baby put a foot in her ribs. She grunted.

Diega watched her closely. "Are you going to be okay?"

Rebekah shook her head. "I think I need to sit down."

"Sit here." Diega guided her to a large stone-carved jaguar that had a flat place on the animal's back. Rebekah was unsure about sitting on the artifact, but Diega was firm. "It's okay. Stay there as long as you need."

The moment she sat on it, the baby calmed. "Just until the light-headedness goes away," she told Diega.

Jonas took her photo.

"Great. Now you've got proof I sat on a Mayan artifact."

"It is called the Jaguar Throne," Manuel said. "I assure you, lesser people have sat on it before this climb was restricted."

Jonas took a second photo. "If you're really worried someone will see these, we can delete them later."

The three of them watched Rebekah. She hated that. "I'm sure I'll be okay." She used her eyes to signal to Jonas that he should distract the others.

Jonas picked up on her cue. "What's in the sanctuary?" he asked Manuel. He moved into the room off the vestibule and began taking photos.

Neither Manuel nor Diega followed him in. They continued to look at Rebekah.

"I'll get up," she said.

Manuel held up a hand. "It is not that. It is ..."

Diega interrupted, "... only that moon goddess worship, which went on in here, celebrated women, fertility … and here you are, a pregnant woman close to delivery, seated on the Jaguar Throne."

Rebekah wasn't sure where they were headed, but she didn't like the attention. "I feel better now." She stood up.

From the other room, Jonas shouted.

* * *

Jonas had hoped his movement into the sanctuary would garner attention from at least one of their guides for Rebekah's sake, but it hadn't worked. He moved about the room noisily, thinking someone would surely follow.

His focus had then been drawn to a faded drawing on one side of the room, of two jaguars moving away in opposite directions. Rebekah will love these, Jonas thought.

He had raised his camera and looked through the eyepiece. He backed up so he could get both jaguars in the picture.

Just when he was poised to take a photo, a focused beam of light—from where it came Jonas wasn't sure except he knew it wasn't his camera—hit the exact center between the two jaguars and spread out, illuminating a set of hieroglyphics that hadn't been there a moment before. Vivid and pronounced the first second, they began to fade the next.

Startled, he took the photo. The hieroglyphics could barely be seen. "Everyone, get in here! You have to see this!"

* * *

Manuel rushed into the little room, no idea what to expect. But he certainly expected more than the two jaguars Jonas pointed at. He'd seen them before.

"It's gone now," Jonas said.

"What's gone?"

"When I came in, there were hieroglyphics on that wall, between the jaguars. And then they disappeared."

"Really?" Manuel looked at the familiar drawing. "There have never been hieroglyphics there."

"I got a picture."

He watched Jonas switch the camera to playback mode. Jonas handed the camera to Manuel and pointed to the LCD screen. "There."

Manuel moved the camera around trying to get a good view of the faint hieroglyphics. Diega and Rebekah, who'd come into the sanctuary, also gathered around the tiny screen. Diega grabbed her brother's hand. "Hold it still," she said.

Manuel let her take the camera. Frustration filled his voice. "It is too small. We need to enlarge it." He walked to the blank space between the jaguars. It looked nothing like what the camera had captured.

Diega, fascinated, stared at the screen. "The camera's playback isn't meant for this kind of work. We need to transfer the photo to a computer."

Manuel watched Jonas squint at the jaguars. "Tell me again what you did at the time the hieroglyphics disappeared," Manuel said.

Jonas backed up and gestured toward the wall. "I didn't do anything. When I came in, the hieroglyphics were there, but then I realized they were fading so I hurried up and took the photo."

Diega looked at Rebekah. When she felt Manuel's eyes on her, she gave him a meaningful glance. Manuel wondered if she had figured something out.

"Perhaps," Diega said, "we should return to your office and find out what it says."

"Our guests may not be ready to leave."

Rebekah surprised Manuel by making a quick concession. "I'm getting tired. Really. Maybe I shouldn't have tried this. We should go."

Jonas seemed puzzled. "Are you sure? You were so excited about this tour."

"I still am. But it may have been too much for me. And the baby. It's time to go."

Manuel was elated to be heading back to his office with the camera, but he didn't want Rebekah to know that. "You could come back tomorrow, and we could go to a different area, one that doesn't have stairs."

"Thank you, Manuel. If I feel able tomorrow, I may take advantage of your offer."

"If not, then you must return after your pregnancy when you are better able to see the complete ruins."

As they started down the stairs, Jonas led with Rebekah behind him. Manuel paused just a moment at the top before following Rebekah.

"What is it?" he whispered to Diega.

"It wasn't what he did, it was what she did." Diega nodded back at the jaguar throne.

Manuel nodded. He knew what she was implying. It all fit and should not have been unexpected. Diega started down the stairs.

Manuel gave one last look at the throne, turned off the lights, and descended the stairs behind the others.

Chapter Sixteen

Cancun, Mexico
The Sagievs' Hotel Suite
December 18, 2012
7:00 p.m. local time

Time to Solstice: 59 hours, 11 minutes

Rebekah loved the suite she and Jonas had been given by the hotel. They weren't in the main building, which was attached to the atrium Jonas had designed, but in one of a series of cottages out on the hotel grounds. The furnishings were modern—the bed was just about the most comfortable thing she'd ever slept on, and as a woman ready to deliver that was saying something—but the décor showed the Mayan influence. The bedroom was accented with reproductions of ancient Mayan pottery, and even the wastebasket looked like it had been purchased from an authentic local vendor. In the large sitting room that served as the entrance to the suite, Rebekah faced a Mayan tapestry depicting the Tzolkin, the ancient ritual calendar. It dominated the wall. An adjacent wall served as a showpiece for three ceramic plates, all painted in the style of the ancients, showing Mayan women planting corn, masked warriors defending their land with long spears, and two elderly men discussing what looked to Rebekah like mathematics, judging from the symbols used. Yet, in the midst of all this, was furniture that looked like it came out of a Pottery Barn catalog. The fact that it melded so well together amazed her. The decorator had truly appreciated both worlds.

The living room also held a work desk, and Rebekah could see Jonas bent over the keyboard of the laptop. He'd been playing with the photos they'd taken at Chichen Itza since he'd returned from a brief meeting the company had held after dinner. She shifted her weight to get a little more comfortable on the couch. Not as good as the bed, she thought. She glanced at her watch. "I'm surprised we haven't heard from Manuel yet about the photo you took in the Temple."

Jonas didn't look up. "Would the hieroglyphics be that easy to interpret? You weren't able to do it."

Rebekah laughed at Jonas' naïveté. "I'm an amateur. Those were more complicated than any I've seen. But Manuel is one of the foremost authorities in the field. I thought he'd have some idea of what it said by now."

As she talked, photos spit out of the printer Jonas had hooked to his laptop. He compared a set of three, then brought them over to Rebekah. "Here're the photos from the Pyramid, the ones I took and the ones the stranger took."

"He was so creepy." Rebekah gave the photos a quick comparative glance, checking to make sure the hieroglyphics she'd wanted were in fact in each photo. But as she examined them more thoroughly she spotted subtle differences. Reaching for a magnifying glass, she examined them closely. "That's interesting."

"What?"

"Look at these photos the creepy guy took, and compare them with the ones you took before his. The symbols have changed." Rebekah pointed out the differences.

"Weird. Maybe it was the flash."

"Or a shadow fell on them at that moment. Maybe both."

"Does that affect the meaning?"

"If I'm right. This is the area where the scribes of the hieroglyphics traditionally leave their mark." She pointed to a spot on the photo Jonas was holding. "In fact, this mark's rather famous. It appears on the Temple of the Inscriptions in Palenque."

"How could the scribe have worked on both monuments? That's hundreds of miles from Chichen Itza."

"I'm not saying it's the same scribe, only the same mark. It's like so many prophecies attributed to Isaiah. People wanted their work to be linked to someone famous. That's why this mark is on a lot of Mayan ruins."

"What does the second set of marks mean?"

Rebekah pointed to a photo taken by the tourist. "This string of glyphs is of the 'thirteen gods.' It's very recognizable. The long count Mayan Calendar, the one that ends in two days, has 13 'baktuns.' These are the gods of that era."

Jonas compared the photos. "We should show this to Manuel." He copied the files from the computer onto a flash drive.

Rebekah shifted on the couch cushions. “Manuel can wait until tomorrow. Right now I need to lie down on the bed. This couch isn’t working for me. How about a massage?”

Jonas removed the flash drive and set it aside. “I’d love one. Thanks.”

“You know what I mean.”

“Will I get a reward for this?”

“Maybe. But you’ll have to wait.”

Jonas put out his hand to help her off the couch. Rebekah was embarrassed when she came up gracelessly, but he caught her in a hug and nuzzled his face in the base of her neck. He breathed softly into her ear. She shivered when he ran his hand down her back. “Waiting is the really tough part,” he said.

“You’ll get no sympathy from a pregnant woman.” She stepped back and gave him a kiss. “But if your massage is as good as I think it’ll be, I might find some other way to reward you.”

“I’m there.”

She led him into the bedroom.

Chapter Seventeen

Washington, DC
Situation Room, The White House
December 19, 2012
3:03 a.m. local time

Time to Solstice: 51 hours, 08 minutes

Jim Harrington yawned in spite of how alert he was. He hadn't been sleeping well and came fully awake with the news General Archer brought him at this hour of the morning. But that didn't mean his body didn't still need rest.

The news was this: Just an hour ago the small platoon in Iraq located a truck very similar to the one their mole had been driving. It had been found in Mesopotamia, quite a distance from where the nuke had disappeared.

"When our men found the dead bodies in the sand this morning and no trace of either truck, we suspected might have discovered our mole," Archer reported. "Whoever's behind this probably suspects we're looking for the nuke."

"Hence the decoy," Major Simmons added.

Jim was getting annoyed by Major Simmons. He was like one of those teacup dogs that owners take everywhere. Archer was never without him. Though Simmons reminded him more of a bulldog. Jim briefly wondered if teacup bulldogs existed. He doubted it.

"You know two other things, too," Jim said. "One, you know how far the other truck could have come, so expand your radius of operation in all directions. And two, you know the President will be anxious for an update."

"We'll find the other truck," Archer said.

"And that's another thing," Jim added. "We have to hope there's only one decoy truck."

"The last transmission before the sandstorm showed there were only two trucks involved," Simmons said. "The next one must have the nuke."

Jim doubted he would get much sleep now. "The sandstorm lasted for a long time and kept us guessing. Who knows what they might have done while we waited it out? Keep looking."

Chapter Eighteen

Cancun, Mexico
The Hotel Kukulcan
December 19, 2012
9:45 a.m. local time

Time to Solstice: 44 hours, 26 minutes

Jonas glided across the terrazzo floor of the atrium. He looked down on the polished surface, pleased with the result. He'd chosen terrazzo because with it he could recreate the look of the stone floor of the Pyramid in a modern sense. He felt almost like he was a part of the hotel's grand opening committee, though his job had been completed months ago. Tonight's gala was the celebratory part of the job, the opportunity to show off the hotel's design. Though the atrium made up only one part, it was the showy one. Jonas stopped just for a moment to take it all in.

His mission in the atrium was to check on the putty-like substance he'd seen on the beam the day before. He'd mentioned it to the head of maintenance, but the man seemed overwhelmed and Jonas didn't believe it would get checked. He trusted he could see it from the floor. He didn't have his pack or rope with him since he was dressed for the meeting he had at ten o'clock with others from the architectural firm.

Before he could cross to the place under the beam, he saw Stephen Bradford heading toward him. Bradford was the president and senior partner of the firm. Jonas felt only marginally comfortable around the older gentleman. Bradford gave off the air of old money with his styled silver hair and expensive suits, but there was a hard driver behind the façade. Though he'd taken to Jonas and gave him the atrium design over others, it would be difficult to describe their relationship as familial. Bradford pushed Jonas to higher highs and lower lows than Jonas had wanted to experience with this project. It had come out well—better, Jonas knew, than if he hadn't been pushed so hard—but the extra hours and heated design reviews with Bradford left him with mixed feelings.

"Jonas! Good morning, I'm glad I caught you. Have you heard we've tentatively rescheduled the ten o'clock meeting for eleven? My secretary just started making the calls."

"Are there problems?"

"Only with the damned airlines. Some of our people are just now getting in. Have you seen today's paper yet?"

"No, why?"

"You're on the front page." He pulled a folded paper out of his briefcase and handed it to Jonas. "You read Spanish, I know."

Jonas opened the paper.

Bradford pointed. "It's under this headline, "Fourth tremor in month warns of major earthquake."

Jonas recognized the scene in the photo right away. Someone had taken a picture of him sheltering Rebekah at the Pyramid after the tremor. He translated the caption under the photo. "Jonas Sagiev, a visitor to Chichen Itza, shelters his pregnant wife Rebekah during yesterday's tremor. Tiny stones from the Pyramid were dislodged during the event." Jonas looked up in bewilderment. He couldn't recall any reporters taking photos or asking for his name. Then it hit him. The cell phones. Some tourist had snapped it and sold it to the paper. "Everyone introduced themselves on the tour bus. Someone must've been taking notes or got my name from the tour company."

"The firm and the hotel got a mention, too. Nice public relations, even if you didn't intend it to happen. I'll see you at 11:00, unless we have to delay the meeting again. You have your cell phone?"

He nodded. Bradford strode off leaving the paper in Jonas' hands.

Jonas checked the company cell to make sure he'd turned it on. He headed back to the villa to show Rebekah the morning paper but stopped short as Diega stepped into the atrium. She spotted him.

"Good morning, Jonas. Nice photo in today's paper. How is your wife today?"

"She's fine. Enjoying room service. I just found out about the photo. I'm on my way to show it to her. What are you doing here?

"Giving some additional tours today to special guests. Like you, they are here ahead of the grand opening. But I also have a message. Manuel would like to speak with you tonight about the photo you took. He would have been here this morning, but he needed to do some additional research."

"It's important?"

"It's complicated. I only know a little. You will learn more tonight."

Though he tried to get more out of her, Jonas was unable to break her conviction that what little she knew was not worth revealing. A couple of Diega's tourists came up and she busied herself with them, deliberately so, Jonas felt. He left and was almost all the way to the villa when he remembered he hadn't checked the beam, but he didn't turn back.

He entered the suite. Rebekah wasn't at the small table in the sitting room, eating the continental breakfast as he expected. Instead he found crumbs on her plate and heard the shower running. He cracked open the bathroom door. Steam rolled out. Rebekah loved hot showers.

"Is everything okay?"

"Everything's fine." She lifted her voice over the noise of the shower. "Jenny Bradford called. She wanted to know if I felt like shopping. Of course I don't, but she is the wife of your company's president."

"You're pregnant, Rebekah. You could have played that card."

"I'll probably play it later when I'm tired, but I figured we wives could use company since the rest of you will be busy."

Jonas stepped fully into the luxurious bathroom. The mist rolled around him. The shower, big enough for two with shower heads at each end, had doors of clear glass. He could just make out Rebekah rinsing off. "The others are getting here later than we'd hoped. Stephen was in the lobby and told me there've been more delays. My meeting's now at 11:00."

The shower stopped. Rebekah peered through the glass and saw him standing there. She paused. "Okay, I'm coming out." She slide the door back and stepped out. She struck a Mae West pose. "Hey, there, big boy. Come up and see me some time."

"How about if I towel you dry?"

"Just don't get any ideas."

Jonas wrapped the towel around her shoulders and moved it slowly down her back. He kissed her on the neck.

"You're getting ideas," she said. She took the towel from his hands. "You know, I've been thinking about the hieroglyphics you photographed in the temple yesterday, what they might mean."

"Nice segue to a completely different topic. I ran into Diega in the lobby. She told me Manuel wants to talk to us about them tonight."

"Good. I distinctly saw the symbol for 'Kukulcan,' and I also saw the symbol for 'birth.' I'd like to hear what he has to say about that." She finished toweling off and then wrapped her hair with the damp towel. "You know I love legends, and Kukulcan being born from the mouth of the feathered serpent is a big one for the Maya. It's possible what you photographed is a prophecy about that."

"Speaking of photographs, there's one of us in the paper. I'm guessing some of our tour companions made good use of their cell phones."

"Where's the paper?"

"In the sitting room."

"I'll catch it later. Right now I need to dry my hair if I'm going to be ready to go shopping with Jenny when she shows up. Why don't you go out and eat that remaining cheese danish so I'm not tempted, okay?"

"Are you trying to fatten me up?"

"The calories would sit on you than me. I'd only have to work them off later. And don't give me that crap about how I'm sexy no matter what I look like. When the baby's born and I'm still twenty pounds overweight, we'll see what you think."

Jonas pulled her into a hug. "Think what you want, but it'll still be true."

He gave her a kiss and went out to look at the danish.

Chapter Nineteen

Washington, DC
Situation Room, The White House
December 19, 2012
12:00 p.m. local time

Time to solstice: 43 hours, 11 minutes

Jim Harrington leaned forward on his elbows, assessing the situation. He pursed his lips, pausing before he said the first word. General Archer and Major Simmons sat across from him. He looked them in the eyes. They were nervous. Hell, he was nervous. The situation wasn't good. He knew that or he wouldn't have had to call this meeting. They would have contacted him hours ago to let him know things were going well. He now knew why presidents aged so quickly in office, and why NSAs didn't fare so well, either.

Jim leaned back in the leather chair. It squeaked sharply, made everyone choke back a laugh. He smiled, too, one of the guys, just for a moment. He wished it could last longer. "It's been nine hours since you found the decoy truck. The President wants to know what you have learned, and why haven't you found the real truck yet?"

Archer cleared his throat. "We've learned almost nothing from questioning the two drivers of the truck. They claim they were hired to drive this cargo through the desert. Their destination was Mosul. They can describe the man who hired them, but they don't have a name. All of that checks out using lie detector tests. What didn't pass the test was their claim to have come from Tikrit. After letting Iraqi intelligence question them, they changed their story to say they came from somewhere in the middle of the Syrian Desert. Actually that didn't pass either, but it could be the methods used by the Iraqis. We're not sure."

"Did they know anything about the second truck?"

"They seemed surprised we suspected there was another. They wouldn't confirm it at first, but then they disagreed on how many trucks there were. No single number passed a lie detector test for both of them."

Jim narrowed his eyes. “So there could be multiple decoys?”

Archer nodded slowly. “If we assume they’re telling the truth about leaving from the middle of the desert, and we use our knowledge of how far their truck made it, we can study the possible vectors for the real truck or any other decoys and assess where their likely positions.” If the General was nervous, Jim thought the general was covering his nervousness well. There was no quivering in his voice.

Archer turned to Simmons, who pushed a series of buttons on his laptop. Maps appeared on screens across the room. The major pointed to a screen showing several circular overlays emanating from a pinpoint in the Syrian Desert. “We have two things to consider. We know this decoy moved ahead of the sandstorm. Did it come from a remote location as part of a strategy to confuse us? If that’s the case, then the truck with the real nuke had to sit out the sandstorm, likely in some cave. Assuming they restarted their journey after the storm ended, and guessing they went at top speed, they should be between here and here.” He used a laser light pointer to indicate two concentric circles. “But, if we assume both trucks started from the same location just before the sandstorm, then the truck we’re looking for could have made it as far. That means, at this time, it could be between here and here.” He pointed to two other concentric circles farther out. “This region up here is hostile, so we’ve had to go slow monitoring it.”

Archer jumped back in. “It’s after sunset there now. That’s the real break for them. We won’t be able to get good visible coverage again until dawn.”

Jim knew he had to play hard ass for the President. “It’s now been over twenty-four hours since we lost contact with the mole. Twenty-four hours! And now you’re telling me that because it’s nighttime, we’re going to wait another twelve without any sense of where this nuclear weapon might be?”

Neither the general nor the major said anything. Jim spoke tersely. “They could get past a lot of eyes at night. Make something happen.”

Chapter Twenty

Cancun, Mexico
Cancun International Airport
December 19, 2012
11:30 a.m. local time

Time to Solstice: 42 hours, 41 minutes

The first thing Talasi Evenhema noticed when she disembarked the aircraft was the suffocating humidity. The heavy air weighed on her like an extra set of clothing. She slowed her pace toward passport control and found herself being passed right and left by other passengers less affected by the oppressive air. Perhaps, she considered, it was the weight of the mission and not the stickiness of the climate. Both were beyond her power to change.

Talasi stood in the long line of passengers preparing to go through customs. She spoke Spanish fairly well, a consequence of growing up in Arizona, even in the northern part, and even on a reservation. She felt her knowledge of the language would be an advantage in getting through customs. She'd packed in her carry-on suitcase some medical supplies she thought she might need, like surgical sutures, her pocket doppler for checking the baby's heart rate, and medications like Cytotec, in case labor needed to be induced or she needed to stem the blood loss following delivery. She hoped there wouldn't be too many questions at customs.

The truth was, Talasi didn't know for sure what her role would be on this mission. Could the ancients have known it would fall to her—not the son her father had hoped for—and that she would be skilled as a doctor? Talasi didn't doubt anything the way events were unfolding.

As the crowd got closer to the customs gates, she examined her choice of customs agents. Which one would be most sympathetic—or bored and unquestioning? Her best prospect, she assessed, was a 40-ish woman with bad skin, a seen-it-all air about her, and a perfunctory snap of the admittance stamp that kept her line funneling quickly. Talasi maneuvered into it, no small feat since most people had noticed the woman's line was flowing like rainwater in a desert wash.

Talasi smiled at the woman when she reached the front of the line. The woman didn't smile back. Talasi considered that maybe she shouldn't try so hard. Didn't want to appear as though she were trying to fly under the radar.

The woman took papers and passport from Talasi. She glanced at the United States logo emblazoned on passport.

"The purpose of your visit?" she asked in perfect English.

Talasi decided answering in Spanish might look suspicious. "I'm a tourist, here to see the Mayan ruins."

"Length of stay?"

Talasi always wondered why the agents asked that question. It was right there on the form. "Two weeks." She really didn't know how long she'd need to be there. Two weeks would get her through the next few days for sure. Once she was satisfied the mission had been completed, she was free to leave, but who knew what defined a completed mission? Perhaps one of the others would know. She had booked a return flight in two weeks so that her story would at least be consistent.

"Where are you staying?"

"The Cancun Hyatt." Talasi had booked a room there for one night. It gave her an answer to the question, and a place to stay the first night. Talasi had no idea where she would be staying for the duration.

"It says here that you are a medical doctor and you are carrying some supplies with you?"

This was the tricky part. "I'm a member of Doctors Without Borders. I always try to be prepared, even when I'm on vacation." Basically true, Talasi thought, but hoped her face didn't give her away. She was a member, but she had no official assignment here in Mexico, so no real reason to be carrying the substances she had. If she'd had advance notice, she might have volunteered to work in a Mayan village, if such an opportunity had existed.

The woman glanced at the short list of medications Talasi had provided. Talasi sent up a prayer to her ancestors. She'd chosen to be honest, because it was far better to answer the questions honestly and risk the Mexican authorities seizing the drugs than to suffer the consequences of getting caught being dishonest. To make it less likely the agent would recognize medications that might trigger questions, Talasi had listed generic industry names, like misoprostol instead of Cytotec. With any luck, the agent would gloss over them.

"Have a nice stay," the woman said.

Talasi watched with a sense of relief as the stamp clicked on her passport. Everything had gone smoothly. Her flights had not been delayed by winter weather, and the medications, though questioned, had not been confiscated.

"*Gracias*," Talasi answered. The woman gave a half-hearted smile as she returned Talasi's passport. No "*de nada*" or other civil response.

Talasi didn't care. She rolled her carry-on bag through the International Arrivals terminal and searched for the correct carousel to retrieve her checked bag. As she approached, she spotted it amid the Where's Waldo of suitcases looping past the waiting passengers, headed toward the return opening in the wall. She shook off her sluggishness and sprinted to the opening lugging her carry-on. She managed to nab the other before it disappeared behind the wall. She checked the ribbon she'd placed between the zipper pulls. No sign it had been searched. That was good.

She hauled her bags through the customs gate. Making a circle through the terminal, she looked for any others who might have been sent to join her. She didn't know how she to identify them, what sign would be given, but she felt she would know. She made two laps.

Perhaps she was the first to arrive. Perhaps others had to travel farther. She sat down to wait.

* * *

Cancun International Airport, 4:20 p.m.

When Colin Noble had shown up at Heathrow for a flight to Cancun, he had no idea how long he might have to wait or what cities he might have to fly through. He only knew he needed to get there as quickly as possible. Money he had, but it would make no difference if the schedules didn't align. He tried Aero Mexicana first, figuring the clerk would help him find the quickest flight, even if it wasn't on that airline.

To his amazement, not only did they have a direct flight to Cancun, it left in three hours. Plenty of time for him to get on an international flight. The only seats available were first class, but again, money was not the problem. On a hunch, Colin booked his return for ten days out. A week seemed too close in, but a fortnight was beyond the holiday he could take without getting into some trouble. Although, he considered, how would the world change after the solstice, after the event came and went in two days? Would his job ever matter again, or was it only this mission that mattered? It seemed prudent to plan for a return to his security job. He'd sweet-talked his superiors into letting him use his accumulated vacation on such short notice. Since he was single and frequently accommodated his married co-workers by changing shifts with them, it would have been ungentlemanly for his superiors to deny him the right to do this one thing.

A disciplined military man, Colin knew how to take sleep when he had the opportunity, and so he had on the long flight. Being in first class helped. He had been able to stretch out, and at 6'4" that was a real advantage.

His seatmate made no attempt whatsoever to talk to him, and Colin was relieved. Maybe it was an understood law in first class. He wasn't used to first class, but if it was always like this, no wonder the rich preferred it. He would resume his frugality after the mission. But this mission mattered too much.

The first thing Colin noticed when he exited the aircraft was the warmth. God, it felt lovely. England was having a typical damp and cold December. He could hardly wait to change into cooler clothing, but he'd have to buy it first. He'd gone to Heathrow straightaway without going home. All he had with him was a briefcase, a laptop, and a single change of clothes he always kept in a rucksack in his car, just in case.

He went down a flight of steps from the aircraft and into International Arrivals. Colin was directed into a large, bland holding area for clearing customs. The split-face block walls were painted ocean blue, and the lines seemed infinite. He knew he'd be in his Heathrow security guard uniform for a while.

The surrealness of the situation struck him as he queued up. It hadn't hit him on the airplane, maybe because he'd slept so much. But the time was here, was now. The possibility of such a mission had been with him since his father first spoke of it, but then it had been with his ancestors for hundreds of years and hadn't come true. The part of him that believed his father expected to pass the mission off to someone else before he died. Perhaps to a son. Or a daughter. He was only thirty years old. He still hoped to meet the right person and settle down. But now, with this, knowing the time was here ...

Doubts began to creep in as he crept forward in the queue. Had what he'd seen in London traffic really been the sign? It struck him as exactly right then, but now that he'd slept and arrived in a country where he didn't speak the language, the weirdness factor hit. It was like watching some kind of movie where the plot devices didn't fit together. He'd just about come to the conclusion he was totally wrong and there was no mission at all when a new queue opened up and he was directed to the head of it. He presented his passport and papers and was shuttled through so quickly he'd barely had time to think.

Striding out of the queue, he looked around the terminal and located the correct luggage carousel, already turning with bags aboard. He spotted his overnight bag and picked it up. It'd been checked only because he'd brought a couple of combat knives with him. He didn't know what he'd need on the mission. He had no idea what his role would be—if this really was a mission and if he really had a role. But he couldn't bring his Walther handgun, so he brought the only other weapons he could think of. He would have to rummage through his bag later to see if it had been searched. He hoped the knives had not been confiscated.

The humidity was making his white polyester shirt collar stick to the back of his neck so he reached back and wiped off the perspiration. As he did, he glanced about the area surreptitiously. If this were real, there would be others, two specifically. Of course, he couldn't be sure when they would arrive or where they would be from. He wasn't even certain how to tell who they were. He scanned those seated, letting his eyes rest on each person for less than a second.

He shifted his eyes away even more quickly from a Native American woman who was gazing at him. He moved on to the next person, a nattily dressed black man. But a movement caused him to look back. The Native American woman got up. She came toward him.

He still had his hand on his neck, rubbing away the sweat, but now he was looking at her. She made a movement toward her neck. Then he saw it. The same strange five-sided birthmark he had. On her neck. The same approximate place. He let his hand slide down to his side.

"I'm Talasi Evenhema," she said, putting out her hand.

He wiped his hand on his trousers and shook hers. "Colin Noble."

"The third one isn't here yet," she said.

He nodded.

Surreal.

* * *

Cancun International Airport, 7:30 p.m.

Yan Zhou's grandmaster had not only provided money but also a few outfits to wear in the West. They were clothes Yan had worn before, traveling to competitions outside the country, but still he found them uncomfortable. Yan was not tall but he was a muscular athlete, and the clothes fit too tightly in the upper legs of his jeans and the shoulders of his shirt, but too loose around the waist of the jeans. He wondered how people viewed him. When he glanced in a mirror in the restroom, he thought he looked like an enforcer for some Chinese gang, at least as portrayed on American television. He would need to find better fitting clothes. If he had time.

Time was the one thing he was fairly sure he was short on. He had been able to make good flight connections, but it was still a long way from his home in Hunan to Beijing, then to Los Angeles, then to Cancun. He did not know who he was to meet, or if they would still be waiting for him. Plus, the time difference was thirteen hours, so his internal clock thought it day when it was night here. He'd tried to adjust, sleeping as he could on the flights, but between crying babies and seatmates who couldn't seem to remain seated, a few hours had been all he could manage. He wondered how effective he would be, for whatever it was he was supposed to do.

It was late at night when Yan arrived, and the lines at customs were short. Non-residents from his flight were the only ones in line. He had checked his competition weapons, standard procedure. He hadn't had to contend with them boarding the plane, but he might have to do that now. When his time came, Yan handed his passport to an agent whose reading glasses perched on the end of his nose. The agent looked over the top of the glasses and asked him a question Yan recognized as being in Spanish.

Yan had grabbed a book of Spanish phrases in the Los Angeles airport, written for English speakers. Although Yan wasn't fluent in English, he had studied it in school and had practical experience using it at competitions. During his sleepless hours of the flight, he'd rehearsed the Spanish phrases he knew he would need. "*No hablo espanol*," he replied. "*Hable usted ingles*?"

The agent did not seem surprised. "I speak some English. What are your plans in Mexico?"

"I am part of a martial arts exhibition, but first I am doing some sightseeing." Yan knew of an exhibition going on in Mexico City while he was here. He hoped the agent would not be interested. Yan especially hoped he would not ask for proof of his participation.

The agent examined the pages of the passport. "You must be very good. I see you have traveled many places."

Yan nodded. "I am a champion in my style. I teach in many places."

"Well, enjoy your stay." The agent stamped the passport and handed Yan his papers. Yan took them, retrieved his luggage and moved into the exit area. He stood and looked around. Other passengers passed by him. He continued to stand as though frozen in his spot. If someone were going to meet him, they would have to know it would be here. But how would they recognize him? Admittedly, he looked out of place in the Cancun airport, an Asian athlete in ill-fitting clothes carrying a small suitcase, but that did not necessarily distinguish him from other tourists in bad clothing.

He did not have to wait long. A white man and a Native American woman walked past, splitting as they went around him, both of them checking his neck. He spotted a birthmark on the man's neck, identical to his own. He tilted his head to the left, revealing his birthmark to the woman. She stopped, then circled round in front. The man did likewise.

"I believe this is all of us," the man said. "I hope to bloody hell you speak English."

"I do my best."

"With any luck that will get us through. My name is Colin Noble. This is Talasi Evenhema."

They shook hands with him. "I am Zhou Yan. Please call me 'Yan.'"

"Nice to meet you, Yan. Ready to leave?"

Yan was puzzled. These two seemed to know so much. "How shall we find the baby?" he asked.

The woman, Talasi, pulled out a copy of the day's newspaper. "We figure this must be her. A pregnant woman who looks ready to deliver shows up on the front page of today's paper at the Pyramid of Kukulcan. And she's a tourist. Feels very much like a sign."

"Staying at the Kukulcan Hotel, too," Colin said. "Grand opening tonight." He looked at his watch. "Probably going on right now. I've already picked up a rental car, though I might give you a scare, since they drive on the wrong side of the motorway here."

"You'll do fine," Talasi said.

Yan followed Colin and Talasi to a parking lot where Colin activated the key fob to blink the lights and unlock a large vehicle, a white Dodge Durango.

They placed their luggage in the back. Talasi sat behind the driver, leaving the front seat for Yan. He opened the passenger door and climbed in. He was still admiring the amount of room he had in it, compared to the little car he drove in China, when Colin put the vehicle in gear and they headed out of the airport.

He still had no idea what he was doing.

Chapter Twenty-One

Syrian Desert, Western Iraq
December 20, 2012
3:45 a.m. local time

Time to Solstice: 34 hours, 26 minutes

Fareed Mohammed had not heard from Vhorrdak for over twenty-four hours, and that concerned him. He didn't think the demon could read minds, but he wasn't absolutely sure. Considering what he was planning, Vhorrdak would most certainly kill him if he knew, and he hadn't died yet. That was a good sign, wasn't it?

He and Ashur had spent the day making slow progress in the desert. They were only to go a few hundred kilometers, so they had spent a good portion of the day going from cave to cave, staying out of the heat and out of sight as much as possible. Three hours of the afternoon they'd stayed in a single cave, leaving there with enough time to reach this cave, which Vhorrdak had given them as their specific location for the night. In fact, it was the stop at the afternoon cave which had given Fareed his brilliant idea. Tomorrow they were to make only a little more progress than today, though by dusk they would be on their way to Syria. With plenty of time in between, it should not be difficult to convince Ashur to help him carry out his plan.

But, if it was so easy, why was he awake in the middle of the night worrying about it?

The satellite phone, his connection to Vhorrdak, was a constant companion and a constant worry as well. During the day, he either held it or had it clipped to his pants. At night, he slept on top of it. It made no sound, only vibrated, so Fareed could not take the chance of missing a call. Now it began to shake.

He sat up. Had his thoughts betrayed him, or was this just his next assignment from Vhorrdak? He pressed the button to connect and then held the phone to his ear, saying nothing.

"The Americans are desperate," the voice said. "Send out the second truck." Like the last time, the call disconnected.

All Fareed knew about the second truck was that its mission yesterday had been much the same as theirs, to spend time making little progress. Vhorrdak had some kind of grand scheme for keeping the Americans from searching too hard for a truck unlike the decoys, that is to say, looking for something more ordinary, like the truck he and Ashur drove. He had no idea where the second truck was, but he knew when he activated the signal, the truck would leave whatever cave it was in and follow the GPS unit until it reached its destination. For some reason, Fareed thought it would point them east toward the mountains. But he wasn't sure.

He made the transmission to the second truck. Wherever they were, the two hired men would receive the signal, wake up, and leave. He wondered if they were sleeping any better than he was.

Chapter Twenty-Two

Cancun, Mexico
The Hotel Kukulcan
December 19, 2012
8:00 p.m. local time

Time to Solstice: 34 hours, 11 minutes

Manuel circulated around the room. It was like being at a University fundraiser, but he didn't feel particularly comfortable. While he knew people and it was nice not to have to push for donations, his purpose was to see Rebekah and Jonas. But how would they receive the information he had for them about the prophecy? Would they believe? He was dismayed they hadn't yet arrived.

The presence of Raz Uris was disquieting. He had come across the antiquities dealer one too many occasions recently. Rumors that the man dealt in Mayan artifacts obtained illegally had been circulating since Raz set up shop in Cancun three years ago. Plus, Raz had an unending curiosity about Mayan legends. In his few conversations with the man, Manuel answered questions that related directly to the topic he hoped to cover with Rebekah and Jonas this evening. Having Raz here precisely at this time worried him. If it were more than a coincidence—and Manuel suspected it was—he would have to watch out for Raz as well as find Rebekah and Jonas.

Raz shook a few hands and settled into a conversation with a woman he recognized as one of the officials in the Cancun government. Raz is well-connected, Manuel thought.

Finally Manuel spotted Jonas and Rebekah at a table on the far side of the atrium. Jonas, dressed in a traditional black tuxedo, was looking up toward the high beams that ran the length of the atrium. Rebekah, in a black formal that accommodated her pregnancy but still had classic lines, looked elegant except that she had her shoes off and was rubbing her feet.

He hurried over to their table. Rebekah was the first to notice him.

"Good evening, professor." She put her feet back in her shoes, looking self-conscious.

He smiled at her. "You were going to call me Manuel, remember?"

"So I was. It's a hard habit to break."

"Admiring your design?" Manuel asked Jonas.

"No. I'm trying to see if something I noticed yesterday was taken care of."

Rebekah rolled her eyes. "Jonas can't leave any of his projects alone, even when they're already constructed. Can you, Jonas?"

"All right. I promise not to let it distract me any more this evening."

"Good. Then sit down," Rebekah said. "Manuel, would you join us?"

As he pulled back a chair, Manuel saw Raz Uris hurriedly exiting the building under the large Mayan arch at the front of the atrium. Manuel was glad to see him go, but wondered what he could possibly put Raz in such a hurry.

Manuel turned to Jonas. "You must be enjoying all the attention tonight. It is well deserved."

Rebekah interceded again. "Jonas is terribly modest. He's delighted that people love his design, but he's not all that comfortable in the spotlight."

Jonas took his wife's hand and kissed it. "You're sweet," he told her, then faced the professor. "Tell me, have you had any luck with the photo?"

Jonas' bringing up the photos relieved Manuel. It allowed him to segue to the difficult topic of the prophecy. He leaned toward the two. "I have. In fact, it is why I'm here."

Rebekah sat up straighter. "What does it say?"

Manuel shook his head. "Too noisy, too many people around. It is a nice night. Maybe we could use the outside tables."

"Rebekah's tired and her feet hurt. Do we really need to move?"

Rebekah touched Jonas on the shoulder. "It's okay." She stood, a bit awkwardly.

Jonas stood with her and she threaded her arm through his. Manuel led them out the back of atrium. They entered the hotel's festively decorated cantina and exited onto an outside patio. Manuel found them an empty table on the perimeter away from the crowd.

When Rebekah was seated, Manuel pulled the photo they'd downloaded from the camera the previous day out of his tuxedo jacket pocket. He pointed to the faint Mayan hieroglyphics between the two jaguars. "What you have uncovered is a prophecy, a very old one, older even than the temple itself."

"You make this sound ominous," Rebekah said.

Manuel did not try to put a different spin on it. "We have a solid translation of the first part, but there is more to work on." From his other pocket he pulled out a folded piece of printer paper. "This is what we have now." He handed it to her.

Rebekah unfolded the note. Jonas leaned behind her to see what it said.

Manuel recited from memory as the two read it. "Near to the end of days/ In the time before the King is born/ Words that bear what has been seen/ You must recover to help survive/ The coming fury of the evil one."

Rebekah held the note at arm's length as if not really seeing it clearly.

Jonas looked puzzled. "What does it mean?"

Manuel paused. "Rebekah, do you recognize the name Chilam Balam?"

"Of course. The most recognized of the Mayan prophets."

"Exactly. This prophecy carries his signature."

Manuel watched Rebekah for a reaction. "Anyone could have written it," she said.

He could hear the skepticism in her voice. He knew she would be aware that many prophecies were falsely attributed to a recognized prophet.

"Yes, anyone could have. But if so, why did it appear suddenly yesterday, and only to your husband?"

"I'd like to know that," Jonas said.

Now Manuel focused on Jonas. "I've been consulting with the elder Maya. They believe it is because you will be the one to find the book Chilam Balam refers to with 'words that bear what has been seen."

"Me?"

"That book must be found if we are to learn the location of the coming king's birth." He paused for effect. This next part was a gamble. "And if the world is to survive."

Manuel watched a series of emotions play across Jonas' face before disbelief settled in. "Well, that's nice," he said slowly, "but Rebekah and I are just a little too busy right now to save the world."

"The world is not yours to save."

"That's a relief."

"It will be your son who does this. You just have to find the book."

Jonas immediately stood. He pulled on Rebekah's arm. "Let's go, Rebekah."

Rebekah resisted. "What book are you talking about?"

"The Book of the Thirteen Gods."

"The reference at the end of Chilam Balam's prophecies? You believe it's not just a myth?"

Manuel heard something new in Rebekah's voice. It was not cynicism. He wondered if she knew more than she was letting on.

"If the image Jonas has captured on his camera is correct, we must assume the book describing the end of our time exists."

Jonas interrupted. "You said, 'Thirteen Gods?' Rebekah found ..."

Manuel saw a startled flash in Rebekah's eyes. She stood up, causing her husband to go silent. In her hand she clutched the prophecy Manuel had given. "You were right, Jonas, we should go. Manuel, if we decide to save the world, we'll let you know."

Rebekah hustled a quieted Jonas off the patio and onto the grassy path that led back to their villa.

Manuel watched them leave. That did not go well, he thought. He toyed with the idea of pursuing them, but he knew it would not do any good at this moment. The two needed time to think and time to talk.

But they would come back. He was certain they would come back.

Or all is lost.

* * *

Jonas knew Rebekah was in a hurry to get away. He was, too, but Rebekah's need seemed to center on something she knew. He waited until they were a good twenty feet away from the patio before he said, "I shouldn't have said anything about the thirteen gods, should I?"

Rebekah leaned in. They continued walking. "Those hieroglyphics from the outside Pyramid did say something about the thirteen gods. I just didn't want Manuel to know about it until I checked it again. So much for first impressions. I guess Manuel may be some kind of a nut case."

"I'm glad you noticed."

They were moving at a good clip when Rebekah stumbled into him. He adjusted, using leg strength to keep himself balanced. He held her upright. But the ground kept shifting. The struggle to stay standing became intense.

Rebekah clung to him. "It's another tremor." He could see fear in her eyes.

He tried to get them away from the building. Just a few more steps and they'd be in the open grassy area that led to their villa. He could hear the noise of the crowd. Some shouted, some cried. A few became hysterical. He heard people screaming 'terremoto,' over and over again.

"I hope it's not an earthquake," he said.

They reached the open area. Rebekah dropped to her knees. Sensing he couldn't keep her upright, Jonas eased her to the ground. He fought the tremor, tried to ride it out like a Fun House floor. He turned back toward the hotel.

Tables and chairs were toppling on the patio. People held onto each other and anything else they could find. Some tried to run. Jonas spotted Manuel holding onto the outside bar that seemed rooted to the ground. Behind Manuel, the hotel swayed. The atrium vibrated with intensity. Jonas heard an explosion.

The atrium collapsed.

His atrium. Crumbled to the ground as he watched. The boom of the wreckage went through his body as the structure dropped to a heap. In the next seconds another tremor threw him to the ground. He shook his head to clear his thoughts. What the hell? He heard Rebekah. She lay near him.

"Oh … my … God." She began to cry.

"Are you okay, Rebekah? The baby?"

As though she'd forgotten the child, she frantically felt for him. A sense of relief flooded her face. "He's okay. Quiet but okay." She looked past Jonas to the rubble. "Your beautiful atrium …"

Jonas choked back a mixture of anger and regret. "It's gone." He crawled next to her. They held each other, both in shock. Minutes passed.

Jonas was yanked from his blankness by the cries. He realized others were hurting, far more than he and Rebekah. He couldn't sit any longer.

"Can you stand? We need to … I mean, the earthquake has stopped … I think I should go help. Will you be all right?" He jumped up and held his hand out to her.

She came up slowly, steadying herself and the baby.

Jonas looked to the building. So many people in need. He started toward them, but he worried about leaving Rebekah alone. And she was in no condition to help.

Rebekah sensed his dilemma. "Go ahead, Jonas. I'll be fine. They need help."

"You're sure?"

Rebekah had her cell phone out and was already dialing. "I'm sure. I'll get emergency help."

Jonas ran toward the collapsed building.

"Jonas!"

He turned around.

"There's no signal. I'll try the phone in our villa." She spotted something on the ground before she left. Reaching down, she realized it was the translation she'd seized from Manuel. She stuffed it in her purse.

As Jonas raced toward the collapsed atrium, Manuel came up beside him. They reached the wreckage and began to work together to free people below.

"I heard something explode," Manuel said.

They shifted pieces of the outside wall away from a woman trapped under some beams.

"I did, too. This shouldn't have happened. The hotel was designed to withstand earthquakes greater than this one."

Jonas heard sirens approaching and saw the lights of fire trucks and rescue vehicles. Manuel hurried toward them.

Jonas looked back over the wreckage. This shouldn't have happened. The explosion must have disrupted the support structure. He should have been more forceful with the foreman to check out the beam with the small gray mass on its side. That mass may have been a bomb.

He came upon the Mayan arch, his centerpiece. The structure was a load-bearing marvel, still intact. He shook his head.

"Jonas ..."

The voice was weak. Jonas looked around. Sheltered under the arch was Stephen Bradford, head of the firm. His legs were covered with debris but his upper body seemed okay. Jonas tore into the wreckage. "Help me!" he shouted. "Help me! This one's alive!" He switched to Spanish and yelled it again.

Jonas knew it was dangerous to move him, but he couldn't leave Stephen there. He hoisted him onto his back in a fireman's carry and tried to climb out of the wreckage when he saw an emergency medical technician approaching.

"Put him down. I need to examine him," the worker said in Spanish.

Jonas laid Stephen onto the debris.

The technician checked him over. "Get me a stretcher and a couple of people."

"Is it bad?"

"Not life-threatening. He must have been in a good spot. His condition is better than most."

Jonas took off over the rubble to get the stretcher and another person. From a high vantage point he paused a moment to look out over the collapsed atrium. It didn't seem real. He wasn't sure when it would. But one thing he knew. It was not his structure that was at fault. Someone else brought it down. And he was going to find the bastard who did it.

Chapter Twenty-Three

Cancun, Mexico
The Hotel Kukulcan
December 19, 2012
8:20 p.m. local time

Time to Solstice: 33 hours, 51 minutes

The Sagiev's suite shook first with the earthquake, then with the collapse of the atrium and now the tremors afterward.

Raz witnessed the havoc they were wrecking in the bedroom. He'd been searching the suite for the clues to the Book of the Thirteen Gods, which Vhorrdak warned him Jonas and Rebekah possessed in photographic form. The earthquake came sooner than he'd expected, forcing him to detonate the explosive. Fortunately, he'd located the photos on Jonas' laptop just before. Now Jonas' neatly packed suitcase was tossed to the floor, the artwork crashed from the walls, and the clock alarm buzzed. Raz couldn't think with the thing chirping. He crossed the bedroom in five steps and banged on the clock. The alarm stopped immediately.

He dashed back to the laptop, shut it, and yanked the cord from the computer. The printer next to it had photos in the tray. Raz grabbed them and put them in his pocket. He hurried to the door. There was a great deal of confusion outside, but no one saw him leave the villa. He stayed deep in the shadows along the front of the building and slipped around the side.

The tremors stopped. Raz took a deep breath. Rebekah and Jonas were nowhere in sight, but hotel security was mobilizing. He spotted a group of three uniformed guards moving around the grounds. He watched them intently, waiting for them to move out of sight so he could leave.

There was something different about them—the way they were positioned, the way they searched. They're not concerned about the hotel, Raz thought. They're looking for something specific. He couldn't take the chance they were looking for someone like him, who'd used the distraction of the earthquake to burglarize a villa. He flattened his back against the wall, trying to make himself one with it.

They crept toward him. He shrank back, trying to get deeper into shadow.

From the direction of the collapsed atrium a figure appeared and hurried across the expanse toward the villa. Raz, already as invisible as he could make himself, held still. But the three guards hurried by him, clearly trying to avoid being seen by the newcomer. They whispered amongst themselves. Raz detected two accents. A Brit and a Chinese, he thought. Those are no guards.

As the figure got closer, Raz determined she was female and pregnant. Rebekah Sagiev. Raz watched her pass by him, unnoticing. He heard the door to the villa open. Raz had to leave, and quickly. He couldn't be caught here. As soon as the door closed, he straightened himself and strode deliberately toward the parking lot.

At least, that had been his intention. But after he moved far enough away to be indistinguishable from any other guest, albeit one carrying a laptop, he slowed and turned around. The three guards were now outside of the Sagievs' villa. They knocked on the door.

* * *

Rebekah dug through the rubble and found the hotel phone buried beneath the bed quilt on the floor. Sitting, she listened for a dial tone. Nothing. She hung up, waited a second or two, tried again. Same result. She tossed the phone aside and leaned back against the nightstand. This night had so quickly turned into a nightmare.

She could hear sirens and felt relieved. Someone had reached the emergency responders.

A knock came at the door. She hesitated for a moment. It surely couldn't be Jonas.

"The hotel is being evacuated," said a male voice in a British accent.

Rebekah snatched up her purse and opened the door.

Two men and a woman stood at the opening. They were dressed in the burgundy and tan uniforms of the hotel staff, but the men's outfits were ill-fitting.

The man with the British accent spoke again. "You need to come with us."

"But my husband ..."

The woman, maybe a decade older, and a Native American from the look of her, interrupted. "He's at the atrium now, but they're moving everyone down to the street. You can meet up with him there." She spoke like an American.

"But ..."

"You need to hurry," the woman said.

Rebekah tried to shut the door on them. "No, I'm going to wait for him."

An Asian-looking man pushed the door open against her, her strength no match for his. The three rushed into the room and shut the door behind them. Rebekah screamed but the Brit grabbed her and held her arm steady while the woman pulled a hypodermic syringe from a small bag and jabbed the needle into her arm. The liquid felt cool as it flowed into her arm.

Rebekah opened her mouth to yell but no words came out. She couldn't believe this was happening. And then everything went dark, the drug smothering her consciousness as if a cover had been thrown over it.

* * *

Colin caught Rebekah as she went slack. Rebekah's purse dropped to the ground. Talasi picked it up. "I'd hoped we wouldn't have to do that," she said.

"I know." Colin eased her over to Yan. "Yan, get her to the van."

Talasi went through the purse. She found a note and glanced at it. A verse of some kind.

"Bring the purse," Colin said. "Is there anything else we should take? What about that backpack?"

Talasi dug through it. "A climber's rope and some other stuff, nothing important." She yanked the quilt off the floor and looked under it. "There's a computer printer but no computer attached to it. Wait a minute. Here's a flash drive."

"We'll take both. We might be able to get something out of the printer's memory, and there might be something important on the flash drive."

Colin watched Yan pick up Rebekah. He did it easily but with care. Colin opened the door.

"What about clothes?" Talasi said.

"If you can find something quickly, get it. But we need to leave."

Yan stepped through the threshold. Colin impatiently watched Talasi sort through a suitcase. When she had two items in her hand, he motioned for her to speed it up. "Let's go."

* * *

Raz followed on a parallel path staying a little behind the three security guards as they carried Rebekah Sagiev toward the front of the hotel. No one seemed to take notice. When Raz could see they were headed for a vehicle in the parking lot, he sped up. He couldn't follow them, since his car was in the back lot. But he could get the license plate number.

Raz watched the Chinese man carefully put Rebekah in the middle row of seats in the Durango. The woman guard got in next to her. The Brit drove and the Chinese rode shotgun. Raz had enough time to memorize the license plate. No doubt it was a rental. Traceable, if you knew the right people, but that wasn't the problem. Raz was certain whoever it was would be using an alias. The problem would be finding the car again. But it could be done.

The car backed out and moved toward the front of the hotel, maneuvered around emergency vehicles and exited onto the main road leading into the heart of Cancun.

Raz shook his head. Someone was crashing his party, and he had no idea who they were.

Chapter Twenty-Four

Cancun, Mexico
The Hotel Kukulcan
December 19, 2012
8:29 p.m. local time

Time to Solstice: 33 hours, 42 minutes

Jonas lifted the head of the stretcher, and he and Manuel took Stephen Bradford to a safe spot away from the wreckage. The emergency worker showed them where to place it so he could work on Stephen.

Jonas paced for a few moments, trying to give him some time, but he couldn't wait. "Is he going to be all right?" he asked in Spanish.

"I am stabilizing him. A doctor will see him soon, I hope. But I believe he will be okay. Are you a guest here?"

"We were at the party, my wife and I. We stepped outside to talk to a friend and then this happened."

"We have been told they plan to evacuate the area. You should find your wife and be ready."

With so much happening in such a short time, Jonas had almost forgotten Rebekah. He wanted to know she had made it safely to the room. He hurried away from the emergency worker.

"Where is Rebekah?"

The question startled Jonas. He turned his head and saw Manuel following him.

"She went back to the villa. I'm headed there."

"Let me go with you."

Jonas made no attempt to stop Manuel from following him. Manuel might have crazy ideas, but he'd proven himself.

They arrived at the villa. Jonas found the door ajar. He pushed it open.

"Rebekah!" He dashed through the suite, stepping over the items thrown to the floor. He checked the bathroom and found no one. He ran back into the sitting area. Manuel stood, watching him.

"She's gone!" he said.

Manuel's voice was shaky. "We will hope that she has been evacuated. It is better than the alternative."

"What alternative? What are you talking about?"

Manuel put up his hand. He nudged his foot though the debris on the floor. "Think for a moment. This mess—is it from the earthquake, or did you have something someone wanted?"

"What do you mean?"

"I mean, look around. Is anything missing?"

"What would someone want in here? And where's Rebekah?"

"Trust me, please. We must search for clues. Is anything missing, in addition to Rebekah?"

Jonas haphazardly tossed things around. He found his backpack and checked it. Everything was there. He hung it on his shoulder. Manuel lifted the comforter that was on the floor and looked under it. Jonas noticed the empty table.

"My laptop is gone."

"Did you make copies of the prophecy you photographed?"

Jonas located the printer. "The prints are gone. Why would someone want those?"

Manuel rubbed his forehead. "Dios mio, I have been stupid! People saw her at the Pyramid, with child. They might have known …"

"Known what? What are you talking about?"

"Someone else knows the importance of the prophecy, Jonas. You and Rebekah are in danger."

Jonas glared at him. "Stop it! We've got nothing to do with your crazy prophecy." He picked up his climber's pack and ran out of the villa. He dashed through the grassy area back to the wreckage of the hotel atrium. "Rebekah! Rebekah!"

The police were trying to take control of the scene. Police tape was strung around the atrium. Four policemen set barriers to keep people back. Jonas had never been so glad to see a policeman. He grabbed one by the shoulder. "Can you help me? My wife is missing!"

The stocky policeman looked at him blankly. Jonas realized he had spoken in English. A second policeman responded. "Please calm down, sir. We are evacuating the hotel. She has probably gone with hotel security."

"Gone where with hotel security?"

"To the pool first. They are moving guests off site from there."

Jonas couldn't remember where the pool was. Manuel took hold of his arm. "This way," he said. "I am certain they mean the pool behind the hotel." Jonas followed him without thinking.

Once he got his bearings Jonas ran. An agitated mob surrounded the pool. "Rebekah!"

No one responded. With the crowd milling, he couldn't determine who was in charge. He spotted a security guard with a phone to his ear. He rushed toward him and the guard stepped into a defensive stance. Jonas slowed.

"I can't find my wife." Jonas said in Spanish.

"If you have searched everywhere and have not found here, she was probably evacuated with the first group."

"How would I find that out?"

"We don't have a list. Our focus has been to clear the area. You need to go to the shelter with everyone else. Most likely she will be there."

Manuel came up behind. "Try your cell phone."

Jonas didn't know why he hadn't thought of it before. He hit a speed dial button and listened. "No answer," he told Manuel. The call went to voice mail. He left a panicked message for Rebekah to call him back.

Manuel pulled him away from the security guard. "Look, there is more I have not told you. It is possible Rebekah has been kidnapped. If she has, finding that book may be the only way to get her back. You should come with me."

Jonas swung the climber's pack from his shoulder and defiantly placed it between him and Manuel. "My wife has not been kidnapped and I'm not going to find your stupid book. I'm going to find her!"

"You need to be protected."

"I'm not going anywhere with you. Get away from me!"

Manuel's voice remained gentle. "Then I will come with you. Try to help you."

"Help me how? Find your damn book?"

Manuel looked him in the eyes. "That may be what will be required. But I will help you find your wife. We will start at the shelter. My car is up front in the valet parking lot. I do not think we will have luck retrieving the key, but I have an emergency one. Come. *Vámanos*."

Jonas hoisted the bag back on his shoulder. He let Manuel guide him away from the scene. He could hear the sirens of the rescue vehicles and see their flashing blue lights pierce the darkness. He could smell the diesel fumes of the news trucks and hear the chatter of the television reporters as they interviewed survivors. He took one last look back at the wreckage that was his beautiful, creative, and—he knew—well-constructed atrium. His eyes filled with tears.

His work was in ruins. Rebekah and their baby were missing. He was being taken to the shelter by a man who suggested his wife had been kidnapped and their unborn baby would be some kind of savior. The same man insisted he was destined to find some kind of book that would reveal where the savior would be born, and if he didn't find it, the world wouldn't survive. And, against all logic, Jonas was trusting that man to help him find Rebekah.

The trip to the shelter was in vain. Rebekah was not there and the emergency crews had no record of her. They suggested trying the main hospital in Cancun, but the switchboard was jammed. Manuel guided Jonas back to the car.

He sat in silence for a long time. Manuel started the car. It snapped Jonas out of his thoughts. "Why would she be kidnapped?"

Manuel's voice was calm. "Many people want this savior to be born. They've been at Chichen Itza waiting for a sign. You and your wife provided that."

"What kind of sign?"

"This will require a bit of faith on your part. Some of what I say will not make sense to you, but it will later. The seat of power in the fourth ahua katun is Chichen Itza. With the end coming, people have been here at the seat of power, waiting for a pregnant woman to appear."

Jonas' voice revealed his skepticism. "Other pregnant women had to have been here."

"None so close to delivery." Manuel paused. "… and none who sat in the Jaguar Seat of the inner temple."

"No other pregnant woman could have gotten in there. And who else would know she sat in it? You set us up."

Manuel shook his head. "Rebekah came to Chichen Itza with you. I had nothing to do with that. She was the one who requested the tour. Diega may have suggested the Jaguar seat, but Rebekah sat in it willingly. And you discovered the prophecy."

Jonas started to get out of the car.

"Please, my friend, stop." When Jonas hesitated, Manuel continued. "It matters little at this moment whether you believe me, that your wife will deliver the great king. What matters is that others believe, and she may be missing because of it. I care about both you and Rebekah. I will help you find her."

"How?"

"Please trust me. Come to my house in Valladolid. I can explain things better there. If you want, you can return in the morning."

"But what if you're wrong? What if Rebekah is out there somewhere and they bring her to the shelter and I'm not there?"

"We have left information at the main shelter that you are looking for her. You have your cell phone. She knows how to get hold of you."

Jonas' shoulders sagged.

"Come. Shut the door, and we will be on our way. You will learn much in Valladolid."

Chapter Twenty-Five

Cancun, Mexico
December 19, 2012
11:30 p.m. local time

Time to Solstice: 30 hours, 46 minutes

Colin had chosen the hotel for its anonymity, not its comfort, and unfortunately it showed. They had taken Rebekah Sagiev from the Hotel Kukulcan, driven away from the fancy hotels to an older area of Cancun and checked into the first cheap hotel he could find. After the door was unlocked, Yan carried the unconscious woman into the room and laid her on the threadbare, ugly beige couch.

Talasi followed Yan inside. The first thing she did was push on the stained couch cushions. She glanced back at Colin. "If this couch was ever in good condition, it was probably sometime before I was born. We should have used the room at the Hyatt I'd reserved."

Colin took in the room—the scuffed and peeling flowered wallpaper, the starving artist paintings not quite centered on the walls, the dark burgundy drapes that didn't quite meet, the water marks on the ceiling—and was himself appalled. But it will do for hiding out, he thought. "We'd be too obvious there. And we won't be here that long."

Colin heard a toilet flush. He watched Yan come out of the bathroom. "We will need bottled water," Yan said. "I do not trust water that comes out of that faucet, even for washing my hands."

Talasi tossed him a bottle. "Here, use hand sanitizer." She eyed Colin. "We'll need more than just bottled water. I'll start a list."

Rebekah stirred.

Colin walked to the couch. "She's coming 'round already."

Talasi knelt next to Rebekah. "I told you the drug wouldn't last long. I had to be careful of the child."

Yan folded his arms over his chest. "What do we do when she wakes?"

"We'll hope she doesn't become hysterical over the surroundings, let alone our presence."

"Look," Colin said, "if I'm going to be responsible for the logistics of this operation, you're going to have to trust my judgment. I'm not telling you how to take care of Mrs. Sagiev."

Talasi's mouth tightened. She thought before she spoke. "Point taken. We agreed we each has a unique expertise. We'll just explain the situation and hope she understands."

Yan's response held an amount of uncertainty. "She is the one, is she not?"

"She fits. Can't you sense it?" Talasi opened her medical bag. "And she had the prophecy in her purse. That clinches it for me." She handed the piece of paper to Yan. He read the brief verse and handed it to Colin.

Rebekah moaned.

Not going to have the chance to study this now, Colin thought. He watched Rebekah regain consciousness. "This is where you take over," he told Talasi. Colin nudged Yan and the two men moved away from the women, retreating to the door of the bathroom to watch from there.

Talasi took Rebekah's hand. Her eyes opened. "You'll be all right," Talasi told her.

Rebekah struggled to clear her mind.

"Colin, get me a washcloth. Dampen it," Talasi said.

The bathroom was as disgusting as Yan had said, but the water didn't look bad to Colin. He wet the washcloth and took it to Talasi. She gently touched it to Rebekah's brow.

Rebekah tried to sit up but sunk back into the couch. "Who are you? Where am I?"

"My name is Talasi Evenhema, but that's not important. I'm a doctor, and I'm here to take care of you and the baby."

Rebekah pushed Talasi's hand away from her face. "I don't need your help. I need my husband." She stared past Talasi and her eyes met Colin's. She shifted her attention back to Talasi. "Who're they?"

Colin spoke up. "I'm Colin Noble, this is Yan Zhou. We're here to protect you."

"Where's Jonas? What have you done with Jonas?"

"We haven't done anything with Jonas." Colin glanced at Talasi.

"The hotel was evacuated." Talasi added. "You were in danger. We're protecting you from people who want to harm you. And your baby."

Rebekah made a second effort to get out of the sinkhole in the couch. Traces of the drug were still affected her. "What people? And where's Jonas?"

Colin kept his tone neutral. "Our top priority was you. Now that you're safe, we'll find him."

"I don't believe you." Rebekah's arms flailed. Talasi gently restrained her.

"In time you will," Talasi said, "and so will your husband." She pulled out her pocket doppler. "Now, with your permission, I'd like to listen to your baby's heartbeat."

Rebekah screamed.

This is not going well, Colin thought.

Chapter Twenty-Six

Valladolid, Mexico
Manuel Patcanul's House
December 19, 2012
11:45 p.m. local time

Time to Solstice: 30 hours, 26 minutes

Jonas stood next to Manuel, watching Diega manipulate graphics on a high-speed internet-connected computer. It was not something he would have expected to find inside the hut they had pulled up to. Though Manuel's place was a little larger than its neighbors in this area of Valladolid, it was still a thatched roof hut based on the traditional *palapas* of the Maya. Inside, the floor was made of wood and the walls of valuable caoba planks, but this one had electricity and a high-definition television. Jonas wondered if the house were an elaborate facade, designed to hide the fact that a highly educated, respected professor lived here.

Diega pointed to a symbol that appeared on the computer screen. The face was Mayan, but masked. "Each of these different symbols represents a Mayan god. The Mayan language is a tricky one. The symbol could literally mean that particular god, or not. In this case very likely it is not, because in context it appears to be communicating a message. In that case, the language is logographic in nature. Each symbol stands for part of a word, but usually not a whole word."

Jonas was concentrating, but it was late and ancient languages were not a subject of interest to him, not the Hebrew of his ancestors, let alone this. He frowned at the screen.

Manuel explained further. "It is like spelling with the English alphabet, except instead of a single letter, Mayan symbols are usually consonant-vowel combinations, 'la' or 'lo' instead of 'l'."

"Please, just tell me what it means."

Diega hit a few keystrokes, magnifying the narrow range of symbols. "I will try. But you must understand, ancient Mayan is no longer spoken, and some of these symbols are new to us."

"And even then, it is prophecy, so you have to interpret what you see," Manuel added.

Again, Diega pointed to the symbols. "This warns about the coming of an evil one." She used the cursor to advance along the string. "And this, that some will turn to him, but not enough to prevent the birth of Kukulcan. This last part talks about the need for two sacrifices."

Jonas reminded himself that Rebekah had trusted Manuel, at least initially. He might be crazy about prophecies, but Jonas didn't think he was dangerous. "What kind of sacrifices?"

Neither answered him.

He assumed the worst. "Human?"

Manuel nodded. "The ancient Maya felt their gods required such things."

Diega interrupted. "This is how it is worded, 'Still blood must twice be willingly shed/once betrayed and once for love/as ransom for the kingly birth.'"

"Is it a sacrifice if it's done willingly?" Jonas asked.

Diega shrugged. She paused for a moment as though lost in thought.

Manuel broke the silence. He said to Diega, "What is your opinion about the lack of information as to where the book is? Is there a clue here we are missing?"

Diega spun around in her seat to face them. "Of course there is that possibility. But I believe they deliberately identified the location of the book somewhere else, somewhere it would be discovered, like this, when the time was right. And by the right people."

Jonas stared past her to the symbols on the screen. He hesitated to say what was on his mind, but the reality was that Rebekah had seen something in the hieroglyphics in the photo taken by the stranger, and now she was gone. If there was a connection, should he keep it hidden? In the end, he decided telling them might hurry them up in finding her. "Last night you called this thing the Book of the Thirteen Gods?"

"Yes," Manuel said.

"I think Rebekah knows where it is."

* * *

Cancun, Mexico

In the attic of his Galeria, Raz kept many secrets. He was quite proud of its clandestine construction, which he had done himself. From the inside, there were no stairways to be detected, no visible way to access it. From the outside, no windows, and most importantly, no records showed that it had even been built. Raz had been careful to do the work at night, under cover of creating an out building for storage during the daylight hours, as well as a new façade for the Galeria. Security was supplied by an array of computers he'd obtained from black market sources and installed as well. These not only protected the entire Galeria from intruders but also controlled the climate in the upper chamber. All this was necessary because the attic held valuable antiquities that had come into his possession illegally and needed to remain off the inventory. As such, he occasionally conducted business that needed to be handled without being traceable.

Raz watched the main monitor at the master control center. He waited for the computer to tell him it had successfully scrambled the Internet Protocol Address so he could upload the video to CNN. As he did, he drummed his fingers on the desk. Sometimes it took a little while. Raz stood and wandered back to the treasures he had managed to accumulate.

Now he studied the artifacts from Palenque. One of them was suddenly valuable to a lot of people, as Vhorrdak had predicted. Having interpreted the hieroglyphics on the computer he'd seized from the Sagievs' suite, he knew it would be the key to finding the long rumored Book of the Thirteen Gods. Now he needed two things. First, to force Jonas underground—and Manuel with him—and second, to get Rebekah. He'd already hired some associates to help him with the second, but nothing would start until he made Jonas a wanted man. The video he'd taken at the Kukulcan Hotel, with some slight enhancements, would take care of it.

"Uploading…" the computer said.

Raz hurried back to the computer and watched the progress of the message with the attached video. As it went to 100% complete, Raz smiled. He signed off the computer and made a phone call, also secured, to the associates who were tracking the vehicle Rebekah's unconscious body had been loaded into.

* * *

Valladolid, Mexico

"How does she know where the book is?" Manuel asked.

"I didn't say she knew for sure, I just think she does. There was a reference to it in some photos."

"What photos?"

"When we were at the Pyramid this afternoon, she wanted me to take a photo of her with certain hieroglyphics. It was right where the shade of the Pyramid hadn't covered the entire side yet."

Diega interrupted. "I remember that. One of the other tourists took a picture of the two of you."

"Yes. If he hadn't been part of the tourist group, I wouldn't have trusted him."

"What about the photos?" Manual asked.

"Later that evening, when we downloaded the photographs to the computer, we noticed a difference between the ones he took and the ones we took."

"Different in what way?"

Jonas stepped toward the computer screen and pointed to the symbols. "The hieroglyphics were like these. Except in taking the photos shadows had been cast over them and changed them. Rebekah could read part of it. It might have referenced the book you talked about. I know for certain she said something about the thirteen gods."

Manuel practically trembled with excitement. "Where are the photos now?"

"We printed them out, but …"

"Let me guess," Diega said. "They were taken from your hotel room."

Jonas nodded. "And the laptop we used to download them."

Both Manuel and Diega let out a slow breath. Jonas could read the disappointment in their eyes. He put his hands in his tuxedo pants pockets as he thought about what to do. He noticed the emptiness of his pockets. Then he remembered something. "Where's my jacket?"

They both looked puzzled. "Over there." Manual pointed to a chair across the room. "Why?"

Jonas dashed to where Manuel had draped his jacket. He picked it up and felt the pockets. What he'd searched for was there and he showed it to them.

"Because I have the camera. And the photos are still on it."

Chapter Twenty-Seven

Washington, DC
Situation Room, The White House
December 20, 2012
12:50 p.m. local time

Time to Solstice: 30 hours; 21 minutes

Jim Harrington's hands rested in front of him on the highly polished mahogany table. The three Information Specialists were in the room operating the equipment, but he paid no attention to them. His mind was wandering. His thoughts had gone from the wildly speculative—what would happen if the nuclear weapon fell in the hands of the Iranians—to the mundane—he'd never seen the table in the Situation Room with handprints on it. How often did it get polished? Momentarily, he laid his head on his hands and closed his eyes. He'd been in the room for the last few hours. Too long.

As the President's representative, he'd felt the need to pressure the military working on intercepting the truck. They hadn't made a lot of progress, so he'd taken up residence in the room. Staff came and went, and phone calls seemed continuous, but no real progress had been made. Since the sandstorm ended, the military had been searching along the vectors they thought the trucks would take, but they hadn't found anything yet.

The door opened. Jim struggled to look awake. With the arrival of someone new, he thought it prudent to emphasize his watchfulness.

The new arrival was General Culver, taking over for Archer, who'd been hospitalized for sudden heart problems. Jim was distressed for his friend, but he also hated that someone else had to be brought in. One more person in the loop. And while Jim liked the affable General Archer, Culver left him cold. The man was like Patton to the troops, but Jim was not one of the troops. He expected personal interaction. Culver gave commands. The two men's eyes met, and Jim hoped Culver caught the dissatisfaction Jim put into his gaze. Culver purposefully ignored him as he consulted with one of his men.

Jim strived to stifle a yawn. He waited until the General turned to one of the screens, but it was big yawn and the general caught him bringing a hand up to cover his mouth.

"I hope we're not keeping you up," Culver said.

"If you'd located the nuke, we could all go to bed."

"We're expecting notification any moment."

"Then it'll be worth my wait."

Culver's arrival had straightened up any casualness that had snuck into the room. The specialists monitoring the screens sat up in their chairs. Even the food had disappeared.

The high definition screens showed various desert locations. One of them displayed increased activity. Troops were on the move. A pilot raced to an Osprey tilt-rotor aircraft which took off like a helicopter and then flew like an airplane. The rotors began turning. Ducking soldiers ran under the blades and climbed into the troop/cargo bay.

The telephone rang. Everyone stared at it.

Major Simmons, wearing a headset, was monitoring the phones.

"Incoming call, sir. Colonel Layton in Iraq."

The general picked up the receiver.

"General Culver."

Jim felt like everyone in the room was straining to hear what was being said. He knew he was. Culver and the phone were far enough away, though, that all he could hear was an occasional word. Jim reflected that Major Simmons, still on the headset, probably knew.

Culver spoke. "Very good news. Keep us posted."

Jim didn't wait for Culver to tell them. He wanted to issue the command. "What is it?"

The General spoke with vindication. "They've found the second truck and are tracking it. We should have someone there in just over an hour."

Chapter Twenty-Eight

Cancun, Mexico
El Hotel de Ruins
December 20, 2012
1:00 a.m. local time

Time to Solstice: 29 hour, 11 minutes

Rebekah lay on the couch faking sleep. She opened her eyes a slit, hoping she would fool her captors. Yan sat at the beaten desk across the room. He was logged onto the computer Colin had brought.

"How are you coming on those Mayan hieroglyphics?" Colin asked Yan from across the room, where he guarded the door.

Yan shook his head but made no audible response.

They'd asked Rebekah about the photos they'd downloaded to the computer from the flash drive they'd retrieved from the Sagievs' suite, but she'd been less-than-forthcoming. The trio was certain something important was on it, since the suite had been pillaged and the computer taken. After dismissing the touristy photographs, they'd settled on the ones that contained hieroglyphics, particularly those taken in the inner Pyramid, the ones that had appeared for Jonas.

Rebekah wished Jonas had password-protected his flash drive. With this experience, neither of them would make that mistake again.

However, Yan wasn't making much progress, which heartened her. Those hieroglyphics were difficult for her to translate, let alone these … well, she wasn't sure what the trio of international travelers were, other than her captors. She couldn't believe the story they told her; unfortunately, it bore a discomforting similarity to what Manuel believed.

She guessed Colin might be a soldier or security expert. He looked like he knew what he was doing guarding the entrance to their hotel room. He was built like a soldier, having stripped down to a short sleeve camouflage shirt that adhered to his thick torso. Rebekah noticed his pants were flannel. Clearly he hadn't been prepared for the weather. When he'd sent the Native American woman out to get food, he'd asked her to look for some short pants or gym shorts and another shirt. Rebekah wasn't sure when Talasi left, but it seemed like a long time ago.

Yan's stomach growled. Rebekah could hear it across the room.

"Did Talasi return to America to purchase food?" Yan asked.

Colin looked at his watch. "I'm with you, mate. I could use a bite to eat. If she's gone much longer, I may send you to the vending machine."

"We have no money until Talasi returns."

"Well," Colin said, "there is that problem."

Rebekah reflected on her chances for escape. Colin's constant hovering at the door blocked that exit. A better opportunity might be to try to get to the hotel phone. She was certain Jonas would have his cell phone with him. She wondered where her own cell phone was. She'd had it in the suite, but then Talasi had knocked her out. Did one of them have it?

She hadn't been in the bathroom yet, a small miracle considering the stage of her pregnancy. She wondered if the bathroom had a window. If it did, and she could get in there and lock the door, she might be able to open the window and crawl out. She put her hands on her stomach. The window would have to have a large opening.

Or, perhaps the best way to escape would be to gain their trust.

A rhythmic knock came at the door. Rebekah recognized the pattern as one Colin and Talasi had rehearsed before she left. Nonetheless, Yan leaped up from the desk and covered the other side of the door, his hands ready in some kind of martial arts stance, as Colin cracked the door open to check. When he was certain it was only Talasi, he let her in.

"Can you believe I found a Subway in Cancun?" She held up plastic bag loaded with food. "Colin, I'm sorry, but there were no clothing stores open this late on a Wednesday night. I searched." She handed him a plastic sack from some Mexican dollar store. "But I found you basketball shorts. They're not stylish."

"I don't care." Colin reached into the sack and pulled them out. They were black with some kind of swoosh logo on them.

"Black works." He dug around some more and came up with a flashlight. "Great. You found flashlights, too."

"One for each of us. Batteries are in there, too. Here's the rest of your money. We'll need to take more out tomorrow."

Colin pocketed the money.

Talasi looked at the clock. "It's Thursday now, isn't it? The 20th. One day left."

"Twenty-nine hours, actually, but don't think about it. Yan, guard the door, will you?"

Colin picked up his rucksack, pulled it over one shoulder and carried it along with the shorts into the bathroom. As he turned on the light, Rebekah was able to see in. No window. Damn. She sat up and stretched as though she'd really been asleep. "Twenty-nine hours until what?"

Talasi started pulling out food. "The winter solstice." She looked over at Rebekah. "How are you doing, Rebekah?"

Rebekah shrugged. Yeah, I'm doing great. Love being here with you. "I'm okay. When are you going to find Jonas?" She wasn't sure she wanted them to kidnap Jonas, too, but she knew she wanted him with her.

"Soon. Yan, how are you coming on that translation?"

"Mayan hieroglyphics are nothing like Chinese."

"Perhaps we could make a deal," Rebekah said. "You agree to let me go, and I'll help you with the translation."

Talasi brought her half of a submarine sandwich. "You're not a prisoner, Rebekah. We're here to protect you."

"If I'm not a prisoner, why are you holding me?"

Colin came out of the bathroom at that point. "Because there are forces out there who want both you and your husband dead."

Rebekah paused. "I think you're all crazy."

"Are we? Have you forgotten your computer was stolen and by your own admission there were also printed photos that had been stolen as well? The person who did that was looking for you, not a computer. If you'd been there, you could be dead."

Rebekah was sorry she'd ever admitted the thing about the photos. "Or they might have taken me, too. Would that be any different than this?"

Colin picked up the other half of the sandwich Talasi had brought to Rebekah. "It would, though you may not believe it." He took a bite.

"I just want to be with Jonas!"

Talasi sat down next to Rebekah. "Don't worry. Now that we have you safe, he's our next concern. The good news is, we think he's out of harm's way for the moment."

Colin swallowed the bite he was chewing. "But that could change in the morning."

Chapter Twenty-Nine

Syrian Desert, Iraq
Approaching An Najaf
December 20, 2012
9:10 a.m. local time

Time to Solstice: 28 hours, 01 minutes

Vhorrdak tried to keep the smile off his face. He stood among the Iraqi soldiers, dressed like one of the higher ranking officers, watching them inspect the second decoy truck. It was indulgent of him to do that, to take time out to watch this. But when was he not indulgent about his own wants and desires? And this gave him so much pleasure, especially after spending most of his day yesterday in Syria, bribing officials for the arrival tomorrow of the very cargo the Americans were seeking. He couldn't allow it to be inspected by Syrian customs. Fareed had been instructed from the start how to get around that, but Vhorrdak's bribes would ensure non-inspection on the docks and on the sailing vessel which would take it to Iran.

So far, Fareed had done everything Vhorrdak had asked of him. The men Fareed had hired had followed instructions to the letter. When Fareed sent the signals, the trucks arrived in exactly the right places to be stopped. They were proving to be an excellent distraction for Fareed's truck, the one containing the actual weapon.

In some ways, it was a shame that he would have to get rid of Fareed. But once the bomb was in Iranian hands, of what use was Fareed?

Vhorrdak's Washington contact was another useful tool. He'd also done all Vhorrdak had asked, and kept him informed on the little triumphs like this one, which had enabled Vhorrdak to be here. Unfortunately that asset expected a payoff fairly quickly. Vhorrdak would give him what he wanted, but in the face of Armageddon, that promotion would do him little good. Of course, the man didn't think the world would really come to an end. Few did.

Once the Americans displayed disappointed looks, returned to the Osprey aircraft and flew away, Vhorrdak slipped back into the medical truck. No one was there. He changed out of his uniform, dropping it onto the body of the unconscious officer he'd taken it from. After that, he disappeared into the countryside. His next stop was the Zagros Mountains.

Chapter Thirty

Cancun, Mexico
El Hotel de las Ruinas
December 20, 2012
1:58 a.m. local time

Time to Solstice: 28 hours, 13 minutes

Rebekah watched Yan run a hand through his short, black hair. He did it about every two minutes. He sat in front of the computer, staring. At his side was a spiral-bound notebook. He did much more staring than writing. He blew out a breath.

Rebekah wasn't the only one to notice Yan's frustration. Colin walked away from his position at the door and stood behind Yan, watching him study the screen.

"You need a bit of a break," Colin said. "Why don't you check the perimeter of the hotel? Talasi can do that."

Yan got up and stretched. "Thank you."

"Yeah, thanks," Talasi said. She had been sitting on the couch next to Rebekah, but now took Yan's seat. Yan stood next to Colin behind her.

Rebekah was tired. Tired because she couldn't sleep and tired of her three captors who treated her nice enough, but were nonetheless captors. And tired of not knowing anything.

"Who are you people?" She wanted to scream it at them, but she settled for a reasonable tone of voice that still conveyed her annoyance.

Colin looked up, surprised. "We've told you. My name is Colin …"

"I don't want your name! I want to know why I'm being held by a Brit, an American Indian, and a Chinese native in a crummy hotel room in Cancun."

Colin started to answer, but Talasi held up a hand to stop him.

"We've told the truth, Rebekah. We mean you no harm. Surely you've seen that in how we've treated you. We're protecting you and your baby."

The thing that drove Rebekah nuts about Talasi was the reasonableness of her voice. She had one heck of a bedside manner.

"Yeah," Rebekah said. "Well, why you?"

Colin, Yan, and Talasi shared looks that Rebekah had trouble placing. It was like they'd never discussed the matter. Colin shrugged. "Are you familiar with the prophecies of Mother Shipton?"

"No."

"She was a 16th century prophetess whose writings were discovered by one of my ancestors. The Shipton prophecies predicted the end of the world."

"And you're supposed to be some kind of prophet?"

"No, not me, though some of my ancestors were. We came to be known as the authoritative interpreters of the fifth century Merlin prophecies, which had a great many similarities to Mother Shipton's. Merlin's prophecies, of course, predicted the return of a king."

"Arthur."

"Yes. Almost every culture has these same kinds of prophecies."

Colin nudged Yan. "The I Ching prophecies of China do," he said.

Talasi peered at Rebekah above the computer screen. "The Hopi legends are similar to the Mayan legends, which I understand you've studied."

Colin continued. "All of our ancestors were told one of their lines would be a witness to the birth. We were marked."

Rebekah watched as Colin turned his neck to reveal a five-sided birthmark. Yan did the same. Talasi, who was wearing a collared shirt, pulled down a collar to reveal hers.

Her eyes widened at the sight of their three marks, virtually identical. Even stranger was their resemblance to the five sided Mayan arch Jonas had been so enamored with, the one he'd used prominently in the Hotel Kukulcan project. "Unbelievable."

"Is it?" Colin answered. "Then let me tell you the next part. If you examine these worldwide prophecies, assume December 21 as the end date and calculate backward, they all can be made to fit together."

"You're making this up. You're involved in some kind of weird conspiracy. I want no part of it."

Talasi spoke in that sympathetic voice of hers again. "I'm so sorry, Rebekah, but you don't have any choice. And it's not a conspiracy."

"So who's behind this? How did the three of you get together to plot this?"

Yan responded as if she hadn't been sarcastic. "Our ancestors passed the mission to us. We were told of the signs that would come. We knew we would travel to a distant land."

Rebekah struggled with Yan's sincerity. She determined soon after being kidnapped that though he spoke well, he wasn't really fluent. He seemed to translate everything to Chinese and then back into English before he spoke. What did it mean that he had taken the question seriously and responded in that manner? That this was real?

Talasi answered as if she had read Rebekah's mind. "The signs appeared. We came. And now we have you and your baby to protect until he is born."

Rebekah stared at them. She slowly covered her baby with her arms, trying to shield him from them.

Chapter Thirty-One

Valladolid, Mexico
Manuel Patcanul's house
December 20, 2012
2:15 a.m. local time

Time to Solstice: 27 hours, 56 minutes

Jonas checked his cell phone again to make sure it was fully charged and that no messages had come through. It was, and none had. In the morning, he would insist Manuel take him back to Cancun. He had every intention of returning to the shelter, and if Rebekah wasn't there, stopping at the police station to report her missing.

Jonas' body was tired but not his mind. His mind was running crazy-fast, attempting to process the data it had accumulated from a very long day. He tried out a half-dozen different scenarios, but he still couldn't grasp what was happening. The day's events made sense only in some fantastical way, a way his mind refused to believe. At least for now.

Diega had rummaged through a drawer and come up with ten different USB cords before she'd found one compatible with Jonas' camera. Once she connected it to Manuel's computer, the photos came up and Jonas had spent half an hour answering their questions about how the photos had been taken and the stranger who had taken some of them. Together, he, Manuel, and Diega examined the differences in the hieroglyphics. Then he watched as the other two ran the characters through a program, compared the results, and worked the process again. Jonas lost count of how many iterations they had done. At first, he'd been curious about their findings and asked, but speculation changed with every version. He stopped asking. He eavesdropped on their conversation for awhile, but when they started using so many Mayan words he couldn't understand them anymore, he stopped doing even that. He'd wandered around the *palapas*, but it wasn't very big and there wasn't much wandering to be done. It was only a large, one-room hut skillfully divided by furniture into three smaller sections, a bedroom, a living area, and a tiny kitchen. He'd found coffee in the kitchen. The three mugs of caffeine-laden coffee were probably the reason his mind was racing.

He heard Manuel call his name. He hurried back to the living area.

"Your wife was correct," Manuel told him. "These new hieroglyphics reveal the location of the Book of the Thirteen Gods."

"Where is it?"

"Palenque, if we are reading it correctly."

Jonas had been to Palenque, another of the major ruins. It was located far to the south, outside of the Yucatan peninsula, not at all close to Chichen Itza. He'd been there during his original tour of Mayan ruins, the one he took before he began design of the atrium, several days before he'd met Rebekah. "Just Palenque? No clues as to where in Palenque?"

Diega answered ahead of her brother, her voice full of exhilaration. "The ancients have provided clues. To find the book, we must 'see in life what Pakal sees in death'."

"Who's Pakal?"

"The greatest Mayan ruler-priest of his time," Diega answered again. "The huge monuments at Palenque were built during his reign."

"What does Pakal have to do with this book? I thought you said it was written by some prophet."

"Chilam Balem referenced it, but he came after Pakal. It's possible Pakal wrote it. Here is what we know. Pakal routinely induced a trance-like state in himself by conducting a ritual. He would mutilate his genitals and use the blood to soak parchment-like paper. Then he would burn the paper to offer his blood as a sacrifice. We don't know if other chemicals were involved in producing the paper, but inhaling the smoke induced hallucinations, allowing him to enter the underworld. It was during one of these sessions when the gods revealed the information that Pakal wrote into the book."

"How are you going to 'see what he sees in death?' "

"That will be the difficult part," Manuel said. "When his burial chamber was discovered, they removed his body."

Diega shook her head. "It may not be so difficult, Manuel. We have photos of the tomb when it was discovered. We could lie down in the same position Pakal held and look up. There must be something on the lid of the sarcophagus."

"It will be far from simple," Manuel told her. "You forget. In death Pakal wore an elaborate mosaic mask with oddly-cut jeweled eyes. To see what he sees in death, we would need that mask."

Diega crossed her arms over her chest. "I had forgotten that."

Jonas had the feeling something bad had happened to the mask. "Why? Where is it?"

Diega answered. "It was stolen from the National Museum of Anthropology in 1985, but it may not be lost."

Jonas rubbed his eyes. The fantastical scenario he didn't want to consider, the one his mind told him to reject, stared him in the face. He had to confront it. "Wait a minute. You expect me to believe that a prophecy that's been on the wall in the Pyramid for hundreds of years magically appears on the same day a shadowy inscription on the outside of the Pyramid suddenly reveals the location of a long lost book of the apocalypse?"

In the face of Jonas' admitted disbelief, Manuel nodded. "Keep in mind we have one coincidental factor. You and your wife were present at both."

Jonas grasped the implications. "Let me just assure you that my wife is not giving birth to some Mayan king. For one thing, we're Jewish, if you haven't figured that out yet."

Manuel was not disturbed. "It is you who do not understand. Kukulcan was never depicted as being dark and Mayan. His symbol shows him with lighter skin. He will do more than fulfill Mayan prophecies. Other peoples have similar end-of-time kings, like the Christian religion with Jesus coming a second time. Your Jewish prophets foretold of a Messiah. Who is to say we cannot all end up with the same King?"

"I'm no Jewish scholar, but even I know our scriptures predict the baby will be born in Bethlehem. We're a long way from Bethlehem."

"A different translation reads 'out of Bethlehem'," Diega said, "which could mean a number of things. Where was Rebekah born?"

Jonas did not want to reveal the truth. Did they know more about the two of them than they let on? "Okay. She was born in

Bethlehem. But the Messiah also has to be from the line of David, and we don't know if that's the case."

Manuel seemed surprised. "You do not know if you are of the line of David? I thought your family had an oral tradition that linked you to David through the 11th century author Rashi."

Jonas paused. So they had done some research on him. Did they have any right to know the truth? They didn't, but maybe if he told them, it would bring this craziness to an end. "Look, I've only told a few people this, but … biologically, I may not be the father."

For the first time since the evening began, Jonas saw doubt creep into Manuel's face.

* * *

Colin was unhappy with the way things were going. They had the paper Rebekah had been carrying, the one that had a prophecy on it. It was fairly cryptic, with its talk of words that must be found. Since there were no directions, Talasi had decided there must be additional verses, but Rebekah claimed she didn't know of any. They also had photos of hieroglyphics they'd found on the computer, now cropped and enlarged. Colin believed they must be of some importance, but neither Yan nor Talasi could figure out what the hieroglyphics meant. Though they used internet sources, none were good enough to help people like them who had no experience with decoding the Mayan language. Rebekah had initially offered to help, but now she'd shut down, refusing to cooperate until they retrieved Jonas. It was a promise Colin had made that he intended to fulfill, but he hadn't a clue how. Damn the ancients for giving them a task without any real guidance. He'd expected that things would fall into place, as they had initially in the mission. They had Rebekah, and that was of primary importance, but now what to do with her?

He stood guard at the door and surveyed the room. Rebekah was back on the couch after having reluctantly used their unsanitary bathroom. Talasi, after accompanying Rebekah to make sure she didn't try something, now worked on the computer trying desperately to crack the code. Yan was out conducting surveillance on the car park. Colin had no reason to believe anyone knew Rebekah was here, but in the absence of any supernatural directives from the ancients—and he wasn't sure that would be forthcoming—he needed to put into action the things he knew to do. If he was in charge of security, it meant securing the perimeter. Yan had needed the break anyway.

Colin looked at his watch. Yan had been gone half an hour. He began to worry about him. The guy was strong and highly skilled in hand-to-hand combat, but that didn't mean he was indestructible. The truth was, Colin was beginning to have doubts about this 'mission.'

A knock came at the door. As they'd agreed, a series of four taps, followed by a pause, followed by a second series of four taps. Colin had his short knife in his hand and slowly opened the door a crack. Yan was alone. He let him in.

Yan was agitated.

"A black sedan lies in wait across the street," he said as he entered. "For over twenty minutes it has been waiting there."

Colin closed the door behind Yan. "Can you see who is in it?"

"The driver I can see from a distance. I did not think I should get too close. Others could be in the back, where the windows are dark. I have the plate number."

Colin stroked the stubble that had grown on his face. "In this part of town, it could be someone in the drug trade. But if it stays there much longer, we may need to take action. We'll wait a half hour, then check again."

Rebekah made an attempt to get off the couch. She had to push herself off from the sunken spot, but after a slight struggle, she made it. "I thought you were going to get Jonas. That's what you said."

Colin forced himself to breathe deeply before answering her. He'd been trying to put himself in her position all evening. She didn't know them, couldn't be sure whether they were protecting her as they claimed or just holding her, and she was separated from her husband. Naturally she would be nervous. Naturally she would demand they keep their word and prove themselves trustworthy. But he was still getting weary of her. "Before dawn we'll return to the hotel and set up a position from which we can watch. He was the architect. He'll be there. He'll want to search out the reason the atrium went down."

"If he knew I was safe, he would. Not knowing that, he'll be out looking for me."

Bloody hell. Why couldn't the two of them been together as we'd expected?

Colin decided to bluff. Act like he knew what he was talking about. Like he'd seen some kind of sign he wished the ancients had sent him. Perhaps it would keep her quiet. "Whether he's looking for you or the reason for the hotel's collapse, he'll be at the hotel. When the morning comes," he added. I hope.

Rebekah crossed her arms over her chest, resting them on her stomach. She turned away so they couldn't read her face. Because deep inside, she had the feeling they were wrong, and she wasn't sure she would ever see Jonas again.

Chapter Thirty-Two

Cancun, Mexico
Outside Hotel de las Ruinas
December 20, 2012
2:45 a.m. local time

Time to Solstice: 27 hours, 26 minutes

Raz sat in the back seat of a nondescript black sedan across the street from a hotel. He watched the sign flicker. Hotel de las Ruinas, he thought. It's certainly that. He pushed a button on his watch making the dial light up. He didn't like what he saw. Time was pressing in on him. Vhorrdak had given him the exact hour and minute at which he needed to be back in the shop, but he had to nab Rebekah first. Vhorrdak was unaware he was fitting that in, too. By design.

It's a good thing I know people who know how to get things done, Raz thought. It was not just respectable people in the upper levels of the government he knew, but also down and dirty criminals, ones who could track cars and sabotage power supplies. It was the latter he was counting on tonight. He checked his watch again. Time is tight.

Raz watched as one of the three men he'd hired for the evening approached his car. He struggled to remember the man's name. Pablo, that was it. Thankfully he didn't have to talk to the other two. It was easier to think of them as Sedan Driver and Electric Goon. Raz rolled down the window. "*Sí*, Pablo. *Diga*."

"The power to the hotel should go down in five minutes."

Raz nodded. "Good. Get the others in position. Once our presence is discovered, we'll have to move fast. No guns."

"No weapons?"

"We do everything with our hands. In the dark we can't risk harming the mother. They won't risk it either. And remember, you don't kill anyone."

"*Sí*. We leave them alive."

But Raz was unconvinced by the tone in Pablo's voice. "Dead bodies would only bring in the police. We don't want them to be able to trace us."

Pablo spoke to Sedan Driver. Raz followed the Spanish easily. Pablo told him how they would invade the hotel room and directed him to take a position in the stairwell outside the room.

Sedan Driver took the night vision equipment from Pablo and headed across the parking lot into the hotel. Raz heard Pablo call Electric Goon on the cell phone. From the one-sided conversation, Raz gathered that Electric Goon was already inside the hotel. Pablo nodded at Raz.

Raz got out of the sedan, finally shedding his tuxedo jacket. He'd already dumped the bowtie, but he hadn't had time to change into clothes better suited for this sort of thing. He looked down at his white shirt. Way too noticeable.

"*Momento*," he told Pablo.

Raz opened the trunk and rifled through a duffel bag he kept in the back. He hadn't opened it in awhile, but he was fairly certain there was a black t-shirt buried among the weapons he kept for emergency needs. Finding the shirt, he quickly changed into it.

"*Bueno*. Let's go." Raz slammed the truck lid.

Pablo handed Raz the remaining night goggles and took the same path Sedan Driver had taken, winding around the outskirts of the parking lot until reaching a burned out security light. A number of decrepit cars were parked there. They ducked behind the cars and moved toward a side door of the hotel.

* * *

Rebekah was tired but there was no way she was leaving the crappy couch for the creepy bed. The couch was bad enough but she'd sat on it so long she felt that it had taken on some of her own characteristics and was therefore somehow cleaner than the bed. Who knew what kind of bodily fluids had contaminated the bed or when it had last been changed? Even the 'comforter,' which she wasn't sure would comfort the homeless, was suspect.

Talasi continued to work on the computer. Colin and Yan huddled by the window. Rebekah had, for the moment, given up any notion of escaping. There was no way to get past her captors. At least they were decent to her. That is, since they'd arrived at the hotel. That they'd drugged her to get her here still had her on edge. And they seemed to be part of this growing number of people looking for a savior to be born December 21. Disturbing. She hugged the baby inside her. Not you, she thought, not you. You're not even ready to be born yet. How can I convince them to let us go?

The lights went out. Completely. Rebekah screamed. She was already on edge.

Talasi responded. "Rebekah, are you okay?"

"Yes."

"I'm coming toward you. I'll be there in a second."

Rebekah heard Colin's deep voice. "Flashlight." Suddenly the room was illuminated. It was like the moon had come out of a thick cloud and pierced the darkness. Rebekah could see the area around Colin. He handed Yan another flashlight from his rucksack.

Then the door to the hotel room burst open. Rebekah screamed at the sound of the splintering doorjamb.

Darkly dressed figures, heavily armed, stormed the room. Once they were in they stopped, confused. They were wearing some kind of headgear.

"Night vision," Colin shouted. "Shine your flashlights at their eyes."

Yan switched his on and joined Colin in blinding the two invaders. The men ripped off their night vision goggles but it was too late. Yan was already moving, using the flashlight as a weapon. He swung it at the one nearest one, cracking him in the temple. The invader staggered back. Yan dropped the flashlight and grabbed for the man's gun. He twisted it away from him.

Yan's movement caught the eye of the second invader just as he discarded the goggles. Reacting instinctively, he threw a left punch to Yan's head. It connected, but Yan deflected it like it didn't have much power. Yan spun into the first man, using him as a shield, and sent a left side kick into the second man's stomach. The man grunted as the force of the blow sent him against the wall. Colin took over and cracked his flashlight over the man's head, but the man blocked the attack with his forearm. Colin and the man traded blow for blow.

The moving flashlight beams produced a strobe-like effect. Rebekah got only momentary glances of Talasi, who had closed the computer, disconnected the cord, and shoved it under the bed to hide it. Rebekah quickly began to assess her chances of getting out the door while everyone was occupied. She didn't recognize the swarthy invaders so her goal was to get away from both groups and try to contact Jonas.

But the area around the door was crowded and dangerous, and it was only getting worse.

The first man recovered from Yan's blow to his temple as Yan spun into him. He wrapped his right arm around Yan's neck in a choke hold. Nearly a foot taller than Yan, he lifted Yan off his feet to let Yan's weight add to the stress he was putting on the neck.

Talasi launched herself across the bed and dropped onto the floor. She lunged for Yan's flashlight rolling across the threadbare carpet. Nabbing it, she jumped up and rushed the man holding Yan. Taking a cue from Colin's earlier command, she shined the light directly into the invader's eyes.

Brilliant, Rebekah thought, comparing the man to Talasi, only slightly taller than Yan. It's the one vulnerable spot she can easily attack.

The man screamed as the light burned into his retina. He aimed a kick at Talasi, catching her in the thigh and knocking her back. She dropped the flashlight. But her quick thinking worked. In a momentary lapse, the man bent forward enough for Yan's feet to touch the floor.

Yan threw the gun to Talasi as soon as he got his balance. Falling away from him, she tried to catch it but missed. She hit the side of the bed with her back and bounced forward. The gun slid under the bed. Talasi saw her flashlight come to a rest near Colin's feet.

Yan pulled down on the man's forearm and ducked his chin under the crook of the man's arm to block the choke. He tried to throw the man over his hip but the man had recovered enough to lift Yan off the ground again, diffusing Yan's throw. The man used his left fist to pound Yan's kidney. Yan twisted wildly, then lifted his right foot hard and caught his attacker in the groin. The man coughed and eased up. Yan's feet once again touched ground.

Talasi stretched out toward Colin and his opponent in an attempt to reach the flashlight. Colin spotted her efforts and backed away a bit. His opponent realized it and tried to stomp on Talasi's hand. She jerked it away in time.

Colin's opponent pulled out a switchblade.

Talasi grabbed the flashlight and crawled back to the bed to search for the gun.

A third invader entered the room, sliding by Yan and his attacker. He strode to where Talasi had her head on the floor, shining the light under the bed. He clamped a boot on her neck.

"Move and I'll kill her," he said.

The words stopped everyone where they were.

"Good. Now get down on the ground."

Both Colin and Yan reacted hesitantly.

"Now."

As Colin bent toward the floor, the man he had been battled cracked him over the head with the flashlight. Colin slumped to the carpet. Yan turned toward his opponent but the man blocked Yan's right arm and delivered a chop to Yan's neck. Yan dropped to the floor and didn't move.

Talasi struggled. The third man pressed his boot harder into her neck. He bent over and picked up Talasi's flashlight.

"Perhaps next time I will hire more qualified help," he told the others.

He reached into a knapsack he carried. Rebekah watched him retrieve a high-tech spray bottle and squeeze it under Talasi's nose. He kept his boot in place until he was certain she'd breathed the spray and stopped moving. He moved to Yan and Colin and did the same to each.

Rebekah shrank into the couch as he swept the flashlight toward her. "There you are," he said.

She smelled ether. "No," she said, pleading. "I'm pregnant."

He stopped and put the spray back in the knapsack. "Don't worry. I'm taking you to Jonas."

Rebekah could hardly believe what she heard. "Jonas?"

"Yes, but we have to hurry." He turned to the others. "We need to go back to using night vision."

The men put on the night goggles. The flashlights went off.

Rebekah felt someone lift her easily from the couch. She struggled, tried to get out of his arms, but once she was clutched against his chest, she stopped. What if he dropped her? What would happen to her baby?

She decided to play along, as she had with her other set of captors. But she wasn't naïve. She knew it was too good to be true to think her new kidnappers would take her to Jonas. All she could do at this point was hope.

* * *

Manuel could hardly believe what he'd heard. This was not going at all the way he'd envisioned. "What do you mean, you may not be the baby's father?"

Jonas shook his head. "I had Hodgkin's disease when I was a kid. I had been told the chemo made me sterile. Rebekah and I wanted to have children so we went to a sperm bank. Everything was set up for them to impregnate her with the sperm, but then … we discovered she was pregnant."

Manuel and Diega looked at each other. Diega said, "So you are not sterile?"

Jonas' voice was thick. "I had the doctors re-check. According to them, I am still sterile. But Rebekah claims she has never been with anyone else."

Manuel wasn't quite sure how to ask the next question. "Have you … checked the baby's DNA?"

"To be certain it's mine?" Jonas spat it out, angry. "No, Manuel, I have not. I love Rebekah, and insisting on some kind of DNA check will only put a barrier between us. The only reason I told you about this was so you would get off this kick that our baby is some kind of grand king."

Manuel paced. What did this mean to their assumption that Rebekah carried King Kukulcan?

But Diega smiled at Jonas. "We are sorry to have made you uncomfortable with our questions. But this does not change anything. It only means it is a miracle." She grabbed Manuel's arm, stopping him in mid-pace. "Think about the Christian parallel. The foster-father raises the child."

Manuel felt as though a veil had been pulled back. "Of course."

"We have confirmation in that others recognize she is the mother. That is why she was kidnapped. Though," Diega said, pausing as she thought it through, "there is no parallel for that."

Manuel felt his moment of clarity slipping away.

Jonas gripped his climber pack. "No one would kidnap Rebekah because of your stupid prophecy. Take me back to Cancun. I'm going to find her."

Manuel looked at Jonas with new appreciation. Jonas' role was doubly important. But still he had to be persuaded to find the book. And to do that, he had to be convinced. "The evacuation was hours ago. She was not at the shelter. You still have your cell phone. If Rebekah had arrived since we left, they would have contacted you. Or me. They have my number, too. And you know she would have tried to get a message to you."

Jonas yanked the cell phone from his pocket. He pulled up a number on the screen and dialed it. He waited a long time for an answer, then closed the phone with a snap. The conflict played out in his face. "Okay. Let's say for a moment she's been kidnapped. How do we find out who has her?"

"We can put out feelers through the Mayan community," Manuel said. "They will be looking for the prophecy to be fulfilled. In the meantime, we must find that book. It will point the way to where they will take Rebekah."

A vein that ran across Jonas' forehead pulsed. "How can we find it? We can't even get the first clue. You said Pakal's mask had been stolen."

"I did say that, but we think we know where the mask is."

"Where?"

"The mask was originally stolen from the museum by a rebel group of Maya known as the Cruzol." Manuel could have added more, but the history of the Cruzol would not have meant to Jonas what it did to him and Diega. The two of them were part of the group, descended from natives of the Chan Santa Cruz pueblo who had fought the Mexican government well into the early twentieth century. Though the movement was thought to have died, it had gone underground and survived. Today it provided resistance in more subtle ways.

"Can we get the mask from them?" Jonas asked.

"Unfortunately, one of the Cruzol betrayed the group and sold it," Manuel answered.

"I trust you know who bought it."

"We suspect …"

"You suspect?"

Diega touched Jonas' shoulder. He turned and looked at her.

"We are fairly certain it is an antiquities dealer named Raz Uris," she said. "He is a former Mossad agent who came here a few years ago to collect Mayan artifacts. He has a shop in Cancun."

"Many copies were made of the mask," Manuel said, "though they were just copies. Until now we have had no compelling reason to risk stealing the mask back," Manuel said. "However, now it has become imperative."

There was a frantic knock at the front door. Diega opened it. A young man of Mayan heritage burst in. "Turn on the television. CNN. Bad news."

Manuel grabbed a remote. Within moments the screen displayed the familiar CNN news desk. Late night anchor Amy Wilson was reporting.

"Police are looking for this man, Jonas Sagiev, an American architect wanted in connection with the collapse of the Kukulcan Hotel," he said. "A video of the man scaling the hotel atrium and planting an alleged explosive device was sent anonymously to Cancun police and other local news media. CNN has obtained a copy of that video."

The four of them stared in horror as a video showed Jonas climbing the rope to a high beam in the Hotel Kukulcan hotel atrium. The time stamp showed it was early morning. From the angle of the video, it was unclear exactly what Jonas was doing.

Jonas edged closer to the television. "I found something up there," he said, talking back to the screen. "Why would I sabotage my own creation? And who made that video?"

"Investigators say the recent earthquake may have been used as a cover for triggering the device, which collapsed the atrium and killed twenty-two people. Police are also searching for Rebekah Sagiev, wife of the missing architect, who is believed to be with him."

Manuel turned to Jonas as the video showed Jonas hanging upside down on the rope kissing Rebekah. "What were you doing up there?"

"I knew that atrium inside out. What I saw must have been the explosive. I was checking it out when Rebekah came in. She doesn't like me climbing now that we're going to have a baby. She persuaded me to have the construction foreman check it out. Which he didn't do, obviously."

On the television, the blonde anchor shifted her notes around. "In other news, the surprise random searching of commercial trucks in Iraq has people speculating on what government officials expect to find ...."

Manuel hit the 'mute' button. "Someone set you up."

"But who? And where's Rebekah?"

"Somehow we must find the answers to both questions. And also find the book, so we will know where the king is to be born."

Diega glanced at her watch. "All in about twenty-seven hours."

Chapter Thirty-Three

Washington, DC
Situation Room, The White House
December 20, 2012
3:50 a.m. local time

Time to solstice: 27 hours, 21 minutes

Jim Harrington had sat through the discovery of the second decoy truck; he understood the disappointment—the chagrin—of those in the room and those in the field at having been duped. The President had dictated that they find the nuke as quickly as possible. Everyone recognized the danger in not locating it. If it fell into the hands of militant Islamic extremists—and they were plentiful in and around Iraq—it would push the world to the brink of nuclear war. This worst-case scenario was what the government had feared since the collapse of the twin towers in 2001 revealed the mindset and the intentions of the extremists. Jim echoed the sentiment prevailing then and now—failure was not an option.

But he was not going to throw out an old cliché in the hopes of stirring anyone. He would wait for the military leaders to respond first. Even more of them had been pulled in now, even more possibilities for leaks. But he sensed the desperation. In the end, he truly hoped more specialists would help. They were in a separate room anyway, plotting strategy. Only those monitoring the satellite feed of various views of the Iraqi landscape stayed with him in the Situation Room. He watched the flicker of the images as they changed on monitor after monitor.

Eventually it was General Culver who returned to the room to face him. He brought Major Simmons with him, but Jim knew Simmons was there for support, not strategic thinking. That was the way Culver ran things.

Culver practically marched to the chair opposite Jim's. He placed his hands on the table as he sat; when he lifted them, damp handprints remained. "We suspected from the start there would be a decoy truck," Culver said. "We just didn't expect two."

Of all the ways to start this conversation, Jim thought. "When I contact the President, I'm sure he'll want to congratulate you on having located the decoys and busting Iraq's illegal auto salvage parts operation," he said dryly. "But as you know our main concern is finding the real nuke."

"Despite the sandstorm, look how quickly we've found the decoys. The real truck is next."

"Culver, don't take me for an idiot. The real one will be harder to locate. And what if they're running more than two decoys? Or what if they've switched the cargo to a completely different kind of truck?" Jim started to get up. "I need some coffee."

The General waved him to sit down. "Simmons will get it."

Simmons looked startled, but he hustled to locate the coffee pot.

"The possibility of alternate transportation for the nuclear weapon has occurred to us," Culver said.

Simmons returned with two mugs bearing the logos of military suppliers and a pot of coffee. He poured coffee for the two men at the table. "I remember that you take yours black," he told Jim.

Jim liked that Simmons knew that. He couldn't remember when he'd had a cup of coffee around him, though. Maybe he should be talking to the major instead of the general. "Have your men been successful in getting anything out of the drivers?"

Culver stiffened. "No. They appear to have been hired for the sole purpose of driving the truck from the desert to a location specified by a GPS unit the driver had with him. The first delivery point was an empty warehouse in Mosul, though they were taking a roundabout route. The second delivery point was an empty warehouse in An Najaf. We're tracking down the owners of the warehouses, but we don't expect to find anything of significance. The drivers claim not to know the contents. They were relieved to learn they carried nothing more than auto parts."

"They don't know who hired them?"

"They gave us a description of the same man, but no names, and we've tried to match up faces, but he doesn't appear to be in any database."

Jim took a sip of his coffee. "So I ask the question again, if there are multiple decoys or if they've switched the payload to a different truck, how will you track it down?"

"We've tightened down security at all the borders," Culver said. "We're checking every vehicle."

How comforting, Jim thought. Like there isn't a huge expanse of desert with no check points.

"Under General Culver's orders we've alerted every agent we have in the Middle East," Simmons interjected.

Culver gave a backward glance. "Thank you, Robert." The tone was not one of appreciation. Simmons scurried off to return the coffee pot to the warmer.

Culver resumed facing Jim. "As Major Simmons noted, we've alerted our agents. Soon we'll know who has it and who's trying to get it."

"It needs to be soon. Too many questions are already being asked. You saw the CNN News feed. Before long the President will be inundated with calls from foreign governments asking what we expect to find."

Jim knew he couldn't exhort them anymore than he already had. It was time to disappear and use an impending return to exert pressure.

"Use every resource," he said. "Call in every favor. I'll be back in two hours unless you have a breakthrough. For now, I'll report what little we have to the President."

He stalked out of the Situation Room, not looking back to see if his exit was having the impact he hoped.

Chapter Thirty-Four

Cancun, Mexico
Outside El Hotel de las Ruinas
December 20, 2012
3:00 a.m. local time

Time to Solstice: 27 hours, 11 minutes

Rebekah rethought her decision not to struggle as she was carried across a darkened parking lot. Was she going from the frying pan into the fire? The man who gave the orders illuminated the way with a high-powered flashlight. They were in a bad part of town. She'd been fairly sure of it from the hotel, but the nature of the neighborhood confirmed it. But other buildings have lights. What does that say about this hotel's blackout? Still, she hadn't been blindfolded or gagged. Did that mean they were trustworthy? If she screamed to get attention, who would come to her rescue?

Before she could decide on a course of action, the group came to a dark sedan and she was eased into the back seat. At least they're treating me with care, she thought. Though the others did that, too. The man who gave orders got in next to her. She scooted as far away from him as she could. The driver started the car and they sped away.

"My name is Raz," said the one who seemed to be in charge. "I'm not going to hurt you."

'Raz,' Rebekah knew, was a popular Hebrew name, and she knew its origin, 'secret.' That didn't give her a good feeling. She wanted to believe him, but she couldn't let herself. "Where are you taking me?"

"Somewhere safe. You'll see."

"Who were those people?"

"I'm not sure. I was at the Kukulcan Hotel's opening. I saw them carry you out of your hotel room unconscious. When they put you in their SUV and drove off, I followed them here. The whole thing seemed suspicious."

To Rebekah, what was suspicious was the ability of someone to organize a rescue operation like this. Was she really being rescued? Now that they were out on the city streets, she could see what Raz looked like. He had military short hair and a fu man chu. His face was hard and lined. He was dressed in black tuxedo pants, well-polished shoes, and a black, short-sleeve t-shirt. He must have come from the hotel reception.

She tried to see into his eyes to determine whether they held any threat for her. Even with the dim light she was confident of one thing. The man is dangerous.

"Why do you care about me?" she asked. "I don't even know you."

"I was at the hotel for a reason. Think of me as being with Security. We thought there'd be trouble."

"Who is 'we'?"

Raz just shook his head.

"How do you know Jonas?"

"Let's just say I'm interested in keeping both of you safe. We'll be at my place soon.

"And Jonas?"

Raz looked at his watch. "He'll be there in about an hour, I would say."

* * *

Between Valladolid and Cancun, Mexico
Manuel's car

Manuel had misgivings about breaking into Raz Uris' Galeria del Sol, even though he had been the one to suggest it, and even though he knew they had no alternative. Their intelligence about him having the mask was solid enough, but this was a risky step. If it backfired, they would find themselves in jail a mere twenty-seven hours before the birth of the king.

Our success has been assured by the prophecy, thought Manuel. Whether biologically or not, Jonas is still the father of the child. He is destined to find the book. Therefore, we cannot fail.

He was glad Diega was good at details such as breaking and entering. Though most regarded him as the 'smarter sibling,' it was all a deception. Diega, the 'tour guide,' was every bit his equal. Plus, they both had strong altruistic natures that helped them rationalize their occasional illegal activity. Secretly they had rescued a number of artifacts that simply could not leave the country. But those thefts had been planned by amateurs. Taking from Raz would not be easy. In fact, that was why they had not tried it before.

Manuel drove past a sign that said, 'Cancun, 40 km.' He could hear Diega in the back, talking on her cell phone and simultaneously clicking the keys to her laptop. Next to him in the front passenger seat, Jonas squirmed.

"You should sleep, Jonas, if only for awhile," he said.

"I'm worried about Rebekah."

"If it makes you feel any better, Rebekah cannot be harmed until she has the baby."

"I wish I could be confident of that."

Manuel mentally calculated the amount of time until they reached the Galeria. Thirty-five, forty minutes, he thought. He was nervous. "Have you double-checked the plan, Diega?"

"And then some. Actually, I am more concerned about how to get to Palenque. It is a long way, Manuel, and the police are hunting for Jonas."

"While you were digging out supplies for this operation, I made calls. Our friends will have a helicopter waiting when we return to Valladolid. Had I known you were worried about that, I would have told you earlier. I wanted you to focus on getting us into the Galeria."

"I am glad you are ahead of me on Palenque. Based on the records I have been able to access about the gallery and about Uris' purchases, I believe I know exactly what security there is and how to get in. But he has been secretive about it. He has done all of the work himself. There must be a reason for such protectiveness. We will need luck here, that I have figured it out correctly."

Manuel's hands began to get clammy. Luck?Why not speak of fate? Or of faith?

For reasons he could not account, the saying, 'Man plans, God laughs,' popped into his head.

* * *

Cancun, Mexico
El Hotel de las Ruinas

Colin sat up, his head pounding, his vision blurred. He shook his head and realized the lights of the hotel room flickered, not his sight. He tenderly touched the place where he'd been hit.

Across the room, Yan helped Talasi to her feet, favoring his right arm. The lights stopped flickering and remained lit. Colin could see the room clearly.

Talasi gripped Yan's good arm. "What happened?"

The noise of other hotel patrons, now coming to grips with the blackout, became louder.

"We were outsmarted," Colin said. "Someone knew we were here, and they knew we had Rebekah."

Talasi looked around the room. "She's gone."

"Yes," Yan replied. "I would wager it is the car I saw outside the hotel. But how could they have stopped the electricity?"

Colin stood shakily. "They were good, no doubt about it. Bloody hell, Yan. I thought you'd be better than that in a fight."

Yan gave him an angry glance, then hung his head. "I am ashamed at how easily we were defeated."

Colin grunted. "I wouldn't call that easy. But I'm embarrassed, too. Your arm okay?"

"It will be fine."

Talasi sniffed the air. "They used some kind of anesthesia on us. Short acting, inhaled." She drew in a breath through her nose. "From the smell, I'd say it's desflurane. In hospitals if we use it, though, it has to be vaporized. How did they manage to administer it?"

Colin waved off her speculation. "More importantly, who were they?"

"We knew there would be people who would not want the baby to be born," Yan said.

"I've heard speculation that even our government is experimenting with how to atomize substances to knock you out. Supposedly the Russians used …"

"Focus, Talasi." Colin wondered if she wasn't still under the influence of the anesthetic. "We need to figure out how to get Rebekah back."

Yan held out a piece of paper. “Trace the license plate number.”

“Right. I’d forgotten you had it. We need to get out of here. The power outage already has attracted too much attention. Grab what you can quickly. Don’t leave anything behind that could identify us. We’ll trace the plate once we’re in the car.”

Chapter Thirty-Five

Cancun, Mexico
La Galeria del Sol
December 20, 2012
3:45 a.m. local time

Time to Solstice: 26 hours, 26 minutes

Rebekah wandered through Raz's dim gallery squinting at various displays. Raz said he stuck to nighttime lighting because he said he didn't want anyone to know they were there. He had Mayan artifacts from all over Central America. She was amazed at the quality of his pieces. She assumed they were authentic—they certainly looked it—and therefore expensive. Only a few had price tags. She strained to see his asking price on a primitive necklace. Several thousand dollars, she thought. Rebekah wondered who could afford it, and even more, why it wasn't in a museum.

"You have an impressive collection," she said.

"Thank you."

"Where's Jonas? You said Jonas would be here."

"I said he was going to be here. And he will. What you and Jonas have to understand is that Manuel is not your friend."

"What do you mean?"

"Manuel belongs to a rebel Mayan cult, the Cruzol. They're entirely focused on the birth of a mythical King they believe will take place at the winter solstice."

Rebekah was relieved to hear Raz belittle the idea, but still it made her wary. She wondered how much she should reveal. "I'm aware that there are some Maya out there who believe that. I know Manuel has spoken with them. He may be a little crazy, but he hardly seems like a cultist."

"Did you expect him to announce it? His cult believes you are carrying the baby to become King."

So, he knows about that too, she thought. She was beginning to believe Raz might be an ally. "My baby won't be born here. I'm only at eight months, and Jonas and I are getting back to the USA as soon as we can."

"That's going to be more difficult than you think. But we'll talk about that when Jonas gets here." Raz checked his Rolex. "It's time we head into the attic."

"Why?" The idea of leaving the gallery and heading into a private place with Raz made Rebekah nervous. Though she was alone with him either way, somehow the size of the space and the fact that the gallery was public made it feel safer, even with the closed sign on the door.

"You're going to have to trust me. Manuel and Jonas are going to break into the gallery shortly. We will rescue Jonas from him and then you will both be safe."

"Jonas would never break in anywhere. Why do you think he would do that?"

For the first time since Raz had rescued her, his manner scared Rebekah. He moved so close to her she could sense the danger that lay right below his controlled exterior. She could also see what color his eyes were now, black. But this was a blackness that reminded her of the absence of light. "If you want to be together with Jonas again, you need to do what I say, and now."

The words squeaked out of her mouth. "Okay."

He put his arm around her and guided her toward a paneled wall. He pushed on a spot about two-thirds of the way down on left side. When he did it, the adjacent panel came loose. There was a slight click. If the gallery hadn't been so quiet and her so focused on what he was doing, it might have gone unnoticed.

Raz pushed on the adjacent panel and it pivoted in the middle, revealing a spiral staircase behind. "Go up ahead of me," he said. It was not a request.

Rebekah gulped but followed his instructions. When she was halfway up the staircase, she heard the panel close behind her. The passageway went momentarily dark, then a few soft, dim lights appeared, guiding her into the attic.

* * *

Cancun, Mexico
Outside La Galeria del Sol

Jonas huddled with Manuel in the shadows of a free-standing store across the street from La Galeria del Sol. He was glad he still wore the jacket of his tux since the temperature had dropped several degrees in the early morning hours. He shivered. Or was it what he was about to do that had him shivering? He thought about the jacket again. Except for the climber's pack, he was dressed rather formally for a robbery. Of course, he had never been an accomplice in a robbery before, but based on what Manuel and Diega were wearing, he was fairly sure formal wear was not de rigueur. At least the backpack was black.

What the hell was he doing here?

Though they were on the edge of a commercial district, the security lighting was not as good as in the States. There were plenty of shadows in which to hide. La Galeria was in a small house that had been incorporated into the district, much like the clothing store they were using for cover. They waited for Diega to return. She had left them while she scoped out the gallery, looking for signs of security measures she hadn't been able to detect through her data base searches. She was also looking for the owner's car. Because the store had once been a house, Diega said there was always the possibility he'd left a bedroom intact and might stay there from time to time.

"There's no sign of his car," Diega said quietly. Her voice made Jonas start. She'd come up behind him and he hadn't detected her. Manuel seemed undisturbed. Jonas wondered how many times Manuel and Diega had done this before. They seemed almost professional. They were dressed head to toe in close-fitting black clothes and spoke in confident, hushed tones. With their dark Mayan faces, they were nearly invisible in the night.

"Good. What about the security?" Manuel asked.

"The building has motion detector lights as I suspected. Those I cannot turn off until we are inside the building. We must hope no one sees us."

Jonas didn't like the idea that once they started across the property, they would be lit up. He was still trying to cope with the concept of what would happen if they got caught. "I can't believe I'm doing this."

Manuel patted him on the back. "If you wish to get Rebekah back, this is the only way. Besides," he added, smiling, "the police want to question you. Why not give them a good reason?"

"That's not funny, Manuel. I didn't sabotage the hotel."

Manuel started to respond, but Diega was all business. "The back door has three security locks, plus a keypad. Once we get past those, I'll have fifteen seconds to deactivate an alarm."

Jonas was incredulous. "Fifteen seconds! You can do all that?"

"Diega has acquired certain abilities over the years," Manuel said.

"It is time," Diega said. "*Vámanos*."

Much to Jonas' surprise, he found himself doing the unthinkable. The three of them raced across the street and onto the property. Their motion set the sensor lights on, but other than finding themselves spotlighted, nothing else happened. They rounded the gallery and headed to the rear door. Manuel and Jonas flattened against the back wall. Jonas watched Diega. She examined the three keyed locks, then pulled out a tubular device like the end of a small flashlight. It came with several different lock picks. She selected one and slipped it into the end of the tube, locking it in place. Then she inserted the pick into the lock and switched the device on. Within seconds it unlocked the first lock. Diega replaced the pick with a different one, unlocked the second, and then the third.

"Now comes the dicey part," Manuel whispered. "We shall see how good our Mayan brothers were in bypassing the security function of this brand of lock."

Diega put the electric lock pick in her bag and pulled out a small computer. She attached a sensor device to a USB port and placed the sensor directly over the keypad so that it covered the pad. She pulled up a program on the screen, then pushed the 'enter' button. Numbers flashed across the screen so quickly they were virtually a blur. The keypad beeped and Diega opened the door. Manuel and Jonas followed her in. She scouted the inside walls. Jonas found himself holding his breath and silently counting to fifteen. He was up to six when she found the device and fourteen when the computer sensor deactivated it.

Manuel passed out flashlights. "Now we find the mask," he said, quiet, matter-of-factly. "It will not be on display. Watch for hidden compartments, a false wall, someplace to keep valuables."

"One other thing," Diega added. "Records we obtained from a supply store indicate Raz brought in a large amount of building materials shortly after purchasing the house. I believe he may have built a secure storage area in the attic. We need to find a way up there, too."

* * *

Up in the attic, Rebekah was mesmerized by the events unfolding on Raz's closed circuit television. She and Raz were seated at a desk from which he could control the security measures he'd put in place. He'd explained some of them to Rebekah when they'd arrived in the attic. At first she was more interested in the rare antiquities he had stored in the small, climate-controlled storage facility he'd built up there. But once he began monitoring the outside activities, she'd stood behind him to watch. He'd switched from camera to camera to capture the invaders' run across the lawn, Diega's swift dismantling of the security system, and now their search of the gallery. She wouldn't have believed Jonas was involved, but he was on the video. Did he know she was here? Was he trying to rescue her? Did he really trust Manuel?

She wasn't sure whom she trusted.

"There," Raz said. "It's all on record. This should keep them in jail until long after the solstice."

"Not Jonas!"

"No, not Jonas. We're going to rescue him, but I need for him to get into place first."

Raz monitored Jonas' progress around the room. Unlike Manuel, who searched the lower areas of counters and cases searching for hidden storage areas, Jonas felt along the walls. He approached the panel with the staircase behind it.

"Come with me," Raz told Rebekah. "Jonas won't behave unless he sees you."

She hesitated.

Raz gritted his teeth. "Listen. You can stay here and be a party to Manuel and Diega breaking into my gallery, or you and Jonas can come with me to Palenque and find the Book of the Thirteen Gods. Let's see. Stay here and get thrown in a Mexican jail, or fly safely to Palenque. Your choice."

Rebekah knew she had no choice. And she desperately wanted Jonas with her.

The two of them descended the staircase. Raz had the closed circuit transmission on his cell phone, fixed on Jonas's location.

At the bottom of the stairs, Raz stood with one hand on the panel. "Just a little closer."

Jonas felt his way down the edge of the panel that contained the switch. Just as his hand passed over it, Raz triggered the mechanism. Jonas stopped. He shined the light on the panel, but couldn't tell that it had adjusted slightly to allow the next panel to move.

Raz stepped over to the panel and motioned to Rebekah to come close to him.

"When I open this, grab Jonas and pull him in," he whispered.

Rebekah nodded. Raz pointed to where she should stand. He pushed on the panel and it swiveled open. Jonas shined the flashlight toward it, illuminating Rebekah. Relief and surprise flooded over him. He reached for her, but she motioned for him to stay quiet. Raz grabbed him and pulled him through the opening.

"What the …?"

Raz hurried to close the panel. Noises erupted from the gallery as Manuel and Diega ran toward where they'd heard Jonas.

"Jonas, shhh." Rebekah hugged him. "We can't stay here. It's not safe for you. Come with us."

"How did you get here? What about Manuel and Diega?"

"I hate to break this up, but we need to get going," Raz said.

"Who are you?"

"My name is Raz. I'm here to help you."

"Yeah. That's what everyone says."

"I'm an agent with Mossad. And I rescued Rebekah."

Rebekah put her finger to Jonas' lips. "He did rescue me. And you."

Raz took the flashlight from Jonas. He shined it on a door just beyond the staircase. A metal case about a foot and a half square leaned against the door jam. “Follow me,” he said. He grabbed the case and opened the door to the outside of the building. Rebekah could see where they’d hidden the car, about a hundred feet from the door.

“Where are we going?” she asked.

“To the car. The police should be here in about ten minutes. We need to be long gone by then.”

“Gone where?” Jonas asked.

“Palenque. We’re going to recover the Book of the Thirteen Gods.”

“I’m not …”

“Please don’t contradict me,” said Raz. “You don’t have much of a choice.”

Rebekah hugged Jonas. “I thought I’d never see you again.”

“A touching sentiment,” Raz said. “Now hurry.”

They ran to the car.

Chapter Thirty-Six

Cancun, Mexico
Colin's Rental Dorango
December 20, 2012
4:17 a.m. local time

Time to Solstice: 25 hours, 55 minutes

Colin hoped his international contacts would have arms long enough to embrace the Cancun police. He'd made contact with his superiors back in England as soon as they'd left the Hotel de las Ruinas and called in every favor he could. He'd given them the license plate number Yan had copied down. That had been over an hour ago. How long could a simple trace take? And yet he knew it was not simple to elicit international cooperation. Not only that, he was counting on his network of friends to drop everything and make the contacts. Did they really understand his rush to get the information, especially when he had to be so vague about the reason why? He intimated a kidnapping, but he didn't want to be too explicit lest the Cancun police get involved. Although, with the emergency rescues still going on at the Hotel Kukulcan, he didn't see how they could have the time.

Yan continued to drive around Cancun. They were looking for a Wal-Mart where they could get a GPS unit. Talasi, who knew Spanish, had asked the barista for directions when they stopped at an all-night Starbucks. It had been her idea to get some coffee, which she claimed she would need if she was going to stay awake for the duration. Colin hadn't cared, as long as they got the directions. As a staunch Brit, he wasn't a huge fan of coffee.

The stop had made Talasi happy, though, and that was a plus. She seemed satisfied to sip her venti latte and hum some kind of melody that Colin didn't recognize. Every once in a while she chanted a few words he assumed were Hopi. He wasn't used to this kind of behavior, but since he'd made the instant decision to come to Mexico, everything familiar felt as far away as the motorway he took to Heathrow. Would he ever see it again? He sipped his Tazo tea.

"There's the Wal-Mart," Talasi said. "And it looks like it's open."

Yan made a quick left into the car park. At this time of night they were able to get a spot close to the door. Colin gave Talasi money from his stash and she went in.

Colin's cell phone rang. He checked the incoming number. It was restricted. "Yes?"

The voice didn't identify herself. She spoke quickly. "The car is registered to Raz Uris. He's a permanent resident but not a citizen. He lists his nationality as Israeli. We have information, not yet verified, that he is a retired Mossad agent. The only listing we could trace for him in Cancun is an antiquities shop for which he is listed as the owner, La Galeria del Sol." She gave him the address and he wrote it down.

He read it back to her. She verified it and ended the call.

Talasi opened the back door carrying a plastic Wal-Mart sack.

"Get in," Colin told her. "We just got the address."

"Great." She handed him the sack as she snapped her seatbelt in place.

Colin cut open the hard-plastic container with his switchblade and pulled out the GPS unit. It took a few minutes to boot up and get going. He typed in the Wal-Mart address from the receipt and then the address his contact had given him.

"I hope it's not far from here," Talasi said.

"Estimated time to destination, ten minutes," the GPS unit announced. It told Yan to leave the car park and turn right.

"The license plate is registered to Raz Uris," Colin said. "He's an artifacts dealer, and might be a former Mossad agent."

Talasi leaned forward. "That's odd. Why would someone like that want Rebekah?"

"Maybe the same reason we had her. We're headed to his gallery."

Talasi verbalized the doubts Colin himself had. "His gallery? We don't know he's taken her there."

"It's the only lead we have. If you've a better idea, I'd bloody well like to hear it."

* * *

Diega repeatedly tapped the wall where Jonas had disappeared. A slight echo came from behind the panel.

"Hollow," Diega said. "There must be a trigger somewhere. Look for it." Manuel could hear the constrained panic in her voice. He felt the same way.

The two of them ran their hands up and down the panel.

Alarms sounded. The noise hurt Manuel's ears. "This is not good," he shouted over the cacophony.

"We should go out the way we came in."

They rushed to the back door to the shop and tried the handle. Locked. Diega examined the keypad, punching in the code she'd used to get in. No success.

"Can you get us out?" Manuel yelled to Diega.

"If we have enough time." Diega quickly retrieved her equipment and began to work on the keypad. "One of us must find a way out quickly."

"I'll go back and check the wall. Maybe I can find the way to open the panel." But he had difficulty concentrating over the noise of the alarm.

"What about Jonas?" Diega asked.

"He is likely a prisoner now."

"But to what is Raz connected?"

"*No sé.*"

Manuel said a silent prayer to the ancients for help. *If this is to be, if Diega and I are to be the ones to help bring this prophecy to fruition, you must aid us. We need a way out.* His hand was two-thirds of the way down the left side of the panel. He felt an uncontrollable urge to press against the wall.

And something moved. It was a small shift, but Manuel detected it. He used the flashlight to check the sides of the panel. His side had detached itself from the next panel.

"Diega, I have found something."

She dropped what she was doing and rushed to Manuel's side. Systematically they began to push on every inch of the panel.

* * *

Raz opened the trunk of the sedan and carefully laid in it the case containing Pakal's mask. Rebekah climbed in the back seat where she'd previously sat. Jonas hesitated, his hand on the open door.

"Get in," Raz said. He made it clear this was not a request.

"It's going to take forever to drive to Palenque," Jonas said. "Rebekah can't ride that long in a car."

Raz spoke through gritted teeth. "We're headed for an airstrip. I have a plane waiting to take us there, and my associate Gilberto is waiting for us at Palenque. The time will go quickly. Now get in."

"Why would Mossad want to help us?"

"I don't have time for this, Jonas. It's all about the book. The one you're going to help me find."

"What if we won't go with you?"

"You're wanted by the police. If you'd like, I could just leave you here and hope they don't throw you and Rebekah in jail."

Jonas threw his pack in the car and slid in next to Rebekah. Before he could reach over to close the door, Raz slammed it shut.

"You're wanted by the police?" Rebekah asked.

Raz climbed in the driver's seat and started the car. "Good question, Rebekah. Jonas, why don't you explain that while I get us to the airfield?"

He put the car in gear and sped off.

* * *

Yan pulled up to the car park of La Galeria del Sol. The headlights shone on a familiar sedan racing away on a side road. He pointed at the retreating vehicle. "That is the car from the hotel."

"Then we'll follow it," Colin said. "Go quickly. I think you can catch him."

Yan's sudden acceleration caught Talasi off-guard. She juggled her coffee cup. "What's that noise?" she asked. "It sounds like an alarm."

"It is an alarm. Someone must've set it off in the gallery."

"All the more reason for us to hurry away," Yan said.

"It couldn't have been going off too long," Talasi said. "There are no police cars here."

Colin glanced back at the gallery. "The police must still busy at the Kukulcan."

Talasi pointed. "Someone's coming out."

Yan momentarily slowed the car. "Could they be Rebekah and Jonas? Should we go back?"

Colin thought a moment. "No, we don't know who's in the car ahead of us but it's unlikely anyone would have left the two of them back at the gallery. Not if they have an inkling of what is going on."

"Even if one of them is Rebekah, we wouldn't want to be there with her when the police arrived," Talasi added. "She doesn't trust us yet. She'd have us arrested."

"Drive on," Colin told Yan.

Yan pushed on the accelerator and resumed the chase.

* * *

Once they'd managed to figure out the pivoting door that allowed them to get into the hidden room behind the wall, Manuel and Diega found the side door and dashed out of Raz's gallery. They saw a car speeding away.

Diega was breathing hard. "We'll never catch them." She bent over at the waist trying to catch her breath. "Should we check the attic?"

"The mask won't be there." He took Diega by the arm. "Come, we must get to the car."

"Where are we going?"

"Valladolid. Raz may be able to fly out of Cancun, but we can't. Not in a hurry."

Diega pulled away from him as though she were headed back to the gallery. "What about our gear? We can't just leave it there!"

"Then we will have to rush." They hustled back to the gallery. The alarms were still shrieking but no police were in sight. Diega struggled with her equipment. Manuel took the bulk of it. "Please, Diega, we must get to the car."

"Are you certain he is taking them to Palenque?"

"Raz has Rebekah, Jonas, and the mask. Where else would they go? And he has the money to fly them there."

"But if we drive to Valladolid first, we will be an hour behind them."

"They may not be able to get access to the ruins this early in the morning."

The two of them began to move faster, Manuel urging Diega along. When they reached the car, Manuel popped the trunk and they put Diega's equipment in it. "I'll drive," he said.

"Manuel, if we know people who can get us into Palenque before it opens, we have to assume he does, too."

"Get hold of Gilberto. Tell him to get over there and watch for them."

Diega got out her cell phone and dialed the number. Manuel headed back into Cancun to catch the highway to Valladolid.

"One more thing," Manuel said. "Tell him not to stop them until after they have the book. With any luck we'll get there before then."

Chapter Thirty-Seven

Cancun, Mexico
A small, private airstrip
December 20, 2012
4:30 a.m. local time

Time to Solstice: 25 hours, 41 minutes

As Raz pulled the car onto the apron of the airfield, he could see the pilot waiting beside the Cessna Turbo Skylane. A single prop airplane, it was powered by a turbocharged, fuel injected Lycoming engine. It wasn't Raz's aircraft, but belonged to Luis Rodriquez, a man who had proven to be invaluable in flying certain contraband artifacts in and out of countries with Mayan ruins. Because the two men had dirt on each other, Raz trusted Luis as much as he trusted anyone.

Raz stopped the car about a half kilometer from the aircraft, well off the field so the car wouldn't interfere with traffic. He sat for a moment to see if the car which had been following them at a distance would go past the airfield. He didn't detect movement but that didn't mean the driver hadn't turned off the headlights. It was still dark. Depending how far away the car was, he wasn't sure he would be able to see it. Part of him worried it contained the trio of internationals who had initially taken Rebekah. How could they have tracked him so quickly? If it indeed was them, he had underestimated their abilities.

"What are we waiting for?" Jonas asked.

Raz was beginning to find Jonas really annoying. Despite what everyone else thought, Raz knew Jonas was dispensable. He didn't need Jonas to find the book. But he did need Rebekah's cooperation, and for now, that meant keeping Jonas around.

"I need to talk to the pilot. Wait here."

Raz got out of the car and opened the trunk. He removed the case with Pakal's mask and jogged the distance between him and the aircraft. His friend Luis put out his hand as Raz greeted him. Raz wondered what Rebekah and Jonas would think of Luis. The man looked like a deposed Central American dictator, with a thick graying mustache and short, salt-and-pepper hair. His face was large and round, matching his frame.

"*Señor*, it is good to see you again. What are we carrying today?"

"People, this time, my friend. And the mask of Pakal. We are headed to Palenque. Will you file the necessary flight plan? I do not wish to attract attention."

"Of course. Where is our cargo?"

"Back at the car. I left them there until I could talk to you. We may have someone tracking us. If so, they are back at the entrance to the airfield. Do you have someone available to watch them discreetly? I don't want them dead, necessarily. I'd like to know who they are first."

"But of course. Let me contact my son Ricardo."

* * *

Jonas waited only until Raz was out of earshot before he began questioning Rebekah. "How does Raz know about using the mask to find the book? You didn't even know about it. That was something Manuel and Diega had figured out from the photos we took outside the Pyramid."

"He just seemed to know."

"And the three people who had you, they didn't know about the book either?"

"No. They found your flashdrive in our room and downloaded the photos, but they weren't making any progress on the translation."

"What about our computer?"

"It was gone when I got back to the room."

"Then Raz had to be the one to ransack our room. Manuel and Diega didn't know where the book was hidden until they had our photos. Raz must have taken the computer."

Rebekah stared out the window at the figures of Raz and the pilot, silhouetted against the airplane. "I've already figured out we can't trust him, but what do we do? I'm not sure we can trust anybody."

Jonas climbed into the front. "We need to open these doors without the lights coming on. That would attract Raz's attention.

I'll try disconnecting the fuses on the car. Then we can get out and make a run for the road back to town. Out there we can find a place to hide."

"Do you even know where the fuses are on this car?"

"Probably the glove box. Or under the dash."

Jonas opened the compartment. In the darkness, it lit up the inside of the car.

"Shit."

* * *

Colin was glad to see Raz walk toward the aircraft alone. "Talasi, look. He left Rebekah and Jonas in the car." The two of them had been sitting in the Durango by the entrance to the airstrip watching the proceedings, while Yan had slipped out and was moving toward Rebekah and Jonas.

"Should we go in?" she asked.

He nodded. "I wonder how far Yan has made it."

"I'm hoping he's almost there. Even with the headlights off, Raz is bound to detect us before we get there."

Colin put the car in gear and eased onto the road leading to the apron of the airstrip. They hadn't gone far when a light appeared inside Raz's car. It illuminated Jonas hunched over in the front seat, Rebekah sitting up in the back seat, and Yan standing near Rebekah's door.

"Crimey! Now Raz'll see everything." Colin pushed on the accelerator and the car lurched forward towards the apron.

* * *

The light took Yan by surprise. He was poised to tap on Rebekah's window and motion for her and Jonas to come with him. Now his presence was revealed to everyone. He opened Rebekah's door and grabbed at her arm. "Come, we must hurry. And your husband, too."

Rebekah did what he did not expect. She screamed, "It's them!" and tried to hit him in the face.

"But we are here to save you!" Yan deflected her fist and spun her around so her back was to him. With a back bear hug, he hauled her out of the car.

"Let go of my wife!" Jonas opened the passenger door. Yan saw him coming around the front of the car. Before he could get close enough to strike, Yan maneuvered Rebekah between the two of them. "We are here to help," he said.

Colin pulled the car up at that moment. The headlights shone on Raz running across the field, waving a handgun.

Colin and Talasi got out of the car to help Yan. "Trouble coming," Yan said.

Jonas crossed the distance to Colin and surprised him with a side kick to the stomach. Colin backed away.

Yan let Rebekah go and stepped toward Jonas, trying to help Colin subdue him. I cannot hurt Jonas, Yan thought. Jonas spun toward Yan and aimed a front kick at Yan's crotch. Yan shifted left, blocked it, and came in at Jonas. His goal was to shock Jonas with flurry of short punches to the midsection, but Jonas came back at him with a double palm heel toward his face. He's had training, Yan thought. That will make it harder not to hurt him. Yan dodged left again and struck Jonas with an elbow in the side as Jonas went past. Jonas groaned.

The blow threw Jonas near Rebekah. He looked up in time to grab onto her and use her weight to stop his momentum. "Get back in the car," Jonas said.

Rebekah lunged for the open door and got inside. She shut the door and hit the lock button just as Talasi reached for the door handle.

Talasi glared through the window. "We're trying to save you!"

Yan heard the sounds of two shots. One of the bullets felt like it grazed his arm. He looked for Jonas and saw him ducking behind Raz's car. Yan dove for shelter behind the Durango. He felt a second jolt to his shoulder. Pain like he had never experienced before pulsed out of his right shoulder muscle.

Colin hunkered next to him.

"I'm hit," Yan said. "Right shoulder."

Talasi started the Durango. She pulled it up, blocking Raz from getting another shot at them. "Get Yan into the vehicle."

Colin clutched Yan around the chest and hauled him into the back seat. Talasi sped off while Colin was still trying to shut the door behind him. He closed it and flattened himself against the floor just as a bullet pinged off the side.

* * *

"I think I got the short one, but I'm not going to follow them to find out." Raz located Jonas under his car. "Are you all right?"

"I think so. A little roughed up." Jonas rolled out from beneath the vehicle and stood. He brushed himself off.

"You know how to fight."

Jonas opened the car door to check on Rebekah. "I had hand-to-hand combat training in the Guard."

"Good thing." Raz tucked the Glock into the small of his back where he kept it hidden. He found his cell phone in the front pocket of his pants and used speed dial to get back in touch with the hired help.

When Pablo answered, Raz started talking immediately. "We've had some trouble. The same ones from the hotel. I never thought we'd see them again. A man named Ricardo will be in touch with you. He's the pilot's son. I'll have him follow them. Then, I need you to make sure we don't ever see them again." Raz closed the phone and headed toward the plane.

"Let's get out of here," he told Jonas. "Hurry."

"Rebekah's pregnant. We'll get there." Jonas was beginning to wonder if they shouldn't have thrown their lot in with the internationals. Under his breath, he asked Rebekah, "You're okay?"

"We have to get away from him. From everyone."

"I know. But we don't have a choice right now."

"You learned to fly in the Guard. We could ..."

"Overpower Raz and the pilot and get shot down trying to fly over the border? I don't think that's our way out. Not yet. Not with the police looking for me."

"What do we do?"

"For now we have to make Raz believe we trust him. Then we get the book. It's the only bargaining chip we have."

"I don't want our baby to be born here."

Raz beckoned them again. “Rebekah, Jonas!”

Jonas ignored Raz. “Play along,” he told Rebekah under his breath. “We have to get that damn book. It’s the one thing everyone seems to want.”

Rebekah seemed to speed up a little. When they boarded the four-seater, Jonas and Rebekah sat in the back, Raz next to the pilot. Jonas hadn’t flown a prop plane in nearly a decade. He watched the pilot carefully as he went through the sequence to start the aircraft. Just in case I get the opportunity to do it. Rebekah’s suggestion was beginning to form into an idea.

Then they taxied down the unpaved airstrip and flew off.

Jonas watched the ground fall away from them. Next stop, Palenque, he thought. A place, with any luck, where all this madness will come to an end.

Chapter Thirty-Eight

Zagros Mountains, Iraq
December 20, 2012
12:31 p.m. local time

Time to Solstice: 25 hours, 40 minutes

Vhorrdak pulled his cloak tightly around him and lowered the hood over his face, protecting it from the wind. At least the sun was shining. That was perhaps the only positive thing he could say about being in the mountains today. This time of year it was cold, and if the sun was shining it was bitter; if it was snowing or raining, it was raw.

He stood well off to the side of the narrow, hard-packed dirt road that wound around the mountain pass. Hidden within a clump of shrubs that barely came up to his shoulder, he was only mildly protected from the wind. Most importantly he had not been seen by the third decoy truck which had just gone by. He had been amused by how terrified the drivers had looked, going around the mountainside at the highest speed they dared. He wondered if they had experienced a slip or two, and it had them rattled. However, he reminded himself not to be smug. After all, he needed them to successfully keep the Americans occupied.

With just a little over twenty-four hours before he moved the nuclear weapon onto an Iranian ship, he could not be more confident. The third truck had made excellent progress. In contrast to the first two trucks, which had been instructed to go at slower speeds, this truck had hurried onto better roads under cover of the sandstorm. It had gone through Al Fallujah and then up to Balad before the Americans had figured out to look beyond the distance they had been covering. By the time the Americans had found the second decoy, this truck was already into the Zagros Mountains.

The Americans were looking in the mountains, but likely not too much. Vhorrdak had primed his contact to hold back on a full-scale search in the event someone suggested it as a possible route. He would soon turn them loose.

But not quite yet. He would wait for another couple of hours. That way, when the Americans began searching in earnest, they would only have an hour or so before dusk. About the time they figured out where the third truck was located, it would go into hiding. He would leave them there until he needed them to cover his move in Syria. Then he would call them out. Or rather, Fareed would call them out. He wanted as few connections to himself as possible.

Half a world away, the other part of his plan for Armageddon was unfolding—the locating of the book describing the final days, making his blueprint complete; and, of course, the birth and death of his enemy, the king. Vhorrdak considered how unfortunate it was that he was not omnipotent and thus unable to occupy more than one place at one time. Though he had discovered ways to move between space and time, he was still limited in what he could do. For that reason, the other piece of business had to be entrusted to an underling. A bright, tough, driven underling, but a human underling nonetheless. All of which reminded him he needed to check in with Raz.

Chapter Thirty-Nine

Cancun, Mexico
A small, private airstrip
December 20, 2012
4:41 a.m. local time

Time to Solstice: 25 hours, 30 minutes

Talasi sped away from the airstrip. They were lucky to have gotten away without all of them being hurt, but her concern was for Yan. Colin was in the back seat trying to stop the bleeding. She'd given him a few instructions, but both of them knew they needed to trade places.

"How he's doing?" Talasi asked.

"Still bleeding. I've gotten it to slow but you need to evaluate it."

Yan groaned.

"I think we're far enough away, Talasi. You don't see anyone behind us, do you?"

"There aren't any headlights."

"Pull over."

Talasi popped the trunk open with a latch up front. She retrieved her medical bag before closing it and climbing into the back seat. She felt Colin put the car in gear and pull back out on the highway.

Yan's shoulder was bloody but not as bad as Talasi had been expecting. Colin had removed his shirt and used it to absorb the blood. Talasi dropped the red, sticky shirt to the floor. She glanced around for something else to use and found nothing. She pulled off her own top, stripping down to an athletic bra. Somewhere in her travel bag was another shirt she'd locate later.

The overhead light in the car was on, but it wasn't good enough. "I need more light, Colin. Where's the flashlight?"

"Hooked to my belt. Just a minute." Talasi felt the car veer. Colin passed back the flashlight. "Here."

Talasi used the light to examine the shoulder. She wanted to probe the wound, but first she needed to numb it. She opened her medical bag, pulled out a syringe, and filled it from a bottle of bupivacaine.

"Yan, I'm going to numb your shoulder so I can explore it." She prepped the area with an alcohol swab.

Yan clenched his teeth as the needle penetrated his skin. Talasi released the fluid into the muscle, removed the needle, and wiped the area again. "I'm sorry, but I can't wait for this to fully take effect, so it's going to hurt."

Talasi admired Yan's grit. He groaned but only cried out once during her evaluation. Finally she was able to say, "I'm done now. You can relax."

"How is he?" Colin asked.

"He'll make it, but we need to find someplace I can operate on him to remove the bullet."

"Will a hotel room do? We can't afford to attract attention."

"We're headed back into Cancun, aren't we? Stop at the first hotel you can find." And I hope it's cleaner than the last one.

Chapter Forty

Mexican airspace
Between Cancun and Palenque
December 20, 2012
4:58 a.m. local time

Time to Solstice: 25 hours, 13 minutes

Raz had never received a phone call from Vhorrdak in the air before. He was wearing his headset so he could communicate with the pilot, and he wasn't clear what to do. The satellite phone had vibrated, but he wasn't sure how to pick up the call through the headset, and he wasn't sure he should even if he could. No one else needed to hear this conversation.

Because he knew it would be bad not to answer the phone, Raz decided to pull off the headset and try it anyway, despite the noise of the aircraft. Vhorrdak always sounded like he was in his ear, anyway.

"Where are you?" Vhorrdak asked.

Damn, it's so clear, Raz thought. I wonder if he can hear me as well as I can hear him?

"Headed for Palenque."

"Pursuing the book?"

"Yes."

"Are there others with you?"

"Yes."

Vhorrdak paused. "But they cannot hear you."

Raz looked at the pilot, Jonas, and Rebekah. They eyed him curiously, but he didn't think they could hear him. Plus, they all had their headphones on. He leaned toward the door, hiding his mouth in case they could read lips. "It's unlikely."

"Have you had any complications?"

"Yes."

"Tell me."

Raz related the story of the three internationals, how he'd taken Rebekah from them, and used her to get Jonas away from Manuel.

"Why do they want her?"

"They claimed to be protecting her."

"You think you wounded one of them?"

"The young Chinese guy. I've sent men after them to eliminate them."

Vhorrdak's voice became so animated Raz was afraid it might blow a hole through his eardrum. "No! In no way are you to harm them. I want you to leave them to me. Call off your men. Now."

"Consider it done."

With no warning, Vhorrdak disconnected. In many ways, Raz was relieved to have him off the phone. But now he needed to call Pablo. The satellite phone might have worked with Vhorrdak's odd powers, but it wouldn't work for this.

Raz put his headset back on. "Get me a phone link," he told the pilot, "and put me on the channel alone. I need to make a call immediately."

Chapter Forty-One

Cancun, Mexico
Hotel de Los Reyes
December 20, 2012
5:03 a.m. local time

Time to Solstice: 25 hours, 08 minutes

Hotel of the Kings, Talasi thought as she spread extra sheets and towels over the bed. Let's hope it's a good sign.

Talasi felt she needed good signs and portents. This would be a most difficult operation. Not because she hadn't seen wounds worse than Yan's—she'd seen plenty worse—but because she hadn't specialized in surgery, really didn't have the right tools, and wasn't working in a sterile environment. She had brought along some antibiotics, fortunately. With any luck, Yan would be able to tell her whether he was allergic to either of the two she had. If not, she'd go with her gut feeling.

"Let's get him up on the bed," she told Colin. Colin had kept the bleeding to a minimum as she'd assigned him. He lifted Yan, careful to avoid putting any pressure on the right shoulder. She'd given Yan a general anesthetic to knock him out for the operation.

She handed one end of another sheet to Colin. She wondered what the maids would think when they found so much blood on them after they left.

"We're going to drape it across like this," she said, demonstrating with her hand. Colin leaned over the opposite side of the bed and tucked the sheet under Yan's body. She used iodine to sterilize the shoulder area to prepare it, then looked at Colin. "I need you over here. You're going to assist."

Colin came around the bed and stood by her, stoically. "I've never done this before," he said.

"And I've never done it under these conditions. But the bullet isn't deep. The damage isn't that bad. We'll both do fine."

"Whatever you need, tell me."

Talasi nodded.

"We've only got about twenty four hours. He'll recover in time, won't he?"

She laughed nervously. "Even if we can find Rebekah again, I'm not sure Yan is capable of being there to see the birth."

"He has to be. We're the witnesses."

"We don't have a manual for this, Colin. Maybe it will have to be just the two of us." She took a deep breath and began the operation.

Colin muttered to himself, but Talasi heard him anyway. He said, "The last time, there were three."

And she knew that was what had been recorded in history.

Chapter Forty-Two

Valladolid, Mexico
Aeropuerto de Valladolid
December 20, 2012
5:25 a.m. local time

Time to Solstice: 24 hours, 46 minutes

Manuel had checked his watch repeatedly on the drive from Cancun to Valladolid. Now, as he pulled into a small airport that served Valladolid, his estimate was confirmed: they would be an hour behind Raz Uris and the Sagievs headed to Palenque. The only good part of it was that Gilberto was a trustworthy man. He'd agreed to keep an eye out for the group arriving at Palenque ahead of its opening, and to delay them or stop them from leaving once they had obtained the Book of the Thirteen Gods. Manuel had assigned Gilberto a dangerous task, but then Gilberto was himself a dangerous man. Manuel prayed it would work out in favor of their cause.

The helicopter was waiting for them, exactly as their friend had guaranteed them. Bartolome, the owner, stood next to a Bell Jet Ranger, painted in the red, green and white of the Mexican flag. He held the door open as he waited for them.

"Bartolome!" Manuel said as he pulled the car to a stop and jumped out of it. "My friend, it is good to see you, but you did not have to wait for us." The two men shook hands.

"I was not sure you would be up to flying. The drive from Cancun has been a long one and it is early in the morning. Have you even had time to sleep?"

Manuel was touched by his words. At seventy-six years old, Bartolome, a Mayan elder, was still capable of flying, but the speed with which they would have to work and the danger inherent in recovering the book was enormous. Manuel smiled and clasped both of his hands around Bartolome's. He looked into the sallow face, once full, and saw the frailty within. "You offer too much, my friend, but thank you. My sister Diega has slept, and you know she is capable of flying. You trained her."

Diega had exited the car, but in respect for Mayan tradition, waited for Manuel to greet Bartolome first. Now, Manuel's beckoning brought her over.

Bartolome beamed. "Yes, I know how capable she is. In fact, she is a better aviator than you, Manuel!" He hugged Diega.

She kissed him on the cheek. "Forgive me, Bartolome, but we must hurry."

"Of course you must. A king is to be born and you have little time. Are you going to retrieve the mother?"

Manuel nodded. "Yes, and more, we hope. The Book of the Thirteen Gods."

"So it exists."

"It does, but many forces are at work to seize either her or the book. And now that we know the book exists, we must have them both."

"I sense danger for you, Manuel," Bartolome's words sounded grave.

Diega looked at the elder. She knew his sight often went beyond this world. "I will watch out for him, *señor*."

He turned to her. "You will be placed in danger as well, my dear. But I sense a different destiny for you. Remember that legend says the king is only vulnerable from the moment of birth. That will be when the adversary will strike. Now both of you must be off. The helicopter is fueled and ready."

Manuel shook Bartolome's hand again, Diega gave him one more kiss on the cheek, and the two of them boarded the helicopter. Manuel heard the familiar whine of the turbine as Diega started the engine and the rotors began turning. The helicopter, powered by a Rolls Royce Allison 250 engine, had good power. Manuel did not know what type of aircraft Raz had, but he hoped they could gain precious minutes as they sought to rescue Rebekah and Jonas from their adversary's grasp. He trusted by now Raz had shown his true colors and the parents of the king knew not to trust him.

Chapter Forty-Three

Palenque, Mexico
December 20, 2012
7:39 a.m. local time

Time to Solstice: 22 hours, 32 minutes

Out of the window of the plane, Jonas looked onto the clearing that included the ruins of the city of Palenque. He could see the Otolum River flowing by the Ball Court, where the ancients played games of life and death. He could see the main Palace, and then the Temple of the Inscriptions, where Pakal was buried. The Temple of the Cross and the huge Temple of the Sun rose over the area south of the river, and there was a set of buildings to the north of the Ball Court. The ancient village, carved out of the jungle, was magnificent from the air, especially in the early morning sunlight.

What Jonas was most concerned with, however, were the thin tracts of land surrounding Palenque that had been reclaimed from the jungle. One of those tracts appeared large enough for a small plane to land, and the pilot was headed for it. Jonas was glad he did not have to attempt the landing. It looked like it was for emergency use only.

He'd no sooner finished thinking that when the pilot began his descent. The lush green of the jungle got closer and closer. Jonas knew—hoped—the pilot's flight skills would allow them to approach just above the treeline as they headed for the strip of land the pilot intended to use as a runway. Jonas heard Rebekah gasp.

"We're going to hit the trees!"

The pilot laughed. "No, señora, we are not. I have done this before."

Jonas would have felt better had he not seen Raz gripping the armrest so hard his knuckles turned white, but the pilot was true to his word. The plane cleared the top of the jungle—just barely, but cleanly—and dropped onto the makeshift runway. The wheels touched down and they coasted to a stop.

Raz let go of the armrest. "Well done." He unbuckled himself and opened the door, dropping to the ground. Then he reached back into the plane and pushed his seatback forward to let Rebekah out. He helped her off the plane. Once she was down, Jonas slung his bag over his shoulder and stared at the monuments of Palenque rising high above the floor of the jungle.

A golf cart approached them. The man driving it had a scarred face. His skin was tough and leathery, and his body had a thick, hardened appearance as well. Jonas wondered just what occupation this man had.

The cart pulled to a stop where Raz stood. "Have you made the arrangements, Gilberto?"

Gilberto smiled. Jonas noticed that one of the teeth was gold, and none of them were straight. He wondered if it was dental hygiene, heredity, or if Gilberto had been in a number of fights. He guessed it was the last. "I have the key, Señor Uris. We are free to go into the ruins."

"*Bien*, Gilberto. "Rebekah, would you ride up front, please?"

Rebekah looked at Jonas for confirmation. All he could do was nod. Though they were both nervous about the situation, they had no choice but to go forward and hope for the best.

Rebekah took the seat next to Gilberto. The back of the cart was more for maintenance purposes, with a flatbed and no seats. Raz indicated that Jonas should get in, so he climbed onto the flatbed. Raz sat close to Jonas. Jonas tried to get comfortable, leaning against the small railing that went around the cart.

Gilberto drove to the front gate and unlocked it. Jonas found it eerie to be entering Palenque with no tourists anywhere. A deserted, ancient Mayan city, and they were alone in the place.

Rebekah must have felt the same way. "This must be how Jose Calderon felt when he stumbled upon the ruins in 1784," she said.

Gilberto returned to the cart in time to hear Rebekah's comment. "So you know something of the history of Palenque, *señora*?"

"A little."

"We are entering from the east gate and coming straight into the Main Plaza," Gilberto said. "The large temple you see in the distance to our right is the Temple of the Cross, which is the tallest of the buildings here."

"We're not here for the tour," Raz said. "Take us to the Temple of the Inscriptions."

"As you wish."

Jonas detected a bit of irritation in Gilberto's response. Gilberto eased the cart across the entrance and pulled in quite a bit before stopping. He walked the distance back to the gate, had trouble re-locking it, then strolled back to the cart.

"It is a shame you do not have more time," Gilberto said. "I'm sure the *señora* would enjoy exploring the Palace. It is quite a complex."

Raz glared at him. "We just need to get to Pakal's tomb. And more quickly than you have taken us anywhere so far."

"Of course."

Gilberto still did not seem to hurry. He drove the cart carefully, even as he took a direct route to the Temple of the Inscriptions.

"Can't you make this lawn mower go any faster?" Raz groused.

"*Sí, señor.*" But the cart seemed to pick up only marginal speed.

Gilberto stopped in front of the large Temple. "From here, we go on foot."

Raz leaped over the rail. Jonas matched his movement on the opposite side, landing on the ground near Rebekah's door. He helped her out of the cart.

Rebekah looked at the five sets of stairs that led up to the top. "Are we going all the way up there?"

Gilberto nodded. "The only way to Pakal's tomb is to go up into Temple and then down a staircase into the heart of the structure."

Jonas remembered now the strenuousness of the trip to the tomb. As steep and as high as the stairs were to the top of the Temple, the way down to the burial chamber was even longer. "Rebekah can't possibly do that."

Raz removed his Glock. "Despite her pregnancy, she looks to be in excellent shape. And we must all stay together. Do I make myself clear?"

If there had been any doubt in Jonas' mind that they'd backed the wrong horse, this took care of it. He looked at Rebekah and read the fear in her eyes. He held her hand. "I'll be right with you."

Gilberto eyed the gun. "It is fifty-two feet to the top. If we must take her with us, we will go slow."

"Then we will go slow. But she will make the trip to the tomb."

Chapter Forty-Four

Cancun, Mexico
Hotel de Los Reyes
December 20, 2012
8:15 a.m. local time

Time to Solstice: 21 hours, 56 minutes

Colin knelt on the bed, near the edge of it, directly behind Yan's unconscious body. He braced Yan's back and held him upright so Talasi could finish bandaging the damaged right shoulder and arm.

"I'll make a sling for his arm when the anesthesia wears off," she said.

"How long will it take?"

Talasi tossed the remaining bandage material on the bed. "Minutes, hours. It doesn't matter. There's no way we can find Rebekah and Jonas. And they won't come with us anyway. Not now. We've failed."

"We haven't failed. We still have almost twenty-two hours. Something will happen."

"Something already has. And it wasn't good."

Colin understood Talasi's frustration. He'd been wrestling with doubts about their mission ever since Talasi began operating on Yan. While she'd been on auto-pilot, issuing orders and being a one-woman surgical team, he'd had little else to brood about. Talasi was just now facing the situation. Naturally, she saw it as grim.

But Colin's initial depression had given way to hope. He knew in the rational world the odds of finding Rebekah and Jonas were slim. He'd prayed about it, sent up silent petitions to his ancestors to help, reviewed the events that had led them to this point. How could we have come this far if the natural world was controlling the events? he thought.

And eventually that thinking had made the difference. It wasn't that he'd received any direct answers, but he felt a sense of peace about the question he'd asked. The natural world wasn't in control here. The spiritual world was. Good battling evil in spaces they couldn't see, in realms where natural laws didn't apply. Something was in the works.

He was confident Talasi would see it, too, once she had a chance to think about it.

"The operation has you strung out," Colin said. "Relax, take deep breaths. We can't do anything for the moment, not with Yan out. But the moment will come. It has before; it will again."

"You're all Mr. Sunshine this morning."

"I don't know how to explain it, Talasi, but this setback won't turn out to be a setback. In the end, we'll see that fate will have taken us from bad to good."

Talasi removed the latex gloves. She gave Colin a withering glance he imagined she'd used on interns who'd said things she regarded as stupid. "Fate could also take us from bad to worse."

But Colin was no intern. He saw himself as the leader of this party of sojourners—at least the one with military planning experience—and he wasn't about to let negativity take over. "In twenty-two hours we'll see that this has been a necessary detour. But it won't go from bad to worse."

I hope.

* * *

Zagros Mountains, Iraq
December 20, 2012
4:20 p.m. local time

Time to Solstice: 21 hours, 51 minutes

Vhorrdak sat in a cave puzzling over the three internationals Raz had encountered. He'd decided to remain in the Zagros Mountains, much as he hated the cold, until he figured it out. He'd located a cave, which took away the chill from the wind, but it still felt cold, at least by his standards.

Who were these people? They'd come from different ends of the earth. There was no way for them to know each other. How then did they each know about the baby, and especially how had they located Rebekah?

Something was missing from the equation.

They claimed that they were there to protect Rebekah and the baby. Had his enemy arranged something special to distract him, as he sought to distract the Americans?

But these were not distractions. These stood directly in his way. They knew about Raz now. It would be difficult to get Raz past them. He needed someone else to kill the baby at the moment of birth. He wished he could do it himself. He would get a lot of pleasure out of it. But that was not within his control, since he was not allowed to kill directly—damn again his enemy. Nor could he be two places at once, and his plans for the nuclear weapon required him to be in the Middle East during the most critical time.

So who could kill the baby?

And then it came to him. A perfect solution. All it would take is a little time in Cancun. And fortunately, he knew faster ways to travel than relying on current technology.

First, though, he needed to contact Washington to let them know about the truck being in the Zagros Mountains. Then he needed to call Fareed and let him know when to send the truck into hiding. He usually liked to call just when it needed to be done, but now he would be busy with this other project.

He was confident Fareed would handle it well. Fareed was one asset he could trust. Well, trust was perhaps too strong a word. He trusted Fareed to do it as long as Fareed knew he was watching.

* * *

Syrian Desert, Western Iraq

Fareed and Ashur had spent yet another day making little progress, exactly as instructed. They headed in a southerly direction, moving cave to cave, driving some distance but resting mostly. Which caves they chose were up to them with the exception of the last. That one had been specified by Vhorrdak. Why, Fareed didn't know, but he knew he needed to be there at the time specified, just as he had been the day before. He thought it might be some kind of test. Perhaps Vhorrdak was watching.

He was very surprised, then, when the satellite phone vibrated before they had left the next to last cave. As before, Fareed did not talk after connecting with the caller.

"Plans have changed."

That didn't seem to merit a response, so he continued listening.

"Alert the third decoy to hide immediately when you reach the next destination. Don't be late. Timing is critical. Tell them to wait until further instruction."

When Fareed was sure Vhorrdak had disconnected, he did likewise.

"What is it?" Ashur asked.

"There is a change in plans," Fareed answered.

This was the critical point for Fareed. He had to sound convincing. He'd been looking all day for a way, for a reason, to hide the nuke before they got to the last cave, the one Vhorrdak had specified, and to make it seem as though they were following instructions. Though Ashur had never met Vhorrdak, Fareed did not to want to underestimate him. He did not know what Ashur would do if he suspected Fareed was encouraging them to go against their employer.

"We are to hide the cargo here. Our employer suspects we have been compromised. He will have another vehicle pick it up. We are now another decoy truck." Ashur did not seem to care. In fact, he seemed relieved.

Though the cargo was not heavy, it was awkward. Fortunately, Ashur was strong. Together they set it down in the back of the cave, where a small alcove was located. They'd found several flat sandstones to put in the commercial truck that would create about the same weight and size as the cargo.

Fareed jotted the GPS coordinates of the cave, adding the month of his birthday and subtracting the date so no one could find it from his note. He checked the cave before they left. From the front, no one would notice the nuke was there. He tried to memorize the placement so he could come back and retrieve it after he'd either fooled Vhorrdak or used it as a bargaining chip to save his life. It was strange how, when he looked at it from the front, the front wall of the alcove melded with the shape of the other side of the cave such that it formed a pointed arch.

That is a good way to remember it, Fareed thought. It is behind the right side of the five sided arch. He looked at his watch.

"Let's go," he told Ashur. "We must hurry to the next cave."

Chapter Forty-Five

Palenque, Mexico
December 20, 2012
8:24 a.m. local time

Time to Solstice: 21 hours, 47 minutes

Jonas, Rebekah, Raz and Gilberto stood at the bottom of the Temple of the Inscriptions, looking up.

Fifty-two feet, Jonas thought. He looked at the Glock Raz had steadied on him. Now was not the time to try any heroics. But he would look for an opening. He still had his pack with him, which gave him some security. He took Rebekah's arm. "One step at a time," he said. He took the first step up.

She joined him on the stone step, using his arm to steady her. Gilberto moved behind her as a buttress in case she fell back. The three of them moved up about ten steps before Raz took his first step up the Temple stairs. Clearly he wanted to be behind all of them.

Jonas wasn't sure if Rebekah was winded or if she was taking a cue from Gilberto's unhurried ways. Raz had been correct in saying that Rebekah was in good shape, even in pregnancy. But the pace was hers to set, and she was taking it slow.

Halfway up the stairs Rebekah paused. "The baby's awake, and he's kicking."

Jonas put his hand on her belly and felt his son's feet thumping against his. He felt a kind of pride that his son was vital, active. But it worried him, too. Soon enough, he thought, you'll be out where you can push and strain and test yourself against this world. But don't be in a hurry. We need to get home first.

"He wants us to go on," Rebekah said.

Jonas wasn't clear how much Rebekah really knew when she said things like that, but the bond between a woman and her unborn baby was a mystery. That much he did understand. He paused to look around. Twenty-some feet up the side of an ancient temple in Mexico with the sun now a ball sitting above the horizon, he almost gasped at how big the earth appeared, and how scared he was of all that was happening. The only world he cared about had narrowed to him, Rebekah and the baby, and it seemed terribly fragile. Back in his little suburb outside Philadelphia, he felt in control of his circumstances. Even at the firm he had a sense of influence. But here and now, he found he had to re-discover a kind of faith he'd let go a long time ago, a faith that, despite the events, they would be okay. There was a plan. He had a hard time believing it was the same plan Manuel believed in, or the plan Raz had involved them in, but there was a plan.

If there wasn't, they had no reason to go on.

The baby kicked him again, right before Raz said, "Enough of a rest. Get going." This time Jonas and Rebekah went up the stairs step by step together, until they finally reached the landing at the top.

Rebekah stopped again to catch her breath.

Raz moved behind them but out of Jonas' reach. "You're halfway there."

Gilberto went ahead to the entrance to the tunnel. "Not quite halfway. We must still descend seventy-three feet to Pakal's tomb."

"Seventy-three feet?" Rebekah sounded doubtful.

Jonas put his mouth to her ear. "We can do this."

He helped her over to where Gilberto had used a key to turn on the lights, allowing them to see down to the first turn of the stairs.

Rebekah stared into the tunnel. "That's steep."

Jonas took the first step. "I'll go ahead of you, like we did at the Temple. I won't let you fall."

Rebekah put her hands on his shoulders. "I know you won't."

Gilberto slipped by the two of them. "Please, it is I who must go first. Lights will need to be lit as we go." His feet clomped on the stairs as he descended. He disappeared around the first corner.

Much more slowly than Gilberto had gone, Jonas led Rebekah into the staircase. Raz followed behind. He stayed close on Rebekah's heels.

Jonas' senses sharpened with each step he took. Ahead of him was the echo of Gilberto's boots as he plodded his way to the bottom. Just behind was Rebekah's labored breathing and the unevenness of her touches as she worked to maintain her balance.

Behind her he could feel Raz's threatening stance, knowing without seeing the gun was pointed at them.

"The air is so sticky," Rebekah said. Jonas knew it would get worse. He remembered the trickling of droplets on the walls outside Pakal's tomb from his earlier visit. Even now he could taste the ancient dampness and wondered if they were somehow ingesting the molecules of kings and warriors. The thought made him gulp at first, but then he became defiant. Then let us be kings and warriors.

Gilberto was waiting at the bottom of the stairs in the antechamber. Ahead of them stood an iron gate blocking the entrance to the tomb. Gilberto looked to be trying every one of a set of keys he had in his hand. Jonas couldn't help but notice that the tomb was in the shape of a Mayan arch. Across the widest part, dividing the tomb in two, was the lid to the sarcophagus, Pakal's resting place. Because of the way the wall had been removed and replaced by the iron-barred gate, they could see into the sarcophagus from the front. They could see where Pakal's body had lain.

Rebekah slowly advanced toward the tomb. She was staring at the glyphs on the lid of the sarcophagus. Gilberto finally located the correct key. It turned in the lock and the iron gate opened. Rebekah inched closer, still staring.

"Can you read those?" Raz asked.

Jonah wondered if Rebekah had even heard Raz. He could tell from her gaze that she was trying to construct a picture. He'd seen her like this before. He likened it to someone mentally solving a jigsaw puzzle, with puzzle pieces flying about and reconstructing themselves in different arrangements. She tilted her head, unsure.

"Yes," she said, "some. I recognize the shield, the glyph that stood for Pakal. And I can read the numbers that elaborately spell out the date. But I can't translate that back into the modern calendar without a computer. Some of the rest of these I think I could do, if I had the time to study them."

Raz sounded disappointed. "Pity, I'd expected you to be quicker. The work you have ahead of you will likely be more difficult. Nonetheless, you will figure out where the book is."

"The way I've heard it," Jonas said, "I will be the one to do that."

"You are irrelevant. Now back up."

Jonas pulled Rebekah away from the tomb with him.

"Not her, just you." Raz secured the gun in his belt in the small of his back and used both hands to unlatch the case containing the mask.

Jonas assessed the situation. With Gilberto on one side of the antechamber and Raz on the other, there was no way to overpower both of them, even though neither had a weapon in hand at the moment. And with Rebekah between them, either could grab her and it would be end game for Jonas.

He studied both men's movements. There must be a way.

Raz lifted the mask from the case. From the way he held the mask, touching it minimally but keeping it secure at the same time, Jonah judged that the mask was heavier than it looked. Perhaps a weapon? But Rebekah would kill him if he wrecked it. Even if it saves us.

Raz extended his hand invitingly toward the bottom section of the sarcophogus. "Now we need to find out what Pakal sees in death. Rebekah?"

Jonas took a step between Raz and Rebekah. "You can't make her do that. She's pregnant."

"None of the rest of us has a chance of being able to read what's written in there. And you know it's completely safe. But I can see it would be best to let you help her into position. That way Gilberto and I can both keep our eyes on you."

Rebekah put her hand on Jonas'. "It's okay," she said.

She gripped his hand and took a step into the tomb area. She squatted backwards toward the sarcophagus that once served as the final resting place for Pakal. When she was seated, Jonas knelt next to her to help ease her onto the tomb floor. He leaned in close. "Create a convincing lie." As he said it, he realized there was a soft echo in the tomb.

"What did you say to her, Jonas?" Raz asked.

"I told her it was safe to lie down."

Raz paused, but he had a suspicious look on his face. "Very well, continue."

Chapter Forty-Six

Cancun, Mexico
Hotel de Los Reyes
December 20, 2012
8:35 a.m. local time

Time to Solstice: 21 hours, 36 minutes

Vhorrdak pulled a black Lincoln Continental into the parking space next to the car Raz's associates had tracked. It had taken Vhorrdak a while to figure out who these interlopers were. Raz's description of them as internationals eventually provided the key. When Vhorrdak finally realized their purpose, he was glad he had decided to take care of them himself. He knew now they were working for the enemy. In all likelihood, if they'd been eliminated, the enemy would already have others waiting in the wings. So Vhorrdak decided to repurpose them. One of them. The injured one.

How convenient that he was injured. No, not convenient. That would imply Vhorrdak was merely lucky. That, he was not. He was an instrument of his own destiny, and fate favored him. Always.

Vhorrdak opened the car door and got out. He was dressed in an expensive suit. To do the job properly, he needed to look good. So he had visited one of the more luxurious hotels and followed a well-to-do businessman to his room, a businessman who would eventually awaken and discover his car and his clothes missing. The guest would be out long enough for Vhorrdak to finish what he needed to do and abandon the vehicle.

Slipping on the dark Ray-Ban sunglasses he'd found in the car, Vhorrdak shut the front door and opened the trunk, pulling a nicely wrapped package from the back seat of the Lincoln.

He glanced at the rooms nearest the car that belonged to the internationals. One of those rooms held his target. But which? And he really needed to get his target alone.

Vhorrdak headed for the lobby with the package.

* * *

Palenque, Mexico

Rebekah eased herself onto the stone slab in Pakal's sarcophagus. The cold, damp feel of the rock went straight through her clothes. She'd been warmer than normal during the last part of the pregnancy, but this chill had her nerves firing instead of providing relief.

Jonas must have a plan, she thought. Critical to it was her ability to convince Raz and Gilberto that there was some kind of clue here, a clue she could understand. Raz's remark that she was slow in deciphering the glyphs on the top side of the sarcophagus made her angry. She only needed enough time to do it. She reached up and ran her fingers lightly on the underside of the stone lid, feeling for symbols. Outside the tomb, where there was artificial light, she could see just fine. But within the sarcophagus, to which normal tourists had no access, it was dark. She could not see any symbols, but her tentative exploration revealed indentations that she thought were purposely done.

The game is on, she thought, and for Jonas and the baby, I must succeed.

"Hand me the mask," she said.

Jonas repeated the message to Raz. Raz passed the mask to him, and he placed it in Rebekah's hands. She was surprised by its weight, but with Jonas' help she maneuvered it in place over her face, the jewels in the eyes of the mask distorting her sight. She shifted the mask back and forth trying to get something to come into focus. She could barely see. She took off the mask and felt the slab to make sure where the characters were.

"Flashlight," she said. She knew Jonas kept one in his leather pack.

Jonas handed it to her.

She lit the characters using the flashlight. Nothing looked familiar. Odd symbols that made no sense. My knowledge is just too limited. Rebekah felt the baby pushing inside her. Not a kick, but a push. I've got to save us. She slid the mask back over her face.

"There's something here," she said, "but I can't make it out."

Jonas had to buy Rebekah some time. "The light isn't right," he said. "We're using flashlights. I'm sure the Maya didn't have them."

Rebekah craned her head up so she could see out into the antechamber. She watched Jonas search the arched entrance to the tomb.

"Here's a place that holds a torch," he said. "And one here and here and here. That's what we need, torches."

"Do you keep torches around here?" Raz asked.

"Only for effect," Gilberto said.

"Will they light?"

"I think so."

"Then get some."

Rebekah eased her head back onto the tomb floor. She felt a few seconds go by without hearing her own breath and realized she was holding it. She consciously breathed out. She took in another gulp and let it out noisily. Was she breathing too fast? She needed to calm down.

Light started to surround her in the tomb. She raised her head slightly again and saw Gilberto lighting torches and Jonas placing them in holders on the walls of the tomb's entrance. Two were high and two were low. The lower ones shined into her area and lit the symbols.

This is like the shadows on the Pyramid, she thought.

She heard Jonas say, "Kill the lights."

Soon the only illumination source in the tomb was torchlight.

Rebekah wasn't sure she could do this. Her breath quickened. She had a sense of being buried alive, the lid of the tomb seemed so close. And now she was going to put some dead king's mask over her face? Who was she kidding?

And then, the baby kicked. Rebekah remembered her life and Jonas' weren't the only ones at stake. She had the baby to think about. They had to escape. She steeled herself, did everything she could to slow her breathing.

She slid the mask over her eyes.

It took a moment, but distinctive hieroglyphics came into view. They were centered above her. There were two flanking glyphs also within her sight, one to each side. The flanking symbols were not part of the series but Rebekah could tell they were related in some way.

"Hand me something to write with," she said.

Jonas pulled a sketchbook out of his pack, along with a pencil. He handed it to her.

Rebekah carefully slid the mask on and off, copying the symbols as best she could. Her mind was racing while she did it, evaluating what was there. She decided not to write down either of the flanking hieroglyphics. She didn't know how much Raz knew about the Mayan language, but he must have some knowledge or access to someone who did, because he'd been able to quickly obtain a translation of the hieroglyphics from the Pyramid, the ones that had led them here.

Rebekah finished and passed the sketchbook and the mask out to Jonas, who handed them to Raz in the antechamber. At the last moment she saw Jonas' flashlight and grabbed it.

She closed her eyes in silent prayer before making her exit. Then she said, "I'm ready now. Help me out, Jonas, please."

She slid forward until she felt Jonas' strong arms lift her out of the tomb. He was careful to make sure her head missed the lid of the sarcophagus.

Raz hardly waited for Jonas to get Rebekah on her feet before he asked her, "What does it mean?"

"I'm no expert. We ought to pass it by someone who knows this better."

Raz eyed her. "But you have some idea."

Rebekah weighed her answer. The best lies, she knew, began with a bit of truth. "It starts with the same glyphs we found on the Pyramid of Kukulcan, the Book of the Thirteen Gods."

"Is the book here?"

"It was once. It was buried with Pakal."

She could tell Jonas was unsure whether or not she was making anything up. Good, she thought. But in reality she hadn't started lying yet.

Jonas asked, "Where is it now?"

Rebekah still held the flashlight in her right hand. She used it to point at the last of the hieroglyphics on the sketchbook in Raz's hand. "This glyph here shows it being taken to the mouth of the underworld."

"Xibalba, the place of Fright," Gilberto said.

"Where is that?" Raz asked.

"Two places are traditionally believed to be entrances to Xibalba," Gilberto answered.

Rebekah knew if the lie was going to be spun, she had to guide this conversation. "One's in Belize, the other's in Guatemala," she said.

Raz turned to her. "Which is it?"

"The glyph for 'east' is in this string. Caves Branch in Belize is directly east of here."

Jonas stood with Rebekah, put his arm around her waist. "You don't need us, Raz. You have the mask and the location of the book. This is too much for Rebekah. She might lose the baby. You have to let us go."

In a swift, easy movement, Raz removed his gun from the small of his back. "You're right about one thing, Jonas. I don't need you. But I do need Rebekah. She's coming with me to Belize."

Rebekah looked at the gun and then at Jonas. She could tell from the way Jonas had his jaw set, this was not going as he had planned.

And for just a moment, she worried he would do something rash.

Chapter Forty-Seven

Cancun, Mexico
Hotel de Los Reyes
December 20, 2012
8:37 a.m. local time

Time to Solstice: 21 hours, 34 minutes

Vhorrdak walked into the lobby of the hotel carrying the elaborately wrapped empty gift box. The registration desk was to his immediate right. He saw no one behind it. Ahead of him the entryway ended in a paisley-wallpapered hall that ran right and left. From somewhere down the hall he could hear the clinking of flatware on dishes, the jabber of voices talking at different purposes, the laughter of children. He smelled chorizo sausages and coffee. A restaurant.

Maybe the motel manager was in there. He didn't have a lot of time.

Vhorrdak heard a door open and a heavyset man appeared behind the desk. He wore a suit that likely fit twenty pounds ago, the jacket unbuttoned. He smiled at Vhorrdak.

"May I help you, sir?" he asked in Spanish.

Vhorrdak had been around long enough to speak in any language. "Yes, I have a gift for a friend of mine. I'm afraid he forgot to give me the room number. He's British, has the look of soldier to him, though he's not in uniform. He's with two others, a young Chinese gentleman and an American woman."

The manager nodded, began to check his computer. Then he stopped and looked up. "The name of the guest?"

"He goes by different names," Vhorrdak said smoothly. "You know how secretive military people can be. He doesn't know I'm surprising him for his birthday."

"I'm sorry. I'll need to have a name."

Vhorrdak showed his poker face—on the surface, undisturbed by the news that the manager, who had to have known which room this trio occupied, wouldn't just give him the information. Vhorrdak rethought the situation. He had used all the correct casual inflections. He knew he was dressed to project a trustworthy image. Perhaps it was the sunglasses that made the manager hesitate. Unfortunately he'd had to use them. The red eyes would have wrecked what he was trying to do.

He gave the manager his best aura of sincerity. "Please."

The manager shook his head. "I'm sorry, sir, but we can't give out room numbers. If you'd like to leave the gift, we'll be happy to deliver it for you."

Vhorrdak kept the annoyance out of his mannerisms, but there was no question how this would play out from here. He had to have the room number. Since he'd anticipated there was the slight risk of this occurring, he'd prepared a nice bribe. Greed was something he knew worked on human beings. He had just the right amount, too, large enough to be significantly tempting, but small enough not to set off alarms in the man's head.

Vhorrdak reached across the black slate desktop and tucked the peso notes into the manager's hand. "Really, this will be a great delight for my friend, and I want to see his face when he opens it. You must let me surprise him. Please."

The man opened his hand, stared at the money Vhorrdak had placed there. His eyes widened. He brushed his mustache with the thumb and forefinger of his empty hand, contemplating the sum of money that could be his.

All people are inherently dishonest, Vhorrdak thought. It's all about the price point.

* * *

Washington, DC
Situation Room, The White House
December 20, 2012
9:40 a.m. local time

Time to Solstice: 21 hours, 31 minutes

General Culver knew he was dozing, occupying that space between consciousness and unconsciousness where the real world and the dream world blended. He didn't care. He'd been up all night—a frustrating night—and the fact that the White House was back in full operational mode didn't matter to him, not at this moment. He was in the black leather chair at the head of the table. His shoulders were braced against the well-padded back of the chair, his head was tilted up, and his mouth was open. A noise like snoring startled him and he sat up. He thought it might have been him who was snoring. He pushed the cuff back on his left sleeve and checked his watch. Another fifteen minutes and that idiot Harrington would be here for another update. He wished he had some spectacular news just to shut the guy up. Harrington acted like his orders came from the President. Well, they probably did—Culver wasn't sure Harrington spoke with the President as often as he claimed—but Culver would certainly rather deal with the President. Harrington was always posturing. Culver hated that. There was no posturing with the President. And the President liked and trusted him a lot more than Harrington did.

The general struggled to remember the dream he'd been experiencing. He had been in the desert, most likely the Syrian Desert since that's what they were all focused on. There were trucks everywhere, scattering in all directions like insurgents in a bombed out Baghdad house suddenly invaded by American soldiers. The trucks, for the most part, looked alike—virtually all of them identical to the decoy truck they'd found earlier in the night—but there was one, maybe two that looked different. More like American semis hauling freight. Ruefully Culver recalled that one of the semis had Joe Camel on the side.

Did the dream mean anything? The Joe Camel image made him smile at the thought. A fusion of the desert, the camels used for transportation, and good old American advertising. When Culver used to smoke, he smoked Marlboro. He couldn't remember if he'd ever tried Camels.

The general felt his side tilt back again. He slipped into the dream again. Joe Camel winked at him.

Culver heard a cough. Joe Camel hadn't opened his mouth. The general opened one eye. Major Simmons stood next to him. Culver thought Simmons had a slight look of disdain, but then it was gone and Culver wondered if he'd really seen it. Simmons drove him nuts sometimes. The guy doesn't even look tired, Culver thought. Does he ever sleep?

The general sat up. "Yes?"

"Our contacts say the nuke is going to Iran over the Zagros Mountains."

Shit. Wasn't it Harrington that suggested it might be the Zagros? That's what Simmons had told him. He hated that. But he pushed the thought aside. "You have a location?"

"Yes, sir. Our troops are headed there now."

Well, at least we'll have something good to tell Harrington, even if he gets all smug about it.

"Thank you," Culver said. "I'll alert the National Security Advisor." Major Simmons left the room.

Culver stretched and smiled at the thought of his dream. Joe Camel winking at him. He shook his head. Then he stood and marched out of the Situation Room to find Harrington. They had news, and he wanted to deliver it to Harrington before the President's representative came in for another damn briefing.

Chapter Forty-Eight

Palenque, Mexico
The Tomb of Pakal
December 20, 2012
8:50 a.m. local time

Time to Solstice: 21 hours, 21 minutes

Raz grabbed Rebekah's left hand and pulled her away from Jonas.

With the gun pointed at his head, Jonas could do little but watch helplessly as his wife stumbled toward the villain.

"Jonas!" Rebekah's plea echoed in the antechamber. Her right hand holding the flashlight flailed in the air as she reached back for Jonas.

Jonas assessed the situation. It was grim. Gilberto was behind him and Raz in front. Raz's gun was still aimed at him. Rebekah, an unwilling pawn, was at Raz's side.

In his mind, Jonas ran through what he had in his pack. Was there anything he could use as a weapon? If so, could he even get to the pack? He'd put it by the tomb after removing the flashlight to give to Rebekah. The flashlight … Rebekah still had it. It made an excellent weapon, and Rebekah knew some self-defense.

A fight could jeopardize the baby's life, though, not to mention her own. But if Jonas didn't encourage her to resist, Raz would take her away, and both her life and the baby's could be compromised anyway. Jonas felt his own life wasn't an issue—if Rebekah left with Raz, it was likely Gilberto would kill him.

He wondered how far behind him Gilberto was. If Rebekah could keep Raz from shooting him, even for a few seconds, he might be able to take out Gilberto and then go for Raz's gun. Gilberto was a sizeable guy, but Jonas was no slouch in the strength department. As long as Gilberto was unarmed—and Jonas hadn't seen any evidence to the contrary—he felt the element of surprise would give him the upper hand. If only he could get Rebekah to do what he wanted.

"Rebekah!" he shouted with his best 'cry of desperation.' He held out his hand toward her. But he wasn't looking at her face. He was looking at her right hand, where she held the flashlight. He then glanced upward at her face.

She looked at him quizzically. Without moving her head, she shifted her eyes down to her right and back. The flashlight twitched in her hand.

Jonas hoped it was a signal.

Raz pulled Rebekah toward the stairs. "Let's go," he said.

Rebekah yanked her left hand out of his right. She started to shift the flashlight to her left hand.

The move was exactly what Jonas had hoped for, but he couldn't have Raz and Gilberto see it. "Wait," Jonas said.

Both men focused on him. He tried to sound reasonable. "Look, you may not need me to find the book, but you'll need someone to take care of Rebekah." He kept his hands out at his side, hoping Raz and Gilberto would register in their minds he was unarmed and not dangerous. "She's not going to be able to move as fast as you want." Jonas took a half-step backward toward the stairs and positioned himself so he could see both Gilberto and Raz. Gilberto was close, but Jonas would still have to take a step toward him. A step was all Gilberto would need to defend himself. Jonas needed him closer.

"Grab him, Gilberto," Raz said.

Jonas looked at Rebekah. Gilberto crossed the single step that separated him and Jonas.

Rebekah slammed the flashlight against Raz's hand. He dropped the gun. It skittered away across the floor. Raz dove for it. Rebekah kicked him in the gut.

Jonas stepped in at the advancing Gilberto. He slipped his right arm under Gilberto's left and around the larger man's back. He shot his right hip in front of Gilberto's abdomen and bent over. As soon as his back was flat, Jonas used his leverage to roll the man over his back, throwing him on top of Raz.

Raz grunted as Gilberto landed. Gilberto scrambled to his knees and went for the gun. It was an arm's length from Raz.

"No!" Jonas yelled.

Gilberto grabbed the gun.

And tossed it to Jonas.

Jonas' mouth fell open. "What?"

Gilberto didn't answer. He twisted Raz's arm behind the man's back and yanked it upward until Raz cried out in pain. Once he had Raz immobilized, he looked at them over his shoulder. "Rebekah, please find a rag to place in his mouth. Jonas, find some way to tie him up. I understand you are good with ropes."

Jonas and Rebekah stared at him in shock.

Then Jonas went for his pack. "Thank you," he said.

"You are welcome. Manuel Patcanul asked me to watch out for you. He was afraid something would happen."

Jonas threw Rebekah an undershirt he kept in his pack. She handed it to Gilberto. "You're not with Raz?" she asked.

He shrugged. He pulled Raz's head back by the hair and shoved the compact undershirt into Raz's mouth. "He should not have pointed his Glock at either of you. When Palenque opens, someone will find him, but that's not long from now. Unfortunately he knows we're going to Belize."

Jonas continued to sort through his pack. He hated to use his trusty climbing rope for something like this. Then he saw the two mechanical ascenders and his carabiners. He cobbled them together into handcuffs. "Well, with any luck we'll already have the book by the time he catches up to us."

"We still must do something about the pilot," Gilberto said. He moved off Raz's back so Jonas could climb on top. The two of them used the make-shift handcuffs to restrain Raz.

"You have any ideas?" Jonas asked.

"The pilot trusts me. I can get close to him. Perhaps I can knock him out and put him somewhere he won't make trouble." Gilberto noticed that Raz was still able to use his legs. "Give me a hand. We're going to have to lock him in the tomb."

Gilberto and Jonas grabbed Raz's legs and dragged him across the ground to Pakal's tomb. They put him inside, and Gilberto shut the barred, iron gate that protected it from tourists. He used his keys and locked it. "That'll hold him. Let's go."

Gilberto crossed to the stairs and started up at a quick pace.

Jonas retrieved his backpack.

"The mask," Rebekah said. "We may yet need it again."

Jonah packed Pakal's mask into its case and carried it across to the stairs. Holding it in one hand, he helped her up the first two steps with the other. She stared up at the steep climb. "I can't go that fast."

Gilberto had already reached the first turn of the staircase when he heard her say it. He looked back.

"Go ahead," Jonas said. "I'll stay back and help Rebekah."

Gilberto charged on ahead. They could hear his heavy footfalls echo down the staircase.

Rebekah put her mouth near Jonas' ear. "I lied," she whispered.

"I guessed that."

"Let's keep going up. I don't want to take a chance Raz will hear us." She waited until they reached the turn to tell him the next part. "The book is not in Belize."

"There really was a message in the tomb?"

"Yes. And the reference it made was not to Xibalba. I used that as shorthand. The glyphs actually used the term 'mouth of the underworld'."

Jonas thought a moment. "They're not the same thing?"

"Slightly different. I wouldn't know except for another symbol, one on the left side, one I didn't copy down because I didn't want Raz to see it. I recognized it easily. Ek Balam."

"The ruins up north, where you worked?"

Rebekah nodded. She motioned for them to continue on the stairs. "Here's what I think. The Mayan world was crumbling around Palenque. They valued the book. They took it to a safer place."

"A cave is a safer place? The underworld entrances were always in caves, weren't they?"

"That's where the writer was clever. The mouth of the underworld at Ek Balam isn't a cave. It's the opening to what's called the Acropolis. Behind it is the tomb of Ukit Kan Le'k Tok'."

"Forgive me if I'm not excited about the prospect of another tomb."

Rebekah ignored him. "You remember I told you the inscription on the Pyramid of Kukulcan carried the name of the writer? Well, this message was written by the same person."

"But I thought you said a lot of writers claimed to be that guy."

"Yes, but now I think it really was him. He laid the clue there for us to find. He might even have been the scribe for Pakal. Pakal's vision was the source for the book."

Jonas had to stop himself from getting caught up in Rebekah's excitement. They had a major problem to handle before they could work on finding the book. "We need to figure out how to get rid of Gilberto. He saved us, but that doesn't mean I trust him."

"Agreed. We can't trust anyone but ourselves. But getting to Ek Balam without drawing attention to ourselves won't be easy."

"Our only hope is to fly under the radar. Literally."

* * *

Cancun, Mexico
Hotel de Los Reyes
December 20, 2012
8:53 a.m. local time

Time to Solstice: 21 hours, 18 minutes

Vhorrdak thought that the hotel manager had stared at the money in his hand for an abnormally long time. Usually this sort of thing didn't take so long. It was a bribe, of course, but a precisely calculated one. What was taking him so long?

The manager finally looked at Vhorrdak with great disdain. "Sir, I am insulted." He handed the money back to Vhorrdak.

Vhorrdak hadn't thought it would require more money, but he had plenty in his pocket. He made a show of adding it to the stash and placing it on the counter.

The manager had a sour look on his face. "I am afraid I must ask you to leave my hotel."

Vhorrdak intensely disliked people with principles. I don't have time for this, he thought. He didn't need his eyes to be red to tamper with a mind, but he always liked the effect it had on his victims. He took off his glasses and stared into the manager's eyes.

The manager's pupils enlarged. His hands began to tremble.

Vhorrdak could feel the fear. It always gave him a rush. But if he collapsed too soon, Vhorrdak wouldn't get what he came for. "Now, about the room number …"

Chapter Forty-Nine

Cancun, Mexico
Hotel de Los Reyes
December 20, 2012
9:00 a.m. local time

Time to Solstice: 21 hours, 11 minutes

Yan was in the middle of a vivid dream. He'd had these kinds of dreams before, ones populated by people from vastly different areas of his life, all brought together in a story line worthy of the most tangled thriller.

In this, he was still a child in the school his grandmaster had sent him to. He was taking a language test, and he carefully penned his answers in the Zhongwen characters of the Mandarin language he'd had some difficulty mastering. Instead of his regular schoolmaster, however, the test was being proctored by Rebekah Sagiev. Colin sat next to him, trying to copy off his paper.

"Stop cheating. Do your own work," Yan hissed to Colin, trying not to draw attention to himself.

"But I don't understand the questions. There are just too many damn characters in this language."

Suddenly Rebekah was next to him. "Is there a problem?" She looked at Yan, then at Colin. Yan could feel his ears getting red. He hated when his embarrassment showed. Later, he would practice with his grandmaster to control this. But for now, he could not pretend.

"I don't understand the bloody questions," Colin said, "and I was trying to get Yan to tell me what they were."

"Did you help him?" she asked Yan.

"No, master."

"He is a guest. Perhaps we can give him a hint. Tell me, Yan, what does this say here?" She pointed to some Mayan hieroglyphics that had appeared on his paper. He hadn't seen them before, nor did he have a clue what they meant.

"I don't know."

"Come now. Think hard. It's where I'm going."

Yan's ears were getting so warm he wondered if they had turned the color of blood. "I don't know where you are going."

"You're going to be there, too. And Colin."

"I … I still don't know."

"Ek Balam."

"I've never heard of it."

"Say it after me. 'Ek Balam'."

"Ek Balam."

"Good. Remember it. I need all of you to be there. Say it once more. This time shout it."

"EK BALAM!" And that was when Yan found himself coming out of the anesthesia, saying the name so loudly it startled him. He saw Colin and Talasi were with him.

"Ek Balam." This time he said it normally. He shook his head, trying to clear his mind.

"What?" Colin asked. The Brit sat in a desk chair pulled up next to the bed. Colin looked at him curiously.

Yan stared back bewilderedly. But Colin had been there, too. Why doesn't he remember it?

"Where they will go," he answered Colin. "You heard it. She told us to be there." Yan raised his good arm to his face, rubbing his eyes.

"Who is 'she'?"

"Rebekah Sagiev."

Talasi stood behind Colin wiping her hands with a towel. "He's hallucinating," she said.

Colin waved Talasi quiet. "Where did you say she was going, Yan?"

Yan tried to move his right arm. It hurt. He looked at it curiously. It was bandaged. He remembered being struck by a bullet. Was the blood his?

Focus on the question. "Ek Balam."

Colin turned to Talasi. "It sounds vaguely familiar. Heard of it?"

Talasi put her hands on her hips, the towel dangling from her hand. She looked like she was contemplating Yan's coherence.

"No, I haven't heard of it. But that doesn't mean Yan isn't on to something. His unconscious mind has been free to roam under the influence. Who knows …"

Colin slapped the chair in excitement. “Who knows if this isn’t the good thing I predicted would happen.” He stood. “I’m going to the front desk to find out if Ek Balam exists and where it is.”

* * *

Washington, DC
Office of the National Security Advisor, The White House
December 20, 2012
10:05 a.m. local time

Time to Solstice: 21 hours, 06 minutes

General Culver didn’t knock but entered the office uninvited. Jim Harrington’s first reaction was one of annoyance, but then he realized that Culver must be bringing some good news. Otherwise, he would have waited for Jim to come down for another briefing. Jim looked at his watch. That briefing would have been in five minutes. Culver must have rushed to get here before he left.

“You have news?” he asked Culver.

“And it’s good. You were right about the Zagros Mountains. Our sources say that’s where the truck is.”

Jim smiled but tried not to gloat for having correctly suggested the route the terrorists might take. No sense in aggravating Culver. He knew the general had swallowed some pride just to admit Jim had been right.

“Have you found it, then?”

“We’re playing a bit of cat and mouse right now. But we know the general vicinity. We’ll get it.”

“I don’t know what your group is hearing,” Jim began, “but my sources are leading me to believe the Syrians are not behind this. Most think it’s the Iranians. I believe the goal all along has been to get this nuke to Iran.”

Culver blew out his breath. “We’re coming to the same conclusion. You know, Jim, we keep throwing around the term ‘Armageddon’ like we really don’t mean it, but ...”

“I know.” He paused. The men’s eyes met, and for a moment Jim felt whatever animosity they had fade away. They were in a lifeboat together, this small, secret group, rowing madly to keep the world from becoming a dangerous whirlpool that threatened to suck everyone into oblivion. The self-righteous ayatollah now governing Iran would rather blow up the world than allow infidels to wield economic power over his theocracy. Culver's point was close to his own beliefs.

"Just make sure we get the nuke before they do."

* * *

Cancun, Mexico

Colin closed the door of their motel room behind him. The daylight surprised him, forcing him to squint. They'd pulled the heavy curtains in the room when they arrived early in the morning, partly for security and partially to control the light for the operation, so he'd become accustomed to the dark. He scanned the parking lot to see if there were any signs that alerted him to danger. He didn't detect anything. He started toward the lobby. A businessman with a wrapped gift came out of the entrance. He wore sunglasses, and Colin momentarily wished he'd had a pair that dark. The sun in Cancun was so much brighter than what he experienced in England.

The businessman turned and walked toward him. Colin felt a bit of unease. As they passed, Colin braced to defend himself, but other than giving each other a glance, they passed without circumstance. The businessman went a few steps beyond him and veered into the parking lot. Colin felt a sense of relief, and yet, something still felt wrong. He shook his head and focused on the mission. He had to find out if Ek Balam existed, if Yan's hallucination was a real sign or if the product of a drug-induced dream.

Colin went into the lobby and stood at the counter. He waited a few moments and no one came. Damn. Why is there never anyone around when you need them? He knew the restaurant was around the corner and thought about trying there.

Colin glanced at the rack of pamphlets across the lobby from the desk. If Ek Balam existed, would there be a brochure about it? He crossed to the wooden display rack and scanned the myriad of colorful pamphlets all screaming for his attention. Some were even in English. How does one go about spelling 'Ek Balam'? Had Yan pronounced it correctly? Was he remembering it correctly? No pamphlet jumped out at him.

He decided to give the desk another try. He scouted for a bell to ring. Finding none, he leaned over the counter to see if anyone was in the room tucked over to the side.

He spotted the manager, face down behind the counter.

"Oh, my God," Colin said. He hopped the counter and dropped next to the man, checking for a pulse. He still had one. Colin patted the man's face. "Hello?" No response.

He pulled out his cell phone and called the room. Talasi answered.

"We've got an emergency at the front desk. I need your expertise."

"What about Yan?"

"He'll be fine for a few moments. Something about this doesn't feel right. Maybe I'm being paranoid, but it's like someone doesn't want us to find out about Ek Balam."

"I'll be right down."

"Make sure the door is pulled tightly behind you."

* * *

Vhorrdak watched from the front seat of his car. The woman exited the room the manager had finally identified. She rushed down the sidewalk to the lobby. The Brit must have found the manager and called her for help.

This made things simpler for Vhorrdak. The ease of it once again confirmed that his destiny, his vision, was inexorably correct. His enemy would not succeed.

No time to waste. Vhorrdak got out of the car and walked quickly to the motel door. He slid the master key he'd taken from the manager through the card reader and slipped into the room.

Chapter Fifty

Palenque, Mexico
The Tomb of Pakal
December 20, 2012
9:15 a.m. local time

Time to Solstice: 20 hours, 56 minutes

Jonas was relieved when he and Rebekah finally reached the bottom steps outside the Temple of the Inscriptions. Rebekah had done better than he'd hoped, given how distressing this ordeal was, how strenuous the climb from Pakal's tomb had been, and then how frightening the final descent from the Temple stairs had seemed. He'd steadied her as much as he could, but ultimately it had been her determination that had allowed them to move as swiftly as they had. They still had Pakal's mask.

From the top of the Temple Jonas had seen people parking their cars in the lot. Employees were streaming through the plaza on their way to their stations. We need to get out of here before someone finds Raz, Jonas thought.

Gilberto pulled up in the golf cart. A large black sack about the size of a body bag lay in the back. "I need to get this down to the tomb quickly," he told them.

"Is it the pilot?" Jonas asked.

"Is he …?" Rebekah added.

Gilberto shook his head. "I only knocked him out. But he will come around soon. I will be back."

Jonas and Rebekah watched him climb the stairs. Even carrying the body of the pilot, he moved swiftly. Jonas was glad he hadn't had to grapple with the man.

Once Gilberto disappeared at the top of the Temple, the two of them hopped into the cart.

"That was too easy," Rebekah said.

"I can't believe he left the key in the ignition. Now if only we're as lucky when we get to the plane."

"Hold on a minute. I need to put the mask somewhere." She laid the case on the flatbed of the cart within easy reach in case she had to stop it from sliding. "Okay, let's go."

While Jonas steered the cart back the way they'd come in, Rebekah turned back to gape at the massive Palace at the end of main plaza, adjacent to the Temple of Inscriptions from which they'd just escaped. "We've really got to come back to Palenque some time."

"Yeah, well, we're not out yet. I hope we don't have any trouble at the gate."

Jonas suspected he might have been driving too fast by the way employees glared, but no one tried to stop him. Fortunately, they weren't all that far from the entrance Gilberto had brought them through. The short distance surprised him.

"Rebekah, remember how slowly Gilberto moved, how he was always delaying Raz? I bet it's because of Manuel. Gilberto's plan was to hold us here until Manuel comes."

"But Gilberto talked about Belize like he planned to go with us."

"Think back. All he said was 'we.' It could have meant who he was working for. And we know that's Manuel. He told us that."

"Manuel can't possibly get here that fast unless he flies."

"Do you really doubt Manuel has the resources to do that?"

Rebekah didn't answer.

A guard suddenly appeared, blocking the gate. Jonas slowed down, but only a little. "Rebekah, pretend you're having the baby."

She clutched her stomach. "Ohhhhhhhh!"

"This woman, she's going to have her baby," Jonas yelled at the guard in Spanish. "Move out of the way! I must get her to a hospital."

The guard's eyes bulged at the oncoming, speeding golf cart. Jonas thought for a moment he wasn't going to move.

"Aleja!" Jonas shouted.

The terrified guard jumped out of the way at the last moment, just before Jonas would have had to slam on the brakes.

He sped through the gate.

Rebekah continued to scream, one hand on the baby and the other in the flatbed gripping the case the mask was in.

"You can stop now," Jonas said.

"You almost killed that guy!"

"In a golf cart? C'mon. It wouldn't even have left skid marks on his back."

"That's not funny!" Rebekah held on as Jonas bounced over the uneven ground toward the makeshift airstrip where the pilot had earlier landed the plane.

* * *

Cancun, Mexico

Colin paced inside the motel entrance, thinking that he shouldn't have called Talasi. They should have left and maybe called an emergency number when they were well away from the motel. No matter what Talasi said, he would not wait for the police. He heard a noise and glanced around, paranoid. Please don't let anyone come to the desk until we're finished.

Talasi rushed in from the front door carrying her medical bag.

"Behind the desk," Colin told her. "Here, I'll help you."

Colin gave her a boost and she slid over the counter. While she crouched behind the front desk examining the manager, Colin crossed his arms and leaned with his back against the counter facing the lobby as if waiting for someone.

Too many weird things are going on, he thought.

Talasi stood up and tapped Colin on the shoulder. "I don't know what's wrong," she said. "He's just out cold. Pulse is fine, breathing is fine. No signs of trauma."

"Is there anything we can do for him?"

Talasi held up her hands. "Get him to a hospital, have them run tests. Things we don't have time to do. Fortunately he's alive."

"Agreed. We have other problems." Colin thought a moment. "Get Yan ready to depart. I'll call for paramedics and make sure they're no videocameras filming this. We don't want anything to connect us."

* * *

Vhorrdak put his sunglasses back on as he stole out of the motel room. This worked out far better than having to eliminate the internationals. Now that he understood who they were, he feared if he stopped them, his enemy would have already arranged for others to take their place. He had realized long ago that although he would never be omnipotent, he could still use his enemy's hope for these miserable creatures—and especially their free will—to work against the divine purpose. With their perpetual penchant to do the wrong things, Vhorrdak could frustrate his enemy's plan. And he would do that, here at the end.

This arrangement with Yan also meant he could now use Raz in a different way, one that allowed him to get around Raz's seeming need to be near the woman Rebekah. Raz would be reassigned to pursue the book and the book alone. Yan would replace Raz and be his agent to kill the baby.

Vhorrdak returned to the car and was seated when he saw the Native American woman come out the motel lobby and head for the room. He watched her slide her key through the key pad and go in. Vhorrdak put the car in gear and left the parking lot. Once the car was returned, he needed to get back to Iraq to manage the other end of the march toward Armageddon.

Chapter Fifty-One

Palenque, Mexico
December 20, 2012
9:25 a.m. local time

Time to Solstice: 20 hours, 46 minutes

Jonas pulled the golf cart near the aircraft, leaving enough room for him to pilot the Cessna away. He helped Rebekah into the airplane.

"Don't forget the mask," Rebekah said.

"Right." Jonas went back for it and placed the case in the back seat of the plane. He threw his pack in next to her. "The keys are here. It's our lucky day."

Rebekah was strapping herself in. "I would hardly call today lucky."

"If we can get to Ek Balam and retrieve this book, it will be."

Jonas climbed in the front seat and did a quick study of the panel. He pushed the propeller pitch control full in, the mixture control full in, and cracked the throttle rod slightly. He flipped the master electrical switch to 'on' and smiled as the instruments and radios came alive. Just as he remembered. He turned the key to the right, pushing in the throttle a little as he did, and the engine started.

"Now comes the really hard part," he told Rebekah.

"What's that?"

"Clearing the jungle." He set the flaps at ten degrees and shoved the throttle all the way in. "Hold on!"

The plane shot down the short runway, bumping as it went. Then landing gear came off the ground and the ride got smoother. The plane rose, but the thick jungle still lay straight ahead.

Not rising fast enough.

"We're gonna crash!" Rebekah screamed.

"No, we're not!" Jonas eased back on the yoke. The nose rose higher. Now he saw the green leaves of the top of the trees. Green won't get us to Ek Balam, Jonas thought. He pulled on the yoke as hard as he could. He prayed. The plane rose more. Jonas could now see over the trees to clear sky. It might work. It better work.

He saw the sky. He held his breath. He felt the landing gear skim the very top of the trees.

And then they were free.

Jonas eased in the yoke to level off the incline and breathed again. He took ten degrees off the flaps, and looked back. "We made it."

Rebekah gasped. "That was close."

"It's still our lucky day."

"Hold that thought," Rebekah said. "Look over there."

Rebekah pointed out her side where a helicopter flew into view. It looked to be headed for the same place they'd landed, but instead of descending, it continued to hover. The pilot turned the helicopter so it faced them squarely.

"Jonas, I think we have company."

* * *

Diega had hurried the helicopter as much as possible to Palenque, sure she and Manuel would get there in time but not wanting to take any chances. They had Gilberto's assurance that he would keep an eye on Raz Uris, and that he would keep Jonas and Rebekah safe until they arrived. Now, as she scouted the landing area, not only were there no aircraft there, one had just taken off. Manuel sat next to her watching the Cessna leaving Palenque airspace. He had his headset on so the two of them could talk.

"Who is flying that airplane?" he asked.

"No sé. I did not have time to look at them as we flew in."

"Nor did I. But I have a bad feeling that aircraft contains Rebekah. We should follow them."

Diega knew to trust her brother's instincts. She started to lift the helicopter out of the hover when she spotted someone below, running onto the makeshift airstrip and waving his arms. "Down there, Manuel. It's Gilberto."

Manuel leaned to the side to look out the window. "So it is. But if we stop, we may lose them. The have a head start and can go faster."

"Gilberto may know where they are headed."

The siblings stared at each, momentarily unsure what to do.

* * *

Rebekah loosened the straps on her seatbelt so she could turn completely around and watch the scene with the helicopter. It had started out of its hovering position to follow them, but now it descended to the ground.

"They're settling back on the airstrip," she said. Rebekah opened Jonas' pack and pulled out a small set of binoculars. "Jonas, they're picking up Gilberto."

"That's good. That'll slow them down a bit. We'd get there before them anyway, but every little bit of time helps."

"I don't think this will take them much time."

"What direction is Ek Balam?"

"Northeast. It has a small airstrip near the ruins. I remember that because we landed there when we went for the excavation. Do you think Raz kept a map in here?"

"Likely he did. I'd have one. Try looking in this pile of stuff between the seats."

Chapter Fifty-Two

Cancun, Mexico
El Hotel de Las Reyes
December 20, 2012
9:50 a.m. local time

Time to Solstice: 20 hours, 21 minutes

Talasi pulled smelling salts out of her bag. She shoved them under Yan's nose. No reaction. She had called Colin. She hoped he got here soon.

The door opened and Colin entered. "How's he doing?"

"Physically, he seems okay, but he didn't respond to the smelling salts."

"Try again."

"C'mon, Yan. Rally!" She shoved them back under his nose. This time he jerked.

"Amen," Colin said.

Yan, eyes half closed, jostled Talasi with his good arm. He pushed away the smelling salts.

"It's Talasi, Yan. Are you okay?"

"Yes. I think."

Colin knelt on the other side of Yan. "What happened?"

Yan's pupils were tiny, the size of a small inkblot. "I had dozed. Or it felt like I was dozing. Someone was here in the room. I remember thinking how much my arm hurt."

Colin glanced around. He got up to check the bathroom. "Someone was here?"

"Maybe not."

"Probably a dream," Talasi said. "The anesthesia could have induced it."

"Go on, Yan," Colin said.

"I heard a voice, a cold voice. It told me I could be whole again. Strong again. Able to defeat enemies. Did I want to be made whole?"

Talasi didn't want to sound worried, but now she was. Anesthesia was one thing, but her culture stressed the importance of dreams. Whether it was under the influence of her drugs or not, the dream state was still important. How Yan responded to the question might impact what she thought about the dream. "How did you answer?" she asked.

He paused. His eyes, which had been looking into hers, shifted slightly to a spot over her shoulder.

He does not want me to know the truth.

"My exact words, I do not recall," Yan said. "I feel that I must have answered as anyone would, after an injury like this."

Which was? Talasi thought.

Colin finished checking over the room. "There's no one here. It must have been a dream, like you said. We need to pull out. Now. Are you able to travel?"

Yan moved his shoulder and arm. He winced, but nodded his head. "Talasi did a good job."

She looked at him, watched the way he moved. Something didn't feel right, but she wasn't going to deny his assertion that she'd fixed him up well. "Then we should go. I'll put my supplies back in the bag."

Colin helped Yan to his feet while Talasi packed up her instruments. The group gathered their few possessions. Yan worked with one hand.

He left the room first, Colin behind him.

Talasi glanced back into the room as she turned off the light. She frowned. What had happened in this room while she and Colin were gone? If it had just been Yan who'd been out, that would have been one thing, strange dream or not. But the manager had displayed the same weird symptoms. Yet, he had not responded and Yan had.

It was puzzling. She would have to think on this.

* * *

Mexican airspace
Between Palenque and Ek Balam
December 20, 2012
10:00 a.m. local time

Time to Solstice: 20 hours, 11 minutes

Rebekah pulled out a straight-edge ruler along with the map she'd found when rummaging between the seats. Per Jonas' instructions, she drew a line between Palenque and Ek Balam to estimate the distance and give them a more accurate sense of direction. She'd known Ek Balam was northeast of Palenque, but Jonas needed a proper vector along which to point the aircraft. Otherwise, he had said, they could miss the ruins.

Of course, it didn't help that Jonas was glancing every few seconds at her clumsy effort. The few times she'd flown with him before she hadn't paid attention to his map. She was fairly sure he'd done it all ahead of time.

"How's it coming?" he asked.

"It would help if you'd stop watching me."

"Sorry, but I need that information quickly. The farther we stray off the right vector the harder it'll be to correct. If I were more familiar with Mexico, I'd feel better about navigating solely from the air. But I'm not."

Rebekah played around with the ruler, gauging the distance. "Looks like it's about 400 miles."

"That's about three hours. What about direction?"

"I'm guessing again, but it looks like about a twenty degree angle from north."

"That's good enough."

Rebekah watched as Jonas rolled the yoke a little to the left, and pushed on the pedals with his feet. She felt the aircraft moving to the left. She looked out the window and could see them headed a little more north of where they'd been headed.

Jonas set the heading bug on the directional gyro to twenty degrees. "That ought to do it."

"Maybe you should check the map over. Make sure I did it right."

"I was looking over your shoulder. I would have said twenty degrees, too." He took her left hand in his and kissed it. "You're my co-pilot in every way."

How could he be so relaxed? she thought. Then she realized, he's bluffing for my sake. "Thanks. We're going to get out of this okay, aren't we, Jonas? You, me, and the baby?"

"We're doing fine so far."

Rebekah was quiet for a moment. "What about the helicopter?"

Jonas turned around and looked back. "I don't see it. Gilberto thinks we're going to Belize. I'm hoping that's where they're headed."

"Could they follow us without being seen?"

"Sure. Especially if they have contacts on the ground watching for us."

"That's not reassuring."

"I know. But I got a look at their helicopter. This Cessna can outfly it. If they're out of sight, and we continue to make a hundred and thirty-five knots, we'll be about twenty minutes ahead of them by the time we land."

"That may not be enough time, not if they know where we're going."

"We've got more problems than that if they know where we're going. They're likely to have another Gilberto looking for us."

Rebekah felt anxious at the thought. It hadn't occurred to her until Jonas mentioned it. The baby kicked inside her. She wasn't sure if the baby was reacting to her sudden rush of worry, or if he would be kicking anyway. He was an active child. Sometimes she wondered if he was a little too anxious to be out in the world. She put her hand on her belly where he kicked and massaged the spot. Your daddy won't let them get us, she thought, aiming it at the baby. The kicking continued for maybe half a minute, then stopped.

"How will we avoid being seen? I don't exactly blend into crowds." Rebekah said it quietly, as if by doing so the baby wouldn't hear it.

"My guess is, if they have someone there, his mission'll be the same as Gilberto's. Watch us. Let us do what we're there to do, but don't let anyone harm us. Then hold us until Manuel can get there."

Rebekah looked down at the Mexican topography they were flying over. Small dirty brown villages cut out of lush green jungle. Off in the distance to her right she could see the ocean. She thought back to what she'd allowed Raz and Gilberto to believe, that the next clue pointed to Xibalba and Belize. "Jonas, what if the book isn't at Ek Balam? What if it's just another clue?"

Jonas shrugged. "We'll figure that out when we get there."

Chapter Fifty-Three

Palenque, Mexico
December 20, 2012
10:02 a.m. local time

Time to Solstice: 20 hours, 09 minutes

Gilberto ducked under the rotating helicopter blades and climbed into the cabin behind Manuel and Diega. He put on a headset.

"Who was in the aircraft that just took off?" Manuel asked.

"Jonas and Rebekah, but Raz is not with them."

Diega knew Manuel would ask more about Raz, but she had a more pressing concern. "Where are they headed?"

"Belize."

"Really?" She rolled some power into the throttle and waited for the main rotor blades to spool up. The eased the nose over slightly and the craft lifted off the ground to a hover. As she pushed slightly forward, the helicopter picked up speed and altitude. Once in level flight, she brought the throttle back to cruise power. Thc advantage the helicopter had over the airplane was that it could safely fly at a much lower altitude, saving climb time.

"Where is Raz?" Manuel asked.

"He is down in Pakal's tomb with his pilot. I locked the gate before I left, but soon they will make enough noise that someone will discover them. Especially now that Palenque is open for visitors."

"How did Jonas get the aircraft?"

"My fault. I didn't think they'd run from me. They took the cart and got to the airplane after I'd taken the pilot to the tomb. I didn't know either of them could fly."

"Jonas seems able to do anything," Diega said. "He makes it difficult to keep track of them." She paused. She could see the aircraft, but it was a speck heading away from them at a high speed. "But he is not headed to Belize."

"That is what Rebekah said they needed to do."

"My guess is that she lied to you. Belize would be east." Diega pointed to the magnetic compass. "Jonas flies mostly north."

"What she said sounded truthful. She even showed me the ancient Mayan symbols she discovered. But you know I cannot read Mayan ..."

Manuel cut Gilberto off. "She copied the message and showed it to you?"

"Yes, but now I think she must have made it up to fool Raz and me …"

"Don't be so sure," Manuel said. "Rebekah is clever, but if she took the time to write it on a piece of paper, my guess is that a message was truly there. She probably misdirected you in its meaning, however."

"What exactly did she say? Can you remember?" Diega asked.

"She showed a symbol and told us the book had been taken to the mouth of the underworld, Xibalba. She said tradition holds that the location for Xibalba was in the underwater caves of either Belize or Guatemala. That is what I thought, also. Am I not right?"

"Yes," she answered, "but one is east and the other is southeast, and they are not going either way."

"Rebekah herself said it was east, at Caves Branch."

Manual paused, considering the possibilities. Then he squinted at Gilberto. "When she first talked about it, did she use the words, 'mouth of the underworld' or did she call it Xibalba?"

Gilberto had to think. "What is the difference? I believe she said 'mouth of the underworld.' It was I who interpreted that as Xibalba. But they are both the same."

"Yes and no, my friend. But you have nonetheless provided the location where they are headed. They are going to Ek Balam." Manuel looked at the speck in the distance. "Can we get there ahead of them?"

"No," Diega said. "And we may well be an hour behind them when they land."

* * *

Cancun, Mexico
December 20, 2012
10:30 a.m. local time

Time to Solstice: 19 hours, 41 minutes

Colin pulled the car into a petrol station and parked it at a pump near the dirty, non-descript convenience store. He turned to Talasi in the back seat and handed her some cash. “We need directions and a map. Use your Spanish on the clerk and see what you can find out.”

Talasi tapped Yan on his good shoulder. “You need anything?”

“A new arm.”

“I’ll see what they have in that section of the store. How about some bottled water or a Powerade? You’ve lost quite a bit of blood. You need to keep drinking fluids.”

“Whatever you think best.”

“Colin?”

“Water’s fine.”

Talasi went into the store while Colin filled up. About the time he finished, Talasi was back out with drinks and a map. “The attendant says Ek Balam is a relatively new site. We go into Valladolid and then turn north. It’s along the coast.”

“Did he say how long it would take us to motor there?”

“The roads aren’t that good. Two and a half hours. Two, probably, if you drive the way you usually do.”

Colin smiled. “Only fast enough to avoid the authorities.”

They got back into the car. Talasi had handed Yan the Powerade she’d bought him, forgetting that he would need help opening it. But as she leaned forward, he shifted the bottle into his right hand, gripped it, and spun the cap with his left. Talasi was surprised. The movement had been done gingerly but naturally. Yan hadn’t even winced. Was that unrealistic?

No, she decided, it was possible. Yan was in tremendous shape, and recovering from a bullet wound like that in his shoulder wouldn’t affect his hand and grip strength. This was all perfectly normal.

She hoped.

Chapter Fifty-Four

Syrian Desert, Iraq
December 20, 2012
Dusk

Time to Solstice: 19 hours, 22 minutes

Vhorrdak stood on a rocky outcropping overlooking the desert. The wind had been active most of the day, but now it was dying down. The temperature had also dropped. It was cooler, but hardly cold. Vhorrdak liked the desert. He loved its searing heat in the day. And at night, the coolness of the desert felt refreshing. For short periods of time.

For two hours now Vhorrdak had been watching the highway that ran through this pass on the way from Nowheresville to Syria. Several beat-up commercial trucks hauling freight through Iraq had gone by. There weren't many on this deserted stretch of highway. And none of them was particularly interesting. They all looked alike to Vhorrdak. He was waiting for a particular truck. It wouldn't look any different either. Vhorrdak was counting on that. What he'd seen so far made him confident his followers had done an excellent job in that regard.

Ten minutes ago a cloud of sand appeared in the desert to the north of Vhorrdak's position. The sand stirred up ahead and settled down behind, the signs of something advancing. Vhorrdak expected it to be the truck he'd been waiting for. It was not on any known road, and it came from the north, headed toward the highway. Very few commercial vehicles would attempt that. Vhorrdak was confident it could only be a truck engineered to survive the nasty conditions encountered on a cross-country trip through the Syrian Desert. A truck that had special modifications, including powerful filters with a twenty-four hour capacity to remove the dust and sand from the air before any made it to the engine.

Vhorrdak lifted the Leupold scope to his eyes, using the binoculars he'd taken off the dead spotter. He checked the commercial truck now in sight, rolling up out of the sands. Good. The vehicle looked exactly like every other one that had gone by him during the time he'd been standing there. He couldn't be more pleased. Who would guess what special cargo it carried? Not the Americans. He was fairly confident of that. He was keeping them distracted with other vehicles, more like the ones they were expecting.

The truck braked as it reached the highway. The driver checked for any activity on the road. There was none, and the driver made the slow turn, pulling the non-descript truck onto the highway headed west. An hour down the road Vhorrdak knew the driver and his companion would encounter a sign that told them Syria was six hundred kilometers from that point. That was Vhorrdak's next destination. He wanted to make sure all went well at that location, too.

Chapter Fifty-Five

Airspace over Ek Balam, Mexico
December 20, 2012
1:05 p.m. local time

Time to Solstice: 17 hours, 06 minutes

Jonas debated when to wake Rebekah. He was fairly certain they were approaching Chichen Itza, but there were a lot of ruins in the north central part of the Yucatan peninsula, and he needed her to determine which was which.

"This son of yours doesn't want to let me sleep," Rebekah groaned. "He's thumping against the top of my ribs."

"I'm glad you're awake. We're getting close to Valladolid, and Ek Balam is north of it. That's Chichen Itza, isn't it?"

Rebekah looked at the ruins they were skirting. "Of course. You can see the Pyramid of Kukulcan from here."

"We've passed a number of ruins with similar pyramids. I wanted to be sure. Why did the Maya have so many small communities?"

"It was the way their society formed. The Maya really weren't empire builders at first. They existed in small groups, each ruled by their own nobility. The people had a common religion, but most were content to have their own dynasties. They built alliances through intermarriage among the nobility."

"Was it the Spanish that brought them down?"

"They had disintegrated somewhat before that. Warfare toppled the Classic Period of the Maya. Most scholars feel that for whatever reason, warfare went from raiding parties that captured sacrificial victims to standard operating procedure. Once they abandoned the arts and invested in building up arms, their civilization came crashing down. I would pause here for you to note the parallel in today's world, but you know how I feel."

"For the most part, I agree with you. But countries have to be able to defend themselves. It's when 'defense' becomes an excuse for toppling regimes that I have a problem."

Rebekah searched around for the map she'd looked at earlier. She compared it to what she saw below and then pointed. "Jonas, there's Ek Balam."

"I don't see any real place to land. A helicopter could set down, but not a plane. There's a short, flat strip over there, adjacent to the property. It looks like agricultural land. But it's short. If we miss, we're going straight into jungle."

"What are our alternatives?"

Jonas gripped the controls. "We don't have any."

She wrapped her hands around the baby inside her. "Then I suggest we pray."

* * *

Ek Balam, Mexico

Talasi and Colin stood in the shadows of "Las Gemalas," twin identical temples just inside the Ek Balam site. It had only taken them an hour to drive from Cancun. The temples stood side by side and each was constructed from stones. Each had a wide central staircase that led from the ground to a large rectangular room, now in decay. Colin estimated The Twins to be about six meters tall and forty meters long at the base. The temples faced east into Plaza Sur, the southern-most of the cities' two plazas. Talasi and Colin had positioned themselves in the area between the two temples, where they could look out onto Plaza Sur in one direction, and southwest toward the archway through which all visitors passed. Yan sat several feet away from them, his arm still in the sling, his back leaning against a stone temple wall.

Talasi glanced at Yan, who appeared to be asleep. She didn't necessarily believe he was and kept her voice low just in case. "What if Yan is wrong and it's not Ek Balam?" she asked Colin.

He shot her a look. "I'll ask you again—do you have a better idea?"

Talasi went silent. She didn't seem to trust Yan anymore. Her distrust had been a sudden thing. Colin hoped he was wrong, that he was misreading her.

"Not to worry," Colin said. "Something will happen.

"I wish you would stop saying that. Your 'somethings' haven't exactly been good lately."

Colin didn't dispute her point.

Talasi pointed in the air. "Have you been watching that airplane?"

"No, I've been looking at the faces of people coming in. Though I will say, there haven't been many of them."

"Look at it. I think it's coming in for a landing."

"Here?" Colin stared at where Talasi was pointing. He began to follow it, shading his eyes from the sun. Talasi was right; it was coming down. "Is the pilot nuts? He'll crash into the jungle!"

"That's what I was thinking. It's the mark of a desperate person."

Ahh, that was her point. "And you're wondering who would be so desperate?"

"Any one of the people we're watching for would be that desperate."

* * *

Jonas braced for the abrupt landing, the non-retractable, stiff landing gear touching down on the bumpy makeshift runway. He'd pulled up on the flaps and dropped the nose to make as steep an approach as practical so his rollout would be short. He was coming down now and all that was left was to bring the airplane to a stop as soon as he cleared the jungle vegetation, which mercifully was not as tall as that at Palenque. Rebekah gripped the armrests of her seat.

They hit the clearing with a thud. Rebekah screamed. Jonas was too busy slamming his feet on the brakes and shutting down the engine to scream. His head hit the top of the cabin as the plane bounced along the uneven dirt. The landing gear plowed through small, scrappy brush growing out of the once-cleared land, jostling the aircraft. But most alarming to Jonas was that they were rushing headlong toward lush green jungle at the end of their very short runway. Rebekah tromped on the duplicate set of brakes on her side of the cabin beneath the instrument panel. "Stop, stop!"

In spite of his somewhat jaded viewpoint, Jonas prayed.

Green leaves filled their view from the windshield. The aircraft slowed as it mowed down some low grass. They stopped just short of plunging into the jungle.

Jonas felt his heart pounding in his chest. He made the engine sputter to a stop. He turned to Rebekah. "Are you okay?"

She was flushed and panting shallowly. "I felt a contraction."

"You're certain it wasn't the landing?"

"No, it was a contraction."

They sat in silence for a moment. Finally Jonas said, "False labor, I hope?"

"We can hope."

"Do you want to go on?"

Rebekah laughed at the situation. "Do we have a choice? Can you fly the plane out of here?"

"We might, if I can turn the plane around. There isn't any damage."

Rebekah shook her head. "We've attracted enough attention with this landing. Let's just get to the ruins and find this book. Manuel and Diega may not be far behind."

* * *

Talasi and Colin watched the plane drop out of sight. They heard the engine noise stop, but there was nothing that sounded like crumpling aluminum.

"What do you think?" Talasi asked.

"I think I'm glad we drove in from Cancun. But they're probably okay."

Tourists and employees alike had stopped to watch the close approach, but no one seemed interested in investigating.

"I'm going to check it out," Colin said. "You stay with Yan and keep watch. Remember, we don't want Jonas or Rebekah or anyone with them to see us first. We just watch. Our goal at this point is to do whatever we can to protect them. They have a destiny. We can't inhibit it without jeopardizing the very reason our families were chosen in the first place."

"You don't have to lecture me," Talasi answered.

"Sorry." He made his way between the temples until he was behind them. Then he took the path leading to the entrance. Talasi watched him disappear from her view when he entered the archway.

She heard a noise behind her and turned to see Yan stand up. He didn't appear to be struggling or making grimaces as he moved his injured arm for balance. He came up next to her.

"At least Jonas and Rebekah will be easy to spot," he said. "Not many tourists here."

"Uh-huh." Talasi took a step back away from him. "How's your shoulder, Yan? You stood up easily."

"It's feeling better," he said.

"Good," she said. "Good."

But she wondered at the speed by which he seemed to be recovering.

Chapter Fifty-Six

Ek Balam, Mexico
December 20, 2012
1:45 p.m. local time

Time to Solstice: 16 hours, 26 minutes

Jonas considered himself fortunate neither Raz nor Manuel had thought to take his wallet from his backpack, otherwise they'd be forced to beg or try to steal their way in. The wallet contained plenty of pesos—Jonas usually tipped a lot in Mexico because of the poverty—which meant they could pay cash and not rely on a charge card. He didn't want to be tracked any more easily than he figured he was being tracked. Since he was being sought by the authorities, Rebekah bought the tickets.

"Got any thoughts on how you'll get the mask past the guards at the entrance?" Jonas asked her.

She shrugged. "Tell them I bought it at Palenque?"

Jonas laughed. "Worth a try. Good thing you know some Spanish. That'll probably help."

The guards proved easier than Jonas thought. They looked inside the case to make sure there were no weapons, but they displayed little interest in the 'fake' artifact. In retrospect, it also probably helped that Rebekah was pregnant and struggling with both her Spanish and the case. No one paid much attention to Jonas. They searched his climber's pack and let him go.

Once past the guards, Jonas took the case from Rebekah. "I can't believe how much progress they made since I was here last," she said. "I wish we had more time. I'd like to go back to the South Plaza and see the Oval Palace. I spent most of my time there."

"We don't have time." Jonas pointed to the huge building ahead of them. It was a massive structure, like a huge ancient hotel. The ground floor was over three times as long as the building was high, and the height had to be a hundred feet or more. The building had five levels, but the third, fourth, and fifth formed a kind of pyramid on top of the second level. A very long staircase led from the bottom to the top in the center. "That's the Acropolis, isn't it?" he asked.

Rebekah nodded. “The places they’re excavating are under the thatched awnings. See the one to the left of the staircase? That’s where we’re headed. The mouth of the underworld.”

The thatched roof ran the entire left side of what Jonas would have called the building’s fourth floor. Jonas hoped they didn’t have to descend into the tomb as they had at Palenque. It would be a long climb to get up there, and Rebekah had already had a tiring day.

Jonas shaded his eyes and tried to see under the awning.

“The Witz Monster guards the entrance to the tomb of Ukit Kan Le’k Tok’,” she said. “Can you see the teeth that run along the bottom?”

Jonas could see a large number of rectangular, upturned ‘teeth’ spaced along the monster’s jaw. “I see them. They’re so white.”

“They’re stucco. This site is unique in that aspect. Most of the sculptures are made of stucco, not carved from stone. If the Maya hadn’t buried the Acropolis, everything here wouldn’t be so well-preserved. Stucco is fragile. Let’s keep moving. I want to get this done.”

But as Jonas helped her up the staircase, he noticed she moved slower, not faster. This is so hard on her. And we don’t have a lot of time.

Once they got onto the fourth level and under the thatched roof, Rebekah seemed to revive. “It feels so much better to be out of the sun.” She led him along the pathway until they reached a stucco façade inside the open jaw of the ‘monster.’ The elaborate façade was adorned with hieroglyphics and life-sized statues of the Maya.

Jonas was less interested in the monster and more interested in the dead king. “Where’s the tomb? In here?” An opening stood in the middle of the façade behind the rough stone column Rebekah described as the nose of the monster.

“Yes, in the second of the two chambers.”

They passed through the opening, through the outer chamber, and then into the inner chamber. “This is where Ukit Kan Le’k Tok’ was buried,” she said. She walked a bare space comparable to a walk-in closet. Jonas thought the tomb was small considering it was built for a king. Still, it seemed a little more spacious than where Pakal had been buried at Palenque.

While Rebekah checked the inner chamber, Jonas stepped into the outer chamber. Passageways went to the right and left, but both came to abrupt halts in small rooms with benches built into the end walls.

Jonas returned to the tomb. "Do you know what we're supposed to be looking for? We didn't get much of a clue at Palenque. Are we supposed to use the mask?"

"I don't know. Help me lay down."

Jonas put the pack down so he could help Rebekah sit and then lay down in the center of Ukit Kan Le'k Tok's tomb.

"Hand me the mask," she said.

He dutifully unpacked it. "I assume you've noticed there's no top to the tomb. You can see daylight through the hole in the roof."

"Yes, I know that. The capstone was removed some time ago. We might be screwed if the clue is on it. Owwww!"

"What's wrong?"

"Another contraction. Let me breathe a minute. It'll pass." She pulled up her knees to take the pressure off her back. She breathed.

"Are you sure you're going to be all right?"

"I'm only at eight months. This has to be false labor."

After a few minutes, she asked for the mask again. Jonas handed it to her.

She looked up, turned to the right and to the left. "There aren't any markings that I can see."

He looked back through to the opening of the façade and thought. He weighed everything he knew about what had brought them to Ek Balam.

"Wait a minute. The clue at Palenque referred to the mouth of the underworld, right? The mouth is the clue."

Chapter Fifty-Seven

Airspace approaching Ek Balam, Mexico
December 20, 2012
2:10 p.m. local time

Time to Solstice: 16 hours, 1 minute

Diega slowed the helicopter as she approached Ek Balam, looking for a place to land. She spotted Raz's aircraft, which was at one end of a short patch of ground with jungle on either side. She had to assume Jonas had used it as an airstrip. She pointed to the plane. "I believe that is the aircraft we have been following, no?"

"It is," Gilberto confirmed. "I have ridden in it many times working for Raz."

Manuel, disturbed by Gilberto's admission, sputtered. "You have worked for Raz?"

"Please, Manuel. You know what I do. In my work I have been employed by many people. He had actually employed me at Palenque. It was why I had his trust. My allegiance here is with you, but you know I will work with others again."

"Probably not Raz."

Gilberto laughed. "No, not Raz. Betrayal comes with a price. I will be watching my back for some time after this."

Diega settled the helicopter onto the rough ground near the plane. "This will block any attempt to leave before us."

She shut down the engine and the rotorblades slowed to a halt. The three of them unbuckled themselves and got out of the cabin.

"Come," Manuel said, "we must hurry."

* * *

Jonas stood with his back to the façade that guarded the entrance to the tomb, thinking. What represented a mouth? The lips and the chin were the outside parts; the jaw, the tongue, the teeth, and the gums as the inside part. Of all of those, only one fit here. The teeth. But did he need to be outside viewing the front side of each tooth or where he was now, inside the mouth viewing the backside of the teeth?

He put the mask to his face and looked through the strange, jeweled eyes. After being momentarily disoriented, he was able to focus on a single tooth. Hieroglyphics appeared. He didn't understand them, but they were there. He pulled the mask back and looked at the tooth unaided. There were blemishes on the backside of the tooth, but only through the eyes of the mask did anything meaningful appear.

"Rebekah, look at this." He handed her the mask.

She looked through it, then handed it to him and walked over to the tooth.She knelt down to examine it. "Wow."

"You saw the hieroglyphics?"

"I did. It's remarkable how they were able to do that. You can't detect that there's any discernable message unless you use the mask."

"Do you know what it means?"

"No. How many teeth are there?"

Jonas counted. "Eight across the front, two on each side of the jaw. What about these that line the entrance?"

"Let me check," she said. She put the mask to her eyes and examined each tooth. "The only glyphs are on the eight across the front."

Jonas retrieved his pack and pulled out a notebook. "Here, copy them down. You're sure you don't know what they mean?"

She glanced over them one more time using the mask. "This is going to require a lot of translation. I can't do this alone."

Manuel, Diega, and Gilberto stepped out onto the path from the stairs.

"Then let us help you decipher it," Manuel said.

Chapter Fifty-Eight

Ek Balam, Mexico

Jonas stepped quickly in front of Rebekah, protecting her. He slid the notebook and pen into his pack, shouldering it. "Stay back," he said.

Manuel remained motionless. "We are on your side."

"What do you want from us?"

"Jonas, you have to recognize …"

"WHAT DO YOU WANT FROM US?"

Manuel hesitated, uncertain. He looked to Diega for help.

She shrugged. "The truth, Manuel. We must persist in the truth."

Manuel retrenched. "We have not lied to you, Jonas. You and Rebekah are destined to be the parents of the King who will guide us through the coming age. If he is not born, and if this Book of the Thirteen Gods is not found, the world will have no hope."

Rebekah moved out from behind Jonas' back. She was holding onto Pakal's mask. Tears streamed down her face. The mask shook in her hands.

"Listen to yourself," she said, her voice filled with frustration. "You're a scholar. Do you know how ridiculous this sounds? Jonas and I, we're ordinary people. And we're not Mayan. I can't give birth to a Mayan King."

Diega put her hand on Manuel's arm to stop him from responding. "I understand how difficult this is for you, Rebekah. We, too, have had to accept roles that defy logic in order to help this prophecy become a reality. As to your question, I will give you the same answer we gave your husband. Kukulcan was never depicted as being Mayan. This King is the answer to prophecies made to peoples from all over the world."

Rebekah gave an ironic laugh. "Now you sound like the three who kidnapped me."

Jonas heard a noise behind him. Past the Witz monster façade was the entrance to another room. Because so few tourists were at Ek Balam that day, he hadn't considered that someone else might be up on the fourth level. But now he heard the shuffling of boots. "Rebekah, back into the outer chamber."

She did as he asked. Jonas did likewise, keeping one eye on Manuel while he tried to form a triangle with the unknown threat.

Before he could look, Rebekah said, "Jonas, those three are here, too."

He glanced from Manuel to the people who'd held Rebekah captive. He recognized them from the private airstrip in Cancun where they had to prevent them from boarding Raz's plane to Palenque. "What do you want?" Jonas asked.

"My name is Talasi," said the woman. "This is Colin and Yan." The three held up their hands to indicate they had no weapons. Yan put up his lone good hand. "We wish you peace. We heard what you said. We're here to help, too. To offer protection, just like we told Rebekah."

Jonas considered their chances of escape. Not good. They were on a ledge on the fourth level of the Acropolis. One group was to the left, one to the right. Behind them was the tomb of the Mayan ruler. Ahead of them—well, it was a long jump down.

His only hope was if they could truly be trusted, if they meant no harm. He would have to test it.

"If all of you want to prove you don't mean us harm, let us go. We'll leave you the mask. You can read the message."

Everyone was silent for a moment. Jonas wondered what other options he had if this gamble didn't work.

Manuel cleared his throat. "It is not that simple, Jonas."

"I DON'T CARE, MANUEL!" Jonas took a step toward him. "You say you won't harm us. Demonstrate that."

Jonas took Rebekah by the arm. Watching that the other group didn't advance, Jonas moved toward Manuel, pulling Rebekah along. He took Pakal's mask from her hands and laid it in front of Manuel. "Here's the mask. We're leaving now."

Rebekah resisted Jonas' pull to leave. "The glyphs are on the eight teeth along the bottom of the mouth, Manuel. There are a lot of them. Directions to the book, I think."

Everyone began to crowd in, trying to persuade them to stay.

Jonas had enough. "STAND BACK!"

They all took steps backward.

Jonas felt a sense a relief as they did. "If you're serious about not harming us, you'll let us walk away."

They fell silent.

Chapter Fifty-Nine

Ek Balam, Mexico
December 20, 2012
2:45 p.m. local time

Time to Solstice: 15 hours, 26 minutes

As they made their way down the Acropolis, Rebekah was a bundle of emotions. But the one emotion that overwhelmed her was love. Great love. Love for Jonas. He had a mental toughness that, if anything, exceeded his physical strength. In the face of tremendous odds, he'd gotten Colin, Yan, Talasi, Manuel, Diega, and Gilberto to back down. They'd stood aside as he guided Rebekah past them on the fourth level of the Acropolis. His backward glances seemed to keep them at bay as the two of them descended the staircase.

Rebekah suspected that Manuel and Diega were now using the mask to decipher the clues left behind by ancient Maya. In some ways, her intellectual curiosity was still engaged. She tried to remember what she'd seen and puzzle out its meaning. But as they headed across the North Plaza toward the Ball Court, she knew she had to let it go.

"I love you so much," she said.

"I wasn't sure you'd think it was a good idea."

"I admit, there's a small part of me that wonders if we're doing the right thing."

"Of course we are. Those people are nuts. Although, the fact that they're letting us go is a positive sign for them."

"What about the book?"

He stopped. "Do you really care about it that much?"

His voice betrayed his hurt. She realized he'd risked having to battle his way out, and to have her question it …. "Not as much as I care about you. It's just that I thought you said it was our ticket to getting out. You're still wanted by the police."

Jonas straightened. It was almost as if he'd forgotten about his predicament. "I say we take our chances with the American Embassy in Cancun. I can explain I had nothing to do with the hotel's collapse."

Rebekah felt something hard and sharp in her loins. She bent over at the waist and groaned involuntarily.

Jonas dropped the pack and clutched her. "What is it? Another contraction?"

"Uh-huh." She breathed shallowly and felt a wetness on her face. She thought it was perspiration but then realized she was crying. She couldn't control her emotions. "Jonas, what if we have the baby now, and what if they make it out to be this King?"

Jonas was silent for a moment. He took her hand. "What we'd always planned, Rebekah. We'll be the best parents we can, however he turns out."

For several minutes they held onto each other. When Rebekah felt no more contractions, she said, "We should go."

"If you feel up to it."

"I feel as good as I'm going to. Are we being followed?"

"No. I've been watching. None of them have followed us, and the tourists don't seem to be taking any notice."

"That's good."

Jonas slung the bag onto his back. They walked through the Ball Court and were behind the Twin Pyramids when another thought hit Rebekah. "What about the aircraft? We don't know that it'll fly."

"I agree. I've already thought of that. We don't have time to fool around. Fortunately we're close to Valladolid and we have money. We'll get a taxi. From there we'll find a way to Cancun."

Once again, Rebekah felt grateful that he was with her and seemed in control of their situation.

They exited the Ek Balam site and scouted for a taxi. None seemed to be there.

"We'll have the ticket booth call for one," Jonas said.

"No, you won't."

Rebekah recognized the voice immediately and knew that trouble had found them again.

She and Jonas turned to face three people—Raz Uris, his pilot, and the driver of the car when he'd originally kidnapped her. "Not you!" she said.

Raz sneered. "Thought you'd seen the last of me, didn't you?"

Chapter Sixty

Ek Balam, Mexico

Jonas didn't have a chance to react before Raz's Glock appeared. He pointed it at Jonas.

"I hoped we'd seen the last of you." She crossed her arms over her chest. "You're not with Mossad."

"I used to be."

Jonas tried to relax his mind. He'd been in a lot of tough situations over the last thirty-six hours. Thirty-six hours! Had it been that long?

Focus, he told himself. Look for opportunity. Trying to make as little movement as possible, he flexed his knees. He wanted to be balanced on both legs, ready to fight if necessary.

Raz caught the movement. "Throw your backpack over to the left, and then don't move. I'll shoot you if I have to."

Jonas did as he asked, staring at the Glock. "I'm not going anywhere."

"Good. But Rebekah is. Come here," he told her.

"No." She hooked her arm in Jonas'.

Raz nodded to the two men. "Get her."

Jonas didn't think either of the men with Raz had a weapon. In some ways it was just like the situation at Pakal's tomb. Except there, Gilberto had been on his side. One glance into the hardened faces of the two men told him neither was likely to be another Gilberto. In particular, the pilot seemed to be angry at him.

Jonas started to move Rebekah behind him to keep the men from getting her.

"I wouldn't do that," Raz said. "It doesn't matter to me if you live or die."

Jonas stopped. In some ways he thought Raz was bluffing—if his life really didn't matter to Raz, he'd probably be dead by now. Raz must have some uncertainty. But should I take that chance?

When Jonas hesitated, Raz told the men, "While you move toward her, make sure I always have a clear shot at Jonas."

The pilot hung back. The other man approached Rebekah from the side.

Rebekah gave Jonas' arm a squeeze. "I'll come," she told Raz.

"Don't, Rebekah."

"I won't see you die, Jonas. Don't make me live with that image." She stepped away from him.

The second man grabbed her arm and pulled. She resisted. The pilot circled around behind them. Raz still had a clear shot at Jonas. The second man began to ease Rebekah away from Jonas. Then he turned and sucker-punched Jonas.

Jonas thought he was ready for about anything but he wasn't. The pain of the blow bent him over at the waist. The pilot kicked him in the groin. Jonas fell sideways, gasping.

"That's for stealing my plane," the pilot said.

Jonas tried to stand but the pain made him roll over and throw up. He lay still on the ground, trying to get his breath back. He forced his mind to stop focusing on the pain.

When he finally stood, the men were gone, and they'd taken Rebekah.

* * *

Manuel stared at the three unknown internationals. The woman had identified herself to Jonas as Talasi and the other two as Colin and Yan. Rebekah knew them.

They looked at him with equal puzzlement.

"So, what are you doing here and how do you know Rebekah?" Manuel asked.

Colin spoke up. "As we said, we're here to protect her."

A British accent. Interesting. "Protect her from what?"

Talasi said, "You brought up the kingship of her baby. You should know there are people who do not want him to be born. We are here to make sure the birth takes place and to be witnesses to it."

They'd used the word 'him.' "And who gave you that job?"

Colin shook his head. "First, tell us who you are and why you are pursuing the baby."

Manuel considered how much to reveal. These people seemed sincere, but was their true allegiance to the king?

Diega interrupted his thoughts. "Manuel! I get it. I know who they are now."

"Who are they?"

"We do not have the time. They are here to protect Jonas and Rebekah, as they said, and we need to let them do that. It is for us to stay behind and obtain the clues to the book."

"What is this book you are all talking about?" Talasi asked. "Rebekah had some clues in the Mayan language …"

"Again, in time, all will be explained. For now, hurry after them. Once we know the location of the book, we will explain all to you."

Yan moved first. He passed them on the ledge in front of the façade and advanced to the staircase. The others followed. Gilberto did not.

While Manuel did not understand Diega's sudden willingness to trust them, he knew that if she had a reason, he should have faith in that. In the meantime, Jonas and Rebekah were unguarded. "Go on," he told Gilberto. "Stay with them. They may need your help. They do not understand this thing we fight."

* * *

Jonas staggered in the direction Raz had taken Rebekah. A wave of nausea hit him and he fell to his knees. He threw up again. He struggled to his feet but couldn't fully straighten. Head bent, he shuffled toward the airstrip.

He heard the sound of a helicopter starting and tried again to hasten his pace. The next thing he knew a black helicopter flew overhead. It headed south, in the direction of Valladolid.

Jonas continued to tramp toward the airstrip. He wasn't certain he was in condition to fly, but he needed to make the effort. Then again, if he could get it going, did he have the time to follow them? Was Raz taking Rebekah to Valladolid or somewhere else? By the time he got in the air, would they have already landed somewhere? It was hard to think.

He heard the sound of people running toward him. Jonas spun to face them, the movement almost setting off another vomiting session. But he stood his ground. He would fight to stay alive, to get Rebekah back.

Gilberto was the first person he saw. Behind him came the three who kidnapped Rebekah. He had to hope they were sincere when they said their mission was to protect Rebekah and the baby.

Gilberto stopped well out of fighting range. "What happened?"

"Raz was here with two other men. They jumped me. They took Rebekah." He pointed into the sky.

The Chinese man muttered something. The Englishman said, "Shit."

Jonas thought for a moment about his own condition and whether he could fly. "How did you get here?" he asked.

Colin said, "We have a car in the car park."

Gilberto said, "Diega flew us here in a helicopter."

"We need that helicopter. Where are Manuel and Diega?"

"They are translating the hieroglyphics," said Gilberto. "I'll go get them." He ran back to Ek Balam.

"I don't have time to wait," Jonas said. "I'm going to the helicopter. If they left the keys, I'll fly it."

Gilberto ran back to Ek Balam.

"I think we should wait for them," Colin said. "You're hurt and you look beat. Are you in any condition to fly? When was the last time you slept?"

When had he slept last? Jonas tried to remember. A couple of hours, maybe, in the plane to Palenque. Before that, a half hour in the car on the way to Manuel's *palapas* in Valladolid. He might have slept an hour after they got to the *palapas*, but nothing more.

"It doesn't matter. I have to find Rebekah."

Everyone knew he was in pain, but no one tried to stop him. Talasi, Yan, and Colin followed as he loped to the clearing.

Jonas saw the helicopter in middle of the short airstrip, effectively blocking the aircraft from using the runway. He worked his way across the nearly barren ground, almost tripping over scrappy roots that littered the rough terrain. He reached the helicopter and yanked open the door. Climbing in made him wince.

"Jonas," Colin said.

Jonas ignored him. He tried to start the engine.

Nothing.

"Jonas, you're not going anywhere." Colin said.

Jonas slammed the door back and got out. “Why not?” He smelled the acrimonious odor of jet fuel.

Colin pointed to the ground under the gas tanks.

Someone had cut into the tanks. Fuel seeped into the dry ground.

“Shit,” Jonas said. He kicked the fuselage.

Chapter Sixty-One

Syrian Desert, Iraq
December 20, 2012
300 km from the Syrian border
11:00 p.m. local time

Time to Solstice: 15 hours, 11 minutes

Vhorrdak peered out from behind the lip of the cave that hid him from view. He re-confirmed that the smaller truck he'd arranged to accompany the commercial truck to the Syrian border was still waiting. It sat along the side of the highway just past the sign which marked the distance to Syria. He was glad he could find weak minds in this area of the world willing to do his work and believe it was for good, that they would be rewarded eternally for it. He could find them in the Western world, too, but they generally wanted money. Vhorrdak ducked back into the shelter of the cave and returned to the fire he'd built using dead scrub from the surrounding area.

Vhorrdak stared into the flames. His plan was coming to fruition, but not without its difficulties. Damn Pakal for having envisioned the end of this age but keeping it hidden. Vorrdak hadn't even heard the rumors about the Book of the Thirteen Gods until after Pakal had died. Impenetrable secrecy surrounded it. The book's existence was confirmed by Chilam Balam, but the great prophet could only tell Vhorrdak in what manner it would be found. The clue is in the shadows of the Pyramid of Kukulcan, two days prior. And so Vhorrdak had waited, waited for the end of the age and the appearance of the woman who would give birth to his enemy.

However, it was all coming together. Raz would soon have the Book of the Thirteen Gods and the king would die at the moment of vulnerability, now that Vhorrdak had planted the instrument for the king's death within the group loyal to the woman. In the end, with the book as his blueprint, he'd have his final victory watching the people of the earth destroy themselves. Evil triumphs over good, at least in this world where mankind rules. He laughed at the flawed creation of his enemy. Yes, he would savor this victory.

Vhorrdak sensed the time was getting close for the arrival of the commercial truck containing the nuclear cargo. He left the shelter of the cave once more to check on the waiting truck. He discovered he was just in time. Through the darkness he could see the glow of the headlights of both trucks. Fareed's commercial truck slowed as it passed the smaller vehicle. The smaller truck, which would serve as one final distraction, pulled up behind it. There were no other vehicles to be seen. The duo picked up speed and disappeared into the distance.

Everything was proceeding as planned.

* * *

"You see the vehicle has closed in behind us," Fareed told Ashur.

Ashur turned in his seat and verified that the vehicle off to the side of the road when they'd arrived was now behind them.

"That is the vehicle which picked up the cargo we left in the cave. When we get to the border, you will see how all this works."

Ashur nodded, and Fareed was relieved. So far the ruse was working. He didn't know how things would go at the border, but improvision was one of his strong suits.

Chapter Sixty-Two

Ek Balam, Mexico
December 20, 2012
3:25 p.m. local time

Time to Solstice: 14 hours, 46 minutes

Colin was glad the Durango he'd rented was large enough to hold six passengers, because anything smaller would have been cramped with Manuel, Diega, and Jonas having joined them. Gilberto had been left to deal with the aircraft and the helicopter.

As they left Ek Balam for Valladolid, Colin drove and Talasi in the middle seat with Yan on the other side so she could tend to him if needed. In the back seat was Jonas and Colin with Diega wedged in the middle. Manuel and Diega conferred about the hieroglyphics they'd found at the mouth of the Witz Monster at Ek Balam. The rest were quiet, allowing the two to work. Colin thought Diega's laptop must have one hell of a battery. He'd never seen her charge it up.

They'd driven about fifteen miles when Talasi asked, Do you havc anything yet?"

Diega just sighed.

"Not much. It is a long set of hieroglyphics, but once we get it, I think it will take us directly to where the book is hidden."

"I am convinced this is the final location for two reasons," Manuel said. "First, the instructions are complicated and extensive. Second, the solstice is tonight. That does not leave us much time. And the book is destined to be found."

"I keep replaying the scene over and over again in my mind, how they took Rebekah," Jonas said. "I don't know what I could have done differently, other than fight to the death."

"Mate, you can't beat yourself up," Colin said. "If you were dead, you wouldn't be here working on how to find her again."

"Colin is correct," Manuel said. "You are an important part of what is going to happen. And you said, did you not, that Rebekah gave herself up, rather than have you fight against what she felt were impossible odds?"

"She did, but she's my wife …"

"To have a warrior spirit is good," said Yan, "but fighting to the death would have had no honor if your wife were no better off. You still have life to continue the fight. Rebekah saw this when she chose the path she did."

Diega looked up from her laptop. "Whatever reasons Raz had for taking her, she cannot be harmed as long as the baby is inside her."

"I'm not a believer yet, but I sure hope Raz is one."

"In time," Manuel said, "you will also come to believe."

Chapter Sixty-Three

Valladolid, Mexico
December 20, 2012
8:00 p.m. local time

Time to Solstice: 10 hours, 11 minutes

As a city, Valladolid had its charms, but this house wasn't one of them. The place Raz owned was a one-story shotgun shack with one bedroom and one bathroom, not a property he visited often. He'd bought it from the family of a shopkeeper who'd died unexpectedly. What he sought was a place in the center of the Yucatan where he could make deals for stolen Mayan artifacts without a lot of oversight. In a large coastal city like Cancun, where he had his gallery, his activities might attract too much attention.

Furnishings in the little house were minimal. The floors were tiled and cold, with tiny rugs throughout. The solitary bedroom had one small bed with mosquito netting draped over it. The first time he'd stayed in the house, he'd gone to bed without a net; now he never did. Sleep was ncarly impossible without one.

Rebekah lay in that bed. He only needed to look at her to know she was uncomfortable, the rustic conditions having little to do with that. She was uncomfortable because she was having contractions.

Raz was inexperienced with childbirth and wasn't certain what to do. He sat in a chair next to her and used a damp washcloth to wipe her face. She breathed shallowly.

She put up with him while the contractions were going on, but was less tolerant when they subsided. She caught him by surprise and smacked the washcloth out of his hand. It landed across the room.

"I keep telling you, I'm not as bad as you think." Raz stood up and retrieved the cloth. "I only want the book. Cooperate with me."

"I don't know where the book is."

"But you and Jonas were on your way out of Ek Balam. You must have read the clue."

"We were leaving Ek Balam because we left the clue and the mask for the others to figure out. Jonas and I just want to get back home."

Raz leaned against the wall. "Well, that's not going to happen. Tell me what the clue said."

"I saw it, but I didn't read it. It was long and complicated. The only thing I remember is a warning that the father alone can retrieve the book."

"The father of the baby."

"I guess."

"Your baby."

Rebekah sat up in the bed. "No! Not my baby! My baby is not what people think it is!"

Raz was tired of being yelled at. Plus, he suspected Rebekah was telling the truth. She really didn't know where the book was. He left the bedroom and walked into the kitchen looking for Pablo. Pablo sat at the table playing games on his cell phone.

"Any movement yet from Manuel's house?" he asked Pablo.

The man answered him without looking up. "I just talked to the driver minutes ago. Nothing."

"He didn't drive into the village, did he?"

This time Pablo turned in his seat. "Of course not, senor. That would be too obvious."

"Good." Raz could just imagine how conspicuous a strange automobile would be in Manuel's neighborhood of *palapas*. "Is he on foot, then?"

"In a manner of speaking. He is staying with someone in the village."

"Willingly or unwillingly?"

Pablo laughed. "Does it matter, sir?"

Raz returned the smile. "No, I guess not."

"Have you been able to obtain the information from her you wished?" Pablo nodded toward the bedroom.

Raz began to pace. "No, I don't think she knows it."

"How do you wish to proceed?"

"Patcanul is in the same position we are. He needs the book, too."

"What is taking them so long, then?"

"Rebekah said the clue was long and complicated. Perhaps they are having trouble deciphering it."

"Or perhaps not."

Raz stopped pacing. Was that possible, that they would decipher the clue, but wait for him to reveal himself first? "I suppose it's possible that they are waiting for us to make a move."

"How much time do you wish to allot them?"

"Before what?"

"Before we go in and take the clue from them."

Raz stared out the lone window in the kitchen. How long?

The small courtyard that he shared with the next house was just outside. Though the neighborhood was far from grand and though his neighbor had little money, he tended the courtyard like it was a prized garden. One of the fruit-bearing trees planted in the courtyard was a papaya. In the moonlight Raz could see the football-sized fruit dangling from it. Patience was required with papaya. It needed to be somewhat yellow before picked, then allowed to ripen indoors. Picked too green, the fruit would not ripen inside. But if one waited too late, the birds would eat it first.

Patience. He would give the good professor a little more time. At the very least, he wanted to be certain the clue had been deciphered before he stepped in.

"This is a delicate situation," Raz told Pablo. "I think we will wait him out. If Rebekah is telling the truth, our best course would be for them to find the book, and for us to steal it from them. They understand the Mayan mind better than we do."

But in the back of his mind was the reality that if he hesitated too long, Vhorrdak would step in. He could not let that happen. That he had Rebekah was both a blessing and a curse. Despite his protestation to Vhorrdak, she was vitally important to him. To allow Vhorrdak to learn that would undermine his own plans.

Chapter Sixty-Four

Valladolid, Mexico
December 20, 2012
11:21 p.m. local time

Time to Solstice: 6 hours, 50 minutes

Colin marveled at the number of modern things Manuel and Diega had packed into their little hut. The siblings worked on a computer with high speed access to the internet. Colin had tuned into CNN International on a high-definition television—a smallish one, but high-def nonetheless. Now he was tired of watching the same three headline stories play over and over.

Yan rested on a bed behind Colin. Talasi examined his wound. Yan had insisted he was fine but yielded to the doctor. Jonas slumped on a couch, trying to sleep. Colin could see he was tired but wasn't sure how much rest Jonas was really getting. At least he looked more comfortable since Manuel had replaced Jonas' tuxedo with a T-shirt, trousers, and training shoes.

Talasi finished the examination. Yan went into the bathroom.

"How is he?" Colin asked.

She sidled close to Colin. "Better than he should be," she said under her breath.

"Isn't that good?"

"I've never seen a wound heal quite so fast." She sounded like this was not a good thing. "But it means Yan will be at the birth."

Before Colin could ask her why she wasn't happier at Yan's condition, Manuel and Diega began to talk excitedly between themselves.

"We have it!" Diega announced in English.

Jonas almost leaped from the couch. Talasi and Colin followed him to the computer. Yan exited the bathroom and joined them.

"What does it say?" Talasi asked.

Diega referred to her handwritten notes. "There are four parts of the final clue. The first part gives us a marker. 'Along the coast upon a hill/where lives a tree shaped by man/for a man shaped by a tree'."

"The tree is clearly a ceiba," Manuel interjected. "Of course, there are lots of ceiba trees shaped like crosses, and lots of hills near the coast."

"So we have to look at the second part," Diega said. "'A new star lights the entrance/below, an arch stands guard/a stone unknowingly marks the spot/with unintended significance'."

Colin felt he was beginning to pick up on parts of this. "The new star could be the comet. It's what brought us here."

"Very good, Colin. We think so, too," Manuel said. "And if the entrance is on the hill, then it could mean it's in a cave."

Colin thought about it more. "But what about the arch and the stone?"

Manuel and Diega shared a look of frustration. "I suspect we will not know until we get there," Manuel said.

Talasi pointed to Diega's notes on the yellow legal pad she'd been using. "You said there were four parts. What does this one say?"

Diega reached out and touched Jonas' arm. "The last part makes it clear Jonas will be the one to find it. 'Dig deep and answers will be found/by the favored father's hand/by him alone can it be touched'."

Jonas pulled away from Diega's touch. "Our baby is not your king." His shoulders bunched up as he said it.

Then his voice quieted. "And ... as I've said before, I'm not sure I'm the father." He turned away from the group.

Diega got up from the computer., "You are the father the baby will know. It is enough."

Colin wasn't sure how to take this, that Jonas was not sure he was the father. Had Rebekah had an affair? What did this mean for the prophecy? Had he, Talasi, and Yan made some kind of error? Diega, at least, seemed certain this did not present a problem.

Jonas stood several feet away, his back to them. His hands were clasped behind, his right holding his left wrist. He stood that way for at least a minute. No one knew what to say.

Finally Manuel crossed the room and stood in front of Jonas. He put his hand on the man's shoulder. "Now we come to this, Jonas. You have heard the clue. We believe you are the one. Where is the Book of the Thirteen Gods?"

They waited for a response. Colin felt the tension.

Jonas lifted his head. A grim smile played on his face. He looked Manuel in the eyes. "I know where it is, but I won't help you. Not until I get Rebekah back."

Chapter Sixty-Five

Syrian Border Checkpoint, Iraq
December 21, 2012
7:30 a.m. local time

Time to Solstice: 6 hours, 41 minutes

When the soldier asked Fareed in American-accent Arabic for his papers, it set him on edge. American soldiers at the checkpoint were unusual these days. He knew his cargo was nothing more than sandstone, but still he had to act exactly as though it were the nuclear weapon, or else Vhorrdak would know the truth. He suspected Vhorrdak was here watching from somewhere. The demon would view this as being too important to leave unattended.

Fareed glanced in his rear view mirror. "Yes. Let me get them." He rummaged around in his cab, despite that he knew exactly where the papers were. He needed to buy at least a minute of time. Per the original plan. "Ashur, where did you put them?"

The comment startled Ashur. His dark eyes looked at Fareed with confusion.

Fareed understood Ashur's puzzlement. He'd never let the roughneck touch their papers. And he'd never shared with Ashur that they needed to stall at the checkpoint.

"They are … here … are they not?' Ashur asked. He pointed to a spot beneath Fareed's seat.

So Ashur had been paying attention to the papers. What else had he been paying attention to? Unconsciously Fareed checked the pocket of his jacket, where he had stored his note with the GPS coordinates for the cave.

Fareed returned to the deception. "Not those papers, the others."

Ashur appeared to be confused. "Those are the only papers I know of."

Both Fareed and Ashur turned each way in their seats, looking around. Finally, Fareed said, "Perhaps you are right. These must be the papers." He reached under his seat and pulled them out. "Ah, yes, these are the ones." He handed them to the American soldier.

Ashur exhaled. His shoulders relaxed.

The American soldier looked them over and handed them to the Iraqi inspector. "They appear to be in order. Your call."

The Iraqi inspector appraised Fareed and Ashur. "These say you carry automobile parts."

"Yes," Fareed said.

"I'll need to look at them."

Fareed had hoped it wouldn't come to this. He had hoped the truck might go uninspected. Now they would have to play it out the hard way.

He checked his rear view mirror again. The second truck, the one which he'd met on the way here, was now in sight two spots behind him. He felt sorry for the driver of that vehicle. Likely the man had also hoped it would not come to this. But, the assignment had been accepted. The man's family would be well-compensated.

"Will this take long? We must have this cargo to the port in just a few hours," Fareed said.

"It will take only a moment if you have what you say you have."

The inspector backed away. Fareed got out. Ashur remained inside with a worried look on his face, which he'd had since the inspector mentioned automobile parts that most certainly weren't there. Fareed shrugged as though it were a mere formality, trying to put his fellow driver at ease. Ashur would need it for what was coming next. The prime directive had been to get the cargo through the checkpoint to Syria.

Fareed moved to the rear. Before he passed out of sight of the following truck, he wiped his forehead with his right hand. Then he moved to the rear and unlocked the doors. He swung one door open and climbed inside.

And dove behind the unopened, reinforced door for protection.

The explosion ripped through the through the cars and trucks in line, stopping just short—as calculated—of doing major damage to Fareed's truck. The Iraqi inspector, wounded in the explosion, drew his gun. Fareed peeked out from behind the closed door and shot the inspector in the head. He jumped down from the truck and kicked the body out of the way. He peered around the side of the truck.

The American soldier, knocked off his feet by the explosion, struggled to get up. Fareed aimed his gun, but Ashur, now in the driver's seat, stuck his Glock out the window and killed the soldier. Fareed lobbed several hand grenades into the compound. The gatehouse blew apart. Chaos ensued in the compound.

Fareed climbed into the passenger side of the truck and slammed the door shut. The truck chugged forward, gained momentum and smashed through the gate at the checkpoint, sending the few remaining soldiers at the gate fleeing, even as they shot at the bulletproof glass on the truck.

Within minutes, the truck was on the Syrian roadway headed through the desert on its way to its ultimate destination on the Mediterranean Sea coast.

Chapter Sixty-Six

Washington, DC
The Situation Room, The White House
December 20, 2012
12:45 p.m. local time

Time to Solstice: 6 hours, 26 minutes

Jim Harrington strode to the Situation Room trying to shake off his sleepiness. Earlier he'd sat on a couch in his office, reading intelligence reports off his laptop. But then he'd dozed off. He couldn't remember what he read. The last few days had felt like a blur. A nightmarish blur.

The straight-backed Major Simmons preceded him down the hall. It had been the major who'd awakened him and advised him they needed him immediately. Jim had the impression the news was not good, or at least mixed. Simmons was tight-lipped and wouldn't reveal anything.

As usual, there were few in the room. Only the Information Specialists at the controls and General Culver at the mahogany table. Jim wished it was General Archer waiting for him, not Culver. Another thing he'd fit in earlier in the day had been a visit to Archer at Walter Reed Medical Center. Clay hadn't looked so good.

Culver didn't look good either, but for other reasons.

"What is it?" Jim asked.

"An IED went off at a Syrian border checkpoint. At least one truck got through uninspected."

"The nuke?"

"We hope not. We're still tracking the other truck through the Zagros Mountains. It'll be at our ambush point soon."

Jim tried to gage the situation. There was something they weren't telling him. "But you don't expect to find the nuke in the mountains, do you?"

"No."

"Why not?"

"It was more than just a car bombing. Hand grenades were thrown at the compound, and the driver of the truck rammed the gate at the checkpoint to get through."

Jim shook his head. "Not a good sign."

"No."

"This could become an international problem. Do the Israelis know about the Syrian border breach?"

Culver nodded. "The President has advised them."

"The President knows? How did he find out?" Jim made the implication in his voice clear. He was supposed to be running the show here. He should have been the one to advise the President.

Culver sat across from Jim, tongue-tied.

Simmons spoke up. "What General Culver would like to say, but not have it go any further from this room, is that we believe someone on your staff, sir, contacted the President."

Jim looked up at Simmons, standing behind Archer, to his left. Having spoken, the Major now stared straight ahead, at attention. Jim was annoyed at the implication. The only person on his staff who even knew the President well enough to get a meeting was Travis Black, his assistant. And Travis would never do that.

Or would he?

Jim couldn't detect anything in Simmon's eyes other than were bloodshot. What caused him to say that? What information did he have? It must have been persuasive, for Culver to let him say that.

Or had Culver known? At times, when Simmons displayed an independent streak, Culver had registered surprise.

Jim would question Travis later. He returned to the problem at hand. "What are the Israelis doing about it?"

Culver seemed more ready to talk now. "For the moment, they're waiting for us to supply them with more intelligence. But you can rest assured that Mossad is on it."

"They'll want to invade. Stop the nuke, if there is one." He paused. "How long before you know about the other truck?"

"It's now morning in Iraq. We have forces all over. We think we'll find them within two hours."

Jim contemplated that amount of time. “If the nuke isn’t in the Zagros Mountains, it could be anywhere in Syria by then. It could be getting close to a Syrian port to be shipped … anywhere.”

Culver nodded. “Like Iran.”

Everyone was quiet.

Jim said, “If the Israelis invade Syria …”

Culver shrugged. “Let’s just say it would be very, very bad.”

* * *

Valladolid, Mexico

Raz hurried out of the kitchen. In the pocket of his jeans, his cell phone buzzed. He needed to be by himself before he answered it. He suspected who it was.

The way the shotgun shack was laid out, Raz couldn’t reach the solitude of the living room without going through the bedroom. Rebekah glared at him as he entered. Raz noticed she did not appear to be experiencing contractions, which was something of a relief. It was still hours before the solstice, and he needed to find the book first.

He closed the door behind him and entered the living room, passing by a couple of paintings he’d bought at the Mercado de Artesanias and slapped on the stucco walls. He dropped onto the less-than-comfortable couch.

The only important thing right now was to learn who was calling him and why. He pulled the cell from his pocket and checked the caller ID. Restricted. That usually meant only one person.

“Hello?”

Raz experienced the same strange sensation that he had with every call from Vhorrdak, of words forming in his mind rather hearing a voice. Sometimes Raz wondered if Vhorrdak even needed a damn phone.

“I have it under control,” he assured Vhorrdak.

“But you do not have the book yet.”

No guess work there. He’d have called Vhorrdak if he had the book. “No, but I have the next best thing.”

“No, you don’t. You have the mother.”

How did he know that? "Yes, I have the mother. I'm using her to get the father."

"You have an interest in her."

"I'm telling you again, no. I have no interest in her or the baby. Only the book."

"You have no choice now. I am pulling you off the second part of this assignment. Your task ends with finding the book."

What was Vhorrdak saying? "You act like you want this baby to be born. I thought you wanted it dead. And you're not even in Mexico ..."

"I have given this task to someone else. Someone better placed to handle it."

Vhorrdak was silent. Moments like this made Raz shudder. "I don't understand."

"It is not yours to understand, only to do as I say. If it is necessary for you to kill to obtain the book, Jonas, Manuel, the Brit, and the Native American woman are fair game, but no one else. Do not fail me."

More silence. Raz filled the silence. He hated it when he did that with Vhorrdak. "I won't fail you."

"Of course not. You understand the consequences, do you not?"

The phone call ended abruptly. Raz closed his cell. He was worried about this new turn of events. About how much Vhorrdak guessed of his plan, and how much he really knew.

And he wondered why any of the internationals were still alive. Vhorrdak had said he'd take care of them.

* * *

Valladolid, Mexico
Manuel's *palapas*

Colin was alarmed at the standoff between Jonas and Manuel. It had been fifteen minutes since Jonas announced his conditions, that Rebekah must be rescued before he would reveal the location of the book. Manuel fumed, but Jonas wouldn't budge.

"Please listen to reason," Manuel said, trying again. "Once we have the book, we will know where the baby is to be born, and then we will know where they will take Rebekah."

"That's not reasoning, Manuel. I'll say it one more time. Our baby is not your King. But if you rescue Rebekah, I'll see this quest of yours through, to find the book, however crazy I think it is."

"How do you propose we find Rebekah?"

"I don't know. That's not my problem. You're the one with the resources."

Colin noticed that Diega had fallen asleep on the lone couch. How could she sleep with all this arguing going on? Colin had given up trying to watch the Military Channel, even though he loved American television.

"If we had the resources you think we have, we would know where Rebekah is right now. I notified my connections immediately after Raz had left Ek Balam with Rebekah. But he was clever. He flew in circles and switched helicopters once. We don't know where he landed."

"He's watching you. You said your own people are sure there's a spy here in this neighborhood. Find the spy and get the information out of him."

Colin couldn't stand it anymore. "Jonas, even if they could find this guy, do you really think he'd just yield the information? How naïve are you, anyway?"

Jonas he spun on his heel and headed toward the bathroom. "Not my problem," he said, disappearing.

Manuel blew out a breath.

Colin came up next to him. "I have a suggestion."

"Go ahead."

"Let's flush them out. We take Jonas somewhere. We know we're being watched. They have to follow."

Manuel considered the strategy. "Will they bring Rebekah? We must have her, or all of our efforts are for nothing."

Colin looked at his watch. "The baby will be born in a bit less than five hours. They know it, too. Until the book is found, none of us know where the birth will take place. They can't afford to leave her behind."

Manuel paused for a long time. Finally he said, "It might work. Where do we do this?"

Colin shrugged. "You tell me."

Manuel thought. "We are close to Chichen Itza. The prophecy started from there, and I can get us in. And yet, I do not know. Should I have a special feeling that tells me I am correct?"

Colin pondered the question. "Special senses, I don't know about. But I bloody well love the idea of it being Chichen Itza. The search for the book detours back to where we started. That sounds to me like the kind of thing the ancients would have loved. Let's do it."

Jonas came out of the bathroom. Colin looked up to see suspicion flash across Jonas' face. He realized that he and Manuel were huddled together as though they were telling secrets.

"What's going on?" Jonas asked.

"We have an idea," Colin said, "and we need your cooperation."

Chapter Sixty-Seven

Valladolid, Mexico
December 21, 2012
12:08 a.m. local time

Time to Solstice: 6 hours, 03 minutes

Raz sat in the front room staring out the window. The full moon gave light to the two squalid houses across the street. Shotgun shacks like his own, but beat down. One had an ineffective security door guarding the entrance, with rusting iron bars in a bent metal frame that hung askew from the door. The thick top hinge was no longer attached. The second house had a screened front door, also ineffective, with large holes in the screen that Raz guessed had been punched through. So far from the courtyard, he could no longer smell the sweet fragrances of the tended garden. In the front room, the stench of decaying trash littering the street prevailed.

Raz would have gotten up, but he felt paralyzed by his conversation with Vhorrdak. He struggled to decide what to do.

Pablo spoke, surprising Raz. Though the man usually made enough noise for three people tromping into the front room, he had apparently slipped in.

Raz glared at him. "What did you say?"

"I said, they've left Manuel's house."

He lurched out of the chair. "When?"

"A few minutes ago. My man alerted us as soon as he could."

"Which direction did they head?"

"West."

The destination seemed to leap out at him. "Toward Chichen Itza."

"Yes."

Raz checked his watch. "It's early yet. Why are they headed there? Surely the book isn't back at the place where they started. Why would the ancients do that?"

"I don't know."

"It could be a trap."

Pablo stood there, rooted in the spot. "Should we go?"

"We don't have a choice. Get the car. I'll get Rebekah."

Pablo went out the front door. Raz's car was parked on the street in front of the house.

Raz ran into the bedroom where the pilot was watching over Rebekah. "Let's move," he told Flyboy.

"What about her?" he asked.

"She has to come. We don't know where she's supposed to give birth yet. We need the book to tell us, and we may not have time to come back."

"But she's our bargaining chip."

"Don't argue with me. Besides, I have an idea."

Rebekah, eyes half closed with exhaustion, struggled to sit up. "What makes you think I'm going with you?"

"You don't have a choice. You could try to fight, but there are more of us. And I'm taking you to where your precious Jonas is, anyway."

A glimmer of hope flashed in her eyes. Good, thought Raz, that will make this easier.

"But you lie too easily. Why should I believe you?"

Raz threw up his hands. "I don't have time for this, and neither do you." He went to pick her up and noticed how sweaty she was. Had she been having more contractions or was it just the heat?

"Bring her along," he said, motioning to Flyboy.

Raz left the bedroom and entered the kitchen. He hurried to his uniquely-stocked pantry. Unlocking the door, he opened it and began gathering a few special items he would need to successfully extract the Book of the Thirteen Gods from Manuel's hands.

* * *

Colin drove Manuel's car along the 180 motorway. Jonas sat in the passenger seat, his open climber's pack on the floor in front of him. Jonas has an odd way of dealing with stress, Colin thought. For as nervous as Colin himself was, he expected Jonas to be even more so. Instead, Jonas displayed little emotion as he methodically wound the rope from his pack into an orderly circle. Then he shook it out and did it again. "Careful, mate, you'll fray that thing if you keep playing with it," Colin said.

"It only makes it more supple," Jonas said, dispassionately.

The man is cool, I'll give him that, Colin thought. He wondered how Jonas planned to use the rope, or if this was just a nervous habit.

Colin's own nervousness stemmed from the fact he wasn't quite sure about Manuel's plan. "I've never been to Chichen Itza," he said, making eye contact with Manuel in the rear view mirror. "You're sure we can defend against them if we hole up in this Temple of the Warriors? With Yan's arm in a sling, I'm our only sharpshooter."

"I may surprise you," Manuel answered.

Yan puffed himself up. He sat between Manuel and Talasi in the back seat. "I can fight and shoot with my other hand," he said.

"Shoot, maybe," Talasi said. "I'm not so sure about fighting. We can't afford to have that wound reopen."

"I am a warrior."

'Well, I'm not," Talasi said. "And I've never handled a weapon."

"Never?" Colin was dismayed to hear her confession. "Not even a knife?"

"I'm good with a scalpel."

"A scalpel is not all that different from a knife."

They zipped along the motorway in silence after that. The moonlight painted the countryside in blacks and whites and grays, dulling any sense of color. Road signs told Colin they were approaching Chichen Itza. He feared the quietness was a sign the team was less than confident, despite Manuel and Yan's assertions and Jonas' calm. The team needed confidence if this mission were to be a success. Colin sent an unspoken plea up to his ancestors. A grand gesture of assurance would be a good thing right now.

Instead, Manuel broke the silence. "Everything will come together. You will see when we get there."

If that's assurance, Colin thought, it's a small one at best.

Chapter Sixty-Eight

Highway 180, Mexico
Approaching Chichen Itza
12:43 a.m. local time

Time to Solstice: 5 hours, 28 minutes

Talasi had watched men and women die before, but not because she'd performed a malicious act on them. That thought occupied her mind as she stared out the window. She could see the comet from this side of the car. Must I be prepared to take a life as well as bring a new one into the world? She wondered if was really any different than withholding food from a dying, comatose patient. And yet she knew it was.

Manuel pushed a button and spoke into his cell phone. "We have left the highway and are on the way to the Chichen Itza entrance. How far behind are they?"

He listened. "Diega says they may be as little as two minutes behind us. Let me just review the layout once more. We'll push through the entrance and down the path to the archeological zone. Straight ahead of us will be the Pyramid of Kukulcan. You all know what that looks like. A few hundred feet beyond it is the Temple of the Warriors, a large, rectangular building built in tiers. If necessary, we can seek shelter amid the columns that line the North Colonnade, which is adjacent to the Temple and somewhat closer to the Pyramid. We must move swiftly to set up at the Temple when we arrive."

"How far is Diega behind the second car of Raz's men?" Colin asked.

"Five minutes. She could be closer to them, but she does not want to forewarn them of her presence."

Talasi had to admit that the plan had been reasonably well-thought-out for something Colin, Manuel, and Diega had thrown together so quickly. Diega had slipped out of the *palapas* and, from a place elsewhere in the village, monitored what happened after Colin had driven out. Diega had uncovered two vehicles following. Now, she trailed behind. If all went as planned, she would recapture Rebekah. If Diega didn't … well, Talasi didn't want to consider that.

She went back to her morose thoughts that she might have to kill someone.

If it came to that, could she do it?

* * *

Flyboy drove the dark sedan with reckless abandon. Raz, sitting next to him, could see the speedometer. His comfort level was being pushed to the brink. Flyboy often pulled wide into curves, veering onto the other side of the highway. So far it had not been a problem since the road was not well-traveled this time of night. Raz almost reminded him that he was not flying an airplane. But speed was a necessity, so for the moment he let it pass.

The air in the vehicle hung heavy with the sounds of Rebekah's breathing. Raz had instructed Pablo and Flyboy to place her in the back as carefully as they could, but despite Raz's continued insistence fighting would do no good, Rebekah fought anyway. He admired her spunk. He wondered if the boy inside her had the same fighting spirit.

"She's in labor," Pablo said, sitting next to her in the back seat.

Tell me something I don't know. "I've heard some women labor for a long time, especially if it's their first kid," Raz said.

"She makes me nervous."

"Deal with it. How far behind them are we?"

Raz heard Pablo tapping buttons on his cell phone. Moments later the cell phone beeped.

"We are about five minutes behind the professor and Jonas."

"How far behind them are …?" He couldn't remember what Sedan Driver and Electric Goon's real names were.

More tapping.

"They are within two minutes. They could get closer but they do not wish to risk being seen."

For once, Sedan Driver and Electric Goon were making smart choices. But Raz needed to be closer to them. It was time to crab at Flyboy. "Can't you drive any faster?"

Chapter Sixty-Nine

Chichen Itza, Mexico
December 21, 2012
1:00 a.m. local time

Time to Solstice: 5 hours, 11 minutes

Manuel locked the gates to the main entrance behind him as the five of them hurried into the archeological grounds, moving like wraiths under the moonlight. Manuel's goal was to get them to the Temple of the Warriors, a huge rectangular structure guarded by rows and rows of upright stone pillars. A long staircase in front of the Temple led to the top. If they could get to there, they'd have a tactical advantage, with places to hide and the ability to survey the grounds their pursuers would have to cross. But he feared they had little time to reach it. Raz and his thugs were too close. The locked gate might slow them, but Manuel worried it wouldn't hinder Raz enough.

They jogged down the path that led from the entrance to the ruins. The five of them were silent, except for Manuel's heavy breathing. They burst onto the main plaza, the massive Pyramid of Kukulcan straight ahead of them with the Temple of the Warriors behind it, when the first shot was fired from behind.

Colin reacted immediately. "Bloody hell! They're aiming for me!"

Manuel wondered if Colin wasn't right. The sound of the bullet ripping through the air seemed to come from somewhere above Colin's head. But it made sense. "With Yan injured, you're the only one with firearms experience," he answered.

"Scatter!" Colin ordered.

Manuel knew their plan was in tatters. They would not reach the Temple. The five of them spread out, making themselves more difficult targets. They raced, zig-zag fashion, across the grounds toward the Pyramid. Manuel worried about Yan's injury and how fast he could realistically run without being able to move his shoulder, but Yan was apparently inspired by the threat of death. He might beat us all to safety, Manuel thought.

"They have rifles, two of them," Colin shouted.

That was bad, Manuel knew. On such short notice, his friends in Valladolid had only been able to come up with two handguns. They were Glocks with limited range and few rounds left in their magazines. Colin had one of them, Manuel the other. But if Raz and his men had rifles, they might never get close enough for Colin or Manuel to use them. Manuel understood—Colin had drilled it into him—that every shot must count.

Yan, Talasi, and Jonas had shared the three hunting knives Colin brought from Britain. Even one-handed Yan had manipulated his with ease, but man-to-man combat was his specialty. Talasi and Jonas had reacted stiffly to theirs.

Bullets nicked the ground around them as they ran. Manuel feared at least one of them wouldn't make to the shelter of the Pyramid.

Even lugging his climber's pack, Jonas reached the massive structure first with Colin immediately behind him. They were at the southwestern corner of the Pyramid, the point which faced the entrance. Once they reached it, the two seemed to blend with the blackness of that side of the Pyramid, hidden from the moonlight. But Manuel knew they hadn't stopped running. They were still exposed to the shooters until they reached the southeastern point. All of them would need to round the back corner to be in cover, at least temporarily.

Yan reached the Pyramid next and also became invisible. Manuel and Talasi reached the Pyramid last. The two of them raced along the edge of the ancient ruin, breathing hard. They turned the corner. Temporarily in cover behind the Pyramid, they paused to catch their breaths.

"We … must keep going," Manuel said. He spotted Yan rushing toward the large stone columns in front of the Temple. Ahead of Yan was another figure, also running. But only one. Either Colin or Jonas was not in sight.

Talasi bent over and spat into the grass, heaving. She looked as if she would throw up.

"I can't … go on," Talasi said, gasping.

"Take my hand."

Manuel reached out with his fingers. Talasi didn't move.

"We've got to do this now … while there's no gunfire." Manuel grabbed her hand and pulled her with him. Together they lurched toward the columns.

And then Talasi tripped over a rock and went down.

* * *

Chichen Itza, outside the Main Gate

Raz had sent his men into Chichen Itza with Pablo in charge. That was not optimal, but he couldn't leave Rebekah with any of them. She was in labor. Not hard labor yet, but labor nonetheless. If all went as predicted, she wouldn't deliver for another five hours, but so many variables were involved. He needed to make sure she was protected.

At least his men had experience killing before, more so than Manuel's group, he thought. Flyboy in particular had a mean streak and was out for revenge from Jonas, who had stolen his plane.

Raz contemplated the makeup of Manuel's team with surprise. As he suspected from Vhorrdak's phone call, the internationals were still alive. At least he'd been fairly certain he'd seen them disappear beyond the gate about the time Flyboy pulled into the parking lot. That distressed him. What the hell was going on? He considered that perhaps one of the internationals now played into Vhorrdak's plans. If so, then he would not rule out killing any of them, despite Vhorrdak's warning. He needed to be in control of the situation. The only suggestion he'd made to Pablo was to take out the Brit first, since he was a soldier and maybe used to killing.

Raz heard shots and recognized they were from rifles. He didn't think Manuel's group had firearms with them. Raz was pleased with the light the full moon provided. It should give his men plenty of opportunity to pick them off. Raz's only disappointment would be that he would not be able to kill Manuel himself.

High in the sky, near the moon, was the comet. Astronomers had calculated how long it would remain bright in the sky, and how long it would stay in this solar system. The brightness would dim in the next few weeks, but it would be more than thirty years before it left the solar system. Thirty-three, most thought. Raz wondered if that held any significance.

Raz heard more shots, all rifles. Good.

Rebekah cried out. Raz assumed it was her laboring again.

"Won't be long now," he told her.

* * *

Chichen Itza, the Temple of the Warriors,
North Colonnade

Manuel helped Talasi to her feet. "Can you walk?"

"Twisted my ankle." She favored her right foot.

"We cannot remain out here in the open. We are easy targets."

"I know."

"Let me help you." Manuel wrapped his left arm around her back, propping up her right side. "We can make it."

The Temple of the Warriors lay ahead of them, but closer still by several hundred feet was the North Colonnade. Hundreds of huge stone columns, four rows deep, extending out from the Temple, formed the Colonnade. If they could reach the columns, they'd have cover. Manuel hustled Talasi toward them as quickly as she could go. She hopped on her good leg, balanced against him.

We're going to make it, Manuel thought. They were within six feet of the first column.

A bullet whizzed over Manuel's shoulder, ricocheting off the column. Manuel instinctively ducked, losing control of Talasi. She tumbled onto the stone platform.

"Aaggghhh."

Manuel dropped next to her. "Can you crawl? We're so close."

Talasi grunted at him. She pulled herself toward the column.

Manuel knew he needed to buy Talasi time. He had to give the shooters a distraction. He got his feet under him and lurched to the right, making himself a bigger target.

It worked. The next two bullets went by him. They missed the colonnade entirely and hit the stone wall behind it. Manuel dove for the column nearest him, several feet from Talasi. He watched her muscle herself to safety.

For the moment, they were okay. But Manuel was certain the killers would move toward them. He pulled out the gun he'd been given and stared at it. He remembered Colin's words that every shot had to count.

But Manuel had never fired a gun before.

He looked to his right. Talasi was upright in the shadows with her back to the column. He could hear her breathing hard. "Talasi," he whispered.

He squinted, trying to make out her reaction. He thought he saw her shake her head, but she said nothing discernable.

Manuel waited a few seconds. He slowly moved his head to the side of the column to look back over the grounds. He tried to see where the shooters were. A bullet struck the column inches above him, sending debris onto his scalp.

"Manuel." Talasi's voice was so soft he had to strain to hear it.

He had to strain to hear Talasi's voice. "What?"

"I'm okay. Leave me here."

"No."

"Yes. Get Jonas to safety. Send Yan back for me. I'll be okay until then."

"What is the problem?"

"My ankle will be okay. But I can't hobble between the columns fast enough to get to the Temple. I'd be shot for sure."

Manuel considered their situation. He was not that far from the Temple, really. They had to dodge between another twenty columns or so. It seemed doable, but Dios mio, he had never dodged bullets before. Even if these shooters were not accurate, sooner or later they would get lucky. He had no idea what to do. He wished he could talk with Colin.

And where was Colin? He had seen Yan reach the Temple and knew someone in front of Yan had also reached it. But was that figure Colin or Jonas? If Jonas had veered off course, was he trying to get to Rebekah? Or, if it was Colin, had Colin developed a new strategy? Either way, things had spun far out of his control. Any moment the shooters could creep up close to their position and get them. He tightened his grip on the handgun.

He decided he would trust fate. He would try to get to the Temple. He needed to talk to someone more skilled in combat than he. Manuel braced himself for a run among the columns.

* * *

Jonas and Yan waited to see movement after Manuel and Talasi disappeared into the columns, but there was none.

"Did they make it?" Jonas asked.

"I do not know. I trust they did. But I worry Talasi was injured in her fall."

"What do we do?"

Yan paused. "Colin said we were to gather here, and then go to the top of the Temple."

"I hate to tell you this, but Colin's plan has fallen apart."

"This I know."

"Where is Colin?"

"Did you not spot him climbing the steps of the Pyramid?" Yan pointed. "He is preparing to shoot down the men with the rifles."

"If he can do that …"

"It would be very good for us. I believe Colin would like to get their rifles. But I am most concerned about where the other two gunmen are."

Jonas could only see the two men with rifles. "What other gunmen?"

"Were you not listening when Colin discussed strategy? This man Raz had four men with him who were no doubt sent after us."

Jonas' heart began to beat faster. "Then where are the other two?"

Chapter Seventy

Chichen Itza, the Pyramid of Kukulcan

Colin balanced himself awkwardly on the stairs. He was lying down, his right hand stabilized by the stone surface; his left unsupported as it dangled off the step. The Glock was in front of him, in his right hand, and he was trying to get a line on the nearest shooter. His positioning was all wrong. He'd never had to shoot like this before. But too much movement might attract attention.

Colin practiced moving the gun between the two targets. Once he shot the first man—provided he was successful and killed him—he would have to shoot the second quickly. Talasi and Manuel had made it to safety behind the large columns, but the riflemen would close in on them soon. He had to do this now.

Colin felt his balance shifting. It was slight, but left leg, half off the step, was slipping onto the lower stair. If he moved, would he be noticeable?

He used his left elbow as a brace. Kept the Glock in position as much as possible in front of him. Shifted his weight back until it was more on the stair. Still awkward, but back on.

His propped-up elbow slid out from under him. He caught himself before his chin hit the stair, but the movement was obvious. The nearest rifleman spotted it. Turned and saw him. Shouted something in Spanish.

Shit!

Colin squeezed off two shots as the rifle swung in his direction. The first one missed entirely. The second shot hit the man in the chest. One down, but one bullet wasted.

No time to think. Colin turned toward the second shooter. He fired three times. Hoping.

The second rifleman went down. Colin breathed out. But he couldn't tell if it'd been a kill. He tried to remember how the man went down, get a feel on where he'd hit him. He couldn't remember.

But he needed the rifles. With him and Manuel having only close-range weapons, they needed a rifle to give them a fighting chance.

Colin hugged the stairs on the way down, trying to make himself as small a target as possible.

* * *

Chichen Itza, the Temple of the Warriors

"Manuel," Talasi hissed. "This is your chance. No one is watching you. Get going."

Manuel hesitated. Talasi had rolled onto her stomach. Her legs were now outside the shadow, making her visible. "Talasi …"

She growled at him. "Now, Manuel, now!"

He took off, dancing past the columns, not counting them, not looking anywhere but straight ahead. He focused on the Temple. He had to reach it. He heard shots but didn't look.

He was running so fast that when he saw Yan and Jonas hiding behind columns ahead of him, he had trouble slowing down. Jonas reached out and grabbed him. He pulled him to the column.

"You're safe," Jonas said.

"Colin shot both of the men," Yan said. "He is getting their rifles. Where is Talasi?"

Manuel took short breaths. "She twisted her ankle. She was afraid to run while they were shooting."

"I will get her," Yan said. "Be alert."

"For what?" Manuel asked.

As if in answer, a bullet chipped the stone platform next to him. It had come from the top of the Temple.

Manuel aimed the gun upward toward the Temple and shot. Not a smart move, he realized after he'd done it. One bullet wasted. And he couldn't see the person shooting.

He looked at Yan. "What do we do?"

"We must get out of his sight, first."

Yan pushed Manuel toward the flat side of the Temple's base with his good hand. Jonas scurried after them. They reached the Temple wall and held tight against it.

"All of us are in danger as long as our enemy holds the high ground," Yan said. "We need to get to the top and eliminate him. How can we do that, without using the staircase?"

Manual shook his head. "There is no way up, other than the staircase."

"We would be too exposed. He would kill us instantly."

"I know this Temple," Manuel insisted. "There is no other way."

Jonas ran his hands along the wall. He glanced up at the top of the first tier, then began to get into his pack. "Yes, there is," he said. "We can scale the walls."

Manuel almost laughed. "You, maybe. Not me."

"I agree with Jonas," said Yan. "He can scale the walls. He should go."

Manuel bit his lip. Jonas was not expendable. He had even had second thoughts about letting Colin give Jonas the hunting knife. "The fight is not his," Manuel told Yan. "His destiny is to survive and to find the book."

"No, Manuel, the fight is mine. They have Rebekah."

"Diega will rescue her. Our mission is to make them think we have the book, or know where it is, so she can do that."

"But we must also survive," Yan argued. "Jonas offers us that chance."

Jonas pulled a collapsible grappling hook out of his pack and began to tie it to his rope. "As long as I can get this to hook at the next tier, I should be okay."

"You will likely reach the second platform without notice," Yan said. "But after that, especially as you reach the top, he may see you."

"I'll do what I can."

Yan stepped in front of Manuel. "Give him the gun," he said.

"Has he ever fired a gun before?"

Jonas didn't bother to look up as he finished tying the grappling hook with a double figure eight knot. "No, I haven't, Manuel." He tied a fisherman's knot to make it more secure. "Have you, before now?"

Jonas swung the rope in an arc and threw it up onto the second level of the Temple's pyramidal structure. He pulled. The hook came to the edge of the tier and held. He yanked on it to be sure it would stick. It felt solid.

"If you don't give him the gun," Yan said, "I will take it from you and give it to him myself."

Manuel knew he had little choice. He worried about Jonas dying, but he also worried that after Diega had freed Rebekah, Jonas would choose to use it on them to take her back. But he handed the Glock over.

Jonas took the gun and tucked it in his pack. "Don't worry, Manuel. Remember, I'm destined to survive. He doesn't stand a chance."

Jonas pulled on his climbing gloves. He yanked on the rope one more time. It still held. He began his ascent.

Chapter Seventy-One

Chichen Itza, the Temple of the Warriors

Yan waited until Jonas was safely half-way to the second tier before he revealed the next part of his strategy to Manuel. The two were side by side, inches from the solid wall of the Temple base, watching Jonas climb. "Someone needs to distract the shooter when Jonas becomes visible on the second level. And someone needs to protect Talasi."

"What do you have in mind?"

"Get to the columns in front of the Temple staircase. The walls will provide protection until you get close. Then you will need to run until you reach a column. This will catch the shooter by surprise. Once you are in safety behind the column, remain there. He will watch you to see what you will do next. At the same time, I will go for Talasi."

"Will you be able to help her back with only one good arm?"

"I am counting on Colin and Jonas to take out our enemy."

"Then why do you need to go back?"

"To protect her. There is at least one more man out there we have not accounted for."

* * *

Chichen Itza, the Pyramid of Kukulcan

Colin swept up the rifle and headed toward the southeastern corner of the Pyramid, running as close to the outer wall as he could, trying to blend in. He prepped for battle as he turned the corner. No one was there.

He used the scope on the rifle to study the situation. The moon was in a good position, producing few shadows in which the shooter could hide. However, he could see a stone structure on top with two rooms. The shooter could move around and surprise him from different angles. How can I lure the bloke out in the open?

Colin worried about his companions. He swung the scope back toward the Temple and saw movement along the smooth wall leading to the second tier of the structure. Someone was scaling the wall. Colin smiled. It had to be Jonas. The man was a climber.

But if Colin didn't know where the shooter was atop the Temple, neither did Jonas. When Jonas climbed onto the second platform, he'd be exposed for a few seconds until he ran to the wall of the next recessed tier. Colin could shoot toward the top of the Temple in an effort to keep the sniper at bay, but without knowing where the man was, would it be effective? Or would it be a waste of precious ammunition?

He had only moments to decide. Jonas was ready to climb onto the platform.

Colin leveled the rifle at the Temple.

And then there was too much simultaneous movement for Colin to keep track.

Jonas threw his pack and himself over the top of the wall, grabbed the hook he'd used, and rolled onto his side. A shot came from the Temple just as someone, likely Manuel, ran away from the Temple wall toward the columns of the North Colonnade. The shot gave Colin a cue to the position of the sniper, and he aimed in that direction and fired. He was fairly certain he'd missed, but no shots came back. A second man, he guessed Yan, ran for the columns from another direction.

In a swift sequence, Jonas used the momentum of his roll to get onto his knees, grab the bag, stand up, and dash across the recess of the second tier to its wall. Colin wasn't sure the sniper had seen Jonas. If he hadn't, Jonas would have the advantage of surprise in getting to the next tier. Colin used the binoculars to check for the sniper's position. The moonlight illuminated most of the two rooms. Still, the sniper remained out of sight.

Colin fixed the site on the second person and saw the sling. Yan must be going to get Talasi. But the way Yan had stopped, Colin guessed the sniper must have a clear shot. Colin used that information to look back at the Temple and try to determine a location. There were three, possibly four, locations where the shooter could be hidden. Even then, Colin couldn't make him out.

One more time he checked for Talasi. This time he saw something that caused him to worry. He picked up the rifle again.

A figure had just rounded the western boundary of the North Colonnade and headed for Talasi.

Chapter Seventy-Two

Chichen Itza, outside the Main Gate

Rebekah felt the labor pains easing again. She wasn't unprepared for this. She knew women often labored for long periods of time before delivering their first babies. But she still feared the idea that this was it, that her baby's birth was coming four weeks early. She blamed the situations she and Jonas had faced here in Mexico for the early contractions. She massaged her midsection, tried to feel the baby, but he was quiet for now. She still hoped, against everything her intuition told her, that she and Jonas would escape this nightmare and their baby would be born back home in Philadelphia.

Raz stood outside the car, listening to the gunfire. Rebekah rued her earlier mistake to trust him. She still wasn't clear what he wanted, other than the book.

At least Manuel had been interested in her welfare, misguided as he was about the identity of her baby. Manuel's crazy vision was having an effect on her. More than once during the past twenty-four hours, when she found herself in and out of a fuzzy, sleep-deprived consciousness, she had seen her son as a fighter, a warrior king. Not Mayan, though in at least one of her hazy recollections he was dressed in ancient Mayan clothing. But not Jewish either. She and Jonas had contemplated naming him David. Rebekah wondered if she were feverish.

Raz threw open the car door. "It's too quiet out there."

"Maybe your side is losing."

"Not likely."

"So you say."

Raz's hands were trembling. How odd, she thought. Just what would happen if he failed to get the Book of the Thirteen Gods? The more she thought about it, the more convinced she became that other things must be at stake here. Certainly the book would be an incredibly valuable find, worth a fortune to museums. But she had the impression Raz was already well-to-do. Was this more of a fame thing? Maybe he was just greedy. Or, were the contents of the book much more valuable than the book itself? If she gave in to the idea that the end of the Mayan calendar was significant, then Raz's desperate search could mean he had a huge stake in the information.

"You know, there's only one way to find out how things are going," she said.

Raz bit his lower lip. "Pablo will be out here soon to tell me of their victory."

"Unless Manuel and his group have already killed him."

Rebekah sat back and waited. She heard a shot, followed by a second. And it was quiet again. She could see the worry on Raz's face.

"If you're thinking that I would escape in the short time it would take you to check, look at me. I'm laboring, can't get far."

"You have a plan. Otherwise you wouldn't be encouraging me to go."

"Or maybe I'm just hoping they'll kill you, too, once you enter the area. As I said, I can't go far."

Raz shut and locked the back door of the car. He opened the front and hit the child's lock button. "You can't get out now. I'm going in. I'll be back shortly."

Rebekah summoned her best acting skills to sound panicked. "But what if the baby comes?"

"He won't." Raz checked his watch. "Not for another four hours. Stay put."

He slammed the door behind him. He opened the trunk and pulled out a submachine gun. Closing the trunk, he gripped the weapon and moved toward the entrance.

Rebekah watched him disappear through the front gate. She began to climb into the front seat. She swung her right leg over the middle and discovered an immediate problem. The car ceiling was too low for her to get over. She was too far along in her pregnancy.

She analyzed the situation. She needed to go sideways so the narrowness of her hips would clear the opening, not her belly.

She heard the sound of a car engine. Someone else was in the parking lot. She couldn't see who it was. Panic began to set in.

She got herself into position. It was awkward.

And then someone pounded on the driver's side door. Without hesitation, she pushed herself into the front seat with a controlled fall. She turned, preparing to defend herself against Raz or one of his people.

Chapter Seventy-Three

Chichen Itza, inside the Main Gate

Raz was in a hurry but didn't want to be stupid. He moved steadily along the path from the entrance to the ruins which ran behind and around the ceiba trees, perfect for cover. He encountered no one. He had hoped to find Pablo or Flyboy or one of the others, heading back to tell him they were set. That they'd secured Jonas. Or the book. Didn't matter to him. But he needed one or the other.

Raz entered the open archeological grounds and looked for a secure position. He spotted a couple of scraggly trees far to his right, within shooting distance of the Pyramid. He started across the field toward them but stopped. A rifleman was set up behind a corner of the Pyramid, aiming at the top of the Temple. One of his men? What the hell was going on here? Raz backed up into the protection offered by the path's trees. He pulled out his binoculars to watch.

Definitely not one of his men. It was the damned Brit. He checked the Temple. Jonas was illuminated in the moonlight, climbing to the top of the Temple. The Brit was firing to protect Jonas. One of his men must be up top.

Raz was glad he'd reserved the H&P Mark 7 weapon for himself. He needed to get to the scraggly trees. From that distance, he'd be in good shape. Though he'd be far enough away from the Brit he'd likely miss with a single shot, with a spray of bullets he was sure to splatter the hell out of the guy.

And the Brit was very distracted at the moment. Raz started across the field toward the trees.

* * *

Chichen Itza, outside the Main Gate

Rebekah let out a huge sigh of relief when she saw that her window-pounder was Manuel's sister. "Open the door!" Diega said.

“I’m trying.” Rebekah’s hands shook. She pushed every button she could find on the door’s control panel while she simultaneously pulled on the handle and pushed against the door. Nothing worked.

“Focus,” Diega said. “One at a time. The door won’t open if you push the button and pull on the handle at the same time.”

“Okay.” Rebekah tried to focus, but her elbow hit the panic button on the steering column. The horn began to toot rhythmically.

Rebekah pounded on the steering wheel where the horn was located.

“Find the button and hit it once. That’ll stop it.”

“Right.” She pushed it. The car horn stopped.

“Good,” said Diega. “Now, try the door again.”

She found the button to unlock all the doors. She pulled on the handle and pushed her way out.

* * *

Chichen Itza, atop the Temple of the Warriors

Jonas poked his head above the ledge and onto the top level of the Temple. There was no one between him and the walls of the rooms. So far no one had fired on him. As he climbed the second and third levels, he’d been able to determine the sniper was shooting at Yan, but he wasn’t sure the sniper knew what he was doing. Yet. That could change when he scrambled onto the top.

In truth, Jonas couldn’t wait much longer. He was strong, but his arms were finally giving out. Using what strength he could muster, he launched himself over the top of the wall and struggled to his feet. Pulling the Glock out of his belt, he ran for the first wall he could see.

Just as he reached it, someone stepped out. The man whacked his wrist, hitting the nerve. Jonas dropped the gun. Before he could react, the man pulled him behind the wall and pointed a gun at his head. Jonas realized it was the pilot of Raz’s aircraft.

The man had a rifle slung over his right shoulder in addition to the gun now level with Jonas’ eyes. “Don’t move,” he said.

And the ground began to shake.

Jonas had no idea why he was ready for it. Maybe subconsciously he had been contemplating escape strategies. But the moment the pilot's gun hand began to waver with the earth's movement, Jonas arched his hand upward in a cutting movement. He didn't have enough arm strength left to knock the gun out of his captor's hand, but he successfully batted the hand out of his face. Jonas brought his right knee up into the pilot's groin, bending the man over. He grabbed the pilot by the ears and slammed the head downward, bringing his knee up into the man's face.

The rifle slipped from the pilot's shoulder, but his hand still held the gun. He pointed it at Jonas' body, the loose rifle complicating his movements. Jonas grabbed the gun hand and twisted it away from him. The gun was pointed toward the pilot's head just as the man pulled the trigger.

Blood spurted from the pilot's face, and he dropped to the floor of the Temple.

Chapter Seventy-Four

Chichen Itza, the Temple of the Warriors,
North Colonnade

The column she hid behind began to move as the ground shook. Talasi backed up. Her mind registered danger. She heard the sound of stone breaking as some of the less stable columns smashed into the platform.

Yan shouted from somewhere behind her. Not a warning to her. A yell of distress. Careful to keep a distance between her and the pursuer, Talasi dodged the vibrating columns. Her ankle had become less tender with rest. She had to locate Yan.

The seconds felt like minutes. She spotted him twelve feet away. He lay on the ground next to a fallen column. Before she could move, a male figure ran toward Yan. He carried a gun.

Thoughts processed through Talasi's mind so quickly she barely had time to grasp them. But she determined the figure was not Jonas, Colin, or Manuel. She circled behind him using the unstable columns for cover, her mind so focused on stealth that she barely registered the danger of the columns falling. The figure reached Yan and aimed the gun at him.

Talasi's rushed toward them, the knife out ahead of her. As she reached the figure, he realized her approach and spun.

Bracing to resist the impact of her body, he never saw the knife plunge toward his throat and rip through his neck.

Talasi fell over the body as it toppled. She screamed in horror at what she'd done. She crawled away from the body but couldn't seem to get away from the spurting blood. She gagged at the sight and threw up.

* * *

Chichen Itza, near the Pyramid of Kukulcan

The earthquake had already begun by the time Raz had reached his position at the trees. Though the shaking would prevent him from getting a good aim at his prey, it didn't worry him. He'd reserved the Heckler & Koch MP7 submachine gun for himself. All he had to do was point it in the general direction of the Pyramid, commence firing, and the damned Brit wouldn't have a chance.

He tried to raise the weapon. The ground began to shake harder. The first tree fell, but it was far enough away it posed no danger, just blocked his view. Though shaky, Raz began to move around it.

The second tree fell toward Raz, so close that one of the smaller branches whacked his wrist and knocked the gun from his hand. The Brit raced toward the columns.

The fallen tree rolled toward him. Raz abandoned the weapon and moved, only to see the tree come to a rest on top of it.

Raz sensed the tide was turning against him. His best hope was to get back to the car, retrieve Rebekah. He could salvage this yet.

He ran back toward the entrance to Chichen Itza.

* * *

Chichen Itza, outside the Main Gate

Diega supported Rebekah as soon as she escaped Raz's car. She guided the mother of the king toward her own vehicle several feet away. The ground shook as another tremor hit the Chichen Itza area, but the latest supernatural sign did not faze Diega. She made sure Rebekah was stable on her feet before she let go of her. "Let me get the door."

Diega yanked on the door handle to the backseat and pulled it open. She eased Rebekah onto the seat. "Stay down. Let no one see you. We will be out of here quickly."

As soon as Rebekah's feet were safely out of the way, she shut the door and ran to Raz's car. She plunged a knife into the closest tire.

The tire flattened. She got into her own care and started it.

Rebekah was breathing in short, shallow breaths. Diega hoped it was from the excitement and not the labor. Not yet, at any rate.

"Where's Jonas?" Rebekah grunted out the question. "What's happened to him?"

"Once we're out of here, I will find out from Manuel. But I am confident he will be fine."

Diega's confidence was grounded in faith, not anything she knew from the battle going on inside Chichen Itza. Because of that, she declined to reassure Rebekah further.

* * *

Chichen Itza, atop the Temple of the Warriors

Manuel had to hold on to the side of the staircase as he climbed. The earthquake and the steepness of the steps made it nearly impossible to climb at a decent speed, but he had no choice. Manuel had seen Jonas make it to the top of the Temple and heard a shot. For the next few minutes, it was not his own life that mattered. Jonas must be saved.

The earthquake subsided as Manuel reached the top of the staircase. The moonlight illuminated Jonas, his arms wrapped around his own body, leaning against the wall of the structure. The body of the pilot lay near him. Jonas had tears in his eyes.

Manuel advanced toward him, watching carefully, evaluating him. "Are you going to be okay?"

Jonas nodded, but tilted his face away from Manuel.

Leaving Jonas to deal with his emotions, Manuel bent down and checked the body of Raz's pilot for a pulse. Nothing. Blood pooled around the man's head. Manuel was careful not to step in it. He pried the gun from the dead man's hand and then spotted the Glock he'd given Jonas near the corner of the Vestibule. He retrieved it.

Manuel realized the gun was cold. Jonas had never fired it.

He turned back to where the dead man lay twisted up near the altar. He reconstructed the scene in his mind and realized Jonas had overpowered the pilot and forced him to shoot himself. He wondered at Jonas' strength and his abilities. This man would make an excellent father for the king. There is much he might teach the child about courage and necessity.

But Manuel had not yet told Jonas everything he and Diega knew. There was a fifth part to the final prophecy; he and Diega had only told him about four. Shortly they would have to reveal what they knew. The implication of the prophecy, he believed, made it doubtful Jonas would survive the events surrounding the birth.

* * *

Chichen Itza, outside the Main Gate

Raz raced back into the parking lot and spotted a vehicle's tail lights going out the exit. He ran to his car, only to find it tilted to one side. The driver's side tire had gone flat. "Shit!"

He scanned the parking lot for other cars. One of the remaining cars was his. He'd allowed Pablo to drive it. He didn't expect Pablo would be need it again. Raz pulled out a duplicate set of keys.

But then he had a thought. He dashed back to his vehicle and pulled out a tracking device. The other vehicle in the lot belonged to the Brit. He placed the tracking device under the carriage, out of sight. Then he returned to the car Pablo had driven. He just needed to get out of sight, then follow the tracking device.

He wasn't sure whether Manuel had the Book of the Thirteen Gods yet—in fact, he believed his men had been lured into an ambush that went bad for both sides. *It was only to get me out of the way and recapture Rebekah. How could I have been so foolish?*

He would have the final victory, though. He'd follow them until they located the book and then take it from them.

And with it, he intended to claim Rebekah, one more time.

* * *

Chichen Itza, the Temple of the Warriors

Manuel carried Jonas' pack. The two men descended the staircase to the Temple of the Warriors. As they neared the bottom, Colin, Talasi, and Yan appeared. Even in the moonlight, Manuel could see that Talasi's eyes were stained with tears.

"Are you okay? What happened?" he asked her.

She started to speak, but choked before she could get a word out.

"She killed the man who was trying to kill Yan," Colin said.

Yan nodded. "She saved me. I had to leap out of the way of a falling column, and when I was down, he had me."

"What happened to you?" Colin asked Jonas.

Jonas didn't answer. Manuel could read a mixture of exhaustion, grief, and bitterness in his face. What comes next will only make this worse, Manuel thought. It will not go down easily.

"Jonas killed Raz's pilot," Manuel said. "He'd managed to get to the top of the Temple."

"He must have been the one who shot at me," Yan said.

"And me, out by the Pyramid," Colin added. "I thought this staircase was the only way to the top of the Temple? How could he have gotten here ahead of us?"

"There's a second entrance, but I didn't think they'd be able to get through that way. There is a steep ravine that leads up to the Temple. Plus, you have to go by the hotel, which would attract attention. Oh, my God! The hotel. They've probably heard the shots."

Manuel's cell phone rang. Diega was on the other end.

"I have her."

"Is she well? Where is Raz?"

"She is fine, but she is going in and out of labor. Raz is gone, but I am not sure where. We pulled off and hid while I made phone calls. Rebekah saw him drive by. I slashed the tires on his car, but he had keys to the other vehicle. I should have done something with it, too."

"Whatever happens is destiny now. You know there have been shots fired here. The police may be coming …"

"My phone calls were to the police. I have put them off, at least temporarily. You should have just enough time to make your escape and retrieve the book. If Jonas really knows where it is."

"My concern as well. I will talk to you soon."

Manuel closed the cell phone.

"That was Diega. Raz is gone, and I am fairly certain the others are dead, or they would still be shooting at us. Diega has taken care of the police for the moment."

Manuel turned to Jonas. "Diega has your wife. She is safe."

"Where are they?"

Manuel shook his head. "I am sorry to be difficult, Jonas, but I must do this. We have done our part. Now you must find the book."

"Damn you people!"

Jonas launched himself toward Manuel. Colin saw the move and blocked Jonas, deflecting the blows meant for Manuel. The two men stared at each other.

"I know you're angry, mate, but I can't let you harm him."

Jonas turned away from Colin, fuming. He crossed his arms over his chest.

Manuel was glad Jonas no longer had a gun. "You can damn us, but you must cooperate."

Jonas spun around to face Manuel. He spat out the one thing Manuel was afraid Jonas would say. "The truth is, I was bluffing. I don't really know where this book is."

Manuel gritted his teeth. Time was running out. "I had been fearful of that. But nonetheless, you will figure it out. Or your baby will be born without you."

Chapter Seventy-Five

Chichen Itza, Mexico
December 21, 2012
1:33 a.m. local time

Time to Solstice: 4 hours, 38 minutes

Jonas lifted his head to the sky in anger. "My baby is not the …"

Why waste my breath? he thought. These people are not going to give in until the book is found.

Jonas stared at the comet, high in the sky. Was it possible all these things were true? He knew Rebekah had been in labor. It was possible his son would be born tonight. At the time of the solstice? Certainly it was getting close.

No, he thought. It's not possible. It's just me. I'm exhausted. That's why I'm having these thoughts. I haven't slept three hours in the last two days.

But do I have a choice? I have to do something, have to believe in something. Can I believe in this?

Jonas faced Manuel. "Very well. If this damn prophecy is true, then the location would have to be someplace I've already been, someplace I know."

"And?"

Jonas racked his brain. He'd already been all over the Yucatan chasing clues to the book. But none of the places he'd been fit the clues they'd found at Ek Balam. Could it be somewhere I've been before this? A previous trip to Mexico? And then it came to him.

"Xcaret," he said. "The place is Xcaret. I mean, Ek Balam, Chichen Itza, and Palenque are nowhere near the coast. But Rebekah and I went to Xcaret the day before we came to Chichen Itza."

Manuel thought a moment. "Some ancient Maya lived in that area, but it was not a major center like Chichen Itza. Why would …"

For reasons he couldn't explain, Jonas felt a rush of euphoria. "Why not, Manuel? If their world were crumbling, they'd hide a valuable book somewhere out of the way." He felt a sense of certainty. It fit the prophecy.

Manuel was tentative. "I suppose an eco-park being built on it could be part of the plan, and some of the ceiba trees there are shaped like crosses. For Jesus, 'a man shaped by a cross'."

"One thing I've learned from my ancestry," Colin said, "is that prophecy is a stab in the dark when it's written and then again when it's interpreted. The prophecy that's considered true either conforms because it fits or because it's made to fit. I don't know which this is, but I say we go to Xcaret."

"Do you have an idea where the book is at Xcaret?" Manuel asked.

"No, but I'm optimistic." Jonas said.

"Then let's get there," Manuel said. He handed Jonas a piece of paper containing the prophecy from Ek Balam. "This is the prophecy. Study it. We will depend on your instincts."

* * *

Port of Tartus, Syria
December 21, 2012
9:40 a.m. local time

Time to Solstice: 3 hours, 31 minutes

Vhorrdak stood on the deck of a sea-faring container vessel, the wind whipping around him. He wore the uniform of an engine room officer. He watched the giant cranes on the ship's deck load ocean-going cargo into the tall slots. Each slot held six containers, three below deck and three above. The storage units were large, measuring approximately six meters by three meters by three meters. In fact, they were much larger than he needed, but such ships carried only uniform containers.

The Iranian vessel, the Mashhad, would shortly be bound for Iran. Vhorrdak could smell the diesel fuel of the engines as they idled. He awaited the imminent arrival of a large semi bearing a container identical to the ones being loading on the vessel. Its smaller cargo, which Fareed had bolted into the uniform container, was the nuclear warhead desired by his Iranian friends.

Another truck, much bigger than the one which had been effective in Iraq, big enough to hold this container, had been needed for the last leg of this journey. Vhorrdak himself had made the arrangements, though Fareed had actually done the transfer and now drove the bigger semi. The shipping of the weapon was the one part of Vhorrdak's strategy that required his personal supervision. Things were far too volatile in this part of the world to leave any of this to his underlings. If adjustments needed to be made, or his special powers required, he needed to be here.

He did not worry about how things were going in Mexico. Raz knew the penalty for failure and was too smart not to obtain the Book of the Thirteen Gods. He had not heard from Raz, but on the other hand, he had not expected him to call, not until the book was in his hands. Vhorrdak glanced at his watch. Raz should have the book soon. The solstice drew near.

The book would identify the location of the birth. The troublesome Manuel didn't know the location, either. He, too, sought the book. In one way, Vhorrdak needed Manuel to have it, so he would have the proper location to take the pregnant woman, Rebekah. She had to give birth to the baby at the time and place the prophecy predicted, so the baby to be born would be the savior, so when his latest ally Yan killed it, it would mean the death of the king. With his enemy's standard-bearer dead, Vhorrdak's victory would be assured.

But he needed Raz to obtain the book immediately after Manuel discovered the location. Pakal's visions contained the blueprint for Vhorrdak's victory. He needed to know what it said. By using the projection of what would happen at the end of time, he would bring his long-desired goal to fulfillment. He would use the free will of his enemy's creation to bring the human race to an end. This experiment with humans would come to utter ruin. Within a short time, not only would they demonstrate they didn't love their Creator, they would destroy their world and every living thing in it.

Just the thought of it gave Vhorrdak an incredible rush. He could barely imagine how glorious it would feel when it happened.

His satellite phone rang. Vhorrdak looked at the number. Washington, DC. He had been expecting this.

"A distraction would be a good idea," his contact said. "They are focusing on Syria."

"Your call is timely. Are they still watching the Zagros Mountains?"

"Yes."

"I have just the thing to keep them busy," Vhorrdak said.

"When will I be promoted, as you promised?"

"Imminently, Major, imminently. Yet today Archer will die. It's already been arranged. The resulting musical chairs will see your star rise. Watch and enjoy."

Vhorrdak ended the call and laughed silently. Simmons' star would last about as long as the Comet Quetzlcoatl's appearance. Which wasn't much longer. Its brightness would begin to fade in just a few days. Vhorrdak was always careful with the deals he made. In the millenniums since humans received free will, only a few hadn't turned out like he expected. And he had learned a lot from those.

Vhorrdak punched in a message on the satellite phone. It told the driver of the third decoy truck that it was safe to leave the warmth of the cave in the Zagros Mountains and to head into Iran. It also directed him to destroy the satellite phone and leave it in the cave before he did. Though the Major wouldn't like it, Vhorrdak set it up so the message would be sent in sixty minutes. That would be when a true distraction was needed. He sent the message himself, since Fareed's semi was just now pulling into the long line for the crane to load the special container into the Masshad. Besides, Vhorrdak reflected, in an hour Fareed will be unable to send the message. He'll be dead.

Vhorrdak didn't like having to send the transmission himself, but it really couldn't be helped. Though it opened up the possibility the call could be tracked to this location, as long as the driver obeyed, the plan would proceed as envisioned. The driver would obey. Fareed had chosen good men who knew how to follow orders.

He did not have time to rethink the decision anyway. He turned his attention back to the dock.

* * *

Between Cancun and Xcaret, Mexico
Highway 307
December 21, 2012
3:05 a.m. local time

Time to Solstice: 3 hours, 09 minutes

Raz had no idea where Manuel and Jonas were going. He kept about five minute's distance from them, so they wouldn't know he was following. They traveled along Highway 180 back to Cancun and then headed south on Highway 307 along the coast. Raz kept looking at the time. This journey had taken over two hours and showed no signs of ending soon. He considered the possibilities. Had he been deceived and had they already found the book? If that were the case, were they now headed to the birthplace? But where was Rebekah?

Raz had been careful when he left the Chichen Itza area. He'd gone a couple of miles, pulled over way off the highway, and let them go by. One car. Just one. Unless the car containing Rebekah was even further behind and now following him.

He couldn't worry about that. Whether Manuel and Jonas had the book or just the clues, there was a secret yet to be revealed that would shake their world. Raz liked that expression, 'shake their world.' With all the earthquakes happening and the ones Vhorrdak told him were yet to come, everyone's world was being shaken.

But not his. His confidence was rooted in the secret he knew that they didn't. It was so powerful that he was convinced he would soon be in the presence of the book.

He trusted it would also mean he was soon to be in the presence of Rebekah. What had Vhorrdak arranged, that he was no longer needed at the birth? No matter, he would have both the book and the boy. Vhorrdak would have to deal with that.

Raz glanced one more time at the tracking device. It showed that Manuel's vehicle was slowing down. Raz started to narrow the gap. They must have reached their destination.

And as puzzled as he was when he realized what their destination was, the location made him even more anxious. Xcaret. It put him at a disadvantage he hadn't anticipated. He had never been to Xcaret.

Plus, he had no easy way in. Damn Manuel. They both had connections, but Raz could not use his connections to get someone there. It would take too long. He would have to find a way to forcibly enter. Either that, or destiny would intervene.

And then he knew the answer. It came to him with a feeling of certainty. Yes, that was it. Destiny would intervene.

* * *

Xcaret, Mexico
December 21, 2012
3:24 a.m. local time

Time to Solstice: 2 hours, 47 minutes

There was no hint of daylight as Colin pulled the car into the car park at Xcaret, but the thought of it scared him anyway. True, the night had been too long, and too much had happened. But when the first bit of glow hit the horizon—and it was coming—it meant the solstice was rapidly approaching, too. They were not prepared for it. They had yet to acquire the book, and Rebekah was far away.

Yet, it had to work out. It just had to. They had no alternative.

"The gates are open," Yan said from the backseat. "How is it that you do that, Manuel?"

Seated in the front, Manuel half-turned to Yan, a wry smile on his face. "The brotherhood of the Cruzol extends everywhere. Diega simply had to make a call."

Colin put the car in park, turned off the engine, and everyone got out. He popped the Durango's boot and pulled out two shovels and five flashlights. He took one shovel and handed the other to Manuel. Then he distributed the flashlights.

Manuel took his. "How did you know to bring these, my friend?"

"When the prophecy said we'd have to dig deep, I figured we'd need them. I got them from your mates back at the *palapas* while you were translating the clues from Ek Balam."

"We could have used the flashlights at Chichen Itza," Talasi groused.

"No we couldn't. We had to rely on the moonlight. Flashlights would have given away our positions, especially as close as they were behind us."

"We cannot fight among ourselves," Manuel said. "We must be united. We have little time. Where is the mask of Pakal?"

"Here." Colin removed it from the truck as well. It was still in its protective case.

Manuel gave his shovel off to Jonas. "Please take this. I want to protect the mask."

Jonas slung his climber's pack over his shoulder and took the shovel from Manuel. Together the group went through the open gate.

"Where to?" Jonas asked Manuel.

"That is entirely up to you. You said you were here a few days ago. How do you interpret the clues?"

Though he knew them practically by heart after studying them for two hours, Jonas switched on the flashlight to read them one more time. Along the coast upon a hill/where lives a tree shaped by man/for a man shaped by a tree. A new star lights the entrance/below, an arch stands guard/a stone unknowingly marks the spot/with unintended significance. Dig deep and answers will be found/by the favored father's hand/by him alone can it be touched.

"The first thing we need to find is the cemetery. It's on the hill, and it has entrances into tombs. That could answer the first part."

"Lead on," Manuel said.

Jonas hurried away.

"Wait. We should lock the gate."

"I will do this, Manuel," Yan said. "I have only one hand and will not be able to help with the digging. Go on. I will catch up."

Without waiting for an answer, Yan turned and ran back toward the gate.

Jonas forged ahead, Colin and Manuel right behind. Colin noticed that Talasi lagged. She kept turning and watching for Yan.

"Come on, Talasi. Yan's a big boy. He'll find us."

"Sure," she said. But Colin didn't think she sounded convinced. Something about Yan clearly bothered her.

* * *

Jonas felt like he was making this up as he went along. He no longer felt the flash of insight that had led him to declare Xcaret the place where the book would be. But he pressed on. At least he could get the clues to fit.

Xcaret's Bridge to Paradise was the elaborate cemetery located on the coast. He and Rebekah had walked this path just a few days ago. Rebekah had remarked that it looked like a beehive, and it did. On top of the hill were ceiba trees shaped like crosses. As Manuel pointed out earlier, 'a man shaped by a tree' could be a Christian interpretation for the clues. His Jewish background aside, Jonas was taking an ecumenical view of the puzzle. After all, his companions represented a variety of religious backgrounds.

Fortunately Yan returned to the group before Jonas issued any orders. They were back at full strength now. Jonas knew they would need everyone searching if they were going to locate the book quickly.

He pointed to the trees atop the hill. "Those trees are the markers. We'll start here with the Bridge to Paradise. The clue says, 'A new star lights the entrance/below, an arch stands guard/a stone unknowingly marks the spot/with unintended significance.' Some of the entrances to the tombs fit, the ones where you can see the comet. Let's try the main entrance first. Everyone look for the other signs—the arch, the stone."

Jonas led the group down the largest chamber toward the center of the hill. As passageways led off from it, he assigned others to check them, which they did and then returned. At the end of the chamber was a tall, cavernous interior carved from stone. Jonas shone his flashlight on the large cross which hung from the top. Hundreds of small, Roman-arched insets had been hewed into the interior in concentric rows. They pulled Jonas' eyes toward the top. All of the insets held candles; most were lit. How long do those candles last? Jonas wondered. He and the others moved quickly around the interior. The group agreed that the arches, not having the five-sided Mayan shape, could be disregarded. They returned to the entrance.

"Okay, we need to split up. Let's check the other entrances into the cemetery. There aren't many on this side of the hill, and the entrances have to face the comet to count. Don't bother to check those that don't."

Jonas ran into a shallow opening. He found nothing more on the inside than a highly decorated gravestone and a pot of flowers that were days past fresh. With few openings that met the clue, his companions were back in just a few minutes. Each gave a negative assessment.

They looked at Jonas for the next step. Something came to him.

Manuel, aren't there catacombs under the cemetery?"

"Yes."

"One of those entrances has to face the comet."

Manuel nodded. "This way."

* * *

Raz pulled into the Xcaret parking lot. He knew he was minutes behind Manuel's group but he wasn't concerned about that. He'd convinced himself they were looking for the book, that they were here for that reason, and he knew it would take time to locate. Besides, he needed to get there at precisely the correct time. Too soon and it would disrupt their thought processes for finding the hidden book; too late, and they might have time to escape. His timing needed to be precise.

But he was worried about the other aspects of time, too. The solstice was closing in, and he had no idea where Rebekah was being held. Plus, he had to worry about Vhorrdak. Although he knew Vhorrdak was tied up with something so critical he was leaving the book to Raz, Vhorrdak would check in soon. If Vhorrdak had reason to suspect he was not following the plan, he could somehow bend space to be with Raz. And that, Raz did not want. He needed to appear to be following orders, to be available, at least for now.

He parked close to the entrance, near the car Manuel's group had driven to Xcaret. Ahead of him he could see the open gate and wondered why they had not locked it behind them as they had at Chichen Itza. Perhaps they felt they had outwitted him, that he would not find them. He liked that idea.

Or perhaps it was an ambush, like Chichen Itza had been.

He still had weapons in the trunk. He removed a Glock and hustled through the gate.

He saw lights swinging intermittently in the distance. He followed the path toward them. Signs along the way told him he was headed toward the cemetery and the Crypt of Sighs. Ominous, but ominous was not always bad, at least not for him. As he got closer he could hear voices calling to each other. He recognized Jonas' voice first, and then Manuel's. He entered the area, taking shelter in one of the tombs when he saw their lights leaving some kind of chapel. They exited the cemetery out the back way.

This required absolute concentration. No mistakes now. He could not afford distractions.

He blew out a breath, hesitantly turned off the satellite phone. He hoped Vhorrdak would continue to be occupied.

He followed them from a short distance into the catacombs.

* * *

Behind the cemetery was a wooden gate, not locked. The group followed Manuel down a wide stone ramp into the catacombs.

Jonas remembered the catacombs from his earlier visit. Even with just flashlights it was easy to see the passageways were well-kept. The ceilings were high, the walls were smooth, and the paths wide enough that in most places the group could walk three abreast without problem. Occasionally they could see stars through holes in the ceiling where the limestone broke away.

"Vines drop into the catacombs from above in places like these," Manuel warned, pointing at a sinkhole in the ceiling. "If you don't spot them with your flashlight you may run into them. Just be warned."

Memories of his visit here, only days ago, made Jonas think of Rebekah. This was a mission to get her back. They could not afford to go slow. "We need to split up again. The passageways break off and lead to different exits and entrances. Find an opening where the comet is visible. There's no one else here, so yell if you find one. We'll back down the passageway from any opening that fits that description. Look for the stone and the arch."

"Be methodical," Manuel added. "Each of us will take a new path when one veers off. That will allow us to cover five of them."

"If I remember correctly, the paths intersect with each other, so it's like a labyrinth. Each path will eventually lead to the outside, so just keep working at it."

Jonas took the first split to the left. He came to several places where the sides of the catacombs had been hollowed out far off the path. A good place to bury something. Like a book. He flashed the light beam over the piles of fallen limestone and into the far recesses of the cave. The beam danced over pieces of driftwood, a reminder that water at one time ran through the passageways. How long ago was that? So far back in time that a book could have been buried here a thousand years ago?

Or had others taken charge of this book sometime along the way? Jonas remembered the Cruzol, the rebellious Mayan group Manuel belonged to. They still had elders who practiced rituals dating back over five hundred years. What if a vision directed them from time to time? What if this hadn't been the original location but been made to conform because someone had a dream that placed it here?

Too many variables to consider.

Jonas found his path intersect with another one. He could hear Talasi talking to herself. "Talasi?"

"Here. Jonas?"

"I just came to your tunnel. Where are you?"

"To your left. I hear you back up there. I've already covered that end."

"I'll join you."

He jogged down the tunnel as fast as he dared, his flashlight beam bouncing along as it revealed the stone path. Talasi showed up in the beam, waiting for him. She wiped her brow with her sleeve. He could see she was perspiring. "Are you okay?"

"I don't like caves."

"Let's go on together for awhile."

"I'm good."

"I know, but we don't really have a choice until we come to the next split, do we?"

He could see she was grateful, but it wasn't long until the tunnel split again.

"I'll go right," Jonas said.

"Okay."

Ahead Jonas could see a light, not like a flashlight beam, but a steady glow. He moved a little faster. He quickly came to an alcove on his left. A ledge of stone had been built in front to separate the alcove from the path. The light Jonas saw was a candle that sat on the top of a solid stone altar back in the alcove. The altar was probably seven feet wide in front but narrowed as it went back. The top of the altar was little more than waist high. There was a notch, probably a cubic foot large, cut out of the top front center of the altar. To Jonas it looked like someone had flipped the stone out of the notch to the back of the altar to create a dual-level 'tabernacle.' More than twenty candles were on the altar, but only one, the top one, was lit.

Jonas stared into the flame and had the same feeling of euphoria he had felt when he'd declared Xcaret to be the location. Something about this place was significant.

He ran ahead. The passageway ended at an opening that dropped off into a river that ran through Xcaret. He could go no further. He looked into the sky. The Comet Quetzlcoatl, bright and unmistakable, dominated the view.

"I've found it! Everyone follow my voice!"

Jonas retraced his steps to the alcove. This had to be it. He put his pack down and stepped over the ledge, examining the altar. He had come around behind it when Talasi arrived, followed shortly by Manuel. Colin and Yan yelled for them to give their location, and Talasi called back in answer. Within a minute, they gathered on the path in front of Jonas.

"This altar," he said. "It's the stone that 'unknowingly marks the spot …"

"'… with unintended significance'," Manuel continued. "Yes, that would fit."

Colin leaped over the stone barrier into the alcove. He pushed on the altar. "This bloody thing won't budge. Even with all of us working on it, it's not going anywhere."

As if in answer, a tremor hit the area. Everyone grabbed for a wall of the cave, trying to steady themselves. Chips dropped from the ceiling, causing Jonas to cover his head.

"Another earthquake," Talasi said.

Manuel shined his flashlight on her. "Just a tremor. But it may warn of more to come."

Jonas, still behind the altar, scanned his beam along the ceiling above him where the rocks had fallen. "Manuel, give me the mask."

"You see something?"

"Maybe."

Manuel removed the mask of Pakal from the carrying case. He handed it to Jonas.

Jonas put it on and looked up where the rocks had fallen. He used the flashlight to illuminate the area. The mark was shadowy, almost ghostly, but it was there. A Mayan arch.

"'The arch stands guard.' It's not under the altar, Colin. It's under here."

Colin held up the shovel he'd been carrying. "Let's dig."

Chapter Seventy-Six

Port of Tarsus, Syria
December 21, 2012
11:13 a.m. local time

Time to solstice: 1 hour, 58 minutes

Fareed could not believe how many trucks were still ahead of his, and how long it took the crane to load the containers onto the ship. He knew it took precision to make certain everything was set for shipping, but he was impatient to finish this job and make good his escape.

Ashur was no longer with him. Well, in some sense he was there; he was in the back of the semi, within the large container that was supposed to hold the nuclear weapon but now held the sandstones. Once the truck following them had performed its suicide mission, Ashur figured out Fareed had lied. Fareed had no idea if Ashur was astute enough to relocate the cave where they had left the nuke, but it didn't matter. As long as someone else knew the truth, that person was a danger to Fareed's plan. He'd surprised Ashur with a bullet to the brain shortly after they'd entered Syria.

He wondered how Vhorrdak planned to kill him. He believed that at some point Vhorrdak would show up to do the deed. He did not plan to be around when that happened, but if he was, he would bargain with his knowledge to get away alive. He'd memorized the GPS location and burned the small slip of paper. Without him, there was no way to trace where he'd hidden it.

Fareed heard a knock on his window. One of the dock officials stood there holding a clipboard. He rolled down the window.

"How many containers?" the official asked.

"One."

"So few?"

"I just drive and deliver," Fareed answered.

"Sign here," the official said, handing him the clipboard and holding up a pen. Fareed realized a second too late how the official pointed the pen at his throat. He tried to swat the pen out of the way, but a small dart hit him in the neck. Fareed grabbed at it and pulled it out, but he felt his actions slowing. Within two seconds he could barely move. He was still conscious, but he was losing control of his breathing as his body became completely paralyzed. He gasped for breaths, but his lungs wouldn't fill with air.

And then his consciousness was gone.

* * *

Xcaret, Mexico
The catacombs
December 21, 2012
4:16 a.m. local time

Time to solstice: 1 hour, 55 minutes

Jonas appreciated that Talasi and Manuel had each taken turns, but he had known all along that the bulk of the digging would belong to him and Colin. He was okay with it. The ground was soft and they'd cleared away a huge section under the arch in the ceiling. Manuel and Talasi sat along the cavern walls. Their sweat had dried. He and Colin continued to drip with the effort as they dug deeper and deeper.

"Pretty soon we're going to hit the bloody water table," Colin said.

Manuel got up and put the mask over his eyes. "You've drifted a little to the right. You need to shovel more to the left."

Colin jammed his shovel to the left of where he'd been digging and pulled up a chunk of dirt. He added it to the pile he'd made and gave Manuel a nasty glance. "Perhaps you'd like to take over." He threw his shovel into the space he'd just made. It hit with a clunk.

Jonas, Colin, and Manuel stared into the hole.

"You've found something," Manuel said.

Yan and Talasi jumped up. Jonas knelt on the ground and began to dig with his hands. He scraped away pieces of the damp dirt, circling a corner of the something that Colin's spade had struck. Gradually he loosened it and yanked it out.

"It's a stone," Manuel said. Jonas could hear the disappointment in his voice.

"Is there anything written on it?" Talasi asked.

"Not another clue," Yan said. "We do not have time."

Jonas threw the stone out of the hole and began to dig under where the stone had been.

Colin retrieved the rectangular rock Jonas had discarded and examined it. "Every stone we find I keep hoping will have Excalibur stuck in it."

"Here's what we're looking for," Jonas said. He had nearly unburied a large object wrapped in a cloth.

"'Dig deep and answers will be found'," Manuel recited, "'by the favored father's hand.'"

A voice came from out of the tunnel behind them. "'… by him alone can it be touched'."

Everyone turned at the words. Manuel's flashlight swung to reveal Raz Uris. He had a Glock trained on him. Does the man never run out of weapons?

"Wrong time, wrong place, Raz," Manuel said. "Rebekah isn't here, and, as you said, you can't touch the book."

Raz stepped over the stone into the alcove. "But you're wrong there, Manuel. Jonas is not the father. I am."

Jonas glared at him. "Impossible."

"Not at all. You and Rebekah went with a Jewish sperm donor. HBW60421. That would be me, and I happen to be of the line of David."

"That's not true, Raz. Rebekah became pregnant before the procedure. It may be a miracle, but she says I'm the father."

Raz sneered. "Please don't give me that miracle crap. Now, back away."

Jonas stayed where he was in the hole. Yan, Talasi, Colin, and Manuel moved away.

Raz took a step forward. "Get out, Jonas. You can't very well save Rebekah if you're dead, can you?"

Jonas still didn't move.

Manuel inched toward the pit. "Please, Jonas, get out of the hole," Manuel's voice was on edge. "Trust me. He cannot touch the book."

Jonas clenched and unclenched his teeth. This book was his ticket to reclaiming Rebekah from Manuel. If he worked it right, it would get them out of Mexico, too, and back to the States. If Rebekah's not in labor. If she's okay.

And that was what made the difference in Jonas' mind. He couldn't take the chance he wouldn't see Rebekah again. He had to at least pretend to comply with Raz's demand.

He climbed out of the hole.

Raz jumped easily into it. "Now before you get any heroic ideas, just remember that this gun fires rapidly and I have a full magazine. I just have to aim in your general direction, start firing, and someone goes down. Do you understand?"

No one said a word.

"I'll take that as a 'yes.'"

Raz reached into the place Jonas had been digging. He grabbed hold of the cloth and pulled.

The ground trembled again, much stronger than it had before. Rocks fell again from the ceiling. Several hit Raz, but he didn't drop the gun. It did, however, make him let go of the cloth. The tremor stopped.

"Don't move," Raz warned again.

He squatted into the hole, his hand groping for the cloth. His last attempt had nearly freed the object from the dirt. He gripped the corner tightly.

And a third tremor shook the ground.

Raz fought for his balance. "What the …?"

Manuel ignored Raz's warning not to move. He put the mask of Pakal back in its case. "You cannot touch the book, Raz," he said with satisfaction. "You are neither the father nor the 'favored father.' Let it go."

Raz pointed the gun at Manuel. "One more word and you die." Raz climbed to the shallower end of the hole. He shifted the gun to Jonas. "I'm not leaving without this thing. Get in here and get it for me."

Jonas jumped in but turned his back on Raz, hiding his actions. He bent down and took hold of the object. No tremor. He pulled it out and unwrapped it. The book was constructed of consecutive panels and unfolded like an accordion in his hands.

"What are you doing down there?" Raz asked.

"I'm having problems getting the book out."

Jonas peered at the first page. He turned it over and checked the last. No good. He couldn't make anything out. There wasn't enough light.

"You have it. I can tell you have it. Hand it up to me. Now that it's been recovered, anyone can touch it."

"Not true, Raz," Manuel said. "The book is sacred. Those who work for evil cannot touch it."

Raz's voice was thick. "Well, we'll know soon, won't we? Jonas, the book."

Jonas breathed out in resignation. He prayed for something to happen. Then he held the book up toward Raz.

And a fourth powerful tremor began.

The ceiling cracked. Slabs of dirt and rock dropped to the ground. Dirt crumbled from the walls of the catacombs. Jonas tried to keep his balance, his arm extended upward. Beams from swaying flashlights played across the interior of the alcove as everyone fought to stay on their feet.

Manuel launched himself toward Raz and shoved him aside. Raz fell backward over the stone ledge and onto the path. Manuel grabbed the book out of Jonas' hand and raced back up the corridor, shifting from side to side as he struggled with his balance.

Just as quickly as it hit, the tremor ended.

Colin's flashlight held steadily on Raz. The ex-Mossad agent seemed dazed. His head had clearly hit the path. Then Raz shook off the blow and rolled into a kneeling position. Two other flashlights trained on him.

Raz patted the path around him. He doesn't have the gun, Jonas thought.

Colin must have had the same thought. Before Jonas could get out of the hole, Colin jumped into action. Raz looked up in time to dodge as Colin leaped over the ledge. Raz caught him with a knee to the stomach. Colin fell and Raz kicked his right shoulder, sending the soldier sprawling onto the path. In horror, Raz saw that he had pushed Colin toward the gun.

Before Colin could recover, Raz turned and ran into the darkness of the tunnel after Manuel.

* * *

Yan had been conflicted during the tense standoff. He knew he had made a mistake back in the Cancun hotel room. Under the hazy spell of the drugs Talasi had given him for surgery, he had made a bad deal. He had suffered injuries before, but not like this, not a shot to the shoulder. He despaired that he would never have use of his shoulder again. A voice had whispered at him. Never to be a champion again. Never to teach others. Never able to practice the sport and the art for which he had long trained. He could not remember a time he felt so distressed. And then the voice promised healing. Almost immediate healing. In exchange for a killing. And he'd agreed!

When he'd learned it was the baby, he'd pleaded the action down to trying to kill. The voice had laughed at him when he'd suggested it. But Yan, under the spell of the drugs, had become so distressed the voice relented. After all, how could he strike the baby with full intent to kill and not succeed? If Yan told someone of the deal to prevent him from succeeding, then it wasn't full intent.

How could he have agreed to such a deal? Surely it was the drugs. To whom could he plead his case, though?

His soul in the balance, Yan had been trying to figure a way out. He had deliberately left the gate to Xcaret open, though it had not been asked of him. He hoped the deal might change if he helped Raz obtain the book. Yan was sure Raz knew the voice, had his own agreement. Maybe if he helped Raz, Raz could talk to the voice. Maybe change things. Yan had even considered intervening in the fight.

And yet, Yan suspected helping Raz would not make a difference.

Yan would rather single-handedly fight off a thousand demons, even die doing it, than to lose his soul. In the seconds after he had made the deal, he had been given a glimpse of the agony his soul would suffer if he did not keep his part of the agreement. But it was after he had made the deal. Could he be held to this?

How could he go against his very being and the quest his ancestors had entrusted to him?

He leaped out of the alcove to chase down Raz.

Arms held him back. He turned, almost fought the person holding him. He knew he could do it—his arm was almost completely healed. He hid it only because he couldn't let them know.

It was Colin who restrained him. "Whoa, there, mate."

"But …"

"Yan, don't," Talasi said. "The Magi have to stay together."

Jonas looked at them with curiosity. "Magi?"

Talasi nodded. "It's a parallel. Not a perfect one, but nothing here has a perfect parallel. I'll explain it later."

Yan looked up the corridor toward the fading footfalls. Raz had likely reached the opening. He wondered now what to do. The options were not good.

Colin tucked Raz's Glock into his belt. "Jonas, I saw you glance through the book. Did you see the location of the birth?"

"I tried, but it was too dark."

Talasi put her arm around Jonas' shoulder. "Then we'll have to depend on Manuel. Come. Let's find our way out." She pointed her flashlight in the direction Manuel and Raz had run. Jonas shrugged off her arm, grabbed his pack, and started up the corridor ahead of them.

"But not too fast," Talasi said, tugging on Jonas' shirt. "We need it to take about ten minutes."

Jonas pulled away. "It's already daylight! We don't have ten minutes."

"Yes, we do. We've arranged for transportation. But first, Manuel needs to take Raz out of the vicinity."

Chapter Seventy-Seven

Xcaret, Mexico
December 21, 2012
4:25 a.m. local time

Time to Solstice: 1 hour, 46 minutes

Manuel found his way out of the catacombs easily. Not a single wrong turn. It was as if he was meant for this moment, to do this difficult thing. He knew Raz trailed behind him, but no longer hearing the pounding of feet, he believed Raz had missed a turn.

The parking lot was empty save for the car Raz had driven and for Colin's. It would have been tempting for him to slash the tires on Raz's vehicle as his sister Diega had done at Chichen Itza. It would have ensured his escape, but he needed to take Raz away from Xcaret. He didn't hesitate to take Colin's vehicle, leaving his companions behind. Colin and Talasi knew it was likely to go that way. Colin had given him the keys. Other arrangements had been made for the remainder of the group, once Raz was gone.

Manuel looked back at the entrance. No sign of Raz. He breathed nervously. It was time to look at the Book of the Thirteen Gods. He had to trust Raz would not show up while he examined it. But Manuel had confidence he would be granted the time. So far, he had bet on the prophecy, and he had won. Though the time was coming when winning would also mean losing, he believed that time was not yet here.

What a moment! The secrets of the ancients in his hands. Manuel opened the car door and sat in the driver's seat facing outward, his feet on the asphalt parking lot surface. He laid the book on his lap. It was constructed exactly as he had envisioned it, like an accordion in the way it opened. The few Mayan manuscripts that had been recovered, like the Dresden Codex he had personally examined at the state library in Dresden, Germany, did the same. Manuel wanted to caress it, to treat it as the treasure that it was.

But he had little time. He knew exactly what he was looking for.

Not everything would be written. There would be drawings. He needed a drawing that would tell him the location of the birth. If this were truly Pakal's vision of the end times, it should start with the birth.

Manuel opened it to the first fold. In the leaf he saw what he needed. The Pyramid of Kukulcan. Except it didn't look quite right. What was different? Was he mistaken? He hands trembled. He almost turned to another leaf when he realized what the difference was. This was the inner pyramid, the one dedicated to the moon, not the greater one built over it.

Perhaps he would have time to study the book later. For now, he had to save it.

He laid the precious Book of the Thirteen Gods on the seat next to him as he turned to sit behind the wheel.

Raz burst out of the entrance.

Manuel saw Raz coming toward him. He slammed the door shut, started the car, and threw it into drive.

Raz leaped in front of the car.

For a moment Manuel froze. Should he run Raz over?

Raz must've recognized the answer, because as Manuel pushed on the accelerator, he dove out of the way.

Manuel made a sharp turn to head out of the lot and watched in the rear view mirror as Raz picked himself up off the asphalt. He braced himself for Raz to shoot at him, but Raz instead ran to his car. Manuel let out his breath in relief. Raz must have dropped the gun. For the moment, it meant he was safe, but Raz could have the ability to re-arm himself in the car. Manuel guessed that was likely to be the case.

He fumbled with his cell phone, managing to push the speed dial button for Diega. He heard it ring on the other end. "Answer, Diega, please answer."

His sister's melodious voice came on the line. "Manuel?"

"I haven't much time, Diega. Jonas recovered the manuscript. I have it. The location is Chichen Itza, as we'd hoped it might be."

"The Pyramid of Kukulcan?"

"Yes, but the inner pyramid."

"Are you certain, Manuel? The sign of the comet will not be seen."

"I am certain, Diega. Perhaps it is not as important as we thought. Or … something else may happen we aren't prepared for."

"The helicopter is ready. Rebekah is in labor."

"Wait five minutes, then come in. Be sure to bring the doctor's medical bag."

"Are you still at Xcaret?"

"Everyone but me. I must lead Raz some place I can hide the book, somewhere he cannot reach it."

"Bury it," Diega said. "Bury it somewhere sacred he could not dig it up."

"I can't think. Help me."

"The waters of a *cenote* are sacred."

As if in a vision, Manuel saw the answer. "Taj Cenote. That is where I will head. Thank you, Diega."

"We will celebrate this moment tomorrow, my brother."

Manuel bit his lip. In his silence, Diega said, "What is it?"

"I believe someone has betrayed me. Raz should not have been able to get in so quickly. He should have been farther behind, should not have known we were in the catacombs. He did not have the clues to the location of the book."

Her voice faltered. "But Manuel ..."

"You heard me correctly. If I have been betrayed, you know what it means." He choked on the words. He wasn't sure he could continue. On Diega's end, he heard her crying. He had to end the call quickly. "*Adios, mi hermana, mi amiga mejor.*"

"Manuel ..."

Manuel pushed the 'end' button. He could feel tears on his face. He reached over and touched the manuscript, felt reassurance sweep over him.

The sacrifice was worth it. The baby would be born. The world would be saved.

* * *

The Zagros Mountains, Iraq
December 21, 2012
12:30 p.m. local time

Time to Solstice: 1 hour, 41 minutes

When the call came, the driver of the third decoy truck moved quickly. He and his companion cleared the brush they'd place at the cave entrance to hide it. The small opening, lit by daylight, looked like a hole into heaven. The transmission had said the Americans were gone and that they were safe. That being the case, it was heaven outside.

But even though everything had gone according to plan and that every order they'd received had been valid, the driver did not understand the order to destroy the satellite phone. The phone was their only connection. Either Fareed did not want them to be able to contact him again, or they were being set up, and he did not want them traced to him. The driver decided to keep the phone, adding it to his fake passport, a pistol, and some money—Iranian *rials*—he kept in a fireproof lockbox under his seat. If they were successful, Fareed would never know he still had it. If they were being set up, screw Fareed.

He put the negative thoughts out of his head. They were close to completing their mission. All along he had imagined he would get to Iran. Now, as he drove out of the cave, he envisioned what he would do with all the money he would receive for making his goal.

His reverie was short. As they rounded the first mountain pass, he heard a helicopter circling. He looked up in disbelief. But the helicopter disappeared behind a snow-capped peak.

At the second pass, however, the driver came to a complete halt. Ahead of him were three heavily armed trucks waiting for them.

They'd been set-up.

Screw Fareed.

Chapter Seventy-Eight

Xcaret, Mexico
December 21, 2012
4:42 a.m. local time

Time to solstice: 1 hour, 29 minutes

Raz had been surprised at Manuel's decision to try to run him over. He had not thought Manuel had it in him. But so be it. He had no choice but to follow Manuel. The professor had the Book of the Thirteen Gods, and Raz needed it. Needed it to find Rebekah and his son.

He knew the baby was his, that Jonas had lied to him. He'd seen the reports of Jonas' infertility and knew they had scheduled the fertility treatment with his sperm. How could Rebekah have become pregnant without it? Jonas, desperate for the glory that was rightfully Raz's, had only tried to confuse him.

Raz would see to it that his son lived. He, and he alone, would guide his son. It was his offspring's destiny to be the long-awaited Messiah and conquer the earth. Raz could scarcely imagine how much power and authority his son would have. But his son needed to know how to make the most of it. Raz would see to that.

And there was that one last item on his agenda. He had to destroy the book, and immediately. If Vhorrdak managed to obtain it—and Raz had no doubt he could—Vhorrdak might be able to use it to frustrate Raz's plans. Vhorrdak had too many eyes, too many hands, and too much power for anyone to think the book could be protected from him. Raz knew he could not make Manuel understand this. Manuel would never see things his way.

Therefore the book must be destroyed. And likely, Manuel with it.

He checked to make sure the tracking device he'd planted on the Durango was still working. It was. He could see Manuel speeding away from Xcaret.

Going south.

What was south of here? Where was Manuel going?

And what of the people Manuel had left behind, Jonas and the trio of internationals? Manuel had abandoned them too easily, especially Jonas. Was Rebekah close? There was so little time left until the solstice.

The closer, the better. Once he had taken care of Manuel, learned the location of the birth, and destroyed the book, he could arrive quickly to snatch up his son and Rebekah and head into hiding.

* * *

Manuel was far enough ahead that he couldn't see Raz behind him, but he had to assume the antiquities dealer was following. It was really the only way the prophecy played out. Manuel fumbled again with the cell phone, this time typing out an entire phone number. The car swerved a bit into the on-coming lane as Manuel pushed the 'send' button. Fortunately this early in the morning there was no traffic. Manuel put the cell phone to his ear and prayed his friend would answer the phone. The man was likely still asleep.

Manuel waited through five rings, panicking. Surely he had not misjudged the location for this showdown with Raz. The decision had been forced by circumstance. It simply felt right. He had no time, no other way in. And his friend was the overseer of this jewel of the Yucatan.

"*Hola.*"

Manuel felt a great sense of relief. He answered likewise in Spanish. "Jorge, Manuel Patcanul. Sorry to bother you so early. I need a large favor. I am headed for Taj Cenote. Can you get there quickly and open the gate for me?"

Manuel could tell Jorge was puzzled, but he must have sensed the urgency of his request because his response was immediate and positive.

"Thank you. Also, I need a waterproof container, about the size of a notebook computer. Do you have something like that?"

Again, Manuel received the answer he trusted he would get. He paused for only a second, then made his last request. "Jorge, I also need a handgun."

At that, Jorge began to pepper him with questions. "NO!" he said, interrupting. "I cannot answer your questions. If you have a gun, leave it with the container. If you don't, I will find another way."

But Jorge would not stop his barrage.

"*Lo siento, mi amigo*. It will be dangerous. I want no more blood spilled. You must leave as soon as the gate is open. I cannot tell you more. When this is over, call Diega, she will explain. Please, just do as I ask. Thank you again. *Adios*."

Manuel closed the phone and sped ahead.

* * *

Xcaret, Mexico
December 21, 2012
5:00 a.m. local time

Time to Solstice: 1 hour, 11 minutes

Talasi hurried Jonas, Colin, and Yan along the path from the cemetery to the parking lot. She wanted them to be ten minutes behind, but they'd had to double back a couple times getting out of the catacombs. Now she fretted they had taken too much time. But as they came out of the trees surrounding Xcaret, she could see the helicopter hovering, preparing to land in a large open spot in the parking lot. They'd heard it when they'd left the catacombs.

"There's our ride," she said.

The group watched as the helicopter landed. Colin insisted they wait until the blades slowed to a stop before advancing. Talasi recognized it as a Bell 407 and knew it would seat them all. She'd flown in helicopters just like them. Some of the larger hospitals used that model for EMS missions.

Colin threw open the double doors.

"Hurry," Diega said from the pilot's seat. "There is not much time."

Talasi went in first and found Rebekah already in the back. The pregnant woman was sweating and breathing shallowly. Talasi sat on one side of her. Jonas got in and took the seat on the other side. Rebekah cried when she saw Jonas.

Jonas wrapped his arms around her. "You're going to be all right. We're together."

Talasi buckled in. "Did you bring my bag?" she asked Diega.

"Next to Rebekah."

Talasi looked around but didn't find it. Jonas located it on his side and passed it over.

"Thanks," she said.

Colin boarded last. He sat up front with Diega. "You know where the birth is going to take place?" Colin asked.

"*Sí*. Manuel called and explained. We are to return to where this all began. The Pyramid of Kukulcan." She started the blades rotating again.

Talasi rifled through her supplies. Thank God Manuel and Diega remembered.

She turned her attention toward Rebekah. "This is awkward, Rebekah, with all these people here. But I have to check to see how dilated you are."

Rebekah hardly cared, the pain was so great.

Talasi was glad Yan looked away as she performed the check. She was still suspicious of him, but at least he had responded with decency in this instance.

She wasn't surprised by the results of her check. "Rebekah's over eight centimeters. We have to get there right away."

* * *

Taj Mahal Cenote, Mexico
December 21, 2012
5:15 a.m. local time

Time to Solstice: 56 minutes

Manuel drove his car through the entrance of Taj Cenote. As he expected, the iron gate was open. He had no time to close and lock it. Raz was less than a hundred meters behind. It would be difficult enough to get to the *cenote* ahead of him.

Cenotes, because their waters came from under the earth where the gods existed, had always been considered sacred by the Mayan people. Few cared about that distinction today, and the beautiful subterranean pools were delegated to little more than swimming pools. But Manuel knew the waters still had the power to stop evil. Taj Cenote was a huge underground cavern with a large pool that had a special feature Manuel needed to keep Raz from obtaining the book.

Manuel pulled up in front of the ticket gate and jumped out, cradling the book to his chest. Jorge had turned on the lights to the attraction. For that, Manuel was thankful. He had no flashlight and otherwise could not navigate the landscaped path down to the *cenote*. Just in front of the path lay the waterproof container, a gun, and snorkeling gear. Manuel smiled. He hadn't asked for the gear, but he was grateful. Who knew? Maybe he would survive this. He could hope.

But if he could manage it, Raz would not survive. Manuel could not leave his enemy alive to cause more problems for Jonas and Rebekah.

Manuel tucked the gun in his waistband, the gear under his arm, and dashed down the path while working to get the book into the container. Once he had it sealed, he reached the edge of the water and threw it in. He could hear someone running down the path toward him.

No time to plan. Looking for cover, he spotted a jagged rock sticking up out of the water two meters to his left. The depth looked to be waist high. If only I can get behind it. He pulled Jorge's handgun out of his waistband with his right hand. He kept it away from the water as he hurriedly splashed toward the rock. In his left hand, he held the snorkeling gear.

"Stop right there, Manuel."

Manuel pivoted and fired at Raz with no hesitation. He hoped for a hit but he mainly needed to keep Raz off-balance. He lunged for the safety of the rock.

A second elapsed before Raz retuned fire. The bullet ricocheted off the rock just as Manuel got behind it. Manuel guessed he'd caught Raz by surprise.

"I have you trapped, Manuel. You cannot escape, and frankly, you're not that good with a gun. You missed me by a meter. Give me the book."

Manuel peered out from the left side. He wondered how much of him Raz could see. The *cenote*'s indoor lighting produced odd shadows, and the jagged rock was situated in one. By contrast, he could Raz clearly. The Israeli ducked his head in and out from behind a pile of stones near the end of the path.

"Even amateurs can get lucky shots, Raz. Do you really want to take a chance?"

In a quick movement, Raz slipped from his hiding place, fired, and ducked back into cover.

Manuel practically felt the bullet go past. It missed me by centimeters. He dodged back behind the protection of the rock.

"Keep talking, Manuel," Raz chided. "It helps me locate you."

Manuel knew he couldn't stay there much longer. Raz knew where he was. As long as his bullets lasted, he could keep Raz at bay. But once they were exhausted, the experienced gunman would come in and pick him off.

Did he have any other option?

Yes. He had one inexhaustible weapon. The waters of the *cenote*. They were why he had come here.

"You are too late, Raz. Whether you kill me or not, the Book of the Thirteen Gods is already in the *cenote*. It is sacred water. You cannot enter without burning yourself up."

Raz laughed. "That's not true."

In the shadows, Manuel began to take off his shoes and put on the flippers as quietly as he could. The last thing he would do would be to put on the snorkeling mask. His timing had to be perfect. He had to swim to where he'd dropped the book underwater, grab a quick breath of air, and then swim through the underwater tunnel into the next cave. The swim would be difficult, even more so with Raz shooting at him.

"You know I am correct." Manuel finished slipping on the flippers. He let his shoes sink into the waters. "You could not touch the book back at Xcaret. You will not be able to retrieve it here, either. You work for the Evil One."

"Again, that's not true. I work for myself. And my son."

Manuel did not believe for a moment Raz was the baby's father. "If you believe in your son, then you'll stop hindering us. You know what he can do for this world. We want to protect him."

Raz fired another shot, but Manuel was fully behind the jagged rock. The bullet pinged off it. "You don't know what's best for my son," Raz sputtered. "He's my son. Under my guidance he can learn to rule the world. I don't want the world destroyed. I want it saved, saved for him. It's why I want the book. What power he'll have! And how can you protect him? You can't even protect yourself."

"If you desire such power that badly," Manuel said, preparing to don the snorkeling mask, "you work for the evil one whether you know it or not. You will not have this book."

Manuel pulled the mask into place. He fired three shots at Raz and sank under water. He swam toward the book.

Raz flattened himself against the stones. He waited a few seconds, then fired once at the rock. When no response came, he realized what Manuel was doing. He raced toward the water's edge.

Manuel already had the book in hand when he saw Raz coming. He stood and used the book like a scoop. A wave of the *cenote*'s sacred water splattered on Raz.

The water caught Raz in the face. He staggered backward, his eyes and skin burning from the touch. But as he did, he fired.

Manuel heard the shot, felt a sharp pain in his stomach. Red swirled around him. He took a deep breath, hugged the waterproof container to his chest and dove backwards into the water. He knew he needed to go deep before Raz recovered.

Five meters underwater, he reminded himself, was all he needed to swim. Getting to the Taj Mahal cave from the nearest entry point required swimming through a five meter tunnel. Manuel had done it before. But not with a bullet lodged in his stomach. He trusted God would provide the strength he needed.

Manuel could hear Raz shooting, but none of the bullets were coming close. He swam toward the tunnel entrance. As long as Raz didn't know where it was, he might have a chance.

As he reached the wall, Manuel almost doubled over in pain. He had never felt such agony. His midsection throbbed from the wound and his lungs screamed for air. Manuel kicked himself toward the surface. He had to get one more breath before he attempted the tunnel. One quick breath.

He came up too fast. His head popped noticeably above the water. Panicked, he gulped down air and ducked beneath the surface. He felt a bullet rip by him, but it missed. No more opportunities. Manuel swam into the dark tunnel.

Using the rocky top as a guide, he propelled himself forward. One arm held the container to his chest, the other felt his way. He was going slow, too slow. Five meters. It wasn't that far. But could he keep this up for five meters?

His lungs began to burn for air. How far was he along the tunnel? His hand still touched rock. Not far enough. He kept going. Tried desperately to kick harder.

His body told him he was not going to make it. He had no air left. He experienced pain that made him want to gasp. A single gasp and his lungs would fill with water and it would all be over. Manuel fought away the panic.

And then he was through. He kicked to the surface, tearing off the mask. Now he gulped air. His lungs were grateful. But the pain didn't stop.

Manuel paddled toward dry land inside the cave. This was it. This was the place of his death. He knew it, understood it to be the first sacrifice required by the prophecy. As he dragged himself onto dry ground, he wondered how much time he had left.

He looked up. The cave was an open one, meaning far above him there was a hole to the surface. If Raz knew about it, he might be able to talk someone into letting him rappel down. Manuel decided he could not take a chance.

There was something directly above him. A ledge that stuck out. Manuel wasn't confident he could believe what he was seeing. The ledge was in the shape of a Mayan arch. He began to dig in the sand and dirt.

It was his God, or maybe the Mayan gods—in his wavering consciousness he couldn't be sure—giving him the strength to keep going. Somehow he dug an opening just large enough to accommodate the container. He shoveled the dirt back over it. He patted it down as best he could. Now he could die.

But first he had to propel himself back into the water. If his body stayed on land, it would point to this specific spot. In the water, at the bottom of the cavern, no one would know for sure. They would have to know about the Mayan arch to find The Book of the Thirteen Gods. At least he hoped. He didn't know anymore. His consciousness was all but gone.

Using his last bit of strength, Manuel pushed himself into a short slide, over the dirt and into the *cenote*. The sacred water.

And then he realized he had left blood on the land. A giveaway to the book's location. Manuel could not think what to do. Maybe wash it off? He began to splash water back on the dirt. He splashed for what he felt was a long time. He could not be sure if it had been effective at all.

He breathed his last. His body slipped below the surface and went into a slow downward spiral to the bottom.

* * *

Raz stood at the edge of the *cenote*, using his shirt to dry his face. It still stung, even after being wiped dry. Manuel, damn him, had been gone a long time. Raz knew he'd hit Manuel with his first shot, and may have hit him with one of the others. Even if it was only the first that connected, it should be more than enough to do Manuel in. Had he sunk to the bottom of the *cenote*? Had he made it to the Taj Mahal cave underwater? Either way, Manuel would die, and he had taken the book with him.

Raz needed the book.

He knelt down, gritted his teeth, and plunged his hand into the waters.

Sheer agony. The burning was insane. He felt it all the way into the marrow of his bones. Raz yanked his hand back out.

How could Manuel have been so sure it would be this way? Raz had been in *cenotes* before. How could he be considered so tainted by evil now that he could not enter the waters?

His satellite phone rang. He looked at the number. Restricted.

Raz knew he would not survive another meeting with Vhorrdak, not with the failure he'd just experienced.

But if he were not alive to say what happened, Vhorrdak would not know. Who would tell him? Manuel? But Manuel was already dead. And what about the other player Vhorrdak expected to kill his son? How would that person know what happened here?

Raz's best defense, he decided, was to kill himself. It would keep the book out of Vhorrdak's hand.

He put the pistol to his head and pulled the trigger. The bullet went into his brain. Death was instant.

The satellite phone continued to ring.

Chapter Seventy-Nine

Port of Tartus, Syria
December 21, 2012
5:36 a.m. local time

Time to Solstice: 35 minutes

Vhorrdak stood on the deck of the Masshad listening to the line on the other end of the satellite phone as it rang and rang. Where the hell was Raz? Why wouldn't he answer? Reasons that Raz would not pick up flickered through Vhorrdak's brain. None of them made sense expect one. Could Raz have failed? And yet, Vhorrdak knew it was possible. If Vhorrdak had to obtain the Book of the Thirteen Gods himself, it would put him behind. Fortunately he was no longer dependent on Raz to kill the baby. The Chinese man was a better choice. He would not be suspected. Vhorrdak thought again about Raz. If it was a blatant disregard to answer the phone, Raz will pay.

The big boom of the crane swung toward the oversized semi carrying the nuclear weapon. The boom lifted the mostly-empty container into the air and brought it to settle in the hold. It was on the top of its stack, the last of the containers to be loaded. The boom released the container and repositioned itself for storage during the trip.

Everything here had gone exactly as expected, but Vhorrdak did not second-guess his decision to stay with the weapon. He was right, as always. The decoy trucks had successfully kept the Americans busy. Fareed was now dead, the last person to know what was in the container. This weapon of mass destruction was the lynch pin to his plan for the end of the world. In the possession of his hand-picked, hard-line Iranian ayatollah leader, the nuke was the main event. Even the birth—and soon to be death—of the king would be but a footnote in history. It was inevitable that Vhorrdak's plan would be successful.

Vhorrdak had only to see that the vessel made its way to Iran.

Down at the end of the dock, Vhorrdak noticed a disturbance of some kind. He could see Syrian soldiers had boarded one of the container vessels. Could it be that they were somehow aware of what was going through their docks? Would the Americans or the Iraqis let that kind of information out, if they had somehow traced it?

Vhorrdak looked at the phone still in his hand. He had taken great care to scramble all signals. Still, if they had obtained one of the satellite phones that had made a call to him, was it possible one of the American geeks could have tracked him to this area? Would someone have dared disobey his orders?

Vhorrdak hurled the phone off the deck and into the Mediterranean waters. Then he went to find the commander of the ship. Whether there were Syrian orders to the contrary or not, this ship was leaving the dock, and now.

* * *

The Situation Room
Washington, DC
December 21, 2012
6: 40 a.m. local time

Time to Solstice: 31 minutes

Jim Harrington had been told to expect a report. Now he waited in the Situation Room that had practically become his home during the last couple of days.

Overnight the situation among the tight group following the situation in Iraq had been difficult. No sooner had they learned of the capture of the satellite phone, when General Archer died of a stroke in the hospital, and General Culver was killed in an automobile accident on the way to see him. Police were still searching for the driver of the car who'd hit the general's.

In the meantime, for the sake of convenience, Jim had put Major Simmons in charge. But the reality was that there was no formal chain of command—everyone in the tactical group reported directly to the National Security Office. Jim and his assistant Travis Black now monitored every detail. After all, it was his ass on the line. He was the President's representative.

Since the captured satellite phone from the Zagros Mountains could not come to the Pentagon for analysis in time, Jim insisted on having the best people in Washington work with the military organization in Iraq. Travis arranged for a secure videoconference between the two groups so the geniuses in DC would be able to see the phone, and the operatives in Iraq would know what the geniuses wanted them to do.

They now had preliminary results. Major Simmons strode into the room.

The officer who never sleeps, Jim thought.

"Sir, we don't have an exact location, but we know that calls were sent to and received from different locations in Syria."

"Is the phone still active?"

"Yes, it appears to be."

"Continue to trace it, but alert the Syrians who are friendly to us."

"Sir, I don't recommend it."

"Why?"

"We don't know who is at the end of this phone in Syria. It may be only coincidence that this decoy truck had a connection in Syria and an Iraqi truck plowed through the border gate a few hours ago. The nuke may still be in Iraq."

Jim hesitated. "I thought you had no other leads in Iraq."

"We don't, but we are working to develop them. Give us a little more time."

"What's the downside to alerting our agents in Syria?"

"Our agents there are not completely reliable. And do we really want the Syrians to know they have a nuclear weapon within their grasp?"

Jim thought again. Should he give them more time?

"Major Simmons, I respect your concern, but I want the alert to go out immediately. We cannot afford to take chances. We'll soon know where the phone calls are originating. I want our spies there quickly. If it is a nuke and the worst happens, that the Syrians seize it, the international community will support us in getting it back."

Jim could tell Simmons did not like the order.

"Very well, sir."

Simmons left, but his gait was not nearly as quick as it had been earlier.

Jim called Travis on the phone. "Travis, I need for you to check up on Major Simmons, make sure he follows my orders to alert our agents in Syria about the current situation. Call it a gut feeling, but he seems to have his own agenda all of a sudden. If he doesn't follow orders immediately, I want you to bypass the military and go to the CIA to get the job done. Thanks."

Jim very much missed General Archer. He hoped he was doing the right thing.

* * *

On the way to Chichen Itza, Mexico
December 21, 2012
5:47 a.m. local time

Time to Solstice: 24 minutes

Talasi had hoped the flight from Xcaret to Chichen Itza would be short, but it felt like it was taking hours. She monitored Rebekah briefly, but Rebekah was doing well. Jonas' presence made a great difference. He helped her breathe through her contractions. Talasi was relieved to discover the couple had taken child-birthing classes.

With Jonas caring for Rebekah, Talasi could address another matter of concern to her. She hoped she might not need it, but she pulled out a syringe out of her medical bag and filled it with methocarbamol, guesstimating how much she would need for someone who weighed about one hundred and sixty five pounds.

Jonas squeezed Rebekah's hand. He looked at Diega in the front seat. "Take us to a hospital. Please. Our baby is not your savior."

Diega shook her head but didn't respond.

Talasi answered instead. "He is the one, Jonas. You're going to have to trust us. We'll get all of you to a hospital as soon as the baby fulfills the prophecy."

"We're not who you think we are."

"We'll know shortly."

Talasi felt the aircraft stop moving and begin hovering.

"Prepare to land," Diega said. "I'll get us as close to the Pyramid as I can. Everyone stay buckled. And pray that there will be no one here to stop us."

Diega landed the helicopter smoothly.

"Don't get out just yet," Colin said. "I want to be sure we're not going to be ambushed." Colin had Raz's gun out and ready.

Rebekah groaned again. Talasi checked her progress.

"She's fully dilated, Colin. We need to get to the Pyramid now if the baby's going to be born there."

Colin looked torn as to what to do. "All right. Let me get out first. Yan, stay close to them as we hurry to the Pyramid."

Colin exited the passenger seat, ran around the front of the helicopter, the Glock poised to shoot. He guarded the rest of them as they got out. Jonas was first, and he helped Rebekah out. Yan followed, Talasi last.

Talasi didn't detect any threat. Diega had gotten them within twenty feet of the Pyramid of Kukulcan. The iron door that guarded the inner pyramid lay open. Talasi supposed that with the connections Diega and Manuel had, she should not be surprised.

"Ready?" Colin asked.

Jonas stuck his head back in the doors. "You promise?" he asked Diega. "You promise to take us to the hospital if we have our baby here?"

"Yes. I will remain here and ready for you."

Jonas turned to help Rebekah.

"Jonas," Diega called, "one thing more. You know that two human sacrifices are required. Manuel asked me to say, if you are to be one of them, he prays for you, for strength."

"Damn, Manuel. We could have overpowered Raz back at Xcaret. Why did he have to run?"

"Because," Diega said softly, choking on the words, "he had to become the first sacrifice."

Talasi wasn't sure if Jonas heard Diega's response, but she did. She almost cried herself.

But Talasi had a different mission. It had to be fulfilled, and now. "Rebekah, Jonas, let's go. Colin, what time is it?"

He checked his watch. "Six o'clock. We don't have much time."

The group moved across the grounds to the staircase to the inner pyramid. Yan went in first, then Jonas and Rebekah, then Talasi. Colin scouted around them, Glock out, ready for battle.

They got to the inner pyramid without incident.

Colin pointed to the staircase. “Up the stairs. Hurry.”

Talasi felt the need to take the lead away from Colin. The safe birth of the baby was the new imperative. “The stairs are narrow. We can’t rush Rebekah too much.”

“I will lead,” Yan said. “Rebekah will follow me, and Jonas will support her from behind. For security, Colin should be last.”

They started up the stairs. Rebekah stopped every few steps to groan and take breaths.

Then a tremor hit.

Everyone grabbed onto the walls for stability.

Rebekah began to cry. “I can’t do this. Let’s go back.”

Talasi knew she couldn’t let that happen. “We’re almost there. It’s easier to keep going up.”

“But my water just broke.”

Chapter Eighty

The Masshad
Port of Tartus, Syria
December 21, 2012
1:01 p.m. local time

Time to Solstice: 10 minutes

Vhorrdak forced his way into the wheelhouse of the Masshad. Eight people were in the control room. They stared at him warily as he entered.

"I must speak to the captain," Vhorrdak said in Arabic.

"I do not have time for you now." A portly man in a military-like uniform turned from the console. "You must leave. You are not allowed in here." He thrust a craggy finger toward the door.

Vhorrdak took a step toward him, revealing a roll of Syrian pound notes in denominations of one thousand. He hid the action from eyes of everyone but the captain. "Nonetheless, we must talk."

The man's eyes opened with surprise. He appraised Vhorrdak, a scowl on his face. "Step into my officc." His whisper was a guttural one. He jerked his head in the direction of small room.

Once inside, the captain shut the door and turned to face Vhorrdak. The promise of quick cash appeared to be changing his attitude. "Now you must tell me what it is you want that can be worth such a fortune."

"All the containers have been loaded. Why are we not leaving?" Vhorrdak asked, ignoring the captain's question.

"The Syrians often investigate the cargo of certain ships. They appear to have chosen this ship today."

"Officially or unofficially?"

"It is a request. I find it useful to accommodate their requests."

Vhorrdak smiled. "I think you will find it more profitable to accommodate my request to leave immediately." He began fanning through the roll of money.

The captain's eyes narrowed at the suggestion. He looked first at the money, then at Vhorrdak. "Syrian money will mean nothing to me if I am unable to return to Syria for disregarding their requests."

"Then consider this a down payment. I will give you this and then double the amount in whatever currency you wish when we arrive in Iran."

The captain's breathing quickened at seeing what must have seemed a fortune. Vhorrdak was delighted to see his appeal to the man's greed was hitting its mark.

The captain licked his lips. "May I see what you are offering?"

Vhorrdak handed him the pound notes.

A wide smile spread across the man's weathered face when he saw how many thousand-pound notes were in the wad. "I need triple the amount. In euros," he grunted.

Vhorrdak would have been surprised if the man had not asked for a bigger sum. He knew how to read people. And he did not come this far to be stopped by Syrian officials. "Done. We leave immediately."

The colonel nodded. He stuffed the fat bribe into his pocket and stepped into the wheel house, the door nearly knocking over his second-in-command.

"I was just coming to get you, sir. The Syrian officials have boarded our vessel. They want to see the documents on a container that we loaded into the front bay."

Before the colonel could turn to look at him, Vhorrdak vanished, snatching the bribe money from the colonel's trousers as he left. Now he would need it on the dock.

* * *

The Pyramid of Kukulcan

Jonas knew it didn't matter if they went up or down. Rebekah needed to get somewhere, and quickly, or they would have the baby in the narrow, dimly lit stairwell. "I'm right behind you, Rebekah. You're safe."

The tremor ended. A few bits of crumbling rock echoed off the walls as they bounced down the stairs. The group began their way back up.

Jonas could make out a thin shaft of light coming from the top of the stairs. Yan reached the top first and offered his hand to Rebekah. She was breathing hard and drops of perspiration peppered her cheeks. Jonas and the others climbed through the opening in turn.

Talasi tugged a thin piece of foam out of her medical bag, unrolled it, and laid it on the ground near the jaguar throne. She covered it with a tightly bound sheet she freed and unfolded. "Here. It's not a hospital setting, but it'll make this a little more comfortable."

Jonas slipped the backpack from his shoulders and laid it aside. He helped Rebekah ease onto the sheet. She breathed through strong contractions that were coming ever more quickly, each on the heels of the previous. He knew it would not be long.

"The baby's coming," Rebekah cried. "I can feel it."

She gritted her teeth and gripped the jaguar paw with one hand, her knuckles turning white.

Talasi threw a second sheet over Rebekah's stomach and legs. "I'll help you remove your pants," she said.

Jonas knelt next to Rebekah. He took hold of her other hand.

Talasi spread Rebekah's legs apart. "It is time. It's all up to you, now. You must push, Rebekah."

Jonas felt Rebekah squeeze his hand as she pushed with the contraction. She let up, breathed again, and pushed again.

Another tremor began.

Talasi ignored it. "Push harder. The baby's coming."

The tremor gained in intensity. The pyramid shook. Jonas looked up and saw their roof, the outer pyramid, start to crumble. "Not an earthquake, not now."

Rebekah moaned.

Talasi urged her. "Keep pushing."

Jonas saw the outer pyramid cracking. His mind raced. He looked to Colin, who was also watching. "I don't know what to do, mate. There's no telling which spot might be safe."

Yan seemed oblivious to the earthquake. He knelt next to Talasi, watching her, waiting for the baby to come. A brief flash of light reflected from something he held tightly.

Talasi reached into her bag, pulled out a syringe. She uncapped it.

"Ahhhh," Rebekah cried.

Talasi plunged the needle into Yan's leg and injected him. He yelped, and swatted at the syringe. The move was uncoordinated. With Yan unbalanced, Talasi easily deflected his swipe and pulled the needle out.

Yan tilted over and slumped. A knife dropped from his hand and clunked on the stone floor.

Colin stooped. He picked it up. "What in the bloody hell is going on?"

"He's got the demon in him, Colin. I injected him with Ketamine. It's an anesthetic. He'll be okay later. Push, Rebekah."

Colin examined the knife. "How do you know that?

"His shoulder repaired too quickly. He had to have supernatural help. Maybe he made some kind of deal."

"I'll kill him."

"No, you won't. He's our third witness. He has to see the baby. Push, Rebekah."

"But if he's in league with the devil …?"

"Who knows? Maybe the baby will cure him. Cast out the demon."

Rebekah blew air through tightened lips. "Isn't he coming out?"

Talasi checked. "The head is almost through."

Rebekah moaned.

"Give another push. Everything you've got. Now!"

Jonas heard a loud crack and looked up. The upper part of the outer Pyramid was breaking apart. The section farthest away from them collapsed first. It fell to the top of the inner Pyramid with a crash. Dust and dirt and stone bits exploded everywhere. Jonas could see the comet.

"Is he out yet?" Rebekah asked. "Is my baby out?"

"Almost."

The tremors continued. Jonas' mind whirled. He examined the structure of the upper Pyramid and realized it rested on a huge Mayan arch, but they were not under it.

Jonas grabbed one end of the sheet and foam pad. "Get off the sheet, Talasi," he yelled.

"No, the baby's almost here."

"You'll all be killed," Jonas said.

He pushed Talasi out of the way and pulled the blanket with Rebekah on it under the large arch. Talasi cursed at him but ran next to Rebekah. When Jonas stopped, she went back to work with Rebekah.

Colin picked up Yan and carried him under the arch. The other corner of the upper pyramid collapsed. Colin sheltered Yan from the dirt and rock that flew into the air.

Miraculously, nothing hit Rebekah or Talasi.

The tremors continued.

Jonas tried to focus on the baby. He wanted to see his son born. But something eight feet above Rebekah got his attention.

A carved serpent's head protruded from the rock of the arch. Its eyes seemed to glow red. It swayed as the wall supporting it began to crumble.

Jonas knew he had no time to move Rebekah again. He would have to get it away from her.

He reached into his pack and pulled out his climbing rope. Making a quick lasso, he threw it up toward the serpent. He caught the lower jaw of the serpent's open mouth.

The only thing Jonas had to use against the heavy carving was his bodyweight. He shortened up his grip, took steps toward Rebekah and then leaped over her, swinging freely on the other side. It pulled the serpent's head toward him. Not a lot. But, he hoped, enough.

The carving gave way and crashed two feet from where Rebekah lay. Splinters of stone skittered across the floor. Most of the serpent's head remained intact. Rebekah was unharmed. The rope slipped off the serpent as it fell, sending Jonas flying into a pile of rubble. He disappeared from sight.

"Got him," Talasi said. "He's a boy!"

Colin stared at the way the serpent's head pointed back toward Rebekah. "The baby was born 'out of the serpent's mouth', just as the legends predicted," he said. "Exactly what Manuel said would happen."

Mentioning Manuel's name triggered Colin's memory. Diega had said there was a need for two sacrifices, and that Manuel had been the first. Was Jonas the second? Colin ran for the pile of rock and stone.

The baby began to cry. Talasi gave him to Rebekah.

And Jonas climbed out of the remains of the upper Pyramid.

"Thank God, mate," Colin said. He grabbed Jonas in a bear hug. "I thought you might have killed yourself and been the second sacrifice. Someone else must have done it."

"Please, you're hurting me." Colin let go of him with an embarrassed grin.

"Jonas! Our baby!"

He went to Rebekah's side.

Talasi stood up when he approached. "How did you manage to survive the fall?"

"I told you all along I didn't believe in those prophecies. I had to see my son."

Jonas knelt down. He caressed his son's head and kissed Rebekah. "It's over now. As soon as you can move, I'm going to make Diega fly us out of here and into the nearest hospital."

Tears of joy and relief flooded his face.

* * *

The Masshad
Port of Tartus, Syria
December 21, 2012
3:23 p.m. local time

Time after Solstice: 2 hours, 12 minutes

Vhorrdak stood a safe distance away, disguised as a longshoreman. He'd been unsuccessful at his attempt to bribe the officials who were determined to get into the container. In fact, they'd hung together so tightly he'd never been able to make them an offer. He held out hopes he could find a way to control the situation later, when he could get one of them alone.

He watched as the container was offloaded. The crane eased it onto the dock so deftly Vhorrdak scarcely heard the thud when it landed squarely in position.

Vhorrdak continued to run through the scenarios in his head. An international incident might be his best offense. He wanted nuclear war. If he couldn't get the nuclear weapon to Iran, perhaps feeding the information to Israel would work just as well. Provided hotter heads prevailed and they invaded, in full view of the other Arab countries. But there were unknowns with that scenario. Damn, he needed the Book of the Thirteen Gods, and he needed it soon. When he finished managing this crisis here, he'd check up on Raz. Find out why the man wouldn't answer his phone. Make sure he had the book, then take it from him and have him killed.

The container opened and a crew of customs officials swarmed it. The first thing they saw was a dead body. Vhorrdak wasn't sure, but he thought it might be Fareed's companion. That didn't bode well. Four officials descended on the body while the others continued to explore. They seemed surprised to find the vast bulk of it empty, but then they spotted the small space the weapon occupied. Though he couldn't see past the bodies of uniformed men who rushed toward it, Vhorrdak could hear their astonishment. The Arabic word they used translated to 'rocks.' He began to run toward the container, stopping only when a guard pointed a rifle at his heart and told him to halt. He found his mortal body breathing heavily as the sea of customs officials parted just enough for his eyes to confirm what he'd heard. Rocks were located in spot where the weapons should have been.

What had the bastard done with the weapon? Anger surged through Vhorrdak.

I cannot be double-crossed. I mastered the double-cross.

Instead, Fareed laughed at him from the grave.

And then the laughing turned to something else. Something more disturbing than Fareed mocking him.

It was the far-off sound of a baby crying.

Vhorrdak blocked the noises from the deck and focused on what he heard in the wind that blew around him. The concentration opened him to a dull echo settling in his ear, as though a conch shell was held to it.

This echo was nothing like the sound of the ocean, though. It was a tiny cry that built into a roar. And the taunt in it could not be mistaken.

It was indeed the cry of a baby. A baby who, if capable of reaching him at such a distance, had avoided death at Yan's hands at the moment of birth.

Vhorrdak's eyes, already red, deepened with anger and desperation.

Epilogue

Taj Mahal Cenote, Mexico
January 4, 2013
11:00 a.m. local time

Two weeks later

Vhorrdak followed a tour group of winter vacationers into Taj Cenote. This was the first day the attraction had been opened to the public since the federales had finished their investigation into the deaths that had occurred there. Their conclusion was that Raz Uris, an expatriate of Israel, had followed University of Mexico professor Manuel Patcanul into the *cenote* early one morning and attacked him, wounding him severely. The professor had managed to swim through the underwater passageway to get away, but the seriousness of the wounds resulted in his death on the other side. Uris had then committed suicide. The two men had known each other socially, but officials could not determine a reason for animosity between them.

The group of tourists was as interested in what had gone on in the *cenote* as Vhorrdak was.

"Where was the body of the Israeli found?" asked a middle-aged, overweight man. From his accent, Vhorrdak knew him to be from a southeastern American state.

The tour guide played up the sensationalism. "Right here," she said, pointing to a spot on the rocky floor of the cavern. "If you look closely, you can still see some of the blood. It just doesn't come off easily, not off of the rocks."

The group of twenty crowded around the spot. Several remarked they could see some of the remaining flecks of blood.

Only in their imagination, Vhorrdak thought. He knew it had been thoroughly cleaned.

"Can we see the spot where the other man died?" asked the man's wife, a blonde with big hair.

"Those of you who brought swimwear and can swim underwater to the other side can see it," the guide said. "I'll swim over with you. But we'll do that later. For now, please follow over to the right where we have a better view of the top of the cave."

Vhorrdak waited for the group to move on. Then he stood over the spot and stared down at the place where an outline of Raz's body had once been sketched into the surface.

After arriving in Cancun, Vhorrdak had set himself to the task of finding out what had happened to Manuel, Raz, and the baby. Raz and Manuel had been the easiest to track down, not only because of the satellite signal emanating from Raz's phone, but also because the news media was in a frenzy over what had happened. The fact that Manuel Patcanul was reasonably well-known helped to sensationalize it.

Vhorrdak now believed that Manuel had obtained the Book of the Thirteen Gods and that Raz had pursued him here to obtain it. Manuel had somehow escaped and taken the book into the waters of the *cenote*, waters neither Raz nor Vhorrdak could penetrate. Why Raz had committed suicide, Vhorrdak could only guess. But the death left him with another loose end to tie up, just like Fareed's. Where was the Book of the Thirteen Gods? As well connected as Diega Patcanul had been, Vhorrdak was certain she had retrieved it. There had been no mention of it in any of the police records, and reports said Diega had identified the body before they moved it. Do the math. And that meant the baby and his parents were also in possession of it, because Vhorrdak also knew she left the country to go to the United States as a nanny for a friend's baby. A nanny. More like a bodyguard and accomplice.

The group of internationals had returned to their homelands. This included the Chinese man, Yan, with whom Vhorrdak had made a deal. And not a very good deal, Vhorrdak thought, stifling his anger, not wanting to attract attention at the *cenote*. The Hopi Indian, by blocking Yan's ability to kill the baby at the moment of birth, had allowed him to be in the act of killing and thus enabled him to fulfill the terms of the deal. By now, I should know better, Vhorrdak thought.

Vhorrdak spat on the spot where Raz died, cursing it. From this moment on, anyone stepping on the site would be destroyed by their own internal demons.

I always get my revenge, he thought. My enemy's goal remains vulnerable, along with these others who stopped my plan. They will die, and I will locate the nuclear weapon Fareed hid from me. The world will still be consumed by fire. My enemy's presence cannot change the hearts of these self-centered mortals. They will ultimately destroy themselves, and I will win.

He turned and stormed out of the cavern.

THE END

Made in the USA
Lexington, KY
08 July 2012